Alexander

E.L. STEVENS

NOTE FROM THE AUTHOR

This book can *not* be read as a standalone. It is deeply woven into the storyline of June, which is deeply woven into the story of Georgia and Constantine.

If you're reading Alexander, you likely know what you're in for. However, please review the mental health advisories. I know my brand is "hurt so good," but I never want to actually hurt you in any real way.

Before Alex's story begins, I want you to know I always try to write from the viewpoint that most people aren't inherently good *or* bad. We are all just people who sometimes do bad things and sometimes good things. In my attempt to portray characters realistically, we are left with multifaceted, messy people who rarely have the benefit of thinking through their actions.

This book will take you on that experience. It will have you asking questions, maybe even relating to the heartbreak and the self-sabotage, but above all else, I hope this book is one you can enjoy.

Happy to have you back in Spearhead, my friends!

MENTAL HEALTH ADVISORIES

THEME OF SUICIDE

RECOUNT OF CHILD ABUSE

RECOUNT OF NON-CONSENSUAL SEX

CHEATING

ALCOHOL ABUSE

OFF-PAGE DRUG USE

OFF-PAGE LOSS OF SPOUSE AND CHILD

IF YOU OR SOMEONE YOU KNOW IS STRUGGLING, PLEASE
CALL 988.
WE WANT YOU HERE.

For my brother, who knew my worth long before I ever did.

Thank you.

CONTENTS

THEN

ONE

ALEX

DECEMBER

Being cold in the desert seems like it should be an oxymoron.

*Well, moron that I am...*I'm here. In another fucking desert. Fucking cold. Again.

For the record, there were a lot of places I didn't want to be right now. Had no desire to be back in the Middle East, bunkered down, taking fire on Iraq's barren plains. *And I wasn't.* Wasn't interested in going back to sleeping on a bed of rocks in sub-zero Afghanistan. *Never doing that shit again.*

And then there was this place, least desirable of them all, and I sure as fuck didn't want to be here.

Yet here I am, kicking rocks down cracked asphalt. In December. In a desert. Cold and alone at night. Albeit, *this* was nothing new to me.

When most people think of deserts, they all seem to conjure the same image. Probably some homogeneous land-

1

scape of sand for miles. Maybe a cactus. A tumbleweed blowing by. And for the most part, that's all true. But this place takes 'desert' to the next level. The strip feels barren in more ways than one.

The land is barren, sure. But the people here feel barren, too. I mean, fuck, it's why I'd come here after Jess told me she loved me, and I...said nothing. I couldn't. I just couldn't.

It had been an unspoken truth, but it was definitive now; both of us knew that as long as there was breath in my lungs, I was never going to let go of the pain. Never let go of what *she* did. Her realizing that was like a serrated blade carving me open.

The pain felt visceral. Still does.

I saw the realization in her eyes when she said, *"Don't call me or text me or come see me."* And there it is again, that pain throbbing in my chest cavity, only increasing as each second ticks by until, eventually, I won't be able to withstand it anymore.

Fuck you, Jess.

The truth is I *don't* know how to let go of the pain. Don't even want to if I really think about it.

What's life if not pain?

So, I'd come here with a plan. Being surrounded by people like me was just a bonus. All of us here seeking some sort of high life back home can't supply. Or maybe it was some sort of relief we sought. Doesn't fucking matter. We came here seeking something, though, only to continue being empty fucks and soullessly barren in a new place. Again.

A strip club in Vegas seemed like the perfect kind of emptiness for an asshole like me. But it'd been too hot and sticky in the club. There were no windows I could count, no clear exits, and simply being surrounded by other lost souls and vacant gazes had my chest caving in under the weight of all the nothingness.

I'd gone there tonight to set a plan in motion; I had a goal in mind. A fucking laughable plan, in retrospect. Because looking around at all the people faking like they were fine set my skin on fire. Everything itched and screamed at me: *Wrong.* The gut feeling was yelling at me to leave the club — *a warning.* So I stood, knocking over the ice bucket filled with vodka bottles, the scantily clad waitress falling off my lap, and I shot Blanks a look. *I can't do it anymore.*

All I could manage was a shake of the head. It said a lot, though. It said: *Don't fucking follow me.* And maybe, from the deepest depth of my soul, a part of me said, *this is good-bye.* But we don't do goodbyes, so I walked out of the night-club, nearly running until the cold desert air hit my cheeks. Only then did I stop, bending over to catch the breath I'd been holding.

My inhales were big and shaky. Over and over. Just trying to shake whatever the fuck this feeling was. Trying to right my mind.

But I couldn't, still can't, because all I hear is: *I love you, Alex.* In *her* voice. Over and over.

My teeth drew blood from how hard I was biting down on my lip. My jaw and fists clenched, hating this feeling, knowing it felt like the end of an era.

Because it was.

So I started walking, which is how I wound up here, kicking rocks down a desert road. Alone. In December. In the cold.

Where am I walking? *Fuck*, who knows? I just know that

once I started walking, my skin stopped itching. The panic attack abated.

For a moment, I think maybe I'll just walk until I can't anymore. Maybe I'll just keep going till I hit fucking Utah, and then I'll only be about a day away from death by dehydration.

What a fucking way to go. Just disappear. Vanish. That's sort of my thing already, isn't it?

I just want it all to stop. The thought makes itself known. Again. And my jaw tenses, my fists clench.

So I start walking faster and further until I'm no longer in view of the bright lights of the strip. I breathe a little easier as I put more space between myself and all those empty people. And then I walk some more.

My body calms, but the pain is still there, thumping against my ribs. Pulsing in my clenched knuckles.

When the well-lit streets turn to dark, empty strip malls and mobile home parks, my walking slows. Because honestly, this is the sort of place that feels like home. It's not where I want to be, but it's comfortable. I'm used to it.

Swallowing past the lump in my throat, I focus on putting one foot in front of the other because if I stop, it feels like the intrusive thoughts might swallow me whole.

'Don't call me.' Jess's voice.

"Hey!" The haggard shadow shouts at me from an alley. I turn and look, but keep walking because if I stop walking, something bad will happen. I know it. I can *feel* it.

'Don't text me.'

If I stop walking, it'll be because I've found myself in a pawn shop, staring down at a case of firearms.

Fuck, this sort of actualization was new for me.

'Don't come see me.'

I just want it to stop — all of it.

My hands shake, and I slip them into my pockets while I walk. I keep walking until the faintest hint of purple lightens the eastern sky, birthing a new day. Another day, I realize I have zero interest in sticking around to see the end of.

I fight back tears that are trying to well, but...fuck this. *Fuck all of it.*

It wouldn't be the worst thing if I were gone. No one needs me. People don't depend on me. The few I care about would all be fine. Blanks would be fine. Wouldn't even need a fucking funeral because who would show? Five people, at most?

I would make sure there's no funeral. No one should be allowed to mourn me in some public display like I'm some fucking hero. I'm not anybody's hero. Don't want to be. I'm a fucking monster.

My loose strings are few. I need to make sure Jess's trust is set. And then, yeah, I could disappear. Step off the face of the Earth once and for all.

And then the pain would stop.

I don't know what's waiting on the other side, but maybe I'll see Tally again.

Fuck, maybe there'd be nothingness.

A lone tear escapes.

Just want the pain to stop. For it all to stop.

My legs cease moving.

I stop walking.

Because I'm ready.

I stand and watch the sunrise — *my last sunrise* — standing in the parking lot of a 24-hour diner.

A last meal. Feels kismet.

————

Emma

"Hun," Dina's raspy voice catches my attention. "Take table 19 for me? I need a smoke break." She scoots past me in the narrow galley, already taking her apron off like the answer is obvious. It is, of course. They all know I'll say yes. Everyone who works at Eddie's knows this. I'll take any shift, any table. All they have to do is ask. Does that mean they all take advantage? Also yes.

"Sure, just, uh, drop this off at table six on your way out?" I pass her a newly filled ketchup bottle, and she doesn't so much as smile or say anything in thanks. God, she's fucking bitter. *You're welcome.*

"George, it's been 13 minutes on the onion rings for table five," I press the only line cook, not also on a smoke break. He looks at me, rolls his eyes, then pushes off the counter and drops a basket in the deep fryer. *I hate it here.*

This isn't forever, Em. Nope. This is just a quick detour. A very quick detour that's turned into three years. I mean, three years could be a really small amount of time if, say, you live to be a hundred. I mean, it'd be hardly any time at all, right?

But then again, if my life ends tomorrow, three years will feel like an eternity to my 26 years of life.

And I'd spent them *here*. I don't even have a good reason

for *why* I'd spent them here. That's sort of my problem, though. Always has been. *I don't know when to leave.*

"Roni, when those onion rings come up, will you take them out for me, please?" I ask the only ally I've managed to make in the last 36 months — as if referring to the past three years in months somehow makes the time seem less.

She looks up from her phone to nod, then looks back down, typing furiously. Her bright purple fingernails fly over the glass screen in a fast *tap, tap, tapping* sound. I can only imagine the latest catastrophe her *latest* boyfriend is putting her through. Maybe I don't know when to leave, but Roni doesn't know how to pick 'em. We're both problematic.

Pulling out my guest check pad, I sigh, then head to table 19, singing softly with the oldies that play on repeat 24/7. Roni hates it when I do this, so I pipe up and sing to her as I walk away. My only goal is to bring a smile to her face.

"Won't you staay, just a little bit longerrr," I sing while swaying away from her.

It works, breaking Roni away from her phone and lodging the smallest of smiles on her face. Not that you could even call it a smile. She doesn't really smile. But a smirk, that's peak Roni right there.

She mouths, *"I hate you,"* and I smile a truly outrageous smile in return. I have the sickest sense of wanting to put my fingers to my face to feel the lines, the way my mouth turns up. I want to behold the fact that my face still knows how to do that. It's still possible. I don't think I've smiled like that in a month, maybe a year. *Maybe three years.*

Turning back towards my newest table, I gulp and stare in awe at the man seated there, drumming his long fingers across the sticky plastic menu as he watches the sunrise through the smudged window pane. My heart seizes at the sight.

At first glance, he doesn't belong here. This man does not belong in Eddie's 24-hour roadside diner that hasn't seen a mop in years. This man belongs on the cover of a magazine or in the movies. Maybe a board room or even a battlefield.

But when he senses my presence and turns to face me, I see *it*. It's etched in the deep grooves of his forehead. The lack of laugh or smile lines. The lack of life in his eyes. Oh, how wrong I was.

This man belongs, just like the rest of us.

Sometimes, I wonder if Eddie's is actually purgatory. Like everyone who's stumbled in here is actually dead, and we're just the holding cell.

Recognizing he's just another broken person, I relax. If he turned around with a megawatt smile, I would have been too nervous to serve him. Roni says I'm a lovesick fool who doesn't know how to act around men. She's right about the last part, but I'm not lovesick. I've never been in love. Can't be lovesick when you don't even know what you're missing, right?

My mouth slides to the side in not quite a smile but not a frown. Just a kindred offering that I hope says, *"I see you. I know this. French fries won't fix your problems, but they might help."*

He nearly mimics the gesture, and so, without letting an awkward silence fall between us, I ask, "What can I get you?" I use a gentle voice. The same soft, delicate sound I would use if I came across a wounded animal in a forest. Not that I spend any real time in forests. But I've certainly imagined it enough.

The man clears his throat, "Uh, a full stack of pancakes. Side of bacon. Three eggs, fried. Side of biscuits and gravy, and..." He eyes the cherry pie sitting on the breakfast bar underneath its clear plastic dome, but he shakes his head, "a glass of orange juice."

I jot down his order, and a second later, he says, "Thank you," awkwardly, like he forgot his manners.

Looking up, I smile at him and offer a sliver of kindness in return. "You're so welcome." Same soft voice for the wounded man.

Double-checking the order before I rip it off the pad to pass to George, I can't help but wonder how a man looks as cut as he does, eating like this. A strange thought tugs at the rear of my mind, but I ignore it, pouring his glass of OJ.

Setting it down in front of him, I turn to leave, but he stops me. "Do you have a pen and paper I could borrow?" he asks.

"A pen, yes. But will I get the paper back?"

His cheeks tinge a light pink. "Well, no. Can I just *have* the paper?" I laugh gently and pass him a spare guest check pad and a pen. It's only after I've passed it over that I realize I've given him my *favorite* pen. Vintage, from the Grand Canyon. On it, it says, *"The biggest hole in the west."* It always makes me want to giggle when I see it. Not that I ever actually do, but the thought that it might is nice.

He scans the pen quickly, and his mouth upturns slightly. "I'll make sure you get this back." He holds up the pen, much to my relief.

"It *is* my prized possession." I'm not really joking, but that doesn't matter. I walk away quickly when one of my other tables motions for me to refill their sodas.

I walk past his table a few more times before his food comes out to bring him a glass of water and drop napkins, that sort of thing. I don't say anything, but each time I pass by, he has another note scribbled on the back side of the blank guest checks.

It's not intentional, but occasionally, I get a glimpse of what he's written. Seems nonsensical at first, but when I deliver his food, he fails to cover the last note before I read it.

No funeral. Please. It's my one request.

Love you, sis. I'm sorry.

Chills run up my spine. My tongue feels thick in my mouth, and this feeling... I've felt it before, and I hate it.

Men like that *don't* eat like this. I don't say anything, not that I could. No, instead, I silently deposit the plates in front of him. But my eyes water as soon as I turn and walk away.

I hate that. I hate everything about it. The long-held ache in my chest cracks open again. I want to sit next to him, and hug him, and tell him everything's going to be okay. But it would be a lie. I don't know anything. Least of all, if things will be okay. Hell, if anything, I've learned the opposite. Just when things couldn't possibly get worse, there was always a way.

This place, Eddie's, feels especially like purgatory tonight. There's a group of degenerate-looking gamblers in a corner booth. Missionaries at another. Several low-life-looking tables. But far and away, most tables are just lonely-looking souls. Too many to count.

My hands turn clammy, and I rub them against the skirt of my uniform.

"God, could Table 19 be *any* hotter?" Roni whispers,

coming to stand beside me while I roll silverware into paper napkins.

Nodding but not saying anything, I keep rolling away, swallowing against the tight feeling in my throat.

This is ridiculous. I shouldn't care. I don't even know him. If this was any other person, would I care? *Or is this just because he's pretty?* Alright, I would care, but I probably care more because he is, without a doubt, one of the most beautiful humans I've ever encountered.

"Have you ever thought about...not doing this anymore? L-like life, I mean? Do you ever just want to give up?" I ask her quietly.

It's silent between us, aside from the sound of silverware clanking against the laminate counter and The Supremes singing in the background.

After some consideration, Roni finally says, "Sure. I mean, look around, Em. This is our life. It's not exactly any better outside this shithole either..." The truth reverberates and hits me deep in the chest.

Hopelessness, I know. Despair, also yes. But could I really give it up? *I don't know.* And if I'm being honest, it's probably because I'm too cowardly to do anything about it. There isn't any nobility in me choosing to live. But to leave on your own terms? That's fucking brave.

"Alright, hun, time to go home," Dina rasp-yells across the breakfast bar top. My shoulders droop. I'm not ready to leave. I'm never ready to leave, but especially today. There's a tug, quietly asking me to stay. But that's nothing new, really.

"Can I please stay through the morning rush, please?" I ask Dina, just shy of begging. My hands actually clasp together as if in prayer. I know my shift is the night shift, but it's undoubtedly the shitiest shift. The worst tippers. The most drunks. The morning rush is solid, though. People heading to work, old people, young people. Families.

Sometimes, if Dina is nursing a hangover, she'll let me stay...but not today.

She shakes her head and says, "No dice, sweetheart." I hate that she calls everyone a nickname like it's endearing. Honestly, I think she does it because she can't remember our names.

I give a fake smile to Roni, who shrugs sympathetically.

Without thinking twice, I plate a piece of cherry pie, write a quick note on Table 19's check, then set the pie in front of him as I clear his empty plates.

"I didn't –" he starts to tell me he didn't order the slice of cherry pie. I shrug and drop his check on the table.

Feather-light so no one else can hear, I say, "Life is short." I give him a soft smile, and without waiting for him to read the check or even respond, I walk toward the back to dump his dishes. I'm slightly embarrassed by my presumptive thoughts, but if there's anything that years at Eddie's have taught me, it's to leave my shame behind. So I drop it, along with my cares, and head for the back office.

When I cash out, I count my tips to discover I nearly worked at a loss after buying Table 19's meal. *But it was worth it, I hope.*

Then, opting not to do my closing work as a little "F you" to Dina, I head towards the back parking lot. Elvis singing, *"Only fools rush in,"* gets cut off as the heavy back door closes, sealing the sound in and me out. In its place, a bird chirps into the freshly risen sun. The brisk morning air cuts through my thin uniform, and I shiver as I walk toward my old Honda.

"Hey," a deep voice startles me.

"Holy *firking* shirtballs!" I clutch a hand to my chest with alarm. Getting caught, alone, with a man in the back parking lot is one of my worst nightmares.

"I wanted to give you your pen back." He extends a brawny arm covered in a baby-soft, long-sleeved sweater. "And you didn't need to pay for my meal." The pen is sandwiched between a couple hundred-dollar bills.

My cheeks feel hot, likely red now. "I wanted to," I say quietly and timidly because: big man, small-ish girl, creepy parking lot.

He thrusts his arm towards me again, but I stand there unmoving. A part of me wants to cry, standing in the early morning sun across from him. *Will I be the last one to see him like this?*

I wonder because, truthfully, what a shame. His sandy-colored hair, a shade darker than mine, is backlit in the first rays of sunlight. His high cheekbones are painted pink above his neatly trimmed beard, like he's been standing out in the cold waiting for me. *Beautiful,* I decide.

"Please, take it," he pleads.

"I can't accept." *Idiot.* I should accept. I should take the money — what looks like four hundred dollars — because I'm broke, and crudely enough, he doesn't need it where he's going.

Even with all that, I can't will my body to reach out. I shake my head reluctantly, and he drops his arm back down to his side.

"If you keep looking at me like that, I won't be able to do

13

it, you know," he says with exasperation and maybe some shame, looking down at his feet while he speaks.

"Maybe it's because I don't want you to..." I say back, soft, like I'm back in the woods and a baby deer is laid out in pain before me.

"I'm not a good person, Emma."

Emma. The way he says my name...that he noticed my name. I mean, it's loud and proud on my name tag, but most people don't take notice.

"Few people actually are," I say in defense.

"Yet somehow, I get the feeling you're one of the few." He looks me in the eyes, and it's like a shock to the system. Like I know his pain without knowing him. I can practically feel it, too.

I shrug because I do think I'm a good person. But did I just cut out on my closing duties? *Yeah.* So maybe I'm not the best person. But decent? A hundred percent. Because I've been around shitty people. Bad people. And I know that I am far and away from being bad people. And so is Table 19.

"I would say the same about you."

He sighs, his broad shoulders rising up before slowly fall-ing. "You wanna know why I'm here?"

Desperately. I would give anything for him to just keep talking. So I nod.

"I came here to find someone to marry. Someone just drunk enough that they would choose me. Just lost enough..." his voice trails off. "I sound like a fucking predator when I say it out loud. And I'm not a predator or a murderer or anything, just to be clear."

"Sounds like something a predator-slash-murderer would say." I feel nothing but relief when he almost chuckles at my remark. It's not fully formed, maybe just a scoff, but it warms me from the inside out. It does more than warm me; it's a singe.

"I swear I don't own any windowless vans." He holds up his right hand in a pledge, in what I think is his attempt at a joke. This time, I laugh involuntarily. It surprises me.

With an almost smile on his face, he drops his hand and asks, "Any chance you'd want to grab a coffee or something since I can't reimburse you for the breakfast?" *Oh*. The look on my face has him backtracking, though. "You know, actually, I forgot it's the week before Christmas, and you probably have somewhere to be or people to get home to."

I don't.

I shake my head. "No. I really don't." I sound quiet and pathetic because I am. I used to have people, but honestly, it's better this way. "I would accept a coffee...on one condition."

"What's that?" he asks cooly, almost as if he's prepared to give me whatever I demand.

"Your name. What's your name?" That same, not-quite-a-smile passes across his lips.

"Alexander."

Alexander.

TWO

ALEX

I wish you'd stay.

That's all she wrote on the zeroed-out check. *I wish you'd stay.*

I'm running again, aren't I? The ultimate escape? *Fuck.*

"Is there somewhere we could walk to?" I ask as she wraps her arms around herself, smirking at my question.

"Not anywhere worth going." *Fair enough.* "Um, I can drive," she volunteers.

I nod graciously. "Alright then."

Leading me to a late model Honda Civic, she sheepishly unlocks the car for both of us.

She pushes back a piece of golden blonde hair that's fallen out of her bun, securing it with a bobby pin, then starts the car. It's clean inside. A fresh green tree hanging from the rearview mirror. No real trash except a McDonald's coffee cup left in the center cup holder.

"So..." She laughs awkwardly. I don't feel awkward, though. Probably should. But I don't. I just made peace with being...gone. Relief feels imminent. And all of *this* feels like it could be a final good deed. Even the score, instead of going out like a selfish prick by letting some waitress pay for my last meal.

"You sure you don't need to get home?" I ask again, making sure.

She laughs, not awkwardly this time. "God, I should probably lie and tell you I have three brothers, all Navy Seals, waiting for me, but, well, I don't know." She looks at me from the corner of her eye. "It feels pointless to try and lie to you. So no, there's no one at home. Not even a cat." *Jesus.* Whisper quiet, she says, "There's barely even a home." My chest pinches tight.

"Hmm," I sort of hum.

"Wh-what about you? Is anybody waiting for you?" *'Don't call me, don't text me, don't come see me.'*

I roll my head back and forth against the headrest, eventually landing on, "No one."

"Yeah," is all she says back. A deep understanding in her tone.

We drive silently for the next 15 minutes. Well, mostly silently. Her radio is tuned to Christmas music, and occasionally, she absentmindedly sings along with the carols, not realizing it, I'm sure.

Eventually, we pull into another strip mall, and she parks near a coffee shop that's just opening.

It's a small place with only two tables and two sofas in the back. *Two exits, three windows.*

At the counter, I motion to let her order first.

"Can I please have a Snickers latte with extra caramel sauce and an almond croissant?" She smiles at the barista, offering her name when asked, then looks to me.

"I'll have the same to drink and an old-fashioned donut." She glances at me, maybe with surprise. *Life is short, right?*

I hand over a hundred-dollar bill to pay, but the barista stops me.

"Yeah, we don't take bills that large." I whip out my card, dropping the hundred in the tip jar instead. "Oh, I mean..." The barista stutters.

I hold my card to the contactless reader and just say, "Merry Christmas."

Emma blushes, holds her purse to her a little bit tighter, and shuffles sideways while we wait for the drinks.

I find myself absently staring at her while we do. Honestly, I hadn't given her even a second glance inside the restaurant.

She's taller than her, with golden blonde hair and fair skin. She's pretty. Definitely seems like Blanks' type. Sweet, too. Genuinely sweet. *If she'd been at that club tonight...*

"Emma," the barista calls out, sliding two to-go coffee cups on the bar and two small bags. Bypassing our order's namesake, I grab all the items and lead her to a table. Sliding a chair out with my foot, I motion for her to take the seat.

"Well, this is nice for a change," she says, watching me set her latte in front of her, then place a pastry bag beside her cup.

Settling in, the ease I feel in her presence surprises me.

"How long have you worked at...the diner?" I don't even know the name of the fucking place.

"Three years. How long have you been in Vegas?"

I glance at the vintage Patek Philippe watch wrapped around my wrist. "16 hours. Vegas native?"

Maybe I'll leave the watch in her car. As a parting gift. That would be a hell of a lot better than the $500 I'd offered her earlier.

"Mostly...yeah," she answers. "Where do you call home?"

It's tit for tat, she's not interested in monologuing. It would be refreshing if I didn't abhor talking about myself. But how to answer this? I have the house in Spearhead, but I don't want to think about the specifics of that right now. I also have Georgia's house, but I don't really spend time in any *one* place.

"I travel a lot, but uh, central California is mostly home."

"Like Bakersfield?" she asks.

I shake my head. "No, I have a lake house."

Lightning fast, I clock her, checking my ring finger. Putting together some story in her mind. Instead of waiting for her to ask, unprompted, I supply, "Not married. Though I was once, but she, uh, died in a car accident with our daughter. Long time ago. More recently, I was engaged, but...it didn't work out."

Emma slowly lowers the coffee cup away from her lips.

"I'm so sorry for your loss." I assume she means Amy and Tally.

"Me, too." *I'm so fucking sorry.* I have to look away, deflecting by sipping on my coffee.

This time, she offers up information without prompting. "Well, it's just me. No boyfriend, no husband, present, or ex. My family is dead...at least to me. And I have one friend, who I'm not quite sure would even call me a friend." I nod, and surprisingly, she continues. "My stepdad was an adrenaline junkie, and my mom is just a junkie. They were both more concerned about where or how they'd get their next fix than they ever were about their kids." *Christ.* "I've bounced around since then and ended up, I guess...stuck."

There's clearly more to the story, but it seems pointless to push. Instead, I make a trade. "I grew up mostly with my dad. He was a mean drunk who couldn't hold a job, an addict that wound up in prison." I sigh, "I vowed I'd never end up like him."

"A-and you think you have?" There she goes again, coming up with a story.

"No. Never," my voice is stern. Emma looks stung for a moment, so I soften my tone, "But he broke me, and I've never really been able to put myself back together again. I don't know that I can..."

She gives me a sympathetic smile before saying, "I know exactly what you mean, Alexander."

I know she knows. She didn't need to tell me her story before I knew it. "You probably think I'm crazy..."

She immediately starts shaking her head. "No, no. I really don't." She doesn't...*yet.*

Setting my cup on the table, I wring out my hands. "I'm gonna make you an offer, Emma."

She straightens in her seat. "Um, what kind of offer?"

"The mutually beneficial kind."

Emma

· · ·

The mutually beneficial kind.

"He what???" Roni screeches into the phone.

"Yeah..." I trail off, placing the phone on speaker and dropping it on the bed so I can fold clothes while we chat. I can hear the faintest sound of "Twist and Shout" playing in the background at the diner.

"So what does this mean???" She's still screeching. I had no clue Roni's voice even went that high.

"It means I'm getting married...today." *Married.*

"Okay, but don't you get like rich, human-slave-trade vibes from this guy?" Oddly, no.

"I should, but I don't. Honestly, it sort of feels like he's someone I've known for a long time." The sigh and invisible eye roll are palpable through the phone.

"Are you just trying to convince yourself this is a good idea? I mean, *Emma*, come on..." I can't tell if she's really looking out for me, like a friend? Or if maybe, she's a little jealous?

"Good idea or not, I-I'm doing it." It's pointless trying to explain this situation to her. I guess the bonus of not having anyone who truly cares about you in your life is that there aren't any judgmental or harsh opinions to worry about. Just your own. And if — more likely *when* — this all goes to shit, I will absolutely be my own harshest critic about it. No one else needed.

"Wow. So when are you gonna quit? Dina's gonna flip her shit." I want to wince about leaving them hanging out to dry the week before Christmas, but again, I'm a decent person, not the *best* person. And I can't bring myself to give a fuck about it.

"Sorry about that." Roni scoffs at my lackluster response.

"Listen, I wanna give you something before I leave. Can you come by when you get off?"

"Uh, sure," she says, sounding anything but.

"K, I'll see you around noon." I can barely finish before she hangs up. If she doesn't come, that's fine. If she does, I plan on giving her a chunk of the money Alexander left with me.

When I dropped him off at his hotel after coffee, he asked me to wait. When he came back, he was carrying two stacks of cash. Just two stacks of *hundreds*, like it was five dollars. Chump change.

"For anything you might need...for the wedding," was all he said. What could I possibly need that would take that much money?

As impossible as it felt to accept, I did because that was his show of good faith. That he would hold up his end of the bargain if I did, too.

His requirements for the marriage were fairly simple: Live with him. Show up at family functions and work events with him. And I would go back to school.

My requirement was that he pay me. Not that I made that demand, but he insisted.

Fairly Simple. Clean cut, right? *I hope.*

Yawning, I take another sip of my overly sweet, now cold latte and make a quick mental to-do list:

1. Pack.
2. Find a wedding dress. (Not a real one. I'm not insane, but a simple white dress. Maybe even pale pink?)
3. Make a deposit at the bank.

4. Cat nap. (Hopefully.)
5. Give Roni her farewell gift.
6. Meet Alexander to obtain the marriage license.
7. Get married.

Just a regular, run-of-the-mill Thursday. My turning stomach has me absentmindedly rubbing at my abdomen like that'll make it go away. *I'm getting married.* To a complete stranger. Who could very well be in the human skin trade or maybe plans to harvest my organs. He could be a serial killer. He could be...any number of entirely unsavory and predatory things.

But no matter what awful scenario I think of, my instincts are telling me: *It's okay. It's fine.* Usually, men — even worse if they're attractive — make me uncomfortable. I struggle to be normal or even-keeled when they're around. But with Alexander, I just...don't. It's not a struggle.

I wasn't lying to Roni; I feel like I've known him a long time. There's no pinpointing the exact reason, but it's a knowing. Like his eyes and mine are the same. Like our souls hear and share the same hurt. His pain knows mine, and maybe that's all it boils down to.

Two people with equally hard past lives meeting, intersecting at a point in time, and deciding life might be easier if you don't have to walk it alone.

And *that* was why I said yes. Quickly. Assuredly.

Scribbling a shopping list on an extra guest check, I head towards the door to find myself a wedding dress.

———

The dress was white, vintage, eyelet-organza, and the second I saw it in Main Street Mercantile, I knew it was mine. The baby blue, cat-eye sunglasses were a perfect addition, and the shoes were brand new and hot pink and didn't match at all, but they were perfect. I have a thing about not buying used shoes. I would if I had to, but not today.

Standing on the toilet in my small bathroom so I can see my whole body in the mirror above the sink, I can't help but think: *I look like a bride. Wow.*

Quick math told me I still had an hour before Roni arrived, two until I would meet Alexander. Somewhere in there, I would have to shower and get ready. But I needed at least 30 minutes of shut-eye.

Lying back on my quilted bedspread, I close my eyes and drift off peacefully for the first time in...I can't remember how long.

———

Bang.

Another bang.

I sit up with a gasp. Roni.

"I'm coming!" I shout at her aggressively loud knocks. My hour had flown by too quickly. It felt like I closed my eyes for a long blink and not much more.

Pulling open the trailer door, I find Alexander standing at the bottom of my steps in a sharp navy suit, looking like money and sex. He looks like someone entirely different than the man who sat at table 19 in the wee hours of the morning. He looks like someone's husband. My husband, though? *No.*

"Oh my god, what time is it?" I ask as my stomach plummets. It'd been more than an hour. I knew it. I could feel it. My long blink had gone way past noon. The sun isn't dead center in the sky any longer.

"It's time to get our marriage license," he says, not sounding pissed off or even slightly annoyed. *Thank god.* "I didn't think you'd forget, but I was waiting outside," he looks down at his watch, then starts ascending the stairs, "an hour and a half, and I thought maybe you changed your mind."

I'm immediately shaking my head because, *no.* No, I wouldn't leave him hanging out to dry like that. And *no, please don't come inside.* But he moves forward, and I make room for him to enter the tight space.

Peeking around the edge of the door to check where he parked, I'm surprised to see another suited man standing outside, equally as striking as Alexander but darker. Dark hair, thick mustache. It was a vibe. *He* was a vibe, leaning back against a fancy Mercedes sedan, his black dress shoes contrasting against the dusty dirt road.

The other man gives me a faux salute accompanied by a salacious smile plastered on his face, and I blush, closing the door quickly.

"H-how'd you know where I live?" I start patting my hair down, searching for the hair tie that's gone missing post-nap. Alexander looks around the small space, his head nearly hitting the ceiling of the travel trailer. And for the first time in a while, I feel ashamed. Someone like him doesn't belong *here* with someone like me.

He shrugs. "It wasn't hard to find out, Emma."

"I'm so sorry. I thought Roni would wake me up..." She hadn't come, though. Not surprising. "Again, so *so* sorry." I hope my tone conveys that because I am. *Fuck!* I wouldn't be surprised if he calls this whole thing off and asks for his money back.

Instead, I watch him eye me, still dressed in my wedding dress and heels, before nodding in his assessment. "Well, do we want to do this or not, Em?" *Em?*

"I do." God, that sounded corny. "C-can you give me ten minutes, and I'll be ready?"

"Sure." His tone gives me nothing back, but I intend to use every second of that ten minutes. So, without waiting, I scoot around him, locking myself in the bathroom.

I hadn't even showered. Taking a thirty-second whore bath wasn't what I had in mind for my wedding day, but to be honest, I never put that much thought into a wedding. Period. Using baby wipes, my hands move frantically over all my extremities. I don't even bother to take off my shoes.

After scrubbing my face, I spray an unhealthy amount of dry shampoo onto my roots. While the curling iron heats, I put foundation, concealer, blush, and lipstick on, tossing the mascara and eyeliner into my small clutch for the car ride.

My car? I'm guessing I'll go with Alexander and *that man* to the Marriage Bureau and chapel. *Would I just leave my car here?*

The time to think about logistics has passed. And honestly, I don't want to anyway.

In six quick sections, I curl my long hair, knowing this will, at most, provide a light wave. *Also fine.* Then, running my fingers from root to tip, I grab my clutch and makeup bag and open the door to Alexander staring into my nearly empty pantry. It's a pitiful sight, just a bag of rice and a box of crusty, old brown sugar.

I blush. Hard. The pit of shame metaphorically knocking

me down a peg or two. It's not like I starve. I just don't really eat here. But it doesn't matter because he closes the pantry and says, "This is nice." There's only genuine authenticity in his tone, surprising me.

"Thanks, um, it's really not so bad..." My fingers nervously fidget with the zipper of my bag. "There's no one that bothers me, and it's clean. All the appliances work, and there's no bugs —" I stop when he turns his back to me, the hit of embarrassment making me feel extra hot and squirmy.

"Can I help you with your bag or anything?" He motions around the sparse space.

It looks as though I've already cleared out. I hadn't. There was nothing to pack besides my duffel of clothes and my toiletry bag. I shake my head, motioning to the few items on the bed beside where I'd just fallen down the rabbit hole.

Silently, we both exit the trailer, and the man who's leaning against the car claps his hands together once like he's applauding with excitement at the show he's about to receive. It makes me uncomfortable, but I say nothing.

Alexander takes my bags, placing them in the trunk while the man with the trash-stache opens my door for me. "Madam," he says, oozing confidence and sex appeal, his persona verging on arrogance. He was the type of man who knew he was hot shit and had never heard the word no before. He was the type of man I couldn't stand.

I don't know how these two go together, but they don't. They couldn't be further on opposite ends of whatever spectrum you put them on.

Light to dark. Good to evil. Happy to sad.

Alexander's bulky and tall, with golden blonde hair and a neatly trimmed beard, brooding yet kind. Then there's *that guy*, a smidge shorter, muscular, but not bulky, with dark hair cut tight to his scalp and the thickest porn stache I've ever seen, sitting over a mouth that doesn't know how to frown.

Sliding onto the black leather seat, I'm greeted by an older man behind the wheel who turns to look back at me with a jovial, "Hiya, miss." *Oh.* And then Porn Stache is motioning for me to scoot to the middle, and Alexander is coming in on my other side.

Sandwiched and snug, Alexander says, "We're ready, Dave."

Dave responds quickly with, "Yes, sir," and at that, we pull away from my tiny trailer.

We all sit in silence, bouncing in our seats as the car bounds over the potholed dirt road. When we hit a particularly rough spot, and I bounce, sending my skull dangerously close to the ceiling, a large hand plants itself down onto my thigh, holding me in place. The firm grip sends heat pulsing where it never has before.

Well, fuck. That's not part of the plan.

THREE

ALEX

"You're positive you wanna do this?"

I shoot Blanks a glare for asking the same question for the fiftieth time. He throws up both hands in surrender.

Straightening my arms, I fix my cufflinks and shudder because this is fucking happening.

I love you, Alex.

I know, Jess. And that's the fucking problem.

The only way I'm staying away from her is with a damn good reason. Cue this insane, knee-jerk plan to find a wife in Vegas.

I thought the plan was moot last night. I would take another route to stay away from Jess. From anyone. But then her.

I wish you'd stay. And the way she looked at me like she saw me. I couldn't follow through with Plan B. It would have to be Plan A. I'd put a ring on someone else's finger and accept that Jess is best left alone.

In a way, I'm trading my freedom for hers. I would do it any day.

The double doors open on the other side of the chapel, revealing Emma holding a small bouquet of cheap flowers. I almost feel bad for the pitiful display, but she doesn't seem bothered by it, judging by the kind smile on her face.

As she walks down the aisle of the sterile chapel wearing an old dress and high heels that bring her to my eye level, I look at her. I give her my attention for a brief moment. She looks pretty. Her blonde hair falls in long waves down her back, and the mini veil that the woman at the front desk hoisted on her is tucked into the crown of her head.

She's undeniably attractive and pleasing to look at, but I feel nothing towards her. Absolutely nothing. No burning desire, no lust. I'm just looking at a stranger who was kind enough to tell me she thought I was worth something. That she wanted me to stay.

Don't get it twisted; I'm feeling things right now, but none of it is about Emma, and none of it is good.

I love you, Alex.

I visibly wince, and Blanks looks at me, but I shake my head to let him know it's nothing. He recedes, standing beside me, hands clasped behind his back, feet wide. He might think this is fucking crazy. And it is. But he didn't try to stop it.

He isn't trying now.

As Emma approaches, I work to control my breathing, to slow my heart rate, but none of my usual tactics work. All I want — *no*. All I *need* is to get this over with as soon as possible. The reality of being in a wedding chapel with someone who *isn't Jess* doesn't sit well with my soul.

Traitor, my inner voice hisses at me.

But I'm done. I'm done with all that shit. The inner voice calling me a traitor. Jess's voice on replay saying '*I love you.*' Saying '*don't call me.*' Soon, that shit will all be over. Soon.

Emma isn't smiling anymore, but she's not exactly frowning as she comes to stand beside me at the front of the altar. The officiant begins, but my ears get hot, and all the sound turns muffled. I focus on an arrangement of faux florals behind Emma to keep me rooted, but then all it takes is one blink, and the officiant is already asking me if I do. And, "I do," I say solemnly, sliding the solitaire diamond ring and its encrusted wedding band onto Emma's finger.

She gasps in surprise at the sight.

And then it's her turn. She says a quiet, "I do," and I slip her the gold band I bought this morning. She slides it onto my finger in turn.

"And by the power vested in me by the great state of Nevada, I now pronounce you man and wife! You may now kiss your bride!"

Emma hesitates, and I shake my head once. *No.* With her feet planted firmly on the ground, I lean forward to place a chaste kiss on her cheek. The officiant eyes us warily, but I don't give a fuck.

I'd just done it. Sealed my fate. Jess would never want me again.

I push down the urge to vomit.

There's no clapping or cheering, and rightfully so. We pose for one photo, taken by Blanks, and then we're standing outside in a strip mall parking lot. Again.

"So..." Emma trails off, unsure what comes next. *Same*.

I check the time on my watch. "We fly out early tomorrow morning. We can just meet in the lobby around 5:00 A.M.?" I got her her own room at the Four Seasons. I'm trying to set a clear boundary that this is a business arrangement. We're transactional.

Blanks is focusing on his phone and not paying attention to the conversation.

I watch as she glances at Blanks and then back to me. "That's all?" I can't discern her expression from her face or her tone.

"If you need something, Dave can take you anywhere." More quietly, I ask, "Or do you need more money?" I haven't had a chance to make the initial deposit to Emma's account, but I will.

"I just thought," her brows pinch together, "that we might get dinner or something." She finally lets the arm that's been holding up her bouquet fall defeatedly.

I pause, letting the opportunity and possibilities play out, but, "I can't...sorry." I tack the apology on at the end. I have a precedent to set that I'm not fucking interested. At all. Not in spending time together, not even in making the most of a fucking weird situation. This fake marriage isn't like it was with Jess. Where all I wanted was Jess, all I needed was her. Like she was the fucking air I breathed. She was an all-consuming, drown-in-her type of love.

This ain't that.

That's all I *had* wanted, at least. Now, all I need is to hurt Jess and not much else.

Pain seems to be our currency. Just a constant, fluid exchange between the two of us. There isn't much I wouldn't give to see her face twist at the sting, to watch her come to the same understanding as me that whatever we could have been is dead. It shriveled under my brokenness but under hers, too. Maybe if she took equal ownership of our downfall, I wouldn't be here, standing next to my wife, who isn't her.

It doesn't matter, though, whether I see it. It changes nothing, and in the end, for every hurt I cause Jess, I would do anything to make it right again. I'm still doing this for her. My freedom for hers. My life for hers. She can do what she wants with that.

Emma watches me skeptically, taking in the thoughts playing out on my face. Reading the deep grooves between my eyebrows, my clenched jaw, or at least she's trying to.

I inhale once and release the tension.

"I think I'll just head back to the hotel then, too..." Emma resigns. I want to ask if she's really okay with that, but I hesitate. Is this one question the stepping stone? That's how it started with Jess. Just a couple simple questions.

How are you?

Fine.

Answering had been indulgent. I see that now.

Blanks slides his phone into his pocket, then offers, "What'd you have in mind for dinner?"

"Um," Emma hesitates to answer, "just wanted to get tacos from this little place before we leave." She averts looking at him to look back at me.

"You should do that," I tell her. "I need some sleep, though. Dave can take you." As anticipated, Dave pulls forward, hopping out to open the backseat door.

"But what about you?" Emma asks. I shrug.

Giving a tight-lipped, not-quite smile, I say, "I'm gonna walk back to the hotel. I'll see you in the morning."

Quickly, Emma goes up on her toes, leaning in to kiss me on the cheek, making me feel like a fucking asshole.

She whispers, "Thank you. I'll see you in the morning," then steps away, slipping into the black sedan.

Blanks shoots me a look I don't have the energy to decipher before joining her. When they pull away, I can finally exhale. Fuck.

Emma

He makes my skin crawl. I literally shiver at the thought. The guy with the lip foliage notices, slipping off his jacket and placing it over my shoulders.

"Oh, thanks," I say, surprised. "I don't even know your name." No one spoke on our way to the wedding chapel. It was just a very somber drive. To get married.

He smirks. "It's Caleb, but you'll soon come to find everyone just calls me Blanks." *A little bit twangy.* I hadn't realized that until now.

"I'm Emma."

"I know," he says.

"Mrs. Palomino?" Dave asks. I don't say anything, waiting, thinking maybe he's on the phone. He seems like one of those guys who always has an earpiece in.

Blanks leans in closer and whispers, "That'd be you." *Oh. Shit.*

"I'm so sorry, Dave, yeah?"

"Just need the address, ma'am." *Mrs. Palomino. Ma'am.* Is *this* an alternate reality? Or maybe I finally passed my purgatory test and slipped into heaven. It could have just as easily been an admin error or glitch in the matrix that landed me in this new place, though. Or maybe I finally arrived in hell, and this would all take a turn very shortly...

"Of course." I shakily pull my phone from my clutch to search for the address, then pass the phone over to the older man when we come to a stoplight.

"Congratulations, by the way," Blanks says as we resume driving towards our destination. He's manspreading in the seat beside me, his knee nearly coming into contact with mine. He's taken a foot and turned it into inches. I watch from the corner of my eye as it narrows to centimeters.

"Thanks, I think..." His tone feels off somehow, or maybe I'm speculating, reading into something that doesn't exist.

The car ride continues quietly until we pull into the parking lot.

"Drive-thru, Mrs. Palomino?" Dave asks. The answer is obvious: this isn't a sit-down restaurant. It's a window.

"Yes, please."

We pull up, and Blanks rolls down his window to order.

"What are you having, Dave?" he asks our driver first.

"Nothing for me, sir." Blanks looks at me, rolling his eyes and shaking his head with a smile, two dimples popping through.

"What would you like, *Mrs. Palomino?*" he asks. *Mrs. Palomino* rolls off his tongue sharply.

"A carnitas taco plate and a Coke. Please." I open my

clutch to pull out money, but he just rolls his eyes again and turns away from me.

A crackly voice asks for our order, and Blanks proceeds, "Three carnitas taco plates and three Cokes, please."

We pull forward to the window, and Blanks pays, then accepts the food, passing me a bag filled with styrofoam boxes and three glass bottles of Coke.

Dave pulls out of the small parking lot, but Blanks stops him. "Find a place to park, Dave." The older man nods, and we pull back off the road a minute later, parking in a shaded, empty lot.

I pass a container and drink forward to Dave, and he quickly vacates the vehicle for privacy. Not that we need it. In fact, I wish he'd stay.

Not waiting for Blanks, I open my box of tacos and dig in. After all, all I've had to eat today was a croissant and a latte, if you can even consider a latte as food.

"He's never gonna fall in love with you." His voice, at first raspy, then harsh, makes my cheeks burn. I want to spit my food out. Instead, I choke, trying to swallow it down, coughing as I do. He reaches a meaty hand over to pat my back, making me shudder.

"Excuse me?" I ask, holding a napkin to my mouth in a sort of horrified manner.

"I said he's never gonna fall in love with you." Blanks leans back nonchalantly, his Coke bottle dangling leisurely from his fingers. *Lord, what must it be like to be a man like him?*

"Yeah, I know that's what you said. But what was the *point* in saying it?" I ask coldly.

"Just trying to prevent you from getting hurt," he cracks back.

"And you know...from experience?" I arch an eyebrow. "Are you jealous?" His cheeks turn pink, and he doesn't answer. *Suspect*. "I'm not expecting love from this situation, okay? If you have any sort of ill will, harsh judgment, or rude advice, honestly, it's a pass for me." I go back to eating because, like hell, am I giving up my last Taco World taco for this.

He chuckles. "Well, fuck, Mrs. Palomino. Maybe I was wrong about you." There's something about the way he keeps saying *Mrs. Palomino*...I want him to stop.

"Maybe you aren't, but I'm not your wife, you're not my husband, and under any other circumstances, I wouldn't be caught dead, alone, in a car with you." I draw a line in the sand, my tone cutting. Whatever this is, I don't need it, and I certainly don't want it from *him*.

"She bites," he hisses, throwing the bottle of Coke back with a laugh.

"Listen," I take a calming breath, "I'm sorry. Maybe I'm hangry, and maybe you're just looking out for a friend. I know he's not...okay. Okay?" Some of the casualness melts off his face at my comment. "But it's interesting you assume I'm the one who'll end up hurt..."

He shrugs, "If I were you, I would just keep my expectations low. Real. Fucking. Low." *Okay...*

I polish off my second taco before reengaging because the more I think about it, the more intrigued I become.

"So, how do you two know each other?" *Are they bosom buddies? Fuck buddies?* "You've piqued my interest."

He doesn't answer until he's finished his second taco.

"Met in the Army, inseparable ever since. Mostly. Alex...well, he likes to run. Or disappear. Just be ready for that." Alex. Hmm. "You ever need any company, don't hesitate to call, though." He winks at me, and the shiver returns.

"Yeah. Whatever." I roll my eyes this time, taking a large swig of Coke to try and ease the sting in the back of my throat. "Any other sage or, you know, *actually* helpful advice?"

"You have an exit strategy?" *Always.*

"Yes."

"Then you don't need any advice at all." He leans across the seat, slipping a hand into the jacket wrapped around me. His inner wrist grazes across my chest, sending an odd sensation zipping along my spine.

He fucking does it on purpose. My cheeks heat, and when he retracts the intruding appendage, he fucking smirks. I despise men like him. Self-assured, handsome, and pretentious. *Men like him take without asking.*

Revealing a thick card with a raised emblem on the front and a number on the back, he places it in my waiting hand.

"Call when you need me."

"Don't wait up," I reply, stuffing the card into my clutch because you don't know what you don't know, right?

―――――

Lying in bed, I push the large diamond back and forth across my finger, twirling the band to the right. Then, back to the left.

The hand in the car, holding me in place. My cheeks flame, and I close my eyes against the wave of nervousness.

Without my sight grounding me, the memory from the car morphs into hands holding me down. *That* memory is like a bucket of ice thrown on me, and the moment is gone.

My eyes fly open as a gentle knock startles me and has me racing towards the door to my suite. I check the peephole in case it's *him*, but sigh with relief when it's just room service.

The server motions me to move aside once the door is open so he can wheel in a dining table with silver-covered plates adorning it. He sets the table up in front of the window, pulling over a chair from the small desk for me. Gesturing for me to sit, I do, and he hands me an envelope before excusing himself and leaving me alone.

> *Sorry about dinner, just needed some fresh air.*
> *Happy wedding night. Wasn't sure your favorite, so ordered it all.*
> *And Emma, thank you.*

Swallowing the lump in my throat, I remove one silver dome after the next, revealing cake slices. All different flavors. I get a sort of thrill looking over the selections, but this feels ridiculous to try and enjoy alone.

EMMA
Thanks for the cake(s). Any chance you want to join me?

It's a lot.

ALEXANDER
No, enjoy. I'll see you in the morning.

Keep your expectations real fucking low.

I will. This is the perfect example.

I turn on the TV, looking for the trashiest reality show I can find. *Hoarders, maybe Real Housewives. Nope, it's gonna be Sister Wives.* And then I zone out while shoveling cake in my face on my wedding night. Alone.

Happily.

FOUR

ALEX

Beige hills. *Jolt. Bump. Screech.* Brakes engage, jostling the small aircraft.

The sun is just beginning to crest the beige hills as we touchdown, and the acid in my stomach is in overdrive at the sight.

I'm facing the music this morning. It'll be the first stop I make.

Telling Britain means she'll immediately turn around and tell Jess. And then, I'll spend the rest of my life with this phantom heart banging around inside my chest. Beating for someone who isn't mine.

"Are you okay?" She always uses the softest voice with me. I noticed that. I noticed she uses an almost harsh voice when talking to Blanks, putting him in his place. It makes me like her a little bit more.

Not that I like her. I don't know her. I'm not even

attracted to her. Sure, she's pretty, maybe even gorgeous, but it's not it for me. Emma would never be her. And I was pretty sure that was it for me.

I give a tight-lipped smile and say, "I'm fine. We just need to make one stop first."

"Yeah, okay," she says back, and I can feel Blanks watching the interaction from the periphery, sitting by himself in the back of the plane.

Emma had chosen the seat right across from mine. She even asked to hold my hand during takeoff because, *"I've never really flown before,"* and I did. And it wasn't horrible, but I'll make no plans of repeating it. If we ever fly together again, I'll ask one of the crew to do it. But after bailing on her last night, it felt especially asshole-ish to deny her.

"Where are we?" Emma strains her neck, looking out the window. But there's no airport, no signage, just 360 degrees of foothills, a landing strip, and a nondescript hangar.

"San Joaquin Valley. Private airfield." If I tell her Prather, is she gonna know where that's at? *No.*

When I started building the house in Spearhead, I purchased the closest airfield I could find. It would still take us 30 minutes to drive up the mountain, but it was better than going to a public airport and then driving an hour home each time I needed to travel. It's even closer to Brit's house on Robles.

Disembarking the plane, I'm reminded how light Emma is traveling. She probably doesn't own a single thing warm enough to be in Spearhead. That point is made clear when we stand on the tarmac, and she shivers in the early morning chill.

She's dressed in jeans, a vintage Van Halen tee, and a

thin sweatshirt over top. I'm curious to know what shit storm she weathered that left her in such dire straits, but also, I can't bring myself to ask. And I probably never would.

The one-woman crew and pilot say goodbye to Emma, and then I lead her toward the hangar where Blanks and I are parked. The keys are still hanging just inside the entrance, and I can hear Caleb groan when he sees I left the Jeep for him.

"Your heat doesn't even work, man!" he yells at me. And I shrug because I don't give a fuck.

"Can't have Emma in the Jeep. Safety thing," is all I say, and he immediately shuts up, ripping the keys off the hook and briskly walking past Emma and me towards the vintage pile of metal. That's all it is. Just a couple pieces of metal forming a box with wheels and a couple seats. There aren't even seat belts.

Jesus, driving around in a deathtrap had been just another cry for help, but no one seemed to have an issue with it. And so I kept on driving it. People think I'm oddly attached to it like it's my baby, but it's not. It's just another way I've tempted fate over the years.

"So, we'll drive in this car?" Emma asks, pointing towards Blanks' Maybach.

I nod, and she opens the passenger door to drop her purse. She starts to walk towards me to help with her duffle, but she's fucking stupid if she thinks I need help with the lightest, and also saddest, weekend bag I've ever seen. I shake my head at her approach, and she retreats, slipping into the front passenger seat to wait.

I'm doing it. Really fucking doing it.

I stand, staring at the trunk, buying myself a couple more

minutes, but Blanks honks his horn, and reality slams back into me.

'Don't call me. Don't text me. Don't come visit.'

The message is clear.

The message has been received.

Sitting in the front seat, with Emma beside me, looking happy to be here, I pull out onto the highway and think of nothing but long, dark hair, hazel eyes, and her words for the entire drive.

———

Emma

Alexander retreated. Like he couldn't get far enough away from me in the small space.

So badly, I want to reach out and soothe him. Somehow. A touch, even a knowing glance. But I don't. I turn my head in the opposite direction and look out the window at the changing landscape. It affords him some privacy and gives me a glimpse at what this place is like.

He said lake house, but I still didn't know if that's where we're going right now.

I don't need to know, though. That's the thing about having nothing to lose; you have the freedom to do crazy, stupid shit because stakes are low. *Almost as low as my expectations.*

As the altitude rises, the roads turn windy, and we slow down to maneuver the steep curves and narrowing lanes. Even with the windows rolled up, blocking the December morning chill, I can practically feel the change in the air. Smell it, too. It's earthy and damp. *Fresh.* Like a Christmas tree lot where all the trees are still alive. So, I guess it's like a Christmas tree farm, which is basically just a forest. So the forest smells like a forest. *You're using all your brain cells today, aren't you, Em?*

The landscape is changing, too. The hills' light brown, dry dirt is being swapped with rich-looking chocolate soil spotted with dried pine needles and moss. We even pass a few meadows that still have tall green grasses growing even though it's December. I wonder what they look like in June when everything here blooms? Probably beautiful. Probably like *actual* heaven.

Inhaling deeply, I lean back against the heated leather seat. *This is going to be my life.* Maybe only for a short time, but still. This is already more than I anticipated. Way more.

I might actually be sad when this ends. Maybe not because of Alexander, but because all this would be gone. Though, with the divorce settlement, I'll probably be able to afford to live here by myself, and that thought is exhilarating.

Finding a job that allows me the option to work from home, a small cabin nestled in the woods. I'll start each morning with a coffee on the porch, watching the deer graze through my backyard and —

"I have to go talk to my sister really quick. I'll be right back." Alexander interrupts the fantasy but stops before he's fully out of the car. "Just promise you'll stay in the car?" I nod.

"Of course," I say, punctuating it with a smile. But he doesn't even look at me, walking briskly towards the large mountain home we're parked in front of. This isn't a lake house. This is a lake *mansion. Lake estate even?* I don't know what I expected, but it hadn't been this. I mean, I should have. After we got on a private jet and flew to a private airfield, I should have expected Alexander and his family to live like this, but I didn't. Because I couldn't.

My poor-person brain had limits. I couldn't fathom how *actually* wealthy people live.

I've never seen anything like this before. The large house is modern yet blends with the surrounding mountains. It's massive, with a separate building for the garage and a guest house over it.

Would I be living in a guest house, too? I haven't really thought about it. I haven't thought about where I would sleep...at all.

Movement in front of me draws my eyes up to see a woman padding down the guest house stairs, then faltering when she sees me sitting in the car. Her face flashes with something like anguish, like she stepped on a nail, before she plasters on a tight smile, giving a small yet genuine wave.

I smile and wave back. *Alexander's sister? Maybe?* Her hair is pretty dark, and she's far more tan, but maybe they have different moms or dads. I'm pretty sure the woman he's talking to at the main house is his sister, though.

That makes more sense. She has long-ish blonde hair, far more petite than Alexander, but with a fair complexion and a similar-looking face shape. I could see that more.

Just as quickly as the woman on the stairs appeared, she disappears, and Alexander is sliding back into his seat beside me.

"So that was your sister?" I ask him softly as he buckles his seat belt.

"Yeah." His voice sounds...broken? Even more so?

"The one you were talking to? Or the one with short brown hair?" I ask, trying to clarify.

"The one I was talking to. The one with short brown hair is just some random friend that works for my sister." Hmm... hard to tell, but it sounded like more bitter words have never been spoken.

"Oh, cool," I say, not meaning it. Because everything about Alexander right now says: *Not cool. Not fucking cool. Not even okay. I may never be okay.* "Where are we headed now?" I ask, trying to gently draw his attention away from whatever just happened.

"Home," is all he says. His tone doesn't improve, but I accept it and don't ask for more because, clearly, he can't take much more.

Home, yay! I keep the thought internal because I...I don't know what to expect, but the guarantee that it's better than anywhere else I've lived before is obvious.

We drive towards the main strip of town before turning to drive up a different mountain road branching north of his sister's house. I only get a quick peek at the shops and restaurants that make up the small town, but it definitely doesn't look overwhelming, or high brow, or somewhere I'll feel out of place. And for that, I'm immensely grateful.

The drive between locations only takes five or so minutes, and when we pull up to yet another mountain mansion that's more like its own compound, Alexander rolls down his window to enter a code into a box in front of a gate.

No way. There's no way *this* is where I'll be living.

It's manna from heaven, like Eden on Earth. It's beautiful, and a stupid tear wells in my eye at the sight. *Pathetic, Em.*

We pull up the sloping drive to park in front of a three-car garage. *Three cars.* And I don't even have a car to drive. This is the point when I should start questioning the last 24 hours. That I really married someone I don't know. Jumped headfirst into a situation with no plan and no immediate escape.

I wasn't lying when Blanks asked if I had an exit strategy. I do. I just don't have one I can execute yet. So, in the meantime, I'll play nice and hope that Alexander keeps being accommodating.

"Are you okay to let yourself in? I need a couple minutes." Alexander passes a key to me as I stand, staring in awe at the house before me.

"Yeah, but are you sure you don't want...some company?" I ask, but he's already backing away from me like I'm the dangerous or crazy one. *Am I?*

"There's a guest suite on the first floor. It's yours. Really, I need to be alone, Emma..." The end of his thought comes out rushed, like he can't wait a second longer. He turns around and strides away from me quickly, heading towards a small clearing on the side of the garage for what looks like chopping wood.

No problem. I wouldn't be too aggressive in caring for a wounded pup, and I'll treat him the same. Because I have a feeling that when Alexander bites, he bites hard. Example: *me.*

I'm not a complete idiot. Alexander doesn't *need* a wife. He also certainly doesn't need to *pay* to find one. I'm some sort of revenge, right? I'm the knife in the back. I'm the final straw. Whoever he was just engaged to certainly did a number on him, and Alexander is doing his own number right back.

A shiver has goosebumps popping up along my arms. Fear about being on the receiving end of Alexander's wrath? Or the chilly December morning? I'll never know, to be honest.

Using the slate pavers, I walk towards the wide, solid wood front door and hesitate to enter. Do I ring the doorbell first? Or just use the key? There shouldn't be anyone home, right? Though I wonder where Blanks is if he's not here...

Inserting the key, I push down on the latch, and the large door opens to a massive yet relaxed space. It's even decorated for the holidays, adding to its coziness. There's garland hung from the stairwell and mistletoe hanging in the entry hall. It smells like Christmas. *He decorates for Christmas?* The thought makes me smile.

The family room lights are off, but when I switch them on, the tall Christmas tree in the corner comes to life, revealing a toy train that circles the tree and has a whistle that blows when it rounds the bend. *Wow.* This place was like my every childhood dream come to life. It's *Miracle on 34th Street*. Like I'm the little princess, and all those wishes I made on first stars and meteors were saved and cataloged for this exact moment in time.

Over the mantle hangs stockings, and I notice there are three. Two large and one smaller than the others.

Oh. Ohhh. The house is decorated for the family-he-should-have-had's Christmas.

A deep sorrow builds in the back of my chest, working up into my throat. How...sad. There's no other word.

Dropping my bag by the stairwell, I walk deeper into the family room. It seems like the perfect place to read a book with a mug of hot cocoa on a cold winter day.

Furs are draped over the backs of perfectly worn leather chairs, and a deep sofa upholstered in khaki, buttery, soft fabric sits between them. Even the ottoman is covered in fuzzy soft-as-a-baby's-butt knit. Who could ever leave this behind? Leave *him* behind? It doesn't make sense. It's not adding up.

Running my hand along the *real* Christmas tree, I bring my fingers to my nose and inhale the spruce scent, something that had only ever come from a candle at our house. Each branch is neatly trimmed with an array of various mercury glass ornaments and brown velvet bows. There's a nostalgic longing clawing at the recesses of my mind. Everything *looked* perfect.

I've never had a tree like this, much less *seen* a tree like this, except in movies. Even the gifts below are wrapped in matching paper with coordinating, gold-trimmed name tags.

Bending down, I flip over a tag that says, "*For my love, Jess.*" I suck in a sharp breath, a little bit shocked.

My cheeks burn, and I drop the tag as the train makes another loop around the tree's base, blowing its whistle. Like a warning: *This isn't for you.*

Understood.

I back away from the family room, finding the light switch that corresponds to the tree, and I turn it off, vowing not to touch it again.

Jess. The name slides around in my mind, trying to make sense of it all. *Alexander and Jess*, I try the thought on for size and immediately dislike it.

I wonder what she's like, what she looks like, what she would have looked like here...opening the gift addressed to her from him. And I feel it for the first time, the pang of jealousy.

Shaking off the unwelcome feeling, I continue my self-guided house tour into an eat-in kitchen with double doors that lead to a deck with another breathtaking view of the lake. The highchair at the eat-in table gives me chills, but I walk right past it, moving into the kitchen and circling the island.

I let my hand glide over the smooth, honed marble that looks like it hasn't seen a day of use in its life. It's like the house is some sort of mausoleum for the undead. Unused and pristine — perfectly preserved. Yet there are no family photos, no real signs of life...anywhere.

My stomach grumbles, and I open the fridge to see how dire the situation is, but again, I'm surprised to discover it's well-stocked. Nothing expired.

I pull out a small bottle of orange juice and crack the seal as Blanks strides through a back door, startling when he sees me in the kitchen.

He sets down a drink carrier on the island as well as two brown paper bags. Then, without words, he takes one coffee cup from the holder and slides it in my direction.

He proceeds to unpack the rest of his goods, revealing a loaf of sticky, pull-apart rolls, several miniature quiches, and a mix-and-match dozen of pastries. I salivate. But first, I have questions.

"How long ago was it?"

Blanks looks up at me, a near-sinister glint in his eye. "Be more specific, Angel." *Angel? Feels aggressive.*

Ignoring him, I ask again, "How long ago was it that Alexander and his fiancé...ended things?"

"Ahh, *that*. Well, a couple things. You have to stop calling him Alexander because I don't know who the fuck you're talking about. He goes by Alex. And second, it's been about," he pauses to think, "three days." I choke on the orange juice.

Three days. Instant dread strangles me.

"It's only been three days?" I ask in a whisper.

"Well, yeah. Technically. It ended months ago, but things were officially done three days ago." He smiles a disingenuous, toothless grin. "The same day he did all *this*." Blanks uses one hand to wave around at all the decor.

My appetite is gone, washed right down the drain. Now, all I want is to go take a shower, crawl in a bed, and hide. Because what was I thinking, living with Alexander as his wife on the heels of his life's implosion?

No wonder he wanted it all to end. If I loved someone *this* much, I'd want the end, too.

FIVE

ALEX

I'd never be able to chop enough wood in this lifetime to ease the barrage of internal insults.

Thwack. The ax comes down. *Crack.* The log splits. *You're a piece of shit, Alexander Palomino.*

Thwack. Crack. Don't call. Don't text. Don't come see me.

Thwack. Crack. You're worthless.

Thwack. Crack. No one will miss you. No one.

And then it all repeats again.

When my hands start to blister, I finally lay down the ax. I don't feel any better, but I do feel tired.

Grabbing the shirt I discarded an hour ago, I head inside the house I've dreaded entering since the second we touched down on California soil. The remnants of my thwarted plan to get Jess back surround me as I walk through the entry, then the great room, eventually ending up in the kitchen.

Fucking mistletoe. I had hung up fucking mistletoe.

Three days ago. I thought, at least I had *hoped*, she would be here right now. In the kitchen, singing a song to Eden while she baked cookies. Or wrapping gifts on the dining room table. Or telling me she loved me while I wrapped my arms around her and held on tight. Because I would have.

I would have held on so goddamn tight if she wanted it.

But she didn't. *Don't forget that, Alex, she didn't want this. Didn't want you.*

She doesn't want to deal with my incapabilities, and I can't blame her, though I try.

This is all Jess's fault. Everything can be blamed on her.

But I'm the one who made her feel stupid.

But then she fucked him.

And I'm the one who blew up her life, outing her to her best friend.

Because she was leaving you.

But I'm also the one who can't forgive and forget.

Because she betrayed you!

I grab the first thing in sight, a ceramic bowl filled with oranges, and fling it across the kitchen, the bowl shattering as it hits the French door frame.

With both palms to my eye sockets, I slide down to the floor, my back to the kitchen cabinets. And I heave, fighting for breath that, no matter how hard I try, never seems to fill my lungs.

Why can't I get oxygen? Why do I just want to disappear so badly? Why???

"*Shhh*, you're okay." The voice she only uses for me is here. "Just try to breathe, okay?" She places a hand on my chest, but it doesn't help.

"I'm here, Alex. I'm with you." I drop the palms from my

face to look at her. I have to fight to hold my hands down, to not curl in on myself and away from her.

Her big eyes seem to look straight through my soul.

"Keep..." I heave, gasping for a large inhale that feels anything but, "talking," I eventually get out on the exhale. She nods. And I focus on her voice.

"I'm not going anywhere, Alex. You're going to be okay really soon. I know it. I promise. Just keep breathing, and I'll keep being here. Blanks will be here. And..." I focus on her face. On her blue eyes.

"We're gonna get better together, okay?" She keeps talking as she rubs both hands on either side of my arms, applying pressure that feels good against my still-burning muscles. I hear her talking, but I only retain half of what she's saying. But even still, I focus on her lips. Pink. *Soft*.

"We're going to be okay. I promise. I've never been so sure of anything in my life." I want so badly to believe her. If I could just will myself into believing her, I think she'd be right. Everything would turn out okay. I focus on the faint freckles and how her cheeks are hardly pink at all right now.

"That's better. So much better, Alex. You're doing so great." Same soft voice. I inhale and exhale. "Do you want to count your breaths?" I shake my head no.

"Keep...talking...about...anything."

She nods, taking a second to think. "I've never been in a forest before today...It's so beautiful here, Alex. It makes me never want to be indoors." She hesitates.

"I used to have these dreams as a kid that I would wander into a forest, and then...I'd just keep wandering. I would just stay in the forest forever. And eventually, I would build a small cabin or house, and I'd have a warm fire every night, and it would be small and cozy, and with no one around, I'd be safe."

"This place reminds me of that. And I feel safe. Here. With you. That says something. About you, Alex." She nods her head at me.

"I'm...so tired, Emma," I get out in almost one whole breath. And then I cry.

I sob with my head hanging low. On the floor of my kitchen.

Climbing onto my lap, Emma cradles my face in her hands, trying to wipe the tears away, but they come too fast and heavy.

Eventually, going to her knees, she straddles my legs and rests my head on her shoulder. As I sob, she holds me, stroking the back of my head.

"You can be tired," she whispers, "because you're not alone. So rest. Just rest."

The bare skin of her shoulder is warm and soft, so I lay my head there, letting all her warmth and comfort bleed into me. Wishing this was enough. Wishing this was Jess. Hating myself for wishing it was *her*.

My hands eventually find her waist, fisting the towel wrapped around her body. "W-would you go lay down...with me?" The words are raspy and strained, but I push them out because all I want, all I *need*, is a warm body holding on to mine. I want a smooth voice whispering comforting words, darkness, and endless sleep.

"Sure," she says softly and without hesitation. She stands and offers me a hand that I take. With my hand in hers, she leads me to her bedroom, turning off the light and closing the drapes.

She motions for me to lie down. So, taking off my boots with trembling hands, I place them beside the bed and lie back.

From the corner of my eye, I can see her drop the towel and slip a large t-shirt down over her body.

She could be anybody. This is just a means to sleep.

She pads softly to the bed and gets under the covers beside me. When I roll to face away from her, she comes closer, letting a warm hand drape back and forth across my back. Over and over.

"You're going to be okay, Alexander," she says, whispering softly, her voice matching the weight behind her touch. "Go to sleep, we'll be here." And that, I believe. I close my eyes, and with one last breath, I drift away.

———

Emma

Long after he's fallen asleep, I stay there, my chest nearly touching his back, and I stroke him gently. The pads of my fingers drag across his broad back, up and down, cresting, before gliding down between his shoulder blades. I don't stop until my own shoulder starts to burn.

Watching him break down and cry had been so... *arresting.* Too beautiful to look away from. So vulnerable. He brings out something in me that just wants to cradle and coddle and stroke him back to the man he could be.

He went beyond beautiful, though. *There has to be a word for something so beautiful it hurts...*

Even after I stop rubbing his back, I continue to lie close to him. Just close enough for our body heat to exchange but not so close we actually touch. And I stay there until the light in the room shifts, growing darker.

"Psst," Blanks says into the dark void. I debate playing opossum, but the fact that I'm starving has me sitting up. Slowly, I move away from Alex so I don't wake him.

His breathing doesn't so much as falter for a half breath, and I sigh out in relief.

"Throw some clothes on," Blanks tells me once I've padded close enough to my bedroom door to hear his whispers. I roll my eyes but do as I'm told, finding my jeans and a bra and sliding on my checkered Vans.

I toe out of the room as quietly as possible, closing the door until it's almost shut to let Alex keep sleeping.

When I turn around, Blanks is waiting for me at the end of the hallway. He's leaning against the wall with his arms crossed. Dressed in dark blue jeans, suede boots, and a v-neck sweater over a white tee. He manages to make basic look lascivious.

Thankfully, he doesn't comment on what he just saw. Instead, he says, "Let's go eat," then thrusts a thick sweater towards me to put on. I want to tell him, *Don't tell me what to do.* I want to tell him to stop being bossy, but I'm exhausted and actually hungry, and this sweater...

It's soft and heavyweight and the perfect shade of gray. I want an entire wardrobe made from just this fabric. Sliding it on overhead, my ring snags on the yarns. My hands and limbs still not used to the added height of the ring.

I'm about to take the rings off when Blanks stops me,

"No, wear it." There's something about his tone. So I leave them on.

"C'mon, kiddo," he says as he fluffs my hair. *God, my hair.* It was still wet when I got in bed with Alex and, hence, dried curly.

"Kiddo?" I question him with a scoff. "You're like, what? Three years older than me?"

"Try ten." That surprises me, honestly. I don't know if it's his boyish charm that makes him seem younger or his looks, but I would've only guessed he was 30 on a bad day.

"Okay, *Daddy.* Tell me where we're going to eat."

The tops of his cheeks blaze. He turns around and starts heading towards the door to the garage, through the kitchen.

"There's only one restaurant in this hick town, Angel. That's where we're going." Oh. And Angel? *Again?*

———

Coltons. Shouldn't it be Colton's, or was that just a quirky small-town thing? Like the name isn't possessive, but some long story would eventually tell me how two brothers decided to open a bar in the middle of nowhere, thus birthing Coltons. Plural. Like this is where you come to find the Coltons. Or, more simply, the apostrophe had been too expensive to add to the sign.

The place is packed. Surprising for a Friday night in December in, seemingly, the middle of nowhere.

"Everyone's home for the holidays," Blanks explains as he watches me take in the boisterous crowd hovering around the jukebox.

With a bit of maneuvering, Blanks pulls me to the last

open bar stools, practically forcing me to sit. He was so pushy. Brutish. *No, he's just that confident.*

A bartender with a man bun drops two menus on the bar top, letting us know he'll come back for our order in a couple of minutes. He looks slammed, so I focus on the menu, making sure I'm ready when he returns.

Blanks doesn't even bother to look.

"Already know what you're getting?" I ask.

He laughs. "Nope."

"Umm, okay." As soon as I pick out an entreé, I ask Blanks the question that's been on the tip of my tongue since yesterday, "So why a mustache? It seems like a statement." He stares at me. "Or a cry for help." *Or attention.*

"Alright, what can I get you two?" *Thwarted by the bartender.*

Blanks doesn't wait to let me order first. He just says, "The special and an old fashioned." *Liar, he did know what he was getting.* "And for myself, also the special and an IPA, any kind is fine." *The fuck?*

The bartender knocks his knuckles against the wood top before walking away with a nod.

"Rude, that wasn't what I wanted. At all." He gives me a wayward glance.

"You don't even know what it is," he quips back.

"*You* don't even know what it is!" He smiles at that.

"Don't need to. Anyways, Angel, the mustache is because I can. I pull it off. Not many can. So it's a fuck you to the non-mustached, of sorts."

"Well, being a non-mustached human myself, I take offense."

He shrugs. "Jealousy doesn't become you, dear." *Dear?* He's worse than Dina.

"You confuse me," I have to say a little bit louder as the crowd surges and the volume inside the bar does, too.

"How?" He raises his voice back.

"I can't tell if you like me...or hate me."

"Well, why can't it be both?" he says with a smile twisting off one side of his face.

He might be unsure about his feelings towards me, but I'm pretty sure I'm firmly on the hatred side of feelings towards him. Rolling my eyes, I avert my attention in time for my drink to be delivered.

Unfortunately, our enthralling banter halts — *joking* — and we sit there in silence. I watch the crowd, and people, and the bartender. And he watches a football game on TV. Though it's technically not silent at all, it's loud. Between the people talking and shouting and the constant rotation of banjo-heavy country music, you can barely hear yourself think.

When our food comes, it's shepherd's pie, and I don't let on for a second that this is exactly what I wanted. We both eat without talking, and then he excuses himself to use the little boy's room.

A woman laughing loudly with a group of men draws my attention, and I watch the slim, dark-haired siren twirl around, dancing to a melody no one else can hear. When she stands beside me, in the spot Blanks just vacated so she can order a drink, I look at her again.

That's right, she's the woman from the stairs this morning.

I'm about to say as much when she interrupts me.

"God, you're just sooo pretty. You know that?" she says, looking at me, leaning against the barstool with a slight, tell-tale inebriated sway.

"Umm, thank you?" I respond. She laughs, tipping her head back, exposing a long neck of flawless olive skin. As her chest rises and falls, the red pom pom fixed to her chest bounces. She would be the type of girl to pull off an ugly Christmas sweater like it's couture.

Turning away from me, she motions for the bartender, who swaggers over slowly.

"What can I do for you?" he asks her.

She motions back to the three men she was just standing with and proceeds to order, "Four — no!" Looking at me, then pointing a finger, she says, "Make that five! Shots of Patron! Por favor!" The bartender glances at me, and I try my best to shake my head subtly, *no*. If he pours her a shot, I think I'll be tempted to take it myself so she doesn't find herself passed out or hanging her head over a toilet at the end of the night.

I watch Man-bun make the shots, pouring water into one that he sets aside. *Smart man.*

"Oh, fuck," Blanks says in horror as he returns from the restroom, immediately withdrawing his wallet and placing a hundred-dollar bill on the bar top. He stares at the woman, dancing alone, yet beside me, and asks, "Did she say anything to you?"

"I mean, she told me I was pretty," I whisper back. "Then ordered me a shot."

"Yeah, well, we're leaving," he says, ordering me with his eyes to get rid of the napkin still sitting in my lap. I lift the napkin, setting it on top of my practically empty plate, and as I slide off my stool, a soft hand reaches out for my left hand.

"Wow! Look at this thing!" The woman hiccups as she holds my hand to stare into the large diamond. The moment isn't necessarily uncomfortable, but there's a certain pity I feel for her. Wasted, the Friday before Christmas, practically alone at a bar.

"Can I take you home? Do you need a ride?" I offer. Blanks is shaking his head at me, though.

The woman laughs again, letting my hand fall. "No, that's okay, Ella. You go home to Prince Charming, and I'll stay *right* here." Ella? Blanks is still shaking his head. I wonder if this is one of his exes. Well, not an ex, but a previous *partner*. That's the best word I can think of to describe any woman getting into bed with him.

With a hand around my waist, Blanks pulls me into his side, tugging for us to go. I feel terrible abandoning her. What if someone tries to take advantage? But just as I'm having that thought, an older woman with long gray hair and a perfect blowout walks over.

"Baby *dollll*," she says sympathetically, wiping a stray tear off the dancing woman's cheek.

The gorgeous woman chokes on a sob, wiping another tear away before she starts laughing maniacally.

I want to turn back, but Blanks is jostling me towards the exit hurriedly.

"What was that about?" I ask as we step out into the cold parking lot, my breath turning to fog as I speak.

"It's nothing. Can we go home now, please?" he asks, not leaving any room for follow-up questions, giving me his back. He opens my car door, sealing me inside, then joins me a second later. Without saying anything, he starts the car, peeling out of the gravel parking lot.

"She could do better than you anyways," I say, staring straight ahead into the headlight beams lighting up the pine trees on either side of the road.

He laughs, really laughs. "That's what you think that was?"

I shrug.

He laughs softer again. "Yup, you're right. She could do better than me." He leaves it at that, and I smile the rest of the drive home.

———

I expect him to be gone when I walk inside the still-dark room. But he isn't. He's rolled over now, facing the doorway in my direction, and I falter. Should I leave him to go sleep on the couch? That feels like the wisest choice. But my heart is telling me to be in this bed when he wakes up.

Taking care to undress quietly, I strip, starting with my shoes. Then Blanks's sweater and my tee shirt come off, still stuck together like a second skin. I pop the button on my jeans to shimmy them down, and like I can sense the weight of his gaze, I bring my eyes up to meet his now open ones.

He stares at me, and I stare back. But I don't stop. If anything, my movements become unintentionally sensual. I unclip the back snaps of my bra, letting my breasts fall from their cups, suddenly feeling unimaginably heavy.

I can feel my heartbeat in my fingertips as I slide a hand under the strap of my underwear to glide them down my thighs and past my feet. The cool air hitting the slick warmth between my legs surprises me. Because all I can think about is *his* thick hand holding me down.

With a heavy swallow, I turn to pick up the baggy t-shirt I'd worn earlier, depositing it back over my body. Feeling myself twitch as my perked nipples graze against the fabric. Feeling the humidity between my thighs.

Everything feels like it's burning.

He's still facing me, and I hesitate to get in bed.

"I can go sleep on the sofa..." I whisper, but he's shaking his head. There aren't any words that form; there's no sound spoken, but the sentiment is clear. *Stay with me, Emma. Just a little bit longer.*

SIX

ALEX

She steps forward, her feet falling soft on the thick rug. Pulling back the covers, she gazes over me, stopping at my waist.

She crawls onto the bed but doesn't lie down. Instead, she moves her hand to my belt buckle, deftly sliding the leather out of its fastening. My breath feels hot against my own skin as she uses both hands to undo the top button of my jeans, my dick swollen and pulsing right beneath her touch. The tip, thick and angry, is wedged between the band of my briefs and my abdomen.

I wasn't expecting to have *this* reaction, but when she's close to me and she uses that voice, I can't *not* start to feel something stirring. Thawing.

Moving over me, she grabs onto both sides of my pants and pulls, bringing them down my legs, then sliding them off, throwing them to the floor on my side of the bed.

As she glides off of me, dragging her heat against, then away from me, I have this insane need to pull her over and push that sweet and soft mouth around my cock.

Fuck. I'm not supposed to be thinking those thoughts about my wife, though.

"C-can I do anything for you?" she whispers, still somewhat over me. No longer straddling me, but not lying down yet, either.

So badly, I want to answer. I want to tell her to make me feel better. To give me her body. I want her lithe frame and big breasts bouncing for me. God, how I want it. But I'm not supposed to.

I shake my head. My dick throbs, and she swallows heavily.

Lying down beside me, she rolls over, her face no longer in view of mine. And that's good. I need that. I just need someone beside me to sleep, nothing more. After tonight, I won't be caught dead in her room. Ever again.

———

It's still dark when I wake. But after years of night missions and working abroad, my sleep has never returned to fully functional. Spending the entirety of yesterday asleep *and* most of the night, my body has had enough.

It takes a couple of minutes for my eyes to adjust, but eventually, I see the covers pulled down to our waists and Emma's shirt riding up to just below the swell of her breasts.

Fuck me.

The swath of creamy skin, the neatly trimmed strip of

hair peeking out from the sheet. She's unknowingly luring me to bury myself in her and never look back.

Fuck, it was only two days ago I planned on dying. Why should I deny myself any final pleasures?

Jess.

Yeah, but somehow, I don't doubt Jess will get her kicks off without me. And more than likely, it'll be with Damian, the man I thought was my best friend. Still probably is. It's just different now. Because he had her first.

No one had *had* Emma, though. No one I knew, at least, and a desire so insatiable rose within me to have this one thing that seemed to like me. Seems to want to make *me* feel better. Wants to be *here*. And the thawing in my chest tells me I want her to be here, too. To make me feel better.

I reach down, feeling the engorged rod between my legs begging for attention. I look at Emma, sleeping with a hand in her hair. The ringlets of blonde curls are splayed out behind her, and I stroke myself once — a tease.

Emma shifts at the motion.

I stroke again, tempting fate.

And she rolls towards me. Flickering eyes find mine immediately, then startle when she realizes she's placed a hand right against her bare cunt, holding it there tightly. Without an ounce of shame, though, she slides the hand out from between her thighs and places it on my bare chest.

"Do you need something?" she whispers into the dark, her words heavy.

This time, I nod.

And we reach for each other at the same time. It's not fast, just a slow gravitational pull towards each other. My mouth finds her neck, her leg slips up to drape over my hip, her hands find my hair and then play behind my ear while my beard rubs against her chest.

Slipping a hand between us, her fingers trail up and down my rigid length.

"Alexander," she says on a soft exhale as her hips grind closer, slowly seeking friction.

"Say it again, Emma," I say back into her neck as she does this thing with her fingers, flicking against the sensitive, throbbing head, making me shudder. *What the fuck is she doing to me?*

"Alexander," she says one more time. "Let me do something just for you..."

I pull away from her slightly. "You'll regret it otherwise," she says, placing a hand on my chest and pushing. Something in the back of my mind says I won't, though, and I shake my head.

"You will," soft as sin, her voice. "Let me just...take care of you." Fuck. *I wish she would. I wish she'd fuck me.* The thought is confusing.

"Stand up," she commands, still using the soft voice.

So I do, and she follows, bringing my briefs to the floor as she moves to kneel before me, then peeling off her own shirt.

Her breasts bouncing as she settles on her knees in front of me has me feeling like a teenager who's never been touched. Every inch of me seems to feel the heat of anticipation.

"I need you to ask me nicely." Her big blue eyes look up at me, demanding. She sits there, leaning back against her heels, her palms splayed flat on her toned thighs, and she says, "Ask me nicely."

And I-I'm fucking stumped. I've never been with anyone

who's commanded me; it was always the opposite. She isn't harsh about it, though, and the internal thoughts wage war.

"Please, Emma. Would you please put my cock in your mouth?" She nods, satisfied with the ask, then moves forward.

Dropping her mouth open and gathering saliva, she lets her tongue lay flat, the visual insanely erotic. With one hand at the root of my cock, she drags my head over her velvety surface, and my hips thrust without permission. I almost fucking apologize when she stops and looks at me.

And then her tongue is back, and this time it swirls while her hand pulls. And then she's releasing my cock to suck one of her fingers before wrapping her lips around my length once more.

I grunt, seeing those sweet lips that say only soft and soothing words wrapping up my dick and tugging at me. She makes eye contact again and then slides the finger she just sucked behind me.

Oh, fuck. I'm about to tell her to stop because I don't like that, but then the pressure is there, from behind and in front, where she has me nearly touching her throat, and I want to cry. I reach down to fist her hair, and she moans against me. Taking the opportunity, she slides the finger out, then in, and I can't help but thrust, feeling my fucking legs tremble.

She would bring me to my goddamn knees.

She licks up and down my shaft, then sucks me all the way to the back, and just when I think the feeling can't get better, she slides another digit into my ass, and I lose it. Bucking my hips, spraying my seed against her throat that vibrates under another moan.

I can't think. I can't see.

But here she is, massaging my balls and slamming two fingers into my backside as her mouth sucks me dry.

She fucked me. Royally.

Loosening my grip on her hair, I run a hand down and over her head in appreciation.

I needed exactly that. And she gave it to me.

I want to give her something, too.

"Stand up," this time I command, and she rises to stand right in front of me, her nipples grazing my bare chest.

Before I can talk myself out of it, I drop my head, and she comes up, our mouths locking. Her soft tongue brushes against mine sensually. Slowly. She tastes sweet, but also, like me, it's somehow familiar and yet foreign. Gripping the back of her head, I fight against the need to deepen it. To throw caution to the wind and consume her. There's a new voice, different, saying, *Do it.*

Disregarding the voice, I kiss her with a hand on her waist and a hand in her hair, feeling overwhelming gratitude. There's a certain comfort about the feel of our mouths against one another. That nagging familiarity. *Soft. Calm.*

Whether she realizes it or not, this isn't something I give away to anyone. She's only the second woman I've ever done this with.

I focus on letting her feel my appreciation. Hoping she knows that I'm not using. I don't want to use her like this. Even if I did before, I don't feel that way now.

Deep strokes with my tongue send shivers down her arms. Her nipping at my lip has my dick bouncing back to life, a burn growing down deep. She strokes at my jaw gently before pulling away.

Don't go, the new voice pleads.

"You'll regret it," she says ominously before walking away from me. I look down at my dick, standing at hard attention again, ready to slide between and deep within her. I'm still feeling the high of what we just had. I'm feeling like maybe I just need this one thing, and it will fix me.

Confused, I follow her into the en suite bathroom, turning on the light switch.

"Regret what?" I ask her back as she washes her hands in the sink.

Our eyes lock in the mirror as she says, "Fucking me, Alex."

———

Emma

He would regret it, sooner or later, because he was a man possessed — and not by me. I know that. If he took my body like he wanted to right now, I know he's the type of man who would regret it in the end.

A lot of people wouldn't, but he would.

I, on the other hand, *will* probably regret not feeling him. Never knowing what it would be like for Alexander Palomino to claim me. To have my husband consummate this thing between us. The hit of sadness surprises me.

I turn off the light in the bathroom after I dry my hands, leaving him standing there. His dick is still hard and standing up, and I want it inside me with each throbbing pulse at the apex of my thighs...but protecting myself is the only thing I'm half decent at.

Putting up walls where necessary and drawing boundaries are things I've gotten good at so that no matter what happens, I'll be okay.

I will be.

I throw on a pair of leggings and my thickest pair of socks — not that they're thick enough — then reach for Blanks' sweater, my ring snagging the yarns again.

I groan and slip the tall set of rings off.

"You don't like it?" Alexander watches me.

"I'm not used to it; it keeps snagging on clothes."

"I would prefer you left it on..." He trails off, standing in my bedroom unmoving.

Looking at him, I attempt to infer what he means, but I'll leave them if it's important to him.

"Of course, I'll leave it," I nod as I slip the rings back down.

"Are you going somewhere?" he asks.

"Umm, yeah," I sort of laugh. "I need to blow off some steam. I'm gonna go for a walk."

"It's only 5:00 A.M.," he says, like that will deter me.

"Which is like my 6:00 P.M. My sleep schedule isn't quite right yet."

He nods, then starts slipping his boxer briefs on. I watch as he gathers his clothes, curious to know where all this would lead. *What would our everyday look like?*

I assume he's home or not working because of the holiday, and that's why Blanks is here, too. But maybe they're just with each other all the time? Blanks said *inseparable.*

Do they even work? When are they traveling next? And am I expected to go?

"I'll be back in two minutes. Wait for me." *Huh?* Alex

walks around me, slipping out my door, clothes and boots in hand, only his tight black briefs covering his backside.

His quads, like thick teardrops, will haunt me... *Fuck*, I want him. I wanted him the second I saw him. I *needed* him the second he laid a hand on me in that car.

I can feel myself clenching, yearning for release, but I won't let myself do anything about it. At least not yet.

Without a beanie, heavy jacket, or boots, I'm questioning if I've thought this walk through when Alex bounds down the stairs in thick khaki pants, hiking boots, and a long-sleeved thermal. He's also carrying an armload of things.

Immediately, he passes over a jacket and knit hat, which I accept without question because what else am I supposed to do? Freeze?

He dons a hat and jacket, and we head for the front door.

Stepping out and into the frigid morning is bracing. There's something about seeing frost lining every little thing yet knowing this will all be gone by the time the first sunbeams touch down. It's like a secret world before the rest of the living wakes. Like in this secret world, anything that exists here stays here.

Like what just happened between Alex and me. This walk. It would all stay in this alternate reality before being bleached away by the sun. And I'm okay with that. Low expectations mean I'm not anticipating what just happened to ever happen again. Even if I want it to.

"I guess, where to?" I ask awkwardly, and he motions for me to follow.

Alex leads me to the clearing, where he chops wood and points to two small paths carved out between the trees.

"This one," he motions to the path on the left, "goes

further up the mountain. I've cleared about 5 miles." Pointing to the path on the right, he says, "This one goes down to a hidden cove. It's about a mile and a half round trip." I nod my head towards the path on the right.

Someday, I'll take the 5-mile trail. Preferably when I'm dressed appropriately and alone.

The path to the cove is rocky in spots, and we have to climb and travel along a ridge before starting the descent back towards the water line. I can't see much because of the lack of sun, but occasionally, I glimpse the glint of moonlight on water through the trees.

I hear the scratch of some nocturnal beast. There's the hoot of an owl on the prowl, and a gentle breeze rustles the tree limbs, sending pine needles to the ground, landing like glitter on the frost.

I've never wanted so badly to reach out and feel everything. The cold moss, the frosted forest floor, the pine cones littered about. I want to absorb every sensory detail: the sight, the smell, the sounds, the feel.

A sense of belonging permeates me at a molecular level. It's something clicking into place, breathing frigid air, bathing in moonlight, with nothing but trees as companions. *Here* feels like home in a way no other place has. Like when I was born, there'd been a crossing of wires, a mistake in the divine order, and instead of being born to a loving family who lived in the mountains, I was birthed into a desert of epic proportions. Everything was dry and drained of life there; people doing anything they could to get a glimpse of *their forest* or life beyond.

Whatever drug they could find, whatever hit they could take that gave them a fraction of what this forest is giving me.

It's an epiphany to finally understand why they did *it*. But I'm still convinced I was never meant for the desert. I'm meant to be in a place like this.

I inhale, and Alex slows his gait, turning to make sure I'm fine. We've been walking in near silence for 15 minutes, and I anticipate hitting the cove any second.

"You good?" *Never better*.

"Yeah," is all I say in return.

At last, we reach a small clearing with another path forking off in a different direction and, in the middle, a massive boulder.

We climb up the large boulder, and when we reach the top, I'm rendered speechless and breathless by the view of navy blue water lapping at the shore. Moonlight hits the water and splinters, splaying itself across the lake. Gray puffs of clouds drift listlessly across the sky, and it's all like a dream.

I sit down on the cold gray stone, and surprisingly, Alexander joins me. I sit criss-cross applesauce, and he sits with his knees bent and his arms slung over the top of them.

We sit like this for probably ten minutes in complete silence. Together. Until eventually, it feels like he's not himself and I'm not me. We're just two people with no history and no past. And nothing laid out before us. Nowhere to be and no future. All that exists is life as it happens, in this moment, in this hidden world of ours.

"My dad used to take me hunting. It was always really early. Like this time of morning." I look at Alex, who is talking but zoned out, looking at the water. "I hated going until I got really good at it."

I keep quiet, curious why he would share this with me.

"I got good at it because I had to. Every time I missed, he would shoot me with an air rifle." I gasp but manage to keep the sound internal. "I got good because I thought he'd be scared of me if I was better than him. But he wasn't. He just got jealous instead."

Jesus.

I scoot closer, trying to decide how to say something without saying anything because talking on my part feels wrong. This is Alex's time to share something in our world, and he can have it. This morning is his.

So I scoot closer, but I stay silent. And while my instinct is to crawl into his lap and stroke his face, I just let my close presence provide comfort this time.

I watch him, memorizing the lines of his face, the way his beard comes in thick and to the exact right spot below his cheekbones. The broad shoulders that carry invisible weights. Beautiful to the point of fracture. A fracturing because a soul claimed this man, then turned around and gave it away. A shattering over parents who inflicted torture. A break, dirty and ragged and beautiful. That's what I see when I memorize his face.

"I would have regretted it, Emma. I'm so sorry." *I know.*

All I say is, "I'm sorry, too."

SEVEN

ALEX

When the sun breaks over the mountains on the eastern side of the lake, I stand slowly. Feeling...different. Better. Not happy, but not like I might die under the weight of my mistakes.

And she did it.

She stands with me, giving me her softest smile that shows no teeth, just a turn of the lips that shifts the dusting of freckles across the apples of her cheeks.

The sun's rays dance off her curls as we turn to head back towards the house. This time with her leading, I watch her ass sway as she traverses the uneven ground.

Torture.

It would be agony living like this. It wasn't the plan to open up to her. To be close to her. But at the moment, it's all I want. To be close to her.

But I'm not supposed to be.

I'm supposed to be mourning Jess. The guilt claws its way back to front and center. With each step we take away from the cove, the weight of that guilt grows. It feels as if by the time we get back to the house, this weight will be a tangible thing upon my chest. Worn like a scarlet letter.

'Don't call me. Don't text me. Don't come visit.' But why the fuck am I feeling guilty when those were her final words to me?

She doesn't want this, Alex. Not you. Let it go.

I have to find a way to let it go. And burying myself deep in *my wife* feels like the best idea I can think of.

But she's right that I would regret it. I'd regret letting go of the pain and letting myself feel even just a second of joy. I already regretted letting her take me in her mouth because I didn't deserve it.

I don't deserve her.

And there lies the source of my regret.

Maybe if I'd met her at some other point in my life, everything could have been different. But maybe I never would have given her a second look. Because without being broken, I wouldn't need her so desperately to fix me.

When we get to the clearing beside the garage, the unofficial trailhead, she turns to stop and wait for me.

"Can you take me somewhere today?" She asks. I nod. "I think it would be good if I had a car, so I didn't have to ask you guys for rides and stuff..."

"Do you want me to just get you a car?" She shakes her head.

"No, I can use what you gave me to buy one." I'm already shaking my head, though.

"No, that's money for you to save. For you. I'll go with

you... Or Blanks will, and we'll get it." Her brow wrinkles slightly.

"I appreciate that, but I need it to be in my name. It's... important to me." I give her the same look of confusion.

"And it will be."

"Okay..." She lets it roll out seemingly against her will. If I can do nothing else right, I can take care of Emma's needs. She should want for nothing while she's here.

There's a small instinct inside me, willing me to make some kind of gesture. A hand on her shoulder or arm, a hug. But then there's reality. My boots feel too heavy. She feels too perfect, and the closer I let myself get to her, the more corrupt and less perfect she'll become.

I want to keep her a certain way in my mind and reality. And the more I touch her, the more muddied she would be. So I keep my distance and bypass her to walk towards the house. She doesn't say anything because she's not expecting anything either.

When we walk inside, I can feel it. The difference. *The absence.*

"Blanks!" I shout into the expanse of the main floor, hearing only the sound of the kitchen faucet in response.

Seething, I walk past the great room, discovering what I knew to be true, then on and into the kitchen.

"What'd you do with it?"

He shrugs nonchalantly, "I took care of it."

"Where is it?" I practically yell. He doesn't respond. He never engages when I get like this. I fume, standing in the kitchen, over the missing gifts. The bottom of the tree empty. *Barren.* The stockings hung on the mantel. *Gone.* Her fucking high chair. *Missing.*

"I didn't ask you to take care of it," I hiss, but he stands there stoically, broad, taking it.

"She's not fucking coming back," he says eventually, breaking the tension. Breaking me.

I want to throw or hit or *anything*, but light shuffling has me halting when I remember Emma behind me.

"Take Emma to get a car today. I can't be here." I watch his face twitch with anger and see Emma step uncomfortably from one side to the next.

I should apologize for the outburst, but instead, I walk away and far. Opting for the trail up the mountain, I hope a small little hope that I never see this house ever again.

———

Emma

"Do you always just take care of him?" I ask Blanks, who loads a glass into the dishwasher, his back to me.

"Someone had to do it." He dries his hands while turning around to face me, then leans back against the large, apron front sink. "Should we have waited till Christmas morning? Opened them even though they were addressed to someone else? Done it after Christmas? Fuck that's depressing. I did him a favor by ripping off that bandaid."

I arch my eyebrows, pursing my lips together, "Well, alright then." I take my jacket to the mudroom, hanging it and the beanie I was wearing on an empty hook.

"So, where were you two love birds this morning?" Blanks asks the second I'm back in the kitchen. He immediately grabs a clean mug when he sees me turning towards the coffee maker, filling the cup for me.

"Uh, we just went for a walk." He watches me, my movements, my face.

Passing the cup to me, he says, "You fucked, didn't you?" It's not crass, just matter of fact.

"No, we didn't." He laughs, but the chuckle has no warmth behind it.

"He turn you down, then?" My cheeks flame at the inference.

"No." My business, and Alex's business, is none of his. "Are-are you jealous?" I stutter out.

He leans forward, crowding my space, then does something that has my panties twisting. He fists the front of the sweater I'm wearing, the material disappearing in his massive hand, and he drags me closer to him.

"Not how you're thinking, Angel. We're leaving in an hour. Be ready." He releases the fabric, and I sway backward, no longer inches from his face.

"Okay..." I whisper when he stalks out of the kitchen.

Having a sister or a best friend could be really fucking helpful right about now. Or just *anyone* to talk to at all.

I'm still thinking about the gesture and confused as hell about it as I blow dry my hair post-shower, setting it back to straight.

Is he jealous of Alex spending time with me? Or me spending time with Alex? I was insinuating the latter. The closeness they share...The never-apart thing... But maybe...

No.

It's confusing. Being here. Surrounded by them.

The hand on my leg. The fist in my sweater. His length on

my tongue. Oh god, I won't make it through the day unless I take care of this. Setting down my blow dryer, I lean against the freestanding bathtub ledge. In only my bra and underwear, I watch myself in the mirror as I slide a hand down, feeling the smooth, freshly shaven skin heat under my own touch.

I'm wishing, *dying*, for it to be someone else's, though. I tip my head back when my finger pad brushes my clit, massaging. But it's not enough. I want pressure, I want movement, I want to be fucked like I'm someone's one and only other half.

That's the only way I'll take it; otherwise, it's not worth it. I turn, straddling the edge of the tub, letting my panties pull tight between my lips, and I thrust my hips forwards, the fabric tugging at my pussy, and my inner walls contract. I rub my clit and think about him holding me down. I think about that fist in my hair and not my sweater. I think of him slipping into my bed at night to do lewd things with me.

I rock back and forth across the tub ledge and rub my clit with a prayer: *let me have someone. Give me someone, please.* "I'm begging you..." I say softly to the universe.

As the heat in my pelvis grows, my inner thighs turn taut, and I rock forward once more, my chest jutting out. My nipples strain against the lace fabric of my bra, and I ride the high.

I turn to look in the mirror to watch myself come undone when his eyes meet mine. *Fucking asshole.* But I don't stop riding it out, fucking myself as best I can all alone. *Though not entirely alone.*

With my thighs and walls clenched tight, I can feel the rush of wet heat. *Fuck! Yes!!!* The thrill of an audience sends me somewhere that's eluded me before. I want to scream, but I hold it.

When I'm done, I slide my hand out of my panties and lick the pads of my fingers clean while he watches me.

Fucking eat your heart out.

Saying nothing, I swing my one leg off the side of the tub to head to the water closet.

"Five minutes, Angel," he says to my back as I walk to the toilet. I hold up one hand in a one-finger salute as I retreat, and I hear a faint chuckle.

———

Sitting beside him in the car should probably be embarrassing for me, but I'm not. He should be embarrassed for not looking away.

He leans across, taking the seat belt out of my hand, and buckles me in, the gesture confusing me.

"For the record, Sweetpea, I'd never leave you begging afterward." I turn my head to face him, and with him leaning over to slip the buckle in, his face is just millimeters from mine. Our mouths would touch if either of us so much as exhaled.

He removes his hand from the buckle when it clicks into place, and my heart skips a beat. Moving his fingers up to my jawline, he drags his tongue across the tip of my nose simultaneously.

I-I don't even know what to think about it. I think my mouth hangs slightly open, and he looks down at it, then in my eyes, but remains silent.

After that, he turns away, fastening his own seatbelt, and then starts the black sedan.

"So, what kind of car are we getting?" He does that a lot. Uses "we" to reference to us. It's so fucking surprising and sounds way more intimate than I think he even realizes it does.

"Probably the same thing I had. A Honda Civic." He laughs at me.

"That's a no." I turn to look at him as we pull out onto the main mountain road.

"Why not?" I ask incredulously.

"Let me ask this: why a Honda Civic?"

"They're reliable, easy to park, and compact."

"And so is a Porsche 911," he says with another laugh. "Meet me in the middle, Angel."

"Ugh, you have to stop calling me these pet names. Does Alex know you do that?" He shrugs.

"Even if he did, he wouldn't care." Just a little hit to the heart. *Ouch.*

"Oh, stop. I want a coffee," I say as we hit the main strip of Spearhead. His mouth turns, not quite in a frown, and the little lines between his eyebrows form.

"How about in town?"

"No, I want to drink it on the drive." I put my foot down.

His left eye twitches, and he concedes, slowing down to pull into the last open spot in front of "The Grounds."

"What do you want?" I ask as I unbuckle, expecting him to wait in the car, but he's unbuckling too.

"Can't let you go in there alone," he sighs. And I roll my eyes with a laugh.

"Am I not allowed to go places alone here? And why?"

"Shut up, Em," he says, tugging on a piece of my long hair when I go to open the door. He glares at me, pushing my hand aside, then comes around to get the door for me.

I like him calling me Em.

The inside of the shop and cafe smells like cinnamon and yeasty bread, and I love it. The floors are checkered linoleum, and premade gift baskets with red bows are littered throughout the space. They even have a table dedicated to a small, live Christmas tree with stars hanging on it. Names scribbled on them.

Shame gnaws at me. Walking over to the tree while Blanks stands in line, I look at the names, ages, and wishlists and pluck the remaining non-claimed stars that are left.

When I get back in line, Blanks sees the stack and slides them from my hand to his.

"I guess I know what we're doing after the dealership," he says, verging on annoyance.

"You don't need to come with me." I go to take the stars back, but he lurches his hand away from me.

"And yet, I will." I give him an eye roll while smiling internally.

We order our coffees, Blanks pays, and as we're walking towards the door to leave, I say, "Look at that! No incidents occurred. No need to accompany me."

But when I turn back around, I nearly run right into a pregnant woman. Luckily, Blanks saves the coffee, taking it from my hands.

"Oh god, I'm so sorry," I say to the woman, who looks at Blanks and then back at me with wide eyes. I examine her, checking I didn't spill any coffee, and when I see none, I give a slight smile, ready to move aside and be on my way.

"Emma, right?" She asks.

Blanks finally speaks up, "Brit, this is Emma. Emma, this is Brit, Alex's sister." My face naturally wants to highlight and smile and exclaim. But then I remember the heated exchange she and Alex shared yesterday.

I extend my hand politely, maintaining a smaller smile, one that I hope is warm and friendly.

And she takes it, mirroring my expression. After she lowers her hand and I lower mine, she turns to Blanks and says, "We'll still see you on Christmas, right?"

Blanks gives me the side eye, then, looking back at Brit with a smile, says, "Wouldn't miss it, Doll." *Everyone gets a pet name. Got it.*

Brit nods, then walks past us to stand in line. It isn't the warm sisterly welcome I may have imagined, but this isn't exactly the marriage of my dreams, either. No use in feeling burned by my fake sister-in-law.

Arching my eyebrows, Blanks nudges me towards the door, handing me my coffee so he can open it for me.

"Tad icy? No?" I say as we get back in the car. Me first, then Blanks walks around to get his door.

"We're 6,000 feet above sea level. What'd you expect?"

I laugh, "No, Alex's sister, you oaf."

He nods, "Just give it some time." I don't even know how long I'm supposed to stick around, so I just shrug and move on. Because as much as I would love a friend, even a sister-in-law who's friendly, I know it's best to keep expectations low. *Real fucking low.*

Blanks hands me the stack of stars, probably 10 or so, and I flip through them as we start our commute.

Jacob, 9 yo
Wants a scooter

Come on, Jacob, dream bigger! This is the first Christmas, maybe ever, that I have money in the bank. More money than I've dreamed of making in a lifetime. And not a single soul to buy gifts for. Aside from these stars.

Teller, 6 yo
Wants a science set with test tubes

Yesss, Teller.
"What are you smiling at?" Blanks asks, checking me.
I shrug, "Just excited."
"About your new Range Rover?" He asks, and I laugh.
"You're so stupid. No. And also, no."
After 15 minutes, I ask if I can turn on the radio, and he lets me choose. We listen to Christmas music and sip our coffees in quiet, comfortable companionship.
"You're sure there's nothing going on between you and Alex?" I ask, zoning out on the beige hills we're now driving through.
"You know what they say about stupid questions, Angel?" *Stupid because I had to ask?*
I couldn't help the eye roll if I tried.
"I'm either driving to the Range Rover dealership or Mercedes. Decide quickly."
"I want a Bronco," I decide fast, even surprising myself. He nods at the compromise.
"Then that's what the princess gets." I hate that nick-name, though. I sock him in the arm.

"I'm not a princess." He gives me a look, in turn, that heats my core.

"Not a princess at all, Angel." His voice is slick, lapping up my spine. "The perk is we can take your top off in the spring."

My cheeks heat, and he laughs. "Off the car. We'll take the top off the car." I sock him again, then turn up the music to ear-bleeding-loud the rest of the drive.

EIGHT

ALEX

She hops out of the raised Bronco with ease, rounding the back to remove bags from the trunk.

Something about seeing her *here*, I like it. It makes sense to me.

Then Blanks practically jogs to her side once he's parked to help.

I don't like that.

They spent the day together, and where I shouldn't have given two shits, I find myself wishing, maybe, it had been me.

Or maybe I'm just projecting, worried history will repeat itself. A best friend, just a little too friendly to someone who meant a little more to me than I would let on.

I let the ax fall with more force than necessary, drawing their attention. Neither acts any sort of way about it. Emma eyes me, giving a soft tilt of the mouth in my direction. And then there's Blanks with a gaze that says too much.

It's on me to insert myself if I want. Or, I can hang back and watch this become something... *More like them become something.*

Dropping the ax, I grab the long sleeve I discarded earlier and wipe my face as I head in their direction.

I should leave them alone.

Yet, I move closer.

Why do I care again?

The image of her on her knees. Her straddling me in nothing but a towel. A hand traveling up and down my back.

I want to burn the images into my mind and erase them at the same time.

Even if I don't, or shouldn't, want anything with Emma, I know for a fact I don't want her to have something with him.

"Busy day?" I ask once I'm close enough.

"Productive," they say it in fucking unison.

Then they laugh about it. I have to fight the urge to turn and walk away.

"Need some help?" I stuff the shirt in my back pocket, reaching around Emma's backside to pick up bags of...toys?

"Sure," she says, her cheeks warming when my chest brushes against her back. I watch as Blanks eyes the interaction, knowing it wasn't a fucking accident.

I slip my hand into the handles of the bags she's holding, moving our hands against one another far more intimately than necessary. I'm gentle with her.

I'm trying to be gentle with her.

Inside the house, I drop whatever all this is on the dining room table, and Emma and Blanks do the same.

So you opening a toy store? I try the joke in my mind, but it sounds fucking lame. Because it is. I'm not exactly bringing much to the table conversationally. Not compared to talk-your-socks-off Blanks. He probably already has some endearing fucking nickname picked out for her.

"I was gonna go shower, but um, do you need help?" That's the best I can do. Honestly, that's all I've got. Maybe it's because I'm a 42-year-old widower collecting failed relationships like military coins, or maybe it's just me, but the tank is fucking empty. I don't have witty comebacks and one-liners to throw her way.

"It's just a lot of wrapping and then dropping it off at The Grounds tomorrow morning." She shrugs, not answering one way or the other. But all I can think is: *I can't be seen at The fucking Grounds.* What if *she's* there?

Living five minutes away from the love of your life you're not allowed to acknowledge is fucked. Who isn't allowing me? *Me.* Yeah. Fucked. Fully aware.

"I can wrap. Just give me ten?" I ask her, and Blanks eyes the fuck out of me.

"Okay!" She says nearly exuberantly.

I beeline for the upstairs, an extra hitch in my step. That is until I walk past Eden's room. Then I'm in *our* room. Staring at the bed. Walking into her closet just to catch the scent of her perfume that lingers. My stomach turns at the reminder.

'I love you, Alex.'

I love you, too.

I should have fucking said it back.

My old friend, regret finds me. Had I said it back within the 30 seconds she gave me, would this all be different right now? Had I said, *I love you, I can't live without you, give me all your chances, because I'll give you all mine,* would we be here together?

I slip my phone out of my pocket and hover over her name, debating.

She wouldn't pick up. Would she?

Would she?

———

"We're done, by the way," Blanks wanders in, not bothering to knock. Yeah, that sounds about right. "We're gonna go pick up pizza..." there's no invite added to the end.

"Is she pissed at me?" I ask him.

"I think she doesn't know what to think of you. Luckily someone's already trained her to expect nothing of people, so when she gets jack shit, it's no skin off her back." My stomach sinks with guilt. But that's what anyone close to me should expect.

"Tell her I said sorry. Something came up." He looks at me, noticing I haven't even showered yet.

Blanks scoffs, "Tell her yourself. Or, you know, don't. Or better yet, leave her alone." It sounds bitter, and I drag my eyes from my phone to meet his that glare down at me.

"Do you like her?" I ask, my brow furrowing.

He runs a hand along his mustache, like a tell. "My answer is irrelevant. But don't fuck with her. Don't play with your food. Just fuck, *Pal.* I don't know why you had to do this." He shakes his head. "I just hope to god she doesn't fall in love with you too." He turns and walks away, leaving me feeling like the Jess-sized hole in my heart is the least of my problems.

———

Emma

Christmas Eve. And I'm sitting alone in the dark, watching flurries unfurl from the sky, appearing like magic out of thin air. My mug of cocoa went cold half an hour ago, but I can't bring myself to move from my spot in the living room to rewarm it. All the lights are off, I'm tucked under a furry blanket, and it's just me, the moonlight, and flurries.

Happiness isn't the right word. *Contentment?* I'm probably content. Safe? Mostly. But happy? *No.* And I probably won't be until after Alex and I divorce someday. Being around him is equal parts pleasure and pain.

His wayward glances are like gifts, but his attention deprivation is like being suffocated slowly. He leaves you aching for the next breath every time you see him.

The best thing for me is to pretend he doesn't exist. It's just me in this winter wonderland. Maybe Santa's out there, too.

There are no stockings hung by our chimney with care, though. And the bottom of the tree is glaringly empty. I have no expectations that will change between now and tomorrow morning. So, the plan is to wake up extra early, cook a big breakfast to leave out for them, and then go for a hike. Alone. And hopefully, for most of the day.

Blanks helped me find some hiking gear, a light pack, and Camelbak. Better shoes, and socks, and outerwear. It's the best gift anyone has ever given me — their time. He spent the better part of the afternoon running errands with me before heading to Alex's sister's house for Christmas Eve dinner and festivities.

The invite hadn't been extended.

For some reason, the back of my throat burned when he left.

It's possible I'm finding myself growing attached to the only person capable of human connection in a three-mile radius, so I'll cut myself a little slack.

Even if I was in Vegas right now, I would still feel this way. A little bit slighted. Lonely. So this is nothing new, except that everything is new.

Maybe I've stayed out here hoping to catch Blanks on his way in for the night, but at 11:30, it's starting to feel less and less likely that I will. So, cradling my cup, I set it in the sink, then head towards my suite tucked away behind the great room.

I hadn't ventured upstairs yet. Am I even allowed to? Or is this like Beauty and the Beast? *The West Wing is off-limits!* I have no clue what's there, aside from Alex. He's always either in his room, chopping wood, or, I guess, just gone because I've hardly seen him since he volunteered to help and then disappeared yesterday.

I haven't even allowed myself to really think about that, or what it means, or how I feel because it hadn't felt good. And that's problematic. So I tuck those thoughts away for another day and time, like maybe my hike, and I curl into a ball on the bed.

I rub my feet together, trying to garner some warmth, but it never seems to come, just like the sleep that fails to arrive as well.

So, instead of sleeping, I lie here, staring at the ceiling, wondering. *Where is Blanks?* I still haven't heard him come in. *If I were in Vegas, what would I be doing?* I would be nearly mid-shift on what is notoriously the slowest night of the year. Why Eddie's even stayed open, I have no clue.

And then, like most nights, I eventually play the game of what-if. *What if I had been born into a more normal family with two loving parents who weren't diseased and dysfunctional? Where would I be? Who would I be? Would I like her? Would she be playing Santa with her husband right now, tiptoeing around our house, filling stockings? Sneaking around the living room, hiding gifts and toys?*

The what-if game is a painful one to play. Because all my what-ifs are wishes. Dreams. Ones that I've never felt so far away from obtaining. The dreams felt closer in Vegas, with no boyfriend and no prospects in sight, than here, married to Alexander Palomino.

I'm already wishing the day away when I hear the faintest of steps in the hall. A quick check of the time shows 1:30. Likely Blanks sneaking in. I wait and listen, and then my door slowly eases open. I hadn't shut it all the way, but when Alexander's head pops in, I gasp at the shock.

"Oh my god, you scared me," I whisper-shout at him, clutching the comforter tight.

"I'm sorry." He's standing in the doorway, shirtless. Sleep pants slung low around his hips.

"Is something wrong?" I ask, propping myself up on my elbows to see him better.

"Can't sleep, and I was wondering..." He doesn't finish, but he doesn't need to. I pull the covers back on the empty side of the bed, scooting over to make room. He slides in, and I roll over to face away from him.

If he just needs someone to sleep beside to make it through the night, that's fine. But I won't be rubbing his back till he passes out. The closeness we shared the other night and morning has faded. Snuffed out by Alex's avoidance.

So this time in bed, it's not intimate. There's lots of space between us, me facing one way, him probably facing the other. Because no matter how much I want to be like that with him, Alex is clearly out of reach. Still madly in love with someone else. *Jess.*

Eventually, my eyes get heavier, my breathing mellows, and I drift off, thinking about snow.

———

The clicking of the front door has my eyes shooting open; just a habit from living alone, and, I guess, natural instincts trying to keep me alive living with two men.

I check the phone on my nightstand. 4:30. I was hoping for another half hour, but it wouldn't hurt to start the oven for the cinnamon rolls I prepped yesterday.

Slipping away from beside Alex, I walk towards the great room but stop short, seeing Blanks and a tall redhead making out under the mistletoe in the entry.

Why do I hate it? And who picks someone up on Christmas Eve? Blanks does, obviously.

I wait a moment, tucked back in the hall until, eventually, he throws open the door to the basement, and the two retreat.

My throat is burning again, I get the chills, and a small part of me wants to cry.

Stupid, really.

So silently, I make the breakfast I planned. I prep some

snacks for my day hike and pack my small bag. I lay everything out on the counter for breakfast and am just writing a
short note when I hear the faint screams of ecstasy from
downstairs, making the back of my eyelids hurt.

"Really?" I question the universe.

It's fine. This is just not my time. It hadn't been my time...
ever. What's another few years? Again, assuming I can make
it to 100 or so.

I get dressed in the mudroom where everything had been
hung up yesterday, and as silently as possible, I whisper,
"Merry Christmas," to *them* as I slip out the mudroom door.

———

After two miles, I stop, sitting on a fallen log to eat my
breakfast and watch the sunrise.

For the last hour, I've moved slowly, working hard on not
slipping on the slick pine needles or damp rocks. It's still dark
out, and the thought of spraining an ankle out here, alone, is a
little more than frightening.

The flurries never manifested into an all-out snow last
night. It was just enough to make everything damp without
leaving a presence behind.

It's cold, but with my blood pumping from the uphill
climb, I'm comfortable.

Pulling out the cinnamon roll I packed, I slowly pick at it.
And I cry.

At first, I try to fight it, swallowing past the tightness in
my throat and forcing the food down. But eventually, I just
stop and let the tears fall freely.

There probably hasn't been a single year I haven't cried

on Christmas. It's always been the most disappointing day of the year. There's always some letdown. My parents. Work. The fact that I'm alone. It's rarely about getting what I want because simply put, I've never gotten much.

A pack of underwear. Something picked up haphazardly from a convenience store. Something I buy myself, then eventually return when the guilt of spending the money weighs too heavily on me. I've gotten used to not getting gifts, at least not anything I want.

But no matter what, or where, or who I'm with, I've never gotten over the disappointment of this day. A day for family and warm houses and happy faces. This is a day I spend alone, tired, and longing for all the things this day has never been for me.

Sure, I could have stayed at Alex's with them, but the idea of being there *with them*, yet still being completely alone, has me crying just a little bit harder.

I knew Blanks would be going to Alex's sister's again. I knew I wouldn't get invited to go. And I have no doubt Alexander plans to spend the majority of his day regretting his life choices. Maybe he'll stay in bed all day, or maybe he'll chop wood till his body gives out, but I can't be there for him today. Not on Christmas when I feel like I'm dying inside.

As the sun peeks over the eastern ridge of the mountains, I sigh, and the tears begin to slow. It's hard to stay feeling shitty in the most tranquil environment I've ever been in. This place is otherworldly, like a fantasy land brought to life.

The pine trees are crowding me in with haphazard boulders sprinkled throughout. Squirrels are skittering around, flying in and out of burrows whenever I shuffle my feet. The birds start singing as the sun starts hitting the tops of the trees. The sound is shortly followed by the dripping and pattering of former frost falling from the heavy branches above.

It all works together to form a symphony. Water falling, birds singing, creatures scurrying.

I can finally swallow without the pain making itself known, so I pick up my cinnamon roll and eat while the sun warms the world for a beautiful Christmas Day.

NINE

ALEX

Waking up to a still, brightly lit room, I know she's gone. I can feel it. And my stomach turns with disappointment. I don't know what I hoped would happen, but her absence is like breaking a seal. Or maybe it's the sunlight that broke the spell.

Don't love it, though.

I wasn't supposed to come back in here; I told myself I wouldn't. But I couldn't sleep.

I was bone tired, but my body just wouldn't let go.

And I felt bad. I'd been avoiding her for two days, so maybe she's the real reason I couldn't sleep because as soon as I lay down next to her, the eyes that wouldn't budge fell. Deep.

I can just barely hear them chatting, forcing me fully awake and out into the great room.

But it's not her.

Some woman sits in Blanks' lap while he feeds her. *Where's Emma?* Blanks and the woman look up at me, and the lighthearted look flies off his face when he sees I've come from her room.

He stands, moving the woman's legs off his own, extricating himself out of their embrace.

"She's not here," he tells me even though I don't ask.

"Where is she then?" I move closer into the eat-in, where he's now standing.

"There's a note." Blanks points to the counter, taking a long sip of coffee.

Merry Christmas. Breakfast's on me today. Going for a hike, be back before nighttime.

I turn to stare at him.

"You knew she was doing this today?"

He shrugs.

"You fucking let her go by herself? Are you fucking insane?" I yell. Don't mean to just the anxiety is instant, directly followed by rage. *What if something happens to her?*

"She's fine," he says calmly.

"She doesn't even own a jacket heavy enough for this weather!" I shout again.

"Yeah. She does!" He shouts back, "Because I bought her one yesterday. Calm the fuck down." He moves in closer, daring to get in my face. I don't like the stinging in my chest because if I spared her more than a glance yesterday, maybe I would know this, too. Maybe I would be the one buying her things, taking her places.

"I think I should go," the redhead interrupts us quietly,

moving off the dining bench, then giving us a wide berth as she heads to find the rest of her clothes.

"And who the fuck is that?" I ask Blanks, pissed as hell.

He laughs, "Does it matter? If you're mad about not getting any, maybe next time, don't turn down your *wife*." I want to throttle him.

We stand, staring each other down, until I finally say, "I didn't turn her down." The sick smile slides off the bastard's face. "She turned me down." *Hate admitting that to him.* I shoulder-check him as I grab a piece of bacon off the counter, then head towards the stairs.

"She turned you down?" he asks quietly as if the question isn't actually meant to be answered.

So I don't bother with an answer, focusing instead on getting dressed as quickly as possible to go find her.

———

Blanks

Everything tastes sour. Immediately, I want to throw up the coffee I've been downing like it's a lifeline.

What does it mean that she turned him down?

Who was she begging for in the bathroom?

Was it me? Why do I wish it was me so bad?

I drag my hand down my face, feeling the burn in my chest. This new yet familiar ache that comes every time I'm around her.

Every time I say I'll keep my distance and then can't, the burn is there.

When I left her alone last night, on fucking Christmas Eve, the burn had been there.

When I brought someone home, knowing she would be getting up for her hike, my chest had been on fire. And not for the redhead, but for *her*. Hoping she would hear me. Wishing it was her the whole time.

Knowing it never would be because she's likely halfway in love with her husband already.

But is she?

Why the fuck is Alex sleeping in there if she said no, and why did it make me want to push him into the freezing cold lake? Why couldn't he just leave her the fuck alone?

I want to punch him in his fucking face over it.

My feet are moving up the stairs before I can even think of it. *Stay the fuck away from her.* Repeats in my head, over and over. Is it that I need to stay away, or him? *Both.*

I barge into his room. We were past the point of a courtesy knock.

"Just leave her alone today, okay?" I say to his back as he gets dressed.

"Give me a good reason to, then." He turns around, zipping up his jeans and grabbing a sweater.

Because I like her, and she's nice, and she doesn't deserve whatever shit you'll end up putting her through. But I don't say that. I can't.

"Because she doesn't like Christmas, and it's a shitty day for her. Just let her be alone. You, of all people, should know how that feels."

I hate him for a second because somehow he'll squander this, burning everyone around him in the process, then wonder what all the smoke is about later. He just doesn't fucking get it, his effect on people. I hate that he's like this.

When it becomes apparent he isn't going to bother replying, I say, "Listen, I'm leaving today. But just try and be nice to her." I turn to walk away, almost forgetting, "Your Christmas present's in the garage, asshole. Merry Christmas."

He stands, staring at me, until finally he says, "Yeah, Merry Christmas."

Rolling my eyes, I blow out of his room, fuming. *Still.*

I need to give Red a ride home, make an appearance at Brit's, and then, I'll say goodbye to *her*.

Emma

He's waiting outside for me. Well, that's the story I'm telling myself because it makes me feel good to imagine a man like that would be waiting for *me*. The thought produces chills.

In my fucking dreams.

My cheeks heat, and I drop my gaze, ashamed. He was fucking someone else this morning. How much more clear could it be that he isn't interested? He's also my husband's best friend.

I walk past him, shooting him a sideways smile but not stopping because everything hurts. My feet. My back. My head. I want a hot shower and to sleep for twelve hours. I'm just praying that a ten-mile hike outdoors will be just the thing to set my circadian rhythm back to normal.

In my eagerness to take the hike, I didn't really compute

that five miles meant five miles there. And five miles back. So when I'm unable to walk tomorrow, I just hope that something in this town delivers food. I hope.

Was it worth it? Standing at the end of the trail, on a ridge that offers a view all the way to Nevada, yes. It was worth it. There's a small clearing that brings you right to the edge of a steep drop-off, leaving you feeling like all the world is below you. The ridge feels like the peak. It's empowering, if not a little terrifying, to look down.

But hobbling home, weary and bone tired, I'm not so sure how *worth it* it was.

"Hey," he says, coming forward so that he's no longer kicked back, leaning against his car.

"Hey," I say back, continuing to walk towards the house.

"I'm leaving." There's that burn again. He's always making me feel uncomfortable in the most unexpected ways.

"Oh." I stop walking to turn towards him. "Um, why?" I thought, well, I guess I thought that the two of them lived together.

"The holiday is over, so it's back to reality, Angel." Why am I going to miss him?

"So you're going home?" *If I keep asking stupid questions, will it keep him here longer? Where is home? Texas?*

He smiles that sinful smile and says, "Maybe. I just wanted to say goodbye and tell you," he hesitates, and I hang on the edge of his word like it's my salvation, "Merry Christmas." *Of course.*

I give him a tired smile and eke out a response, "Yeah, same to you. Merry Christmas." *I guess.*

Staring at him as he stares back at me, I want to say something more. I want to hear him say something more, but the front door is opening, and Alex is coming for us.

"Well, bye then." I give a stupid sort of wave and start walking towards the house. Again.

I anticipate walking around Alex, leaving room for him to pass, but it quickly becomes clear he's walking towards *me*, surprising me.

When I turn to look back at Blanks one last time, he's already getting in his car. *Yeah, okay.*

Whatever. Just another disappointing Christmas.

The hiking euphoria is fading, the exhaustion taking over, so by the time Alex gets to me, I feel like I'm barely standing upright.

He reaches around, taking the backpack off my shoulders, and leads me into the house.

There's dinner set on the table and a fire roaring in the great room. And all I want is to cry.

"How was it?" He asks, maybe uncomfortably.

"Long." My voice nearly cracks at the utter defeat that I feel about this day. "I'm just gonna shower and then lay down."

"Oh." He looks over to the table and then back to me. "I can bring your food to your room for you? If you want?" I sort of shake my head. *No.* Then bypass him to leave my coat and hat in the mudroom.

I'm stripping before I ever step foot in my room, leaving a trail of clothes that starts at the door and trickles all the way to the bathroom.

I want a bath, but the thought of sitting down just to have to get back up is too daunting. So I shower faster than I've ever done before. Using shampoo only, I lather head to toe, unwilling to take an extra step to open the body wash.

Fuck conditioner. Screw brushing my hair. I wrap a towel around myself and climb into bed, giving zero fucks that I left the light on in the bathroom. It'll just have to stay that way. I close my eyes, waiting for the relief of resting to find me, but I miss him already.

The endlessly lonely days seem to stretch out in front of me, and I wonder what the fuck have I done coming here?

I swallow against the knot in my throat and wait for sleep to take me.

———

When the light gets flicked off in the bathroom, I startle, and he stops moving at the reaction.

"Sorry," he whispers, "I thought it would be easier to sleep without the light on." I nod, assuming he can see the motion in the dark. I can just make out his body movements, but not his face.

"Can't sleep again?" I ask, and he nods back, moving closer to the bed.

"Can I?" He doesn't need to ask.

I pull back the cover for him, realizing I'm naked, the towel lost at the bottom of the bed. He doesn't notice, or if he does, he pretends to give me privacy by looking away. He takes off his flannel sleep pants and gets into the bed beside me, bringing warmth and his woodsy scent with him. He must have showered recently, and the smell of his body wash is like balm to my skin. I want to melt into him.

But I don't. I roll over, expecting a repeat of the night before. Plenty of space, no touching, just two souls who can't seem to make it through the night without each other.

A warm hand on my hip sears and stings at my cool skin, the heat of his touch nearly unbearable.

"I was worried about you today," he whispers, sending shockwaves bounding over me at how close he is.

"I-I'm sorry. I was fine." When his hand squeezes at my hip, a full-body shiver shakes me.

"Can I touch you?" He whispers again.

"Yeah," I whisper back because my lonely little soul is desperate for human touch. I would beg him to rub my back or run a hand into my hair. I would do anything for him to pull me into his chest and hold me. *Please.*

And then he moves closer, the front of his body sliding against the back of mine. Fitting to me like a glove. Two puzzle pieces locking together. It feels right.

I shiver again, not from the cold but from the thrill, and he notches his arm tighter around my midsection, pulling me flush.

Oh my god. My touch-deprived body burns. He has no idea that this, right here, is getting me hotter than any foreplay ever could.

"I-is this okay?" He stammers. I simply nod, the back of my head rubbing against his chest, and his breathing starts to even out.

Eventually, mine falls into the same rhythm.

"You don't have to ask, Alex. If you want to sleep in here, you can." If my only human interaction would be this, I'd take it where I can.

"Okay," it's the last thing he says before his breathing drops low and slow, and like the sweetest lullaby, I fall with him.

TEN

EMMA

JANUARY

Today marks our one-month anniversary — not that we're celebrating — but it's a notable day for other reasons. Alex's sister, Brit, gave birth to a healthy baby boy this morning. *Technically, my nephew?* I'll never say that out loud, though, because everyone would know it isn't true. I don't even know them.

Aside from our brief encounter at The Grounds, I still haven't *officially* been introduced to Brit. But I tried to do the polite thing and sent Alex with a gift to the hospital.

Again, I wasn't invited, which is, *again*, nothing new. For a man whose marriage requirements of me included attending family functions and social events, he never goes to anything, and if he does, it's clear that I'm not welcome to come with. He never does it in a mean way, but it's always: *I'm leaving, be back in a bit.* Then he'll end up telling me he met up with his brother-in-law. Or his brothers — not blood-related. Or Constantine, his mom's partner.

So that means I'm always either at home or at school. There isn't much in between. I haven't made any friends, and I've hardly met another person, but I keep busy enough.

Alex and I have formed a routine of sorts that's amiable.

Every day, we wake up and go for a walk in the woods. When we get back, I shower and get ready for class while he makes us breakfast. It's my favorite thing he does for me. Monday through Friday, I drive down the mountain for my classes at the local community college while he holes up in his office, working at the house. Then, when I get home, I make dinner for both of us.

We don't watch TV together, or hang out in the evenings, or go out to eat, but every night, he slips into my bed so we can sleep.

We only cuddle occasionally, like on days that are particularly rough for him. Sometimes. I rub his back for a bit, then wake up later to his body wrapped around mine. I like it, but I never count on it happening again. Because everything about being with Alex feels fleeting and temporary. Like each time he does something could be the last time.

I never know what his mood will be for the day until we're in it, but I've learned to read him. When he wants space, when he needs comfort, when he wants to talk. It's still rare, but he's starting to talk to me more. Mostly, on our morning walks, when we sit on the boulder, that's like our safe space. Our secret world.

Those early morning hours, still dark, looking out over silent waters and frosted trees, are for us. He'll tell me things about his mom or dad or even Constantine, a man whom Alex looks up to like the father he never had.

One day, he told me the story about how his sister was... *conceived* and how he ended up living with his dad in Arizona. The rest of the day was hard after that. He was quiet and brooding. But when I went to bed that night, it was the first time he didn't even attempt to sleep in his own room.

He came with me to bed, even brushing his teeth beside me in the bathroom. And when we crawled beneath the covers, he didn't hesitate to pull me into him.

But that hasn't happened since. It's almost a week later, and he's back to sneaking into my bedroom and leaving me alone.

Before Alex comes to my bed at night, I spend a lot of time thinking, mostly about Blanks. I wonder where he is or what he's doing. I wonder if he wonders about me. And then I end up berating myself because I know he doesn't.

Alex doesn't bring him up, and I don't ask. We've created a very quiet, insulated life for ourselves together. It's comfortable and companionable, but I wouldn't say either one of us is blissfully happy. In fact, that's not the goal here. I'm sure of it.

After a month of visiting our spot for morning chats, he still hasn't brought up Jess even once, which tells me it's still too painful. I'm not exactly eager to hear about it anyway.

There isn't some overt burning desire between us, at least not one we're acknowledging, but that doesn't mean I'm not slightly jealous.

I'm jealous of who Alex could be when he isn't like *this*. When he isn't damaged and bleeding out for someone else, who is he then?

Does he smile? Real smiles? Does he laugh, big booming

laughs? Does he talk? Does he ask questions? Is he avid about living?

I want to know that man, but instead, I've been given this other version of him. And that's fine. I have a feeling most people wouldn't put up with his highs and lows, but I can manage. I can be soft and helpful when he needs me, then give him space like it doesn't bother me. I can do those things for him because I know it's what I've always wanted someone to do for me.

The funny thing is, Alex shares more with me than I do with him. Sometimes, we'll be sitting at our spot for so long that it'll be on the tip of my tongue to say it, but inevitably, he'll beat me to the punch. Like yesterday, I almost gave in, but then he started talking about Georgia, his mom.

He doesn't call her mom; he calls her by her first name, and I think it's the most interesting thing, the way he talks about her. Like she's a saint or something. And not like she abandoned him just as much as his father neglected or tortured him. I always end up mad when he talks about his mom or dad.

I'm mad *for* him. Maybe he got tired of being mad a long time ago, but not me. I'll be so angry sometimes that I have to go cry in the shower. Otherwise, I won't be able to shake it for the rest of the day.

Then I'll step out of the shower, get dressed, and go have the waffles or French toast or whatever ridiculous breakfast my husband has made for me that day. And I'll be grateful for him.

No matter how broken he is, he still finds ways to take care of me and show affection in his own way. Maybe affection isn't the right word. *Appreciation.* That's more accurate.

Like how he checks the air pressure in my tires three times a week. Or how he makes me coffee to-go every day so I don't have to stop. In his own way, he cares.

It's quiet. And I like it. More than I should, so I try to temper my feelings and distract myself by thinking about something else. Anything else. The "else" is always Blanks. Or Caleb, as I find myself thinking more lately.

If I think about *Caleb*, it's because I'm dreaming. Daydreaming about a life where men like him are into girls like me. Caleb would have watched me come apart on a fucking bathtub and not been able to keep his hands off me. He would have fucked me against the tile wall, making me scream obscenities.

The back door opening has me exhaling, cleansing the thoughts away.

As I turn to look, Alex walks in, hanging his keys next to mine in the mudroom. We were domesticated like that now.

He walks into the kitchen where I'm cooking and immediately picks up a piece of bread I just finished slicing.

"Hey," I say, giving him a smile. A gesture that he returns, warming me. "How is everyone?"

"Good," he says, still smiling. I love it. He seems almost... different.

Trying to soak up every second of *this* Alex, I keep asking.

"What's his name? How big?"

"His name is Constantine Alexander Millar." His eyes get misty, and my heart beats loud in my ears.

"Wow, that's-" I'm at a loss, "a beautiful name, Alex. You should be so proud." My eyes get misty, too, and my heart thaws a little for the woman who has made no attempt to meet or get to know me but named her son after her brother.

He just nods, then goes on. "He's big," he actually laughs. "Like nine pounds and 21 inches long." I have no frame of reference here, but the way he says it makes it seem like that's a lot.

"Wow!" I exclaim back, stirring the pan sauce that's simmering in front of me.

He picks at the asparagus still on the baking sheet and keeps going.

"When Tally was born, she was six pounds, five ounces. She was this squatty little thing. A little bean." He smiles, softer this time, and *oh my god*. If I could ever pinpoint a moment in time that I would regret, it would be this very second. Because the way he's smiling and looking at me like he's happy, I feel myself take one step, then another, and then I fall. For him.

"I love that name, Alex. *Tally*." I say it for him again. So he knows his daughter's name isn't a bad word.

"Short for Tallulah." He gives a sadder-looking smile, but he's still smiling nonetheless, and all I want is to hug him, and kiss his forehead, and tell him he's the most handsome man I've ever seen. He's a good man. I want to tell him that most of all.

But I don't.

"That's a beautiful name, too," I tell him instead.

ELEVEN

ALEX

The clap of thunder is jarring. I have to focus hard on where I am. Who I'm with.

Home. In bed. Emma. Safe. And the adrenaline subsides.

She's cuddled up next to me, a leg draped over mine. My arm, beneath her head. We fell asleep just like this, talking past midnight. We talked for hours, lying like this.

She's become my safe place. No matter what I do or how I act, Emma keeps showing up every day, month after month, with a smile for me. Using her soft voice when she knows I'm close to losing it. She can read me, and it pains me that I can't do the same for her.

She listens more than she talks. It's my first time being with someone who talks less than me. She'll answer questions and tell me about her day and classes, but more often, she just gives me space and time. She'll wait for me.

When the thunder rolls again, I slide my hand into her curly blonde hair, touching a kiss to the top of her head.

My sweet girl.

It's taken six months of marriage, but slowly, we've warmed to each other. The first few months were admittedly rough. I was still thinking about Jess. A lot. Was still struggling with being...*here*. But that's fading. The scar is closing. I'm healing. And it feels like it's all because of *her*. Aside from the fact that we aren't intimate, it's the healthiest relationship I've ever been in.

Do I wish we were fucking? Most days, yeah. Every time I touch myself, I see Em on her knees. For me. *Only me.* When I shower, and my cock is hard, begging for touch, I see her. I don't know when I stopped seeing long dark hair... *Or more so when that stopped surprising me.*

But everything with Emma feels good. Just like it is.

We have routines and weekly plans now. After...*she* moved away, I introduced Em to Brit and Liam. And CT, too. We have dinner with Constantine at least twice a month. We go camping on the weekends whenever the skies are clear, and we hike to the hidden cove daily. The edges of our two lives have blended over the months, seamlessly.

So, on our sixth-month wedding anniversary, I've already decided: I'm going to ask my wife out on a date.

"You're awake early today," she whispers against my chest.

"It's storming out."

"Nooo," her disappointment is obvious. We were supposed to hike to a camp near the hot springs this weekend. It was her "reward" for acing her finals. She chose it, not me.

"What if, instead, we...go out...on a date?" I can feel her body tense beside mine.

"Are you sure you're ready for that?" Her whispered question is almost as startling as the loud thunder that follows it.

I thought I was. *Aren't I?*

I am. "I like you, Emma. And I thought, maybe you liked me too?"

"I do, I really do, it's just..." She trails off. "If things don't end well...well, we would have to get divorced. And we could never go back to being like this." She's not explicit, but I know what she means.

We're friends who do things that friends don't do. We think about each other in ways friends don't. Dating would be a step away from what we are, but maybe a step in a better direction.

I hope.

———

Emma

Being stood up by my husband feels very on-brand for me.

Worrying my bottom lip between my teeth, I check the time on my phone again. He's 58 minutes late now.

EMMA

Everything okay?

ALEXANDER

Cant make it. Sry.

What the actual fuck? I look around at the house I'm currently waiting in. He can't make it home? To his own house? It's a bad joke. Done in poor taste, without a doubt. My skin itches, and I want to claw this stupid dress off my body.

And then cry a little bit.

Scooting off the couch, I pick up the heels I kicked off a half hour ago and drag my ass back into my room, shutting the door to *my* room. It isn't really mine anymore, though. He's practically moved in. His clothes are folded in the dresser drawers beside mine.

His toothbrush is at the sink right alongside mine.

I undo the zipper on the back of the dress that had taken me 15 painstaking minutes just to figure out how to get up on my own. I can't be bothered to hang it neatly like it was. I just kick it off, letting it land in a far corner of the closet.

I grab a pair of leggings, a baggy flannel shirt, and my slipper moccasins and get dressed to take myself to dinner.

Ugh. He hadn't even spelled out "sorry." It was just "sry." I wasn't even worth an extra finger stroke.

It's hard to say what's making this feel so fucking shitty. Is it that he isn't here right now, or that whatever we had is now dead? I was so worried about it because I knew.

I knew it would never work out. I even knew that whatever we *were* wasn't going to last. It was too fragile; he and I were always on the precipice. Always teetering on the edge of the next thing or nothing. I wasn't ready to leave the shore, but Alexander Palomino said jump with me. And I did. Because I've fallen in love with him.

This ranked high as one of the stupider mistakes I've made.

Grabbing the keys to my car, I feel even more idiotic when I think about Blanks. He said they were inseparable, but he was nowhere to be found. He hadn't shown up. Alex hardly even said his name.

I stopped missing him when I realized he really wasn't coming back, but I still feel a twinge of longing whenever I drive my car or wear the jacket he bought me.

Stupid, Emma. So stupid.

Coltons looks packed tonight, the summer crowd officially infiltrating the small town. I wouldn't be heading there in slippers, alone, on a dead night. Meaning, there was no chance in hell of me going when they were slammed. I also hadn't been since Blanks took me. Alex didn't venture out, and I sort of took his cue and didn't either. So I turn right at the fork and pull into a parking space outside Maggio's.

We've ordered pizza from here a handful of times, never staying to eat. But I can't be at home tonight. *I hate that I call it home.*

I step into the pizza "parlor" that feels a little ancient, but in a homey way, and honestly debate ordering a large pizza just for myself. It's that kind of night.

An older man scribbles down my order: *medium pizza with jalapenos and artichoke hearts, and a beer. Cold, don't care what kind,* then he gives me a sympathetic smile when he asks, *"For here, or to-go?"*

And I say, "Here, only need one plate."

Definitely that kind of night.

Me, my beer, and my one plate sit at a table in the nearly empty establishment. There are a couple teenagers at one table, but other than them, the place is empty. They don't even notice I'm here, which is just fine too.

I left my phone in the car — on purpose — so I sit with nothing to do and no one to talk to until someone walks through the door of the pizza joint, and my stomach falls out of my ass. *Fucking amazing.* I simply don't have it in me to people or small talk right now.

"Emma," he says, almost surprised, maybe awkwardly. Okay, definitely awkwardly. The baby is strapped to his chest, and I smile at him. CT smiles and coos when he sees me.

Now, CT is my kind of person. He smiles a lot and doesn't talk.

"Hi, Liam." I wouldn't say I've gotten close to Brit and Liam because I haven't, but I know them now. Enough to say hi if we run into each other out in public. But I wasn't calling to hang out with them, and they weren't calling me, probably because we don't even have each other's numbers.

"Waiting for your pizza?" He asks, bouncing the baby who's making grabby hands for me.

"Yup." The one plate is looking really sad right about now.

He notices and says, "Sorry," sounding actually, really sorry.

I laugh awkwardly because I'm embarrassed and say, "For what?"

"I mean, I was a little worried Alex wouldn't take it well." I shrug, avoiding saying something stupid because I have no fucking idea what he's talking about.

"Just give him time to cool down. It's not every day you find out your ex is dating your best friend." I swallow the stomach acid threatening to come up and nod, like I get it, but I don't. He shoots me another sympathetic smile, then greets the older man working the counter, picking up his three large pizzas.

I have never been more jealous in my entire life.

I'm jealous of the smiling baby he's holding. I'm jealous of the three pizzas going home to a full house. I'm wildly jealous that the whole lot of them always seem *actually* happy. Just gorgeous, rich, and sickeningly happy. *That's not the life for you.*

When he leaves, he shoots me a sympathetic look, and I want to crumple on the spot.

I don't, because that would be poor form. Instead, I wave and say bye to CT.

Once he's gone, I finish off my beer, staring into the depths of the empty glass, and pray that it'll refill itself.

After wolfing down my three slices and another beer later, I call it quits on Maggio's.

The nervous energy thrumming in my veins pushes me out the door. It drives me home. It knows what I'm going to do before I'm even doing it.

With shaking hands, I head upstairs, treading lightly like I'll get in trouble if I get caught.

He never said *not* to go upstairs, but it always felt implied. Even now, I feel like I'm breaking a rule. Maybe even the cardinal rule. What's he going to do, though? Kick me out? *Okay.* Divorce me? *Fine.*

All the doors are suspiciously shut, making me want to roll my eyes that I'll have to snoop actively. I can't just wander.

Opening the first door in the hall, I'm preparing for the worst, but all I find is a completely nice and unused guest room. *Oh.* It's decorated plainly, without a single personal touch.

I open the second door to the same thing. It's honestly all boring. There are no skeletons or creepiness detected. Just well-made beds that look like they've never been slept in. I debate not even bothering with the last two rooms, but where's the fun in that? It's not like I'm getting my kicks off any other way.

My heart stutters when I open the third door to a child's room. *It's beautiful.* Magical even. Framed against floral wallpaper is a painting of a swan. There's even a chandelier with lilac crystals hanging from its arms. Toys are gathered on the carpet, still diapers and wipes in the changing table caddies.

Whoever *Jess* is, I hate her.

She had everything: the family, the man, the house, and I hate her. For having everything I want. And *god,* how I want it all.

I close the door to the room that makes my empty uterus ache and walk down the hall to the primary bedroom. Well, I assume. It has double doors at its entrance instead of a single door like the other rooms have.

The double doors spread, opening to a large space with a big bed and a fireplace. It seems grand but still inviting, in a way. It makes my bedroom downstairs look like a shanty.

Why the hell are the two of us sharing the smallest room in the house when this is up here?

Walking into the private hall to the large bathroom, I pass dueling closets, *his* and *hers*. His is full, not surprising, but when I turn to look at "hers," I find it's filled as well. Clothes hanging up. *Gorgeous* clothes. Shoes line the shelves. Everything smells expensive, like a classic floral perfume and a hint of leather. There's even a suitcase tucked around a corner. It's all still here. *Like a shrine.*

No wonder he never invited me up here. It would feel like a betrayal.

The bathroom is the same story. All his toiletries line the sink beside *hers.*

The monogrammed makeup bag is what does me in, though. *JD.* My gut twists. *Jess D-something.*

Fuck, he's sick. And I am, too. Sick for being here, thinking I could have any effect against *this.*

He isn't ready. *And he likely never will be.*

It's been six months, and he's still holding on to every fragment of her he can. Would he have kept the Christmas presents under the tree if it hadn't been for Blanks? *Probably.*

I have a hard time believing Blanks is the one she's with, but maybe it is him. Maybe all these people are fucked up, and I can't see it because I hadn't wanted to. Or maybe I couldn't because I'm fucked up too.

Yeah, this is hell. Just more and more of the same. Always wanting, but never having.

I walk downstairs, wishing like crazy I hadn't come up here at all. I should have heeded the unspoken rule. Now that the wool has been pulled back from my eyes, I can't unsee it.

I grab my phone, change into a baggy tee, and head for the basement to watch a sad movie when I pause.

Slipping the diamond ring and its matching band off my finger, I set them on my bathroom counter as pain radiates throughout me. *Okay.*

Sad movie night can now commence. Maybe I'll watch Steel Magnolias or something like that. I feel ready to be gutted by someone else's pain for once.

———

Alex

It was certifiable; I'm a piece of shit.

I stare down at her, asleep on the basement sofa, cradling her phone with the screen still unlocked, where she'd been looking at flights. I don't blame her. Maybe that's what I should do: just buy her the first ticket out of here. Anywhere she wants to go, she could.

I take a seat next to her on the sofa and hang my head down, my elbows resting on my knees. *I don't deserve her.*

Her phone clicking locked draws my attention. She's staring at me, and I'm looking back, tears already brimming in my eyes.

The sympathy she usually reserves for me is lacking, her stare vacant. Her ring finger is naked. She chews on her bottom lip, fighting back whatever it is she really wants to say.

"I didn't deserve this," she finally manages to get out. *I agree.* "I don't even want to be your friend right now." *But fuck, that hurts.*

"Okay. C-can I explain?" She stares blankly but doesn't reply. It tumbles out of me before I can stop it, "Jess-she fucked my best friend, and I never got over it."

"Blanks?" she asks. I shake my head.

"Damian. When things ended between us, I sort of thought it was only a matter of time before they... And it was because she's with him now. Finding out this afternoon...it was bad timing, I know."

"Bad timing?" She scoffs. "My whole life is bad timing,

Alex. I literally can't listen to you tell me some sob story. Not tonight. Go find someone else to pretend to be your wife, okay?" She pushes the blanket off her and moves to stand.

But I'm standing with her. "I'm sorry, Emma, okay?"

"Is that a sorry with an 'o' and two 'r's'? Or just an s-r-y?" She turns around to leave, but I grab her arm.

"I'm *sorry*, Emma. You didn't deserve that. I *know*, and I said I'm sorry."

"I don't think you mean a single word that comes out of your mouth," her tone is mean. She shakes my hand off her arm, flustered. "I hate you, Alex. Because I knew my life was shit before, and I'd accepted it. But then you bring me here," she motions around, tears clouding her eyes. "And I see how amazing life could be with you," she sighs. With a lower voice, she finally asks, "But how can anyone be with you when you're still with her?"

"I'm not with her," the words are ground out between clenched teeth.

"Because you don't want to be?" Emma asks the one question I can't answer honestly. When the words won't form, she looks away, then says, "That's what I thought."

She retreats upstairs, likely to her room, but I just keep standing there, frozen. I wish I could go after her and tell her it's different. But she's right. About all of it.

———

I make sure to head upstairs early so I won't miss her because I know what's coming.

At 8:36, she opens her door, carrying her weekender bag over her shoulder.

It isn't rocket science that she's leaving. She should.

We make eye contact. She gives me a sympathetic smile, and I give her a sorry one.

I made her favorite for breakfast, motioning to the stack of blackberry pancakes waiting. Fuck, I'm going to miss this. *A lot.*

"Thanks." She sets down her bag by the stairs and comes to sit beside me at the eat-in table, putting a pancake and some bacon on her plate.

I'm not hungry, so I just sit with her. My leg bounces, and the knot in my throat feels uncomfortably tight.

"It should go without saying that I don't want you to leave." She looks up at me, tears pooling around her blue irises.

"I-" she starts but pauses.

"I know why you can't stay, Em. I do." So badly, I want to be this person for her, a better version of me, but I just can't fucking do it. I can't keep the tears in, and neither can she. "But it doesn't mean I don't still need you." I wouldn't have survived without her. I know that for a fact.

I wish you'd stay.

"You don't need me, Alex," she says softly, the tears running slowly off her face. I grab her hand, holding it tightly, and shake my head.

"I wouldn't be here if it weren't for you." That's what's so fucking painful. She brought me back to life, and I killed her in turn.

She sort of nods along, knowing the truth of the matter.

"You can call," she concedes, "if you ever really need me. Just-can you please not make a habit of it?" I nod, knowing I would call her. "It hurts to love you right now, but maybe in the future, it won't." She shrugs, gutting me because I fucking love her too.

I pull her into a tight hug, and I tell her. "I love you too, Em." She cries hard on my shoulder, and I cry, too, until we both run dry.

"You don't need me," she says, pulling away, "you need a dog...and maybe some therapy." She smiles, and I laugh.

"Yeah. I think you're right."

TWELVE

ALEX

JULY

"Ohhh, now that's a good boy!" Constantine praises the corgi sitting at his feet, wagging his tail. "This one could be good." I narrow my eyes at him, and he bursts out laughing.

"I'm not getting a fucking corgi, Connie."

"Why not?" He asks incredulously.

"His legs are too fucking short for long-distance hikes, that's why." He dramatically rolls his eyes, patting the corgi's head for good measure, flipping over the dog tag to read its name.

"Sorry, Milton. Maybe next time." *I should get the dog for Connie.*

We walk around the kennel, stopping at a couple different crates, when Connie gestures for me.

"Now I know this is cliché, but c'mon, look at this little

guy." A German Shepherd puppy is huddled in the corner of his crate. I take one look, and I'm a fucking goner.

"Yeah..." I get down on my haunches and hold my fingers up to the crate. "Hey bud, look at you." I make a clicking sound, and the pup slowly rises and pads over, his tail tucked between his legs.

"It's alright," I coax him. One of the volunteers at the shelter comes to stand beside me.

"Oh yeah, the little guy just came in two days ago. Maybe 14 weeks old."

"He's perfect," I say.

"What're you going to name him?" Constantine asks.

Well, since we were already a walking cliché, "Delta." I smile when he finally makes it to me, his wet nose pushing against my hand. "You wanna go home, bud?"

Connie asks the volunteer to get the paperwork going, and I open the crate to let Delta roam. He sniffs and explores, his wet nose running up my arms and over my pants and shoes, making me smile.

"She's gonna love you."

———

Calling feels like the right move. So I tap her name and wait.

It's been almost a month, and I haven't called or texted outside of making sure she settled into her new place without issues. After that, I left her alone, hoping we could meet on the other end of things to start over. As friends.

Maybe I still want more than friendship...but I would take what I could get.

On the second ring, she picks up. Whispering, she asks, "Is everything okay?" She sounds worried.

"Yeah, everything's fine, just-why are you whispering?"

"Because I'm at work."

"Why are you working?"

"If this isn't an emergency, can we talk later, please?"

"Yeah, call me or text if you want, you know. Whenever." *Fuck.* Didn't come out sounding as cool or as calm as I had hoped.

"Okay, bye, Alex." She hangs up. The sting over her hanging up burns. Maybe it's still too soon.

> **EM**
>
> Sorry, I've been meaning to call back. Just busy.

> **A**
>
> It's too soon, I get it.

> Yeah... Sorry.

AUGUST

> **A**
>
> Semester starts next week, right?

> **EM**
>
> I actually transferred to State, so I have an extra week.

> **A**
>
> That's awesome.

> Any chance you want to grab a coffee or something?

Ask me next month.

Will do.

——————

SEPTEMBER

A

Pumpkin Spice Latte?

EM

For me or for you?

Yes.

That's surprising, honestly. When?

This weekend, if you're free.

Sure, you can come see my new place.

——————

Her building is downtown, an older one recently converted to condos. The area is artsy, and it suits her. I like to imagine her walking to get coffee in the morning at the bodega down the street, picking up fresh flowers at the farmers market on the way home. I hope she has a nice life. Hopefully, she's happy.

"Guys, chill." I tug on their leashes, and they both stop trying to get the chihuahua walking across the street.

When we walk up to the entrance, she's standing there waiting to let us in.

Her blue eyes go wide, and she smiles from ear to ear.

She *looks* happy. I don't know if it's to see us, but she looks healthy and happy. She's still sporting a tan in late September, and her hair has been cut a little shorter. She's wearing it curly, too. I love her curly hair; it's my favorite version of her.

"Oh my god. Who are these!?!" She squeals, falling to her knees to pet the two dogs.

"The well-behaved one is Delta. And the one who can't keep it in his pants is Milton." Milton is on his hind legs, licking Emma's face. Delta patiently waits his turn, tail wagging.

"You got TWO dogs?!" I laugh, watching both dogs lose their shit over her.

"I make no claims to Milton. I'm dog-sitting. But uh, yeah, Delta's mine." She looks up at me and smiles. Like she's proud of me or something, and my stomach knots.

"Okay, well, come on." She takes the drink carrier out of my hands so I can manage the dogs, and then leads us to an elevator.

"Do you like it here?" She shrugs at my question.

"It's not Spearhead..." Her words seem edged with sadness. I want to tell her she can come back anytime, but I'm aiming for light and easy today. Selfishly, I hope this meetup might lead to another because I do miss her...and I still love her. Not having her in my life is more challenging than I imagined it would be.

It's not Jess-soul-crushing hard, but life hasn't been the same with her gone.

Delta helps, but we're sleeping in her bed...still. The two of us. So there's that.

"It's cool." I look around at all the original Art Deco features.

"There's a rooftop pool," she says with a smile.

"Sounds like you're living the dream." I mean it, but she laughs disingenuously and rolls her eyes.

"Yeah, the dream."

We're quiet the rest of the way up to her condo on the fourth floor. There are only two units per floor, so as soon as we exit the elevator, we turn, and she unlocks the door on the right.

"Neighbors, okay?" I ask because I worry.

"Yeah, she teaches pilates. So pretty quiet. She likes her sleep. It's great for me." *Thank fuck.* "So this is it."

The plain door opens to a modern space. White painted walls, all white or light wood furniture, but there's still pops of color. Bright art, a purple throw blanket, a huge bouquet of wildflowers in a turquoise vase on her coffee table. It's very Emma, yet somehow she still doesn't belong. Not here, at least.

"You've done a lot." I look around the space.

"It's been three months now..." Yeah, it has. An awkward silence falls over the room.

"Do you mind if I let them off their leashes?"

"Oh my gosh, of course, please." She immediately bends down to help Delta off leash while I do Milton's.

With the dogs loose, I pull off my backpack and set it down on a chair to get out the bag of pastries, dog bowls, and treats.

"Look at you. You're like a real dog dad." She laughs as she watches me pull out a water bottle to fill the travel bowls. I look up at her from where I'm crouched down and smile.

Her cheeks turn pink, and she whips around to start moving the pastries out of the bag and onto a plate.

I watch as she goes on her toes to reach for glasses off a shelf. Her legs are toned and tan, and I can't help running my eyes up and down her body. Fuck, I miss those limbs tangled with mine at night.

"So I want to hear about...everything." The house is considerably quieter without her nightly anecdotes about professors or lab partners she can't stand. There are no clanging pans in the kitchen in the evenings. No one to make blackberry pancakes for. I mean, except for Delta, who eats better than I do.

"Okay, like what?" She laughs, nervously pushing a piece of hair behind her ear as she takes a seat, pushing a chair towards me to do the same.

"Well, where are you working?" I think I choose the most basic question first, but she has to think about it like she's debating not telling me.

"The library, on campus." I nod.

"You know, you don't have to work. If you need money–" She raises her hand up to stop me.

"I don't, but I can't be alone that much. It's not healthy for me. Work helps. I know..." I watch as she counts them off in her head, "Four more people now." The awkward laugh comes again. "I haven't made any friends, but this way, I at least have people to talk to." God, just a fucking dagger to the chest. I've never wanted to hug someone so bad in my life.

"When I'm not at work, I'm in class or studying. And then I joined a rock climbing gym. And Sarah, the next-door neighbor, roped me into doing pilates a couple times a week.

So, I think that pretty much covers everything." Her life sounds full, but somehow, she still seems empty.

"Are you happy?" I ask. Her sort-of-smile fades. We both look at each other for nearly a whole minute.

"You know we're basically the same person, Alex," she says, looking away. "So I'll ask you the same. Are you happy?" She picks at invisible lint on her shorts.

I opt for the truth. "I was happier when you were there."

She does the same, "I was too."

It seems like a no-brainer; we're happier together, but I also know I'll likely hurt her again.

And again.

Eventually, she digs into the almond croissant I got her.

"So, how long have you had Delta now?" The dog trots over at the mention of his name, and she rewards him with pets.

"Two months."

"You should've led with that when you called! I can't believe I've missed out on two months of puppy! Do you have pictures?" I smile, knowing I definitely should have led with Delta, but that would have been playing dirty.

It still might be too soon for us.

"Of course." I hand over my phone, already open to the folder in photos dedicated to my dog.

"Wow, CT is getting big," she says as she swipes through the photos, stopping at the one of Delta and my sister's dog, Luna, chasing around a crawling CT.

"W-what'd you tell your family? About us?" She looks up, passing the phone back to me.

"Nothing." It's the truth. They asked about Emma a

couple times, and I told them the truth. *She's busy with summer courses.* "Well, except for Connie. He knows you moved out." I don't need Brit feeling sorry for me that while I'm getting a divorce, Jess and Damian are planning a wedding. That news had been fun to navigate. Having Delta helped. Made sure I got out of bed, forced me outdoors. Eventually, it started to feel like whoever Jess is isn't someone I know anymore.

"About that..." She trails off. We haven't gotten divorced. It's also only been a few months since she moved out. I wasn't even thinking about it, to be honest. "Do you want to get divorced?" The answer is clear to me. *No.* But that was me being a selfish fuck. I know.

What I say instead is, "Whenever you're ready or want to, just say the word." It isn't an answer, but I don't see the rush. Maybe we wouldn't work out right now, but who's to say it wouldn't eventually? Emma and I were good partners at the end of the day. We have similar interests. We like the same things. We click together.

"Okay," it comes out quieter than I would have liked.

The impulse to tell her I miss her is there. To ask if she would think about making this hanging out thing regular. I want to take her face in my hands, kiss her, and say, *"I love you. I want you to be happy."* Not that we kiss; hadn't since that first day, nine months ago.

Instead of doing any of that, we sit, eating in silence. When Milton starts whining, she suggests a walk.

"Let's do it." I would love nothing more. I smile at her, and we grab leashes, but before we walk out the door, I pull her in for a hug.

Wrapping my arms around her shoulders, I put a hand in her hair to bring her closer. Her hands are on my back, bracing me, and we stand, breathing each other in. As I drop a kiss on her forehead, Delta barks. *Jealous fucker.*

We both laugh and smile, then head out the door.

THIRTEEN

EMMA
OCTOBER

ROB

> Something came up tonight. Raincheck, okay?

EMMA

> Sure!

Rob and I met at the gym. Both of us regulars on Wednesday nights. He has a daughter named Jade, and he's maybe a little younger than Alex but older than me. He's attractive in a different way. His nose is crooked, and he isn't ripped like my husband. But when someone is nice and can make you laugh, they immediately become a ten.

I don't know why he canceled on me, but I realize I'm only disappointed that I'm not *actually* disappointed. It's obvious I wasn't that interested in dating him, but I was willing to try. He seemed normal, and again, he could make me laugh. A normal life with someone who can make you laugh doesn't seem so bad.

What does seem bad is being stood up for the second time in a row. Once is a fluke, twice has me wondering what the fuck is wrong with me.

I'm already dressed and ready to go, though. I mean, there's still a few hours before the game starts... Knowing I'll probably regret this, I send him a text.

EMMA

> I know it's last minute, but I have tickets to the State game tonight. Wanna go?

It's truly a shot in the dark. If Alex doesn't want to go, I doubt I'll go alone. There's no use fighting traffic and crowds when I probably have a better view of the game at home. Not that I'll watch it.

The smarter play would have been to invite Sarah to come with me, but the thought of her bringing chia protein balls to snack on for tailgate is a turn-off. Not that her chia protein balls are crap. They're tolerable, but I was hoping to go all in on the experience. Beers, BBQ, shenanigans. I've never been to a college football game before.

And the last time Alex and I hung out, it was fine. Good. Better than good.

It reinforced what I already knew: I miss him. I'm not proud of that.

The first 20 minutes were awkward, but once we were outside, walking the dogs, it was the same as before. *Before, he reminded me that he was still in love with someone else. Before he crushed me.*

We talked about my course schedule and the four people I now knew. That number didn't include Rob. I left Rob out of the equation on purpose.

He told me about adopting Delta and how they're working on building up to a long backpacking trip. He even shared a picture of Delta wearing his own pack. God, it was so fucking cute.

He's cute. And I loved seeing him love something unconditionally and have the love returned. He deserves it. Regardless of what happened between us, I still think he's a good man.

I still think he never deserved half the awful things that have happened to him, either.

He told me Constantine misses me, which I think might have been code for: *I miss you.* But he didn't say that, which is fine. I wouldn't have said it back, even though I would be thinking it. I know what it means to love Alexander Palomino now, and I don't think I'll have the courage to ride that ride anytime soon.

Be his friend? Sure. Root him on, support him? Absolutely. Date him? Can't. Unless I feel like hurting myself again, I can't. And he isn't exactly asking me, either. He told me he loved me too, but I have a feeling he meant like a friend.

I love you like a friend, Em. I can practically hear his deep voice saying it aloud, ruining me. Because his 'I love you' is certainly not: I'm *in* love with you, desperately. It isn't: wear my ring, carry my babies, *you're fucking mine.* Which is what I want. It's all I have ever wanted, to be claimed. Alex has already staked that claim on someone else.

To be clear, I'm not sure I want Alex to love me like that.

I love him, but being with him might kill me. His presence, his demons, it can be all-consuming. I worry it *would* consume us. Well, at least me. He would take up so much space that, eventually, I would be snuffed out. And I have my own demons. I'm still broken, too. It hasn't escaped my notice that he never asked about my past or my story. He asks me things in conversation, but it's just about the here and now.

Crap, I shouldn't have invited him. The knot in my stomach is already forming, the pangs of regret ringing.

But life is short. Next month, I'll be 27, nearly a third of my life already gone. Maybe more. I can't spend the next sixty years sitting inside alone.

> **TABLE 19**
> Yeah, I'll pick you up in an hour and fifteen. That work?

> **EMMA**
> Yep, see you then.

> Out front.

I grab the bright red sweatshirt and my crossbody bag and head downstairs, expecting to find an old Jeep parked out front.

No, no, no. My nipples harden at the sight in front of me. Alexander Palomino on a motorcycle is like the steamy porno of my dreams. I've always imagined that I'm the type of girl who could have made it as an old lady. Also, Jax Teller has been the star of way too many wet dreams. Well, Alex has, too.

"When did *this* happen?" He's just full of surprises lately.

He outstretches an arm, holding a helmet out for me. "Christmas present from Blanks." *Blanks*. I swallow hard, biting down on my lip so I won't ask about him.

While I adjust and buckle the chin strap, it slips out anyway. "How *is* Blanks?" *I don't want to know. I really don't.*

"Fine. Last I heard, he's dating another model." Right. Of course, he is. He would always be dating *some* model.

I force out a laugh and say, "Good for him," plastering on one of the fakest smiles I've ever mustered.

Luckily, I don't have to hold it for long because I'm climbing on the back of the motorcycle, my legs hugging his hips, my chest against his hard back, and with my body pressed against his, it's impossible to think of anything but him.

"Wrap your arms around me, Em." I do, and it feels comfortable. Natural. My hands slide against his dark hoodie, taking hold. He's wearing a black hoodie and dark jeans, and somehow, he's perfect just like this.

Even though it's October, the valley hasn't cooled down yet. The heat hangs in the air tonight, but on the motorcycle, with the wind whipping around us, I get a chill and hug Alex a little tighter. Maybe it's for warmth. Maybe it's because I miss having someone to touch.

"You good?" He places a large hand on my thigh at a stop light. I nod against his back and fist my hands in his sweat-shirt a little tighter. It's dangerous, getting this contact high off him.

At the next stoplight, I adjust how I'm sitting, moving my hips against his backside, and a hand comes back to hold me. His hands holding me are a weakness. I knew it the first time he touched me. In the back of a black sedan on the way to our wedding.

I want to beg him not to do it and, in the same breath, beg him to never stop. In the end, I say nothing. But each time we stop, the hand comes back to hold me. To give my knee a squeeze, to rub my calf. I don't think he has any idea what he's doing to me. More than likely, he's just as touch-deprived as I am.

The sexual tension eases as we get closer to the stadium, and I start watching the debauchery unfold on fraternity row. I thought it was only like this in the movies, but as it turns out, the movies don't hold a flame to real life.

I've driven past the strip of what looks like old motels turned into fraternities and sororities nearly every day this semester, but they never looked like this before.

People are drinking on roofs. Kegs bob, floating around in pools. Every house has a DJ and some sort of extravagant balloon installation. College hasn't been like this for me. At all. For one, I'm *almost* always the oldest person in my classes. Not in community college, but at State, I'm like a pariah. The weird girl who works in the library and is too old to hang out with.

I don't think 27 is old in general, but when my classmates aren't even legally old enough to drink, the gap feels vast.

We wait in a long, slow-moving line to turn into the main field for parking, but it's not boring. Not in the least. I watch as the sea of red seeps into the field from every direction. College students, but also families. Older people and people somewhere in between, too. I love that all these people have a reason to belong here. To come together. It's not something I've seen before.

I'm not counting the times I've gone to my mom's shows. She's a degenerate, and so are the crowds that follow her around. Like every person at the bottom of the barrel has been attuned to Darla Strait's siren song.

Eventually, the start and stop become steady forward movement, and we enter the tailgating field after Alex shows the attendant a special pass. We drive down the grassy, makeshift roads towards the tent village that's amassed outside the stadium.

The air smells like tri-tip and BBQ sauce. Smoky and sweet.

He eventually pulls behind one of the tents into a reserved area and puts the kickstand down. I take a look around and realize the proximity to the stadium is far above my cheap seat general admission.

"This is the brothers' tent," he motions to the left while he unbuckles, then hangs up both our helmets. *The Brothers.* That's how Alex refers to Max, Niko, and Silas. I know there's one more, but he doesn't talk about him.

I hadn't met the brothers, but I heard about them plenty, and I've seen pictures at Constantine's house. Meeting them in real life feels like unlocking another layer to Alex.

"Cool, can't wait to meet them."

Taking my hand in his, he leads me through the slightly bumpy grass to the front of the tent. There's a large sign for "The MS Group" out front, and inside are rows of long tables covered in red and white checked tablecloths. They're mostly full, too.

I spot Connie about the same time he sees me, and he breaks out in a grin, raising a hand for us to join him at the other end. So I tug on Alex's hand, that's still holding mine, and motion over to the direction we should go. He takes the lead, not relinquishing me the whole time.

I notice one or two people glance at us curiously, but for the most part, no one pays us any attention. Even though I don't know anyone here, it doesn't feel awkward. Yet.

"Hey!" Connie greets us, opening his arms for a hug from me.

"Hi, Connie," I greet back as he releases the embrace, turning to give Alex the same bear-sized hug.

"We've missed you at dinner, kiddo." I blush, not sure what to say. Alex said he knows the truth, but that doesn't make it any less uncomfortable.

"Anytime you want to have dinner, Connie, give me a call." I shoot him a wink, and he laughs. I notice him give Alex a look, but I don't know what it means.

"Get the girl a drink while we catch up," Connie instructs him.

With a gentle hand at my back, Alex asks, "What do you want?"

"Beer, please?" He gives me that signature half-smile before slipping away.

"How's school going?" *I miss Connie, too.*

"It's good. Just busy. I'm working in the library now."

He makes a sort of clicking sound and says, "Gosh, the two of you are so alike, you know that?" I nod because I do know. We're *too* alike.

"You're still married?" He doesn't beat around the bush. He just goes straight for the jugular. I roll with it, though, because I love this old man.

"Hitting on a married woman, Connie?" I tease, and his cheeks turn pink. I know that's not how he means it. He's literally checking in to see if we're divorced yet. We aren't. I can't really give a reason why.

"If I was thirty years younger-" He's stopped from finishing the sentiment by a tall, dark, and handsome man with a buzz cut and tattoos peeking out from the collar of his shirt. He looks familiar, probably from the photos at Connie's.

"Fuck, Dad, please don't finish that sentence." The man rolls his eyes, then turns to me. "Please, pardon him. He's mixing Coors light and prune juice tonight, clearly it's taking its toll." Connie laughs, and I do, too.

"Niko, this is Emma," Connie gestures towards me. Niko extends a hand, and I move to take it. When a young boy runs between us, sending Niko stumbling towards me, he has to use two hands to hold us both upright.

"Cool points: gone," Connie laughs at Niko.

"Hands off my wife, please." *His* voice, speaking those words, is like kerosene on my internal fire. *He did not.* No, he did. Because Niko rights me in a respectful manner, double-checking my ring finger that's naked.

I smile at Niko and say, "It's nice to meet you, I've heard a lot."

"None of it good, either," Alex busts his balls, then passes me a cold beer.

Niko shoots him a faux dirty look and says, "How the hell do you end up with tens?" Redirecting the question to me, he asks, "For real, how much is he paying you?"

I choke on my first sip of beer.

Alex's laugh is big and beautiful, and I have to bite my lip to hold my own laugh in. But damn, the joke was a little too on the nose.

I blush a little but finally say under my breath, "Not enough."

Connie starts howling at the hit while Alex grabs me around the waist and pulls me into his side, staring down at me with an almost mischievous smile.

I think he's on the verge of saying something, but instead, he kisses the side of my head before releasing me.

"You must be Emma," another dark-haired man, bigger than the other, joins our small group. He's dressed up in slacks and a button-down. Even though it's a football game, he oozes seriousness in a way his dad and brother don't.

He extends a hand, saying, "Max. I've heard a lot about you. Pleasure to meet you in person, Emma." He is polite to a fault, yet there's a rigidity.

"Of course, same to you." We shake, and I give him a half smile, but as soon as he releases my hand, his phone is out, and his brow wrinkles.

"Excuse me," Max bows out.

What is in the fucking water around these parts? Even Connie, in his late sixties, would be considered classically handsome. I just call him hot, to be honest.

"Do you want to walk around?" Alex asks, and I nod gratefully. Small talk isn't really my thing. *Is it anyone's thing?*

"You'll excuse us?" Alex asks Connie and Niko, and they both give polite goodbyes.

We exit the tent and turn to walk down the rows of trucks with beds down and grills out. Cornhole tournaments pop up left and right, and then there's a group of people roaring over a makeshift plywood table for beer pong. It seems fun, just not really my kind of fun.

I sip on my beer as we walk until, eventually, Alex asks the question I hoped he wouldn't.

"What's his name?"

"I'm sorry?" I play dumb.

"Your date tonight, what was his name?"

I twist my lip to the side, embarrassed at what I'm about to admit.

"Rob. He canceled at the last minute."

"Hmm," Alex grunts his disapproval. I shrug.

"I'm not surprised he blew me off. I was the one who asked him out. And maybe he just didn't have the heart to turn me down in person." Alex eyes me skeptically.

"You...asked him out?" I don't know if he's surprised, shocked, or angry by that fact.

"Yeah, I did." I shrug again. Clearly, my picker is off. The only men I really want are completely unattainable, so I picked a regular guy, and that was a failure, too.

"I'm surprised you're dating," Alex says somberly.

"I mean, am I not supposed to?" We haven't talked about it, but I figured with me moved out and him still in love with Jess, there isn't a need to define the lack of relationship between us.

He thinks about it. Which is surprising because I would have thought the answer was clear. But I thought wrong because he says, "I'd prefer if you didn't. Until we were divorced."

My stomach flips.

"Oh. Well, are you ready to get divorced then?"

"No," his answer is resolute.

"Okay..." I trail off, expecting him to say more on the issue.

"Okay," is all he says back. I actually stop walking, but he keeps going, and I have to quicken my steps to catch up.

"So what does that mean then? I need you to be explicit, Alex."

He turns, stopping, gripping my waist with one hand. "It means I wish you would wear your ring...And I wish you'd come home." *Home.* The burn within me is building to unbearable levels. I want his other hand in my hair, on my ass. I want him to fuck me in his room at home. I want him to be thinking of me and only me.

But he would never.

I ask the question that will prove this. "If you could be with her right now, would you?" His gaze darkens, and I prepare for my insides to be scorched. For him to blow me up with his answer. *Gut me, Alex, so I can turn you down. Make it easy for me to walk away. Please.*

"I wouldn't, Em." *What?* He steps closer and says quietly, "I want to be with someone who chooses me. With the person who asked me to stay. I want to be that person for you, too. So stay with me, Em. Please."

Fuck. "I want to believe you mean that..." God, do I ever. With his breath skating against my cheek, my body yearns to be touching him. "If I came back, would we stay in my room, both of us?"

"If that's what you want." It isn't.

"What if I want to stay in your room? With you?" It's time for Alex to put his money where his mouth is. Could he actually relinquish the shrine? *This* I doubt most of all.

He looks me in the eyes, knowing I've seen upstairs. I've seen his past frozen in time.

"Come home tonight and find out." The hair on the back

of my neck stands. My arms break out in goosebumps. My eyes widen, questioning. He just stares back down at me, heat building in the small of my back, my inner thighs pulsing to know.

He leans forward, our lips nearly touching. "Think about it."

And then, I don't know if he comes down or I reach up, but his lips are on mine, warm and slow, feeling like the softest place to land. It's only our second time kissing, and I feel like I can hardly even remember the first.

The nearly empty beer slips from my fingers and falls to the ground with a gentle thunk.

Moving a hand up to my neck, he holds me while I brace his biceps. And he kisses me soft and deep, angling his head to reach new depths. *Fuck the football game.* I want *this*. Not in my wildest dreams did I picture this turn.

But can he do it? Actually relinquish her?

It seems like Alex is finally willing to make the break, though.

I pull away, biting my lip, my nerves making me shake.

"Are you sure you're ready this time?" I have to whisper to conceal my shaking voice.

"Positive," he says back. I don't give him an answer because I can't. At least not honestly.

"I'll think about it."

He sinks his mouth down over mine again, and I know. I'll go back to him. Probably time and time again.

FOURTEEN

ALEX

The ride home is cold, with the sun finally tucked away. So, I rub her legs at each stoplight to try and warm her up. I make sure her hands are slipped inside the pocket of my hoodie for extra warmth. I even pull her more snugly into my backside.

Still, when I pull up to her building, she's shivering. Instead of stopping out front to drop her off, I pull into the garage, snagging the last guest spot, hoping she'll invite me in.

I'm not ready to say goodbye. My chest aches just thinking about not knowing when or if I'll see her again.

With the kickstand down, she swings both legs around and off the bike, unbuckling the helmet with lightning speed. Yeah, I can figure out where this is heading. I let loose a sigh, not bothering to unbuckle my helmet.

"Thanks for coming with me," she shivers, then places both hands around her arms to try and get warm.

"Thanks for the invite..." We stare at each other, seeing one another. I see a woman that's trying to heal just like me. I see someone I love, someone I want to love and do my damndest to make happy. I see someone who could be my partner, my other half if she isn't already.

She finally turns to leave, but I stop her before I start the engine on the bike again. "Hey, Em?" She turns back to look at me. "In case I don't see you. I love you." Her terse smile fades, and we're back to staring silently.

I won't be the first to break. She can leave or say something back, but as long as she wants to stand here with me, I'll be here.

"Where did you go that night, Alex?" I know what she means. She doesn't have to say, *'The night you stood me up.'*

I wasn't proud of where I'd gone, what I'd almost done.

"I hiked to the ridge." Her face loses color. "The only reason I came back was for you..." She starts to move towards me.

Then she's hiking a leg up and over the bike. With one leg over the top of each of my thighs, she straddles me, then pulls me in for a kiss. A desperate one. Not soft and safe, like I tried to give her earlier.

So I pull her harder against me, and she gasps when she feels my hardened length beneath her. She pushes her tongue in like she wants to drown me. It's not necessarily nice, and I get it.

She wants to remind me she still gives a fuck even when I don't. And I fucking love her for that. My hands are at her waist while hers dig into my hair, into my scalp. She bites my lip, and my dick throbs.

She pulls back to whisper, "If you leave me, I'll hate you, Alex. I mean it." She doesn't look me in the eyes. Instead, she stares at my lips, avoiding eye contact to keep the tears at bay. I don't want to scare her, but she's the only thing that's kept me here. I nod, and she nods with me.

I wipe away a tear that travels down her cheek.

I won't make false promises, but I know what's at stake. What I could lose. Emma had become my best friend and my favorite person. She was the only thing that kept me going as I hiked 5 miles in the pitch-black rain to come home to her. *To her*.

"Come inside," it's a command. One I take.

Sliding her back, she drags across my dick, and I lift her to stand. Dismounting, I hang my helmet on the handlebars, then pick her right back up again.

Her legs straddle my waist, and I sink my tongue deep inside her. I hold her with one hand on her round ass and one at her neck, in her hair.

"Em..." I moan when she sucks my tongue, my dick dying to plunge itself into her.

"Start walking." So I do. I walk us into the lobby, where we make out against the wall while we wait for the elevator.

In the elevator, she grinds her hips against mine, and my body jerks with a newly forming obsession.

In the hall, we struggle to grasp reality and find the keys to her condo. With her legs still around my waist, she leans over to unlock the door. I kick it open just to turn around and kick it closed.

"Last door at the end of the hall." She instructs me, pulling off her sweatshirt as I walk her back. The sweatshirt and tee come off as a pair, giving me a view of her full breasts held by a lace-trimmed bra. Breasts I still think of every time I touch myself. The way they bounced...full and begging me. Fucking tempting me.

The door at the end of the hall is already open, so I cruise in, dropping her on the bed. With her hair splayed behind her and her limbs sprawled out, I know exactly what I want. I start to undo the button on her jeans, and she squirms.

"This is all I think about, Emma." It has been. I wanted my face between her thighs, worshiping her existence ever since she sucked my cock like I was the fucking king of England. It was an award-winning performance. One I don't think I'll ever forget.

My dick jumps as I begin to pull down her tight jeans, leaving red lacy panties behind. *Fuck me.* There's something about my sweet girl wearing this naughty as fuck underwear...

I can feel Em watching me as I admire her body. When I meet her gaze, she and I wear the same look. *Need.* After I slide her panties down her legs slowly, I tuck them in my back pocket. They're mine now. *She's* mine now. Her breath catches as she watches me run a finger between her bare lips.

Everything about her is so fucking soft. These lips...

And she shaved for him? The jealousy ignites a monster in me, dying to be set free. I don't want anyone else to see her like this. *Not ever.*

"Was this for him?" I run a finger through her slit again, pressing down on her clit. She bucks her hips and gasps. "Tell me, baby. Was it?"

She bites her lip, swallowing. "Yeah, it was." Wrong fucking answer, Emma.

I grab her chin, yanking her forward, and leave her with a kiss that has her grinding mercilessly, making a mess against her sheets.

"Do you wish it was him right now?" She shakes her head, still held by my hand. "If it was him, would you be wishing it was me?" This time, she nods. And I reward her with another kiss, driving my tongue in her mouth, making plans to claim every part of her body. I release her chin, place a knee on the mattress, and lean forward to unclasp the bra hiding her beautiful breasts from me.

"I would have given anything for it to be you tonight," she says as I look down and memorize each inch of flesh. The creamy length of her abdomen that leads to those soft, pink lips. The lines of her quads in her thighs that I want to see flexed and wrapped around my head as I indulge in her.

Well, it's going to be me tonight. And tomorrow. And the night after that.

I rip off my sweatshirt and tee but leave my jeans.

Putting my other knee on the bed, and with one hand at her waist, I push her further back on the mattress. Her breasts bounce, and my cock mimics the motion.

Ten months of marriage, and I still haven't had my mouth on those lips. I haven't felt inside her, haven't claimed her. But I will.

There's this primal need flaring inside me, and all I want is to mark her. I want the world to look at her and know she's mine. How? How would I do it? *You know how.* The small voice says, tempting me. I'm a fucking monster, but I'm not sure I can do that to her. Especially when she might finally be opening back up to me.

I know I can't. But, fuck, why do I want *that* so bad?

I push her thighs apart, spreading her wide, and she fists the sheets. Coming down between her, I run my nose between her legs, up one side and down the other, mapping her. Watching her clench as I get closer until my mouth is placing a gentle kiss.

For as soft and quiet and gentle as Emma is, I already know she'll be able to take whatever I throw at her. I start slow, though. A lick here, a peck there, a nudge inside. She's so fucking sweet. Everything about her is sweet and soft, but this especially. *Fucking nectar.* I want to savor it, make it last. For her, but also for me.

But she's writhing for more. She wants pressure; she wants it hard, and my body recognizes that. So when I finally suck her clit in, my hips thrust against the bed, begging for friction, too.

When she grips my head, her fingernails digging into my scalp, I thrust, feeling the rough denim drag against my cock.

I moan when she pants. She screams when I bite down. She bucks, and I thrust. Holding on tight to her hips and ass, she grinds as I grind.

"I love you," I say as I suck her in and hump against nothing.

When she screams out, "Alexander!" bucking and writhing against my face, I lose it hearing her say my name, my whole body on fire for her. Thrusting down and against the mattress, the ropes of cum leave my body sticking against my briefs.

So sucking and biting more, I send her into another orgasm. This time, she wraps her thighs around my head, and I keep grinding down against the bed to get every last drop of cum released. Hers and mine both.

She trembles when I finally release her, her arms falling back against the mattress in defeat.

"Come home, baby," I whisper to her as I massage her hips and legs where I might have left bruises.

With big eyes and pink cheeks, she nods. And I smile.

"Good. Get dressed."

———

Emma

His hands on me are a weakness I can't overcome.

So when he says, *'Come home, baby,'* I realize him calling me baby is my undoing. I don't want to refuse. So I don't.

"Good. Get dressed."

"Wait, what?" I ask as he stands up, grabbing my legs and pulling me to the edge of the bed. "You don't want..." I motion down to his groin, confused about how the hottest oral sex of my life could leave him not wanting anything in return.

He adjusts himself slightly and chuckles. "I'm taken care of." Then he blushes. *Did he?* Like a virginal teenager?

"Did *you*...?" I ask, and he laughs.

"Yeah, I did, baby. Don't make it weird." Oh god, never. *And baby?* Again? I've never loved the sound of anything more.

"No, no! It's not that, it's-holy shit, Alex." I reach for him to come to mc, and he does. Stooping down to hover over my naked body, I slide my arms around his neck. "That's the hottest thing I've ever heard." Good lord, I want him so bad. The affection I have towards him surges.

He kisses me, then demands again, "Get dressed." I make a fake pouting face, and he leaves me to use the bathroom.

I slowly roll off the bed, my limbs languid and lazy.

"Where are we going?" I call out to him. It's not exactly late, but it is nine o'clock already.

His head pokes out around the door while he washes his hands.

"Home." *Oh*.

Throwing on a sports bra, a pair of leggings, and a long-sleeve thermal, I ask, "Do I need to bring anything?" When he walks back into my bedroom, he's fully dressed and ready to go.

"I'd say bring everything." We're really just going to skip dating and everything in between and go back to being married people who live together?

"Hold on," I grab his arm to stop him from going to my closet. "Maybe we should start slow. Maybe we should have that date that never happened..." I trail off, remembering the searing pain when he said what he'd done that night. He went to the ridge with no plans to come back. I hated every second, every word. He came home, though, and I told him I hated him. I hate myself for that.

"Em," He inhales deeply, holding my chin in his hand. "I don't know how to be normal and just *date*. But I do know that being with you is easier than breathing." His exhale is shaky.

"I don't fall in love with anyone, Em, but I did with you. I think about all the things that had to happen that night for me to find you." He places a soft kiss on my lips. "It wasn't an accident."

"It wasn't," I whisper back because I've thought about it a hundred times. For whatever reason, I was supposed to meet Alexander Palomino that morning. I don't know if it was fate, or destiny, but it wasn't an accident. I know that.

"I was somewhere I didn't want to be, and something told me to get up and leave. And it told me to keep going and not stop until there was you. And you were perfect. In every way. You *are* perfect, Emma." The air leaves my lungs with a gasp.

"I love you, Alex," I say it for the first time, officially, and there's tears in his eyes. "But I'm scared." I'm nervous that this is temporary, which might be okay. Except that my temporary is months or years, Alex's is an hour. Could I accept that, knowing how fleeting this probably is? Do I even have a choice?

I could say no, but all he would have to do is touch me, and I would be back to yes.

"I might hurt you, but you could hurt me too, so I guess we have to decide to take that chance together?" He's not perfect, but neither am I.

"Promise me, if you ever stop wanting this, you'll just tell me?" I ask him, fear lacing each word.

"I promise," he says back with conviction. And I believe him. At *this* moment, I wholeheartedly believe that he believes that, too.

———

I wake up with a hand furled around my curly hair, a leg

draped over my hip, and the deepest burn between my thighs. And we're in *his* room. Not mine.

The fist seems to tighten, and the leg grips me tighter, sending his thick length deeper into my backside. *Oh god*, it hadn't been a dream.

My greedy body angles my hips higher, and a hand comes down to my abdomen, holding me in place.

More. I want to moan; I want to arch my back, driving his length deeper.

"Emma," his voice is hoarse and strained.

"Alexander," I say back, my tone mirroring his.

"Can you tell me what my little wife wants?" *Little wife.* The hand on my abdomen grips and tightens before releasing me.

This time, I'm not noble enough to stop. I want to feel the weight of him on top of me; I want him feasting on me, claiming me, and I want it now.

I pull his hand down, easing it between my legs, and he exhales slowly, the hot air skirting over the side of my face.

"God, you're beautiful, Em," he says as his hand dips lower, gliding against my bare skin.

My nipples pull taught as I look down to watch his large hand dip between my thighs, forcing them open.

He lifts his leg off mine and hitches it higher so he can reach me, sending his dick sliding between my legs in turn. But he doesn't try to enter me. Instead, he slides a thick finger between my lips, finding me hot and wet for him. *Am I really going to let him fuck me?*

"Alex..." I say softly, and he moves the finger down, swirling around my entrance before coming to rest the finger over my clit. God, I want to buck against that finger. I want to praise it for existing, then ride it into tomorrow.

"Yeah?" he asks, his face pressing into the curls at the back of my head.

"I've never...been with anyone...before." The hand between my thighs disappears, and I freeze with embarrassment, rolling my eyes up to keep from looking stupidly at the absence.

"How do you mean?" He asks while holding his hand away from my body.

"I mean, technically, I'm a virgin." I hate that word and what it implies. Hate that I'm a 26-year-old virgin because I've been waiting for the right person, and they haven't come. They don't want me. They aren't dreaming about me like I am about them.

When he doesn't say anything, I start to scoot away from him. Giving him an exit, but his hand is back on my hip, holding me close to him.

"You've never..." Oh god, he's going to make me spell it out.

"I've never had sex with anyone. Is that what you wanted to hear?"

"Jesus, Emma. I-I don't know." I sigh because here it comes. *Well, maybe we shouldn't do anything then.* Like I'm fucking diseased or a toss away. "Just tell me what you're comfortable with, then." This time, I freeze.

"You're not...weirded out by that?" I ask, hopeful.

"Are you kidding?" His dick pulses, twitching between my thighs. "I fucking *love* that it's gonna be me. *Only* me." My chest burns at the possessiveness in his voice.

He scoots back, rolling me onto my back so he can look at me. But I don't want to.

The tears are coming in, my cheeks hot with embarrassment.

"Do you want to have sex right now, Emma?" I nod because I did. I do. But suddenly, I'm scared to death I'll look stupid and won't know what I'm doing. I was never even brave enough to use anything besides my fingers on myself.

"You're fucking perfect, Emma," Alex says as he pulls me into his side, then moves over the top of me, peppering kisses across my body, starting with my chest.

Then they're on my abdomen and then my clit. "Relax, baby." I hadn't realized how rigid I was, knowing what's coming.

"You don't have to if you don't want to..." I tell him as he prepares to go down on me. Again.

"Shut up, Em. This isn't a fucking chore," he looks at me, "it's a privilege." He spreads open my lips and sucks, sending my hips off the bed. He puts a palm on my stomach to hold me down, and with his other hand, he starts to slide a finger in. *Yes, fucking, please.*

The longing for the feeling of fullness there is overwhelming. I want his fingers slamming against me. I want his cock thrusting in me. I want to be fucked like I've watched others be for years.

Alex is gentle at first, but then he adds another finger, and they curl, rubbing against my inner wall as his tongue laves at my clit on the outside.

"Fuck, Alex!" I cry as he quickly brings me right to the edge of orgasm, then retreats, leaving me gasping and wanting more.

He opens his nightstand and pulls out a condom. "Put it on me," he instructs. Sitting up and leaning forward, I take the foil packet in my shaking hand. He kneels on the mattress before me, then guides my hand in his, steadying me. Stroking me.

When I put the condom at his tip and start to run it down his length, he leans forward and whispers. "Fucking perfect, Emma. Everything about you."

My confidence surges, and I arch up to kiss him.

He gently pushes me to lie back, and then he's spreading my legs, moving between me, and positioning himself.

"Tell me you want it," Alex says, looking me in the eyes.

"I've never wanted anything more." It's true.

"It'll hurt." I don't care. "But you're mine, Emma." Of course, he knows exactly what to say, as if I'm not already burning up inside.

I nod, reaching around to pull his mouth down to mine. I want his cock driving into me at the same time his tongue fucks my mouth.

I can feel him at my entrance, and I brace for the discomfort. At first, there's pressure, then a piercing feeling for two seconds, and I bite his lip in reaction, but then it just stings.

"So good for me, baby," he soothes, pushing in further until he's fully seated in me. *Finally full.*

"God, Alex." I gasp at the feeling. The feeling of him and me... *Us*. The thought alone brings me to the edge.

"Are you okay if I move?" I nod my head vigorously. All I want is for him to ride me hard. I want the pain. I want to feel alive. And I do for the first time in a long time.

"I want my husband to fuck me. Hard. Please?" I ask, finally giving him what he wants.

"I love you," he says before pulling out to slam back in. The stinging is back but not as sharp. Then he's pulling out to come back in again. He's gripping my neck, and I hold a hand around his arm while my fingernails mark his back.

It's more instinctual than I thought it would be. When he comes forward, I lift my hips, and when he grinds against my clit, my thighs tense. "Yes," I beg, writhing, arching my back underneath him, anything that will bring him to that spot again.

"Harder," I beg.

"Who's fucking you, Emma?" He asks, moving over me as aggressively as I asked him to.

"Alex." He shakes his head.

"Who am I to you now?"

"My husband." He nods.

"Is your husband fucking you well, Em?" I nod, too. "Come apart for me, *wife*." I actually picture myself falling. I fall deep. In love with this feeling of belonging. I'm someone to somebody. We *belong* now. Actually.

"Alex, please!" I shout. He slams into me, grinding down, and my thighs tighten, and my abdomen tenses, and then I'm spasming around his thick length. A full-body orgasm rocks me. Heat spreading to each limb, my release coating his cock.

I throw my head back and moan as he fucks me through it.

"Look at me, baby," he pleads for my attention, then proceeds to lose it, thrusting hard against me as his dick releases.

I can feel the convulsions, and I wish there wasn't a barrier between us. I crave his cum deep inside me. The thought that follows is sickeningly embarrassing: *ours*.

As both our breathing calms, he rests his forehead against mine. We stay like that until our heart rates return to normal, the connection feeling profound in the moment.

"I love you," he says gently.

I lean up for a quick kiss and say, "I guess we're really married now," with a smirk, my attempt at holding my cards a little more closely.

"I guess so," he says back, a genuine smile painted on his beautiful face.

FIFTEEN

ALEX

I test the bath water first. Then, walking over to her side of the bed, I pick her up and carry her to the tub.

"You don't have to do this." No, but I want to.

"Shut up, Em." I smile down at her, and she smirks back.

I place her in the tub first, then climb in behind her so her back is to my chest.

The suds bloom, and I let her sit and process before I ask any of the hundreds of questions I want to.

How, at 26, was she a virgin? How was she giving a world-class BJ but never had sex? How had she not had sex?

"Do you want to talk about it?" I ask her. She shrugs.

"I'm sure you have questions..."

"It was a surprise, but I don't want you to think I'm mad or upset in some way...at all." It's fucking embarrassing how proud I am to have been Emma's first. It's a fire burning deep

168

in the pit of my soul that I'm the only one she's ever been with. *Mine.*

"My mom is...Darla Strait. Have you heard of her before?" I had.

"I know who your mom is, baby." She turns around to look at me, surprised. Like I wouldn't run a background check on someone I marry.

"Okay...well, I told you before that she's an addict. But it's not just that, it-it's her entire world. I don't feel like addiction fully encompasses the level of...*devotion* she has to it." She starts talking, and I pull her in tight, running a hand up and down her arm, letting her know she's safe with me, too. I can be her keeper, too.

"As soon as a penny comes in, it's back out the door. Or up her nose or in her stomach in the form of pills and hard liquor. But...what's really fun," her voice catches, "is when there isn't any money, and you still have to get to the next high..." I hate knowing where this will lead.

"When I was little, there was a revolving door of men in the house even when my stepdad was still around. My sister, Carrie, tried to shelter me, but by the time I was eight or so, I figured it out."

"And then, when I was a little bit older...and so was Darla, they weren't as interested in her, and she–" she pauses, and I give her a supportive squeeze. "She started offering up my sister... It wasn't...optional. So the second Carrie turned 18, she bolted. She tried to get me to go with her, but I was too scared. She left anyway, as she should, and my mom... turned to me to fill the gap."

"The first time was just hands. I hated it, but I didn't have an option to say no. I want you to know that, Alex. It was do it, or have it done. I didn't want it." She sniffles, and I hug her from behind, wishing someone, anyone, had actually looked out for her. I'm also fucking pissed, but for now, I just focus on her.

"And then after a couple of times, they wanted me to use my mouth, and I wouldn't do it... So they held me down." Bile rises in my throat. "She let them do that to me. Even when I vomited, they held me down. And she let them. The only reason they didn't rape me was because she was planning to sell that to the highest bidder." An actual fucking monster.

"I guess I never really thought sex was all that special until someone was taking it from me without permission. And if that was my only power," she shrugs, "I didn't want to give it away...I left the next day. With no money, no home, and no real friends." She laughs bitterly, "I was 16."

"I'm so sorry, Em." I kiss the top of her head and hold on tight. I think of all the times we sat in the mornings, and she just listened to me tell her about all the awful things that have happened to me, and she had this. Festering.

I hold her tight like I'll never let go.

"This is why you needed me to ask permission...the first time." She nods. It wasn't because she's a domme, it's because she's a fucking sexual assault survivor.

The tears run down my cheeks, thinking about her on her knees for me. Giving me something sacred to her.

"I want you to know, Em, what you've done for me..." my voice cracks.

"There were a dozen times I wanted to tell you..."

"And I'm sorry you felt like you couldn't." I'll do better. I have to. "You're safe with me; you know that, right?" I feel her tense for a fraction of a second.

Then she says, "You make me feel safe. I know."

"Did you ever go to counseling?" She shakes her head.

"You mean how did I go from *that*, to giving a killer BJ?" She teases me, and I pinch her leg under the water. "No, I didn't go to counseling. I was homeless at times. I barely had money for gas. When you found me, that was the absolute best I had done for myself. I honestly thought I peaked, and it was all gonna be downhill from there. I didn't have dreams or aspirations. It was just, keep myself alive. I might not have been..." She doesn't want to say the 's' word, "But I know what it's like to have nothing to live for."

She *is* just like me. She's said it before in different ways, but it sinks in for the first time that she's truly just like me. A blow job isn't just a blow job, and a kiss isn't just a kiss. Even from the first time, we'd given each other something. It hits hard, the feeling of inevitability that's Emma and me. Like no matter what, our paths were bound to cross.

"I've never told anyone this actually...but I was pretty determined to not let it ruin me. So, I started reading *spicy* books that reaffirmed loving relationships existed. That someone could give oral sex and have it be a safe experience." She lets out a soft chuckle before saying, "Libraries are fucking amazing."

"And then...I started watching porn..." she laughs again, nervously, "this is like so fucking embarrassing, Alex." She puts her hands over her face, even though I can't see her as it is.

"Stop," I pull her hands away, sliding my fingers in hers. "I want to hear this."

"Ugh, fine. So, I watched a lot of...porn. I found what I liked and kept reading, and it stopped being such an aversion...And I've had a boyfriend before..." I want his name and to kill him. "But it wasn't like this. There wasn't a future for us. It was just..." I don't want to hear about how she practiced her way to the queen of head.

"You're amazing," I tell her. Because she is. "And I hope you feel like you have so much ahead of you. No matter what happens, you should be so fucking proud of how smart, and kind, and empathetic you've turned out."

"I could say the same thing about you," she answers back.

After that, we just sit in the tub, holding on to one another until the water turns cold.

"I have to go pick up Delta. Do you want to come?"

"Yeah." I help her out of the tub, watching her walk to the empty sink, then dry off. All of Jess' things went to the dump after Emma moved out. It didn't seem fair that Jess got to stay, but Emma was gone.

I still get a weird twinge in my chest, picturing Jess in this space, but Emma... Every time I think of Emma, I'm happy. I'm happy she's here. I *love* her being here. And I don't foresee that changing anytime soon.

"What are you looking at?" She asks in the mirror's reflection, where she sees me watching her from the tub.

"My wife's ass." Her cheeks turn pink as I smirk. "And how fucking beautiful she is." She laughs, ducking her face.

———

Emma

. . .

"I can't believe you got rid of the Jeep," I tell him as I climb into his new truck.

"It was time. Plus, it didn't seem right to make Delta ride around in a tin can." I had the same thought.

"Right, had to do it for the dog," I laugh, mainly in an attempt to bring us back to normal. I'm still feeling a little raw from it all, and I can feel Alex treating me more delicately than needed.

Definitely more affectionately, but I can't tell if it's because we just had sex for the first time, because we're actually together, or because I just trauma-dumped on him. His hand extends across the cab, and he threads his fingers between mine.

"So we're really doing this, then?" I lift our entwined hands where my wedding ring has been reinstalled. After he got out of the bath, he set it on the counter for me, then waited till I put it back on.

"Happily," he says. I still have questions, but it feels real. Like we are actually married. Sleeping in the primary bedroom of the house. Having sex. And we're certainly acting like a couple. We also just happen to be married.

"Okay."

"Do you want to stop for a coffee? Or anything?" Who even is he? I look at him with wide eyes.

"Who are you?" He laughs, then picks up our hands and kisses the top of mine. "No, I'm good on coffee since I'm sort of hoping someone will make me pancakes when we get home..."

"Deal," he says.

We sit in silence the rest of the drive because while Alex may be in a good or better mood, he still has the radio turned off in the car. I'm used to it, though. So I lean back and watch as we drive through the pines, inhaling the distinct mountain air that permeates the truck's cab.

I feel a little apprehensive stepping up to Brit and Liam's house. I haven't seen them since the night I saw Liam at Maggio's...

Alex knocks, and a few seconds later, Brit answers.

"Oh, you brought Emma." *Her tone.* I don't want to dislike her, but she makes it hard. She's never warm or overtly kind to me. She's always just polite *enough*.

I smile at Britain anyway as she opens the door for Alex and me to come in.

The second Alex's boots hit the hardwood floors, Delta comes flying around a corner. No traction on the smooth floor, just like a cartoon character who runs as fast as they can but never goes anywhere. Alex gets down, and the two embrace like long-lost pals.

"You should have told us you were coming..." she draws it out, looking at Alex.

"You knew I was coming to get the dog?" The coding is there, in between the lines, that he should have told them *I* was coming.

"I think we're going for a hike, so we're turning right back around," I try to say it with a smile. "Right, Alex?" He looks surprised by the turn of events, seeing as we don't have a hike planned, but he hides the look from his sister surprisingly well.

"Yup."

"I was hoping you'd stay for Sunday dinner..." I want to roll my eyes at her; just so done with this dance. It's clear that I'm never going to be *enough* to be included. I don't know if it's because I don't ooze rich-people vibes, or we just don't have anything in common, or maybe she thinks I'm not good enough for her brother. I don't know, but I'm done trying to care.

"How about this," I say, overly chipper. "I'll just take Delta home, and Alex can stay for dinner?" I look between the two of them. Britain's eyes go large, and Alex's brow furrows.

"You're being rude, Brit." He stands, grabbing Delta's leash off the entry table. "Thanks for watching the dog," he says a bit insincerely, grabbing my hand and the leash to go.

"I'm sorry, Em," he says as he walks me to the door, but I just shrug. What else can you do? I don't have any girlfriends, and maybe there's a reason why. It always seems like I'm the odd man out when it comes to being "one of the girls."

Or maybe I just don't like other women in general. There's my mom. And then there's my sister. Maybe I'm the problem.

We walk out into the crisp fall day, the sun shining, the breeze blowing, and I get over it.

"I still want pancakes, for the record," I tell Alex as he opens my door, then Delta's too.

"Any flavor you want."

———

We have chocolate chip pancakes because it's been a while since Alex has gone to the store for fresh produce. So, while I read and try to catch up on school work, he does a grocery run. It feels hugely domestic of us. I do, however, have plans to reward him when he gets home later.

The doorbell ringing surprises me. There's a gate, so if anyone makes it to the door, they must have the code. Delta and I unfurl ourselves from the snuggly ball we were made into on the couch.

Going on my tiptoes, I check the peephole as Delta sits beside me, whining. For a split second, I think of *him*. My heart rate increases, and my palms grow damp.

But it's not him.

I open the door, and Britain extends a large vase of flowers in my direction.

Tentatively, I accept the vase, expecting her to tell me they're for Alex or some crap.

"I'm sorry," she says. I stand, holding the flowers, with the door open, and wait for the rest. An explanation, something.

"Is that it?" I ask as politely as I can.

"Can I come in?" she asks. I hold the door and motion her in. "Is Alex here?" I shake my head no. "Already back from your hike?" She sort of laughs at the end.

"There was no hike, Britain. I was just trying to save you from being uncomfortable in my presence." My jaw is tense, my molars grinding together, and I'm ready for her to leave.

"It's...hard. To be around you. And it's not because of *you*. It's just because of who you are to him." This sounds like a 'her problem,' not a 'me problem.'

"I guess it's hard to feel like it's not because of me. You know?" Maybe she doesn't get it. I bet she has whole gaggles of friends. Her wedding party was probably eight people deep, with a long line of backups. She gives off cool-girl, you-can't-sit-with-us vibes in the worst way.

Britain rubs her hands together and shifts uncomfortably. "Jess is my best friend." *Well, fuck.* "It feels like I'm betraying her even when you just...come over." The pain in my throat is a full burn. My mind spins, recalling a memory.

That's just some random friend who works for my sister.

God, you're just so pretty.

Go home, Ella.

"She has short, dark hair. Really pretty?" Britain nods. "Okay." That's all I can say because...what? The fuck? I end up sucking my cheeks in, trying to hold back a tear. He drove us over there that day, knowing Jess would be there.

Did Blanks take me to dinner that night because he knew she'd be there too?

I almost forgot that I was here to make *someone else* feel like shit.

Does Alex even love me? Or is that to make her feel bad, too?

"I'm sorry, Britain. I don't know what you want me to do. I can't stop existing, but I can stay away from you as much as possible."

"Emma, I'm so sorry. That's–no. Please accept my apology, and I hope you'll please accept an invitation to dinner. You're my family, too. And I've forgotten that. So, really, I hope you'll forgive me."

"Sure," I say, mentally having checked out of the conversation.

"Okay..." she trails off awkwardly.

"I should get back to studying," I point to the living room, where my textbooks are on the sofa waiting for me.

"Got it."

I quickly set the vase on a side table and lead her back to the door.

"You'll come for dinner sometime soon?" *No.*

"Definitely, just let us know." I hope she's just bullshitting because I definitely don't want to have dinner with them. Wondering all night if they're comparing me to her. The petite woman with flawless skin, classically gorgeous, who dresses impeccably. I look like a slob compared to her. *Jesus.*

I smooth out the front of my henley and self-consciously berate my tired leggings and shirt. What does Alex even see in me? *Nothing.* Just a means to an end, I suppose. I was just the wrong person in the right place at the right time.

"C-can I give you a hug goodbye?" Brit opens her arms awkwardly, and I move in for the most uncomfortable hug of my life.

When she finally releases me, I give a toothless smile and open the door. She gives a wave and a smile that looks like it clawed its way out of the dark to be here.

Once I can finally shut the door, I lean back against it. The inside of the house doesn't feel warm and cozy anymore. It feels cold and empty. I head to the mudroom to grab a jacket and beanie when the flashy invite hanging on the pinboard catches my attention.

Mrs. and Mr. Palomino are cordially invited to the wedding reception for Damian Scott and Jessica DiAngelo.

Is this why he wants me back? I finger the edge of the invite on handmade paper, feeling envious of everything she is and I'm not. My wedding...was laughable in my thrift store dress. *Jesus.* All I have to show for the day is a photo, singular...and I don't even have it. I know they took one photo, but I've never seen it.

It's been a long time since I've felt this sort of misery. I hang my head against the wall and fight the urge to cry because I gave him the only thing I had of value. I told myself he wouldn't hurt me. I told myself I was doing this for the money. *Lies.*

I'm an idiot.

"You wanna go for a walk, Delta?" I call the dog, not realizing he's never left my side. "You're such a good boy. Let's walk." I slip his lead on, then head out the mudroom door. We head for the clearing and straight to the hidden cove pathway.

We go nice and slow since it's been a while since I've walked the trail. It's slightly overgrown, at least compared to the last time I was on it. *I wonder if Alex isn't using it much.*

It's mid-afternoon, and the sun is just past the middle of the sky, sending beams of sunlight shooting horizontally off the damp trees. I inhale the earthen scent, waiting for relief to find me from the turning in my gut. But it doesn't come.

I wonder what he really thought when I told him I was a virgin? I cringe.

What was he thinking when I told him I was used by dealers? Shame gnaws at my insides.

Maybe he isn't out getting groceries; instead, he's running away. I laugh out loud, and Delta looks back at me. I could just picture him at Jess' house, knocking on the door. Begging for her to take him back.

And then I remember her at Coltons that night. The way she danced like no one was watching. The way she tried to bury her pain in — *oh my god* — the brothers had been there that night. That's where I remembered them from. *Jesus.* Were they all in on it?

Like an arrow straight through the chest, I remember her crying, then laughing hysterically, and how bad I felt for her because she was so obviously dying inside.

She was dying on the inside. And he was dying on the outside.

Alex isn't dying for me. No one is. It was likely no one ever would.

When we get to the boulder, I don't climb it to sit and view the lake. Instead, I stand and stare at the spot that I thought was *our* hidden world. Where the secrets were spilled, and the bond was forged. I thought I was special.

But I'm just a bandaid.

And she's the cure.

SIXTEEN

ALEX

"Emma!" I call out after hauling in the last load of groceries. She doesn't answer, so I start unloading, putting the produce and meat in the fridge. Restocking both our favorites, the Red Vines, in the pantry, I smile because she's back.

"Em!" I call out again, refilling the egg container.

"Delta!" I call, but there's nothing that answers me back.

I slip out my phone, and press her name, then wait.

Her phone rings in the great room, and I wander over to where she'd been sitting, flipping the blanket back to see "Table 19" incoming call on her screen.

Table 19?

"Emma!" I call again, but it's silent.

I walk out to the back deck and call for them, but there's still no reply. Don't love that she left without her phone even if it was just to walk Delta.

Heading back inside, I pull out the chicken breasts for

dinner to start marinating while I wait. But 30 minutes later, I'm still waiting.

I walk out the front door, this time to look around. Calling out, to no response.

I *hate* this. I'm on the verge of leaving to walk the trails in search when Delta's bark draws my attention up to Emma, who looks like she's been crying.

"What's wrong?" I jog to her, taking her face in my hands, checking to see if she's hurt, but she kind of pushes my hands away. And there's that gut feeling telling me something's wrong. "Tell me, please?" I plead with her because my chest aches to see her like this.

"You brought me here to hurt her, didn't you? At least in the first place, that's why you needed a wife, right?"

I take a step back at her words. The short answer is yes.

So I tell her the truth. "Yes."

"I figured as much..." She lets out a shaky sigh. "I had no clue she was your sister's best friend. No wonder she hates me." She sniffles.

"Did Brit say something?" I ask, wondering how she knew.

"You know, I saw her that night at Coltons. While you slept in my room. Blanks took me to get food, and she was there." My hackles rise; not sure where this would go. "Jesus, she was the prettiest person in the whole fucking place. And she was *dying*, Alex. For you. She was a dead woman walking. And I had no clue it was her. She called me Cinderella, you know?" She laughs through the tears. Not a happy laugh.

"I sort of thought she was deranged, but she was just in love with you, which maybe, that's the greatest sickness of all." *Ouch.*

"What are you talking about, Em?" Hate every second of this.

"Do you really think you could be happy with second best?" She asks, and the flames in my chest erupt.

"Is that what you think?" I ask.

She motions up and down her body, sniffles, and says, "I mean, look at me. I'm about to be 27 years old, and I have nothing to show for it. *And* I'm damaged goods. I wore a dress from the thrift store to our wedding. It was 29 dollars, Alex!"

"You are not second best." I grind out my words. "Does what I said to you this morning mean nothing to you?"

"I just don't know if I can believe it..." she says back quietly, eviscerating me.

"When I'm with you, Emma, I don't say a single thing I don't mean. I always tell you the truth, even to my own detriment. Even when it hurts, I tell you the truth. I don't just love you, Emma; I'm in love with you. And I didn't even want to be! But how the fuck was I supposed to not fall in love with you? Huh?"

Her eyes go wide at my confession, but I keep going. "I slept in your bed with the dog for three months. That's how much I missed you. Fuck, when I got Delta, the first thing I thought was: Emma would love him. I'm always thinking about *you*. I'm thinking about you first, not second. When I wake up, first thing, I wonder what you're doing. I wonder if you're happy. I wonder if I could make you happy."

"And today, I was thinking how fucking proud I am that you're mine. And that you gave me something, and I have nothing to give back to you. Except to tell you I love you."

"Fuck! And then I think about your family, and I want to

burn the world down. *For* you!" She listens, just taking a large gulp.

"I don't *have* to *do* anything, Emma. But I choose you. This is all a choice, you know. You could leave at any time. I could go too. You told me to tell you if I ever stopped wanting this, and have I told you that?"

Her answer is hesitant, "No."

"Give it a chance, Em. Please." I grab her face in my hands, clearing the tears where I can.

"Please, Alex, just please promise the second you don't want this anymore, you'll tell me? I can't live with a question hanging over me."

"I promise," I mean it. If that's her one ask, I can respect that. She nods and wipes the rest of the tears away.

"Okay." She starts to walk around me, but I grab her hand and stop her.

"It goes both ways, Em. You have to promise me because you could stop wanting this too."

"I promise," she says.

———

I cook dinner so she can finish reading, then bring a plate to her in the living room.

"Thanks," she gives me a tired smile to go with it.

I go back to the table to give her space, but she joins me a minute later.

"My eyes are gonna start bleeding. I need a break." I just nod. "I'm sorry about earlier," she says, not looking me in the eyes.

"Nothing to be sorry for," I lean over, putting a hand on her thigh.

We go back to eating silently until she asks, "So how long were...you and her together?" I have to clear my throat to force the food down.

"Not very long."

"Hmm," she hums. "Are you going?" The tightening in my stomach has me sitting up straighter.

"What do you mean?"

"Their wedding, are you planning to go?"

"Probably not."

"Okay," she leaves it at that. I hope.

It's a few more minutes of silence when I remember and ask, "Why am I saved as Table 19 in your phone?" She sort of smirks.

"That's what table you were sitting at the diner that night." *Cute.* I give her a warm smile that she gives right back. And then we're back to normal. Our normal.

She tells me about the art history book she's reading. I tell her about driving past the pumpkin patches when I got groceries. And then she asks what I'm doing tonight.

"I don't know. If you're going to study, I'll probably just go downstairs."

"No, let's hang out." This would be new territory. It wasn't that we didn't hang out before; it was just always around dinner, and afterward, she would go her way. I would go mine, but we'd meet back for bed.

"I wanna watch something, go brain dead, and veg," she says, stretching her arms overhead, then yawning.

"What are we watching?" I ask, picking up my plate and

hers to put in the dishwasher. She follows behind me, grabbing water bottles for both of us from the fridge.

"Dealer's choice," she winks, slipping into the pantry, then squealing when she finds the packs of Red Vines.

Holding up a pack, she says, "I love you." I shake my head and laugh.

She grabs the goods and heads for the great room while I clear the rest of dinner, start the dishes, and hit the lights.

She's back to her corner of the sofa, and I take the seat beside her. Then, without much thought, my arm is around her, and she's cuddling into my side. It's just easy with her.

After the second episode of Alone, she tells me, "This was basically my dream, growing up. I wanted to just get lost in the woods and build a little shelter. In my mind, it was cozy, but watching this..." She shudders. "I don't think I could stomach the parasites."

I pull her in tighter, feeling warm that she shared something from her childhood with me.

"I had similar dreams, to be honest." Probably driven by a need to feel safe and free, something neither of us had. She turns to look at me, running a hand up into my hair, and I tell her, "Look at you now, baby. You have your cozy house in the woods." Her nose scrunches, and she sort of shrug-nods.

We go back to watching the show until she asks quietly, "Did you build this house for her?" I shake my head.

"I built it for me," she's content with that answer, nodding. It's not a lie. I built it for the family and life *I* wanted. What that looks like has changed, but this house was built for *us*.

"I like talking to you, Alex."

"I like talking to you too, Em," she yawns, stretches out her legs, and cozies back in. She's asleep five minutes later.

———

Emma

"Let's go for a walk." My eyes flutter once. *Sleep. More.* "We can make the sunrise, come on." And then the covers are pulled away from me, and I'm freezing.

I gasp at the cold air while he hovers over me, looking at my naked body like I'm Botticelli's Venus.

"Alex!" I scold him.

"Emma!" He mocks me right back.

Sitting up slowly, I say, "Fine, get off me, and I'll get up." He gives me a quick peck, then climbs off the bed.

I drag ass right behind him.

I can't even remember going to bed last night. The last thing that comes to mind is cuddling on the couch. Yesterday had been a long day, though. *Really long.*

"Did you put me to bed?" I ask as we stand in opposite closets and get dressed. It still feels weird for me to use *her* space, but going downstairs every time I need a fresh pair of underwear doesn't make sense.

"Yup," he says, sliding a belt into the loops of his jeans. His chest is still bare, and I have to swallow. *Damnit.* I had plans for him last night.

My inner thighs throb, not from soreness but with desire.

But then I yawn. My sleep schedule had finally adjusted to normalcy, and here I am at the ass crack of dawn, going for a quick hike. Even though I feel deathly tired, I'm thrilled. I missed this. These were some of the best parts of my day: walking with him to the lake.

I throw on a thermal and fleece-lined leggings, then grab a beanie and some thick socks. During the day, Spearhead would warm to 50 degrees or so, but in the morning, it's still slightly below freezing.

Delta dances around Alex's feet with excitement.

"We're going, bud," he says to the pup.

We finish putting on our outer layers in the mudroom where the invite hangs, haunting me. There's something about it that irks me. The way it hangs, front and center, like a reminder. That it's hanging at all. It feels more like a jury duty summons than a wedding invite. Alex said he doesn't plan to go, yet he hasn't thrown the invite out...

"Ready, baby?" He asks, pulling my beanie over my head for me, then kissing me quickly. I blush, loving him like this. If it could be like this forever, I would give him every last day of my life.

"Yeah," I smile.

Delta barks when we stand there staring at each other with loving eyes, taking too long.

"We're going!" I tell him with a pat on his head.

We open the door to a still-dark morning. The air is brisk, and our breath comes out in puffs as soon as we step outside. No amount of caffeine could ever replicate this feeling. *This.* This is the high I was weaning for yesterday that never came.

I actually skip to catch up to Alex and Delta.

We walk silently, just like we used to until we get to the boulder. I climb up first, then take Delta's leash, who bounds up, followed by Alex.

He sits down, spreading his legs, then motions for me to sit between them. With my back to his chest, we sit facing the lake and wait for the show. Soon, the purple will pale. Then, an orange will creep up. The clouds will turn pink, and before you know it, we'll be bathed in the first morning light.

"How'd you sleep?" I ask him once we're settled and Delta's busy chewing on a stick.

"Great." He squeezes me from behind. Me too.

And then it's silent again, aside from the sounds of our easy breathing and the dog gnawing and the light breeze tangling the pine boughs.

I wonder, "What are you thinking about?" Usually, we'll just sit here until one of us shares something, but now, I want more. I want to know everything.

"I was wondering...if you're sore." My cheeks, my chest, everything heats. I shake my head no. "Good," he says.

"Then I was thinking about your birthday." *My birthday?* That would be a first — maybe ever — that someone was thinking about my birthday, and no less before it even happened. "Any special requests?" I shake my head again because I don't need anything.

"Okay. Don't make it easy for me or anything." He pinches me, and I screech. "But then I thought about your mom. And..." He sighs, "I'm trying not to make a big deal of it, especially if you don't want to, but I'm having a hard time letting it go." Ugh, my heart.

"I know exactly what you mean because I'm not going to lie. I hate your mom and dad more than just a little." We sit there a little longer before I finally say something.

"I've had time, a decade really, to process everything and work through it. It's not holding me back, at least not

E.L. STEVENS

anymore. Okay?" I let him know that, and then I wonder if it's the same for him. If he's worked it all out.

"Did you ever go to counseling?" I feel him nod behind me.

"More counseling than you could ever imagine, and still, it's a struggle." I weave my hand between his fingers, my bare hands through his gloved ones.

"What were you like as a Dad?" I can tell he isn't ready for the question. Maybe it was the wrong time, or I asked it in the wrong way, but I'm curious to know what Alex was like with Tally.

"I don't know, Em, every time I think about it...I just think about how I failed her." A deep aching fills my abdomen.

"What's your favorite memory of her?" I ask something more specific to try and see him *with* her.

"Probably her first birthday, watching her eat cake for the first time." I picture a one-year-old sitting in a high chair with cake — everywhere. And I picture Alex laughing, maybe with his wife, but I focus on the look I can imagine on his face as he cleaned off little hands and wiped down a face.

"I feel like a terrible father because there's so much I don't remember. There was a lot I missed, traveling for work. And that's the hardest part of it all. Not remembering when all I want is to relive each moment."

"Do you feel like, in the future...you'd want to do it? Again? That is, have kids? And a family?" My question comes out disjointed and wordy. My heartbeat practically halts in anticipation.

"Yeah, Em. It is." I close my eyes, able to breathe again. "Is that something *you* want?" His voice is low.

190

This time, I reply with more than just a nod. I say, "Yes. I-I worry about being like my mom, but I don't think I'm anything like her. Really."

"You're not," he says.

"Just like you're not like your father," I tell him.

The clouds overhead start to tinge pink, and once the sun is fully up, I know we'll turn back to head home.

"I think I've done more healing sitting on this rock with you than I have in 20 years of therapy." God, that was a compliment in the highest degree. "Because sitting here with you, all I keep thinking is that I could do it again. With you. We could be a family, Em."

I want so badly to believe him. My ovaries ache, my empty womb yearns, and I want it. With him, too.

"Maybe in a couple years..." I say, tempering expectations because would we even make it a couple years? I'm not sure, though I hope.

When we start needing to squint against the bright sun, I stand, holding out a hand for him to take.

Before I climb down, he pulls me in around the waist and kisses me. It's a kiss like none other before, like he's giving me something just now. Like he wants an imprint of this moment on his soul forever. I want one, too. I want more than just an imprint.

I picture a blonde-haired baby on our hip. I picture hikes to the cove in the mornings that take twice as long because someone's learning how to walk. I picture the both of us standing around a high chair, cleaning up cake, and laughing.

I picture a life with him. A life I would love.

SEVENTEEN

ALEX

NOVEMBER

Pushing her back into the shower wall, I hoist her legs around me, then bring her down on my cock. She tips her head back and moans, digging her fingernails into my neck.

"Is that what you want, baby?" She nods, then lifts her hips to grind her clit against me. "God, you feel so fucking good." She does. Tight and wet, a good fit. Perfect even.

"Alex...harder," she tells me, sending blood racing down to my balls, that are already drawing up high and tight. My girl likes it rough. She claws at my back, her hands in my hair.

Our mouths meet, and our tongues tangle like we're each trying to suffocate the other. She wants to consume as much as me. I push her harder into the wall and start sucking on her neck, leaving a mark like we're in fucking high school.

It isn't the indelible mark I really want to leave, but it satiates the feeling for the moment.

"Alex." She tenses, and I push harder.

"I'm not stopping till you come apart on my cock."

"But-"

I stop her, "Come, baby," my voice thick with desire and need. And then she's arching her back against the wall. And when I look down to watch her breasts bounce, my dick plunges deep inside her, and I grunt — slamming my seed into her body. Well, into the condom in her body. It's not even over, and I'm already wishing for more.

She's still tense even as the pulses fade. When I lean back and say, "Happy Birthday, baby," her expression throws me. Her eyes are wide, pupils blown, but she doesn't look like she's coming off the high of an orgasm.

"Alex..." she taps my shoulder and points. I turn my head to find Blanks walking out of the bathroom. *What the fuck?*

"*Fuck*. I'm so sorry, Em." She shakes her head.

"It's okay."

"It's *not* okay." I slide out of her as I set her down on the tile floor. "Shouldn't have happened. I don't even know what the fuck he's doing here." She trembles as I move away from her. *Fuck.*

"I'm so sorry."

"It's okay, Alex."

"I'll be back, okay?" She nods, moving under the hot spray to wash her hair. I toss the condom, grab a pair of lounge pants and a t-shirt, and head downstairs.

He's standing in the kitchen, making coffee.

"What the fuck, Caleb! You can't just walk in like that anymore!" I shout at him for making Emma feel uncomfortable in her own home.

"I knocked, and no one answered," he says nonchalantly.

"Because we were fucking busy," I glare at him, feeling like I could punch him for seeing her like that.

"You mean busy *fucking*."

"She's my wife. Is that a crime?" I narrow my eyes, watching him.

"Not in a court of law," he says it low and slow, the disdain apparent.

"Why are you even here? I haven't seen you in almost 11 months." He shrugs again, pulling the coffee cup out from underneath the drip.

"Someone has to work, in case you've forgotten. Then, I was in the neighborhood and thought I would check in, see if the honeymooners are still going strong. And apparently, you are." He holds his mug up, cheersing me.

What the fuck? I still work. Just because I was done doing his good ol' boy shit, though, he's pissed?

"What's that supposed to mean? I told you I was getting too old to do that shit anymore, and you are too. We're just supposed to keep going until one of us dies?" I'm fucking done toting the "Chets" and their packs of fraternal fuck buddies over mountain peaks. Where the fuck is this coming from?

Looking past me, he smiles and says, "Happy Birthday, *Angel*." I turn around and find Emma blushing as she draws her damp hair up with a clip.

Angel? He's always had nicknames for people. He calls Brit, Doll Face. I tolerate it because she doesn't mind, but him calling my wife, Angel...fucking *hate* it.

"Her name is Emma," I say in a clipped tone, trying not to make a scene. Not sure whose sake that's for.

"Alex," she puts a hand on my forearm, "it's okay. It's

fine." Looking at Blanks, and with hardly any warmth, she says, "Thanks for the birthday wishes." She moves past me, then him, to get a mug out to make her own coffee, and Blanks' fist twitches like he's about to reach out and do it for her.

Has it always been like this? Or am I just seeing it for the first time?

I look at him, my brows furrowed, and he arches an eyebrow, waiting. Daring me to make the accusation.

My nostrils flare in frustration, and I run a hand down my beard. I'm being paranoid. The glint off the foiled wedding invitation hanging in the mudroom catches in the light like a reminder.

"Just fucking knock, then leave if no one answers next time."

"Understood," he says. "Well, as much as I'd love to sit and chit-chat with the two of you, Alex. We need to have a word."

I nod towards my office.

Shutting the door behind him, I ask, "What is it?" He sits in my chair, putting his mug on my desk as I hover by the door, waiting.

"Scott Technologies." *Yeah.* "It's time to turn and burn." *Fuck.* The plan has been to disinvest for months, but now that the time is here, all I can do is stare at the ceiling, thinking.

"You're worried what'll happen to her, aren't you?" *Yeah.* I would likely never stop worrying about her. I stare at him, though. His look, in turn, is a blatant accusation that I still love Jess enough to lose millions. And I do.

"We're not gonna do it," I say with finality.

Blanks scoffs at my decision, shaking his head. "It's like you hate money."

I don't hate it. I just don't care about it. Certainly not more than I care about her. He leans back in the chair, "So we're just gonna keep funneling millions into his company until we run dry?" *No.*

"Tell the board we want a new CEO, give Damian a golden parachute, and then we'll sell it." No one gets hurt.

"So much for revenge..." he trails off. It was never about revenge, at least not until recently. I bought Damian's company so my sister could take half its worth and leave him.

When he and Jess got together...maybe the focus shifted. The new goal was to chunk it off, sell until nothing was left, sink the ship, and devalue the company.

I can't put Jess through that, though.

"Jesus, you still love her that much?" I'll likely never stop. I can't. I know because I've tried. It's not that I don't also love Emma because I do.

"Why does it matter to you?" I ask.

He shakes his head, shoving the chair back as he stands. He pushes past me, slamming the office door shut on his way out.

Two things could be true at once. I know that. But why do I feel so fucking guilty for loving both of them all of a sudden?

Emma

. . .

When the door slams shut, I scurry into the pantry, pretending to look for the granola. The bag of granola that's right in front of my face.

When I turn around, he's there. He steps inside the walk-in pantry with me, and my heart stops beating altogether. I can't breathe, and every sense is heightened. The smell of him. The gleam of his blue eyes. The sound of his ragged breath. It's like I can see every fiber on his flannel shirt pressed against his hard chest. My skin practically vibrates. With anticipation, with want, with pain.

"You should have run away from him when you had the chance, Angel." He shakes his head, the disappointment apparent. "Take care of yourself. And when he burns you..." He pauses, swiping a thumb along my jawline, "I just hope you can land on your feet." I want to reach out and hold onto the hand that's nearly cradling my face.

"And what about you?" I ask his back as he turns to leave me.

"I'll always be fine, Angel. Don't worry about me." He misunderstands my question. I wondered if he would be there, on the other side, but he thought I was asking if he would be okay after Alex's burns.

But he would be fine, wouldn't he? There was always *some* model, right?

There was Kate, the brown-haired goddess he took to the Met Gala.

There was Irene, who spent the month of July at his house in the Hamptons. She absolutely ate in her red, white, and blue bikini.

And then there was Anya, his on-again-off-again ride-or-die.

I didn't know Blanks was a socialite until a quick Google search showed more Page Six mentions than I had time to read. Maybe socialite isn't the right word. New York's fuck boy is more accurate.

And he nails it. Fuck, he could nail anything, I bet.

I can't bring myself to say goodbye, and he doesn't say it either. He just walks out of the pantry and out of my life. This time, I have a feeling it's for good. And *that is* for the best.

Because his eyes, watching me come apart...I've never come so hard in my life. I wanted to scream, an almost feral energy radiating through me, but I stayed silent, not wanting to take my eyes off him, looking *at me*. Looking at me like he hated me but, in the same breath, wanted to be the one inside of me.

God, he confuses me. Makes my skin crawl. And yet, I've never wanted to forget him. Not for one second because every time he talks, looks, or touches, I feel this spark of energy. Like I'm actually living and not just going through the motions.

"Sorry. About that." Alex finds me in the pantry, looking like I'm hiding.

"It wasn't a huge deal." I swallow the guilt and finally grab the bag of granola off the shelf.

"Think you're still up for our hike?" I smile tightly and nod. It'll be the perfect distraction. *Or the perfect opportunity to ruminate on seeing him again.*

"Yeah, definitely."

———

Today, we're hiking to the ridge, my first time since being back. The burning in my limbs feels good. The cool air is refreshing, and I *feel* good.

Except when my mind drifts to him.

I'll never see him again. I can't stop the thought from recurring.

He came *today*, of all days — my birthday. I wonder if it's a coincidence. Has to be.

We're just cresting the final turn when Alex stops me, pulling out a blindfold.

"You're kidding me," I laugh. I've been here before. It's not like the view was going to be a surprise.

"Humor me," he says, stepping forward to tie the black fabric behind my head. Once it's secure, he tips my chin up and places a peck on my lips that I savor.

He grabs my hand, then leads me slowly up the last climb, stopping several times to guide me around a fallen tree or rock.

He positions me, turning my body to face a certain direction, then loops around to undo the blindfold.

When the black fabric drops, I see it. A vintage Airstream is parked in a now-clear area. I look at Alex with a smile.

"What's this?"

"A birthday present." He smirks. "A cozy little house in the forest." And my heart melts.

"But how? How did you even get it here?" I ask with astonishment, my heart warming at the thought of how much trouble it would have been to even get it here.

"Magic...and also we cleared a makeshift road." He points behind himself where the trees have been removed, just enough to form a narrow road. "It's only a 1/8th of a mile from the highway if you head west. But I plan to replant the trees, so it'll be like a hidden hideaway. Just for us." It really is like a secret clubhouse. Tiny, tucked away, with the exception of the gorgeous view.

I can imagine, after a full day of hiking, stopping here to retire for the night. With soft pillows and a fluffy comforter, nestled in warm and snug. It would be a dream.

"Go inside," he nudges me.

I go up the trailer steps, but before I open the door, I ask, "You own this land, right?"

He laughs, "Yes. We do."

I open the door to a modern, amenity-filled space. There's an electric fireplace built in, a leather-covered sofa, and a small kitchen. There's a shower and bath at one end and a large bed on the other. It's perfect.

I turn around and throw my arms around him, hugging him tight.

"Do you like it?"

I nod as he wraps his arms around me. I do really like it, just...something feels off. I don't know if it's him or me. I want to rewind to this morning, in the shower, when I'd been head over heels in love. I want him telling me, *"Happy birthday, baby,"* as he fucks me against our shower wall.

"You okay?" He pulls back to ask. My tears well, and I shrug.

"This is...you've done the most, and I feel bad that I don't have anything to give to you." It's not untrue; it's just not the whole truth.

"Well, it's not my birthday, Em," he says, laughing at me. I smile. He's so sweet to think of all this, to go through all the trouble. It's beyond, and I'm a terrible person for standing here, still thinking about *him*. *His* eyes. *His* touch.

"I was thinking, if you want, we could cancel dinner with Brit and hang out here, maybe spend the night?" he asks, wrapping an arm around my waist.

The idea sounds amazing. I just don't want to be alone with him right now. I want distractions and mind numbness. I don't need solitude and silence.

"I feel bad, though. We've blown her off three times now, and what if she did something like make a cake for my birthday, and then we don't show up?"

"Well, first of all, Carly would have been the one to make you a cake, and really? You want to go?" Who even has a chef in this economy? *The Millars.*

"I think I should try. Make an effort?" I scrunch my nose because the idea of going there is contradictory to my being.

"Okay," he says it slowly. Skeptically.

"We have to pick up Delta anyways." He isn't ready for a ten-mile hike just yet.

His smile is slight. *Fuck.*

I bite my lip and go to my knees with a desperate need to let him know I'm grateful. He doesn't have to do any of this. And I do love him. I love him a lot.

"What are you doing, Em?"

"Saying thank you," I start on his belt buckle. His touch is warm and gentle as he threads a hand into my hair. I haven't done this for him since telling him about my mom and everything that happened. He never asks or pressures me.

"I love you, Alex," I say as I pull his briefs down enough to bring his length to my face.

"I love you too, Em."

E.L. STEVENS

I lick my lips, then his tip, and then I swallow him to the back of my throat. I can feel him resisting the need to thrust. But I want him to. Today.

I release him and let him know, "You can do it. It's okay." He strokes my cheek appreciatively.

"You're so good, Emma." I nod, then let him thrust, his hips moving towards my face. He's good too. A good man. Kind, giving, respectful, and gentle. So why the fuck do I still have this need for someone else?

———

I'm trying, I really am. I zip up the burgundy dress and slip on a pair of black kitten heels. But maybe this is too dressy? I haven't really perfected the same laid-back, cool, 'I'm rich' vibe that the Millars and the Scalas seem to have down pat.

But I'm trying to fit in.

I'm trying too hard. I kick off the heels and unzip the dress. *This isn't me.* I throw the outfit back towards the box it came in.

Jeans and a sweater will have to be enough.

"You look good." Alex comes up behind me in my closet, gripping my hips. *He* looks good. His hair is longer now, nearly hitting his shoulders, and his beard is thick but trim. He has that rugged mountain man charm. Thick forearms, broad shoulders, and sun-tanned skin. He's beautiful.

I turn, slipping my arms around his neck, and pull him in for a kiss. I'm already unbuckling his belt when he stops me.

"Really? We'll be late." *Really.* I need him to take the edge off. I want to walk in there feeling like I'm his. Like I belong. I want to carry his scent, his cum. Desperately, I want to be *his only*.

"I want you to fuck me, bare, babe," I whisper in his ear, feeling his grip on me strengthen. "I want to feel full of you."

"Are you sure?" His voice is hoarse, asking back. It wouldn't be the worst thing. A little ahead of schedule, maybe. I don't want to start actively trying, but I want this one thing — a final birthday wish.

"The only thing I really want for my birthday is to feel your cum running down my legs." And then he's backing me against my closet wall, ripping open my jeans.

His mouth is on my neck as he works my pants and panties down. He lifts me, pinning me to the wall with his thick thighs as he frees himself. Already pulsing with need.

"Tell me you need it." His voice is thick with strain. "Tell me you're sure." I nod, but it's not enough. "Coming out of your mouth, Emma, I need to hear it, damnit."

"I want you to pump me full of your cum, Alexander. I fucking need it."

EIGHTEEN

ALEX

I'm not exactly getting any younger. And I love Emma. Fuck, I even like her. I could see us having a family. It's not a stretch of the imagination.

Jess.

It flies through my mind, but I ignore it. Like I've been learning how to do. It gets easier each time she breaks my heart. The last time had been the wedding invite.

"I need it, Alex." As I go to push in, her phone rings, and we both freeze.

Emma's phone hasn't so much as vibrated once since I've met her. Aside from when I've called her. It seems like a once-in-a-lifetime occurrence, like she should take the call. I can see it on her face that she wants to, too.

Setting her down, I grab her pants and underwear, and while she reaches to answer the phone, I help her step back into them.

"Hello?" Emma answers, then holds onto my shoulder to step one foot at a time into her panties.

"Hi…Mom," she says uncomfortably. I only hesitate for a second, then keep helping her get dressed. If she wants privacy, she'll walk away. But she doesn't. She keeps holding onto my shoulder for balance. For support.

I'll be here.

"Umm, thanks?" I can't hear what her mom says, but I hope it was 'Happy Birthday.'

"I don't think I've heard from you in a decade. Is there something you need?" I button her jeans as she talks.

"Oh." It's somber.

"Wow." Bad news?

"For how long?" She nods her head.

"Maybe, but I have to go to dinner. My husband's family is having a thing." She's shaking her head now.

"Yeah, almost a year." She waits. "His name is Alexander, um. But I should go. He's waiting for me."

"I don't think he would say the same," she pauses, "Yeah. We'll see, but I need to go. Bye." And then she hangs up.

My heart rate spikes wondering what the fuck that was about.

Her hands tremble as she sets the phone back down on the closet shelf.

"She said she's in rehab." My brow furrows. "And she called to wish me a happy birthday…she wants to meet you, and she wants me to come visit."

I wait, hoping there's no fucking way. But when I keep waiting, I ask, "Are you?"

"I don't honestly know…" I sigh, then with a hand around

the back of her neck, I pull her into me and hold her while she processes.

The car ride to Brit's is silent, and I just hold her hand the whole time. When we arrive, we end up having to park on the road with all the other cars filling the driveway.

As we're walking to the front door, I tug on her hand, pulling her to a stop. "We can cancel this. I'll just tell Brit I'm sick." She looks at me, smiling for the first time since the call.

"I've never had a birthday party or even a family gathering for my birthday. Her call reminded me of that. I'm not going to let her derail my night." There's my girl. I give her a quick kiss on the forehead, and then the front door opens before we even make it to the porch.

"Uncle AL!" Elodie squeals before running towards us. "Oh my Gawd, you're like a real-life Rapunzel! I'm so excited to meet you, Emma." I love Elle. She's the exact right person to greet us tonight, and just like this. My chest swells with pride over how charming and kind my niece has turned out.

"Emma, this is my niece, Elodie. Elodie, this is Emma." Elodie immediately reaches in for a hug.

"You smell like vacation. Coconut oil?" Emma laughs at Elodie's question before answering.

"Yeah, it's good for the curls. Also, it's nice to meet you, Elodie." Linking arms with Emma, Elodie pulls her the rest of the way into the house, and I follow.

"Why aren't you at school?" I ask.

"No reason..." *Suspect.*

"Huh," is all I say back.

Elodie proceeds to chat up Emma, "My sister isn't here because she hates this place, so you won't get to meet her. But don't worry, you're not missing out on anything."

"Since when-" I'm stopped from asking, "*since when does Caroline hate Spearhead?*" Because the front door is opening and the crowd inside the house all shout, "HAPPY BIRTH-DAY, EMMA!"

Emma's face lights up in surprise. Glad my family could get it together and not treat her like shit today. Constantine is the first to her, giving a big hug.

The brothers all made it. Then there's Brit and Liam, the baby, and Luna. Liam's mom and dad are here, and so is their chef, Carly.

And then there's Delta sitting right beside Emma, waiting for his human to notice him.

"I see you, boy," she kneels down, letting him lick her face. I love that they love each other. "I missed you, sweetie; I did!" She croons out.

After the crowd disperses around her, Sandy drags her to the kitchen to show her her cake. I let her go, planning to catch up in a couple minutes.

I hug Connie, say hi to the brothers, and then my sister taps my shoulder and points to Liam's office.

I follow her, and she closes the door.

"Thanksgiving," she says somberly. I figured I'm not getting an invite this year. Hundred bucks says Jess got one, though. "Jess and Damian are coming." *Winner winner chicken dinner.*

My stomach sinks. Still not prepared for it.

"If you and Emma want to come...we can make it work. I'm not going to *not* invite you. Because you're my brother, and she's my sister now, too." Wonder how long it took Liam telling her that to get her to that conclusion?

"Nah, that's okay, Brit." I give her a side hug so she

doesn't feel too bad. Emma has a break that week, so maybe I'll take her somewhere. Traveling isn't something we've really done together, aside from coming here from Vegas.

And Emma was right; it's been almost a whole year. We're just a month shy of our wedding anniversary.

"I feel bad about it. I really do." I shake my head, though.

"Don't." She eyes me skeptically, like I'm taking this too well.

I am. But then I think of Emma. It sort of soothes the sting.

"Things are going good between you two then?"

I nod. "Yeah." I don't have any complaints.

"Wow. okay. I just didn't think it would happen. I had money on you guys divorcing before your first anniversary," she laughs.

"That's fucked up, Brit." Regardless of the accuracy of the assumption, I don't like that I'm doomed to fail at every relationship in their eyes.

She laughs again, "No! I'm sorry, I just meant. I thought you were doing it to get back at Jess. I didn't realize that you two were, like, actually...*happy*...together. Okay, fine, I'm an asshole. I guess I'm just happy you're happy." *Happy*.

Yeah. I am happy.

Am I the happiest? Hard to say.

I think I'm the normal amount of happy. A good amount. Healthy. There isn't any back and forth. There's never any shouting or fighting. The sex is fucking amazing. Emma is amazing. And we both exist peacefully together. We give each other a level of companionship we haven't had before. That's what you're supposed to want in a life partner.

Isn't it?

———

Emma

The kitchen is overwhelming. Carly maneuvers between a crawling baby and a bunch of hot Greek men tasting every dish she touches.

"Put down the spoon, Silas, or so help me god..." The brother I haven't met before drops the spoon.

He doesn't look like the rest of his family, the opposite of a black sheep, really.

"Emma, right?" I give him a smile and nod.

"Yeah."

"I'm Silas," he extends a corded forearm to shake my hand. He isn't serious like Max, and he's not goofy and assured like Niko. But he seems nice. Genuinely.

"Can I help with anything, Carly?" I ask as she swats Niko away from the cake she just frosted.

"Help remove the heathens from my kitchen?" She asks with an apologetic look, like it pains her to ask for help.

I'm about to ask them to make me a drink as a distraction when a booming voice from the back hallway says, "Get out of her kitchen!"

Max, with a phone in his hand, busy typing away, walks through, and everyone clears out of the kitchen, including me.

But he stops me, "Not you, kid, sorry. Also, happy birthday." I try to do my part, though, and pick up CT from where he's corralling bits of broken pasta off the floor.

"Yuck," I tell him as I brush his hands off over the sink, then rinse the bits of dried food away. He giggles.

"Christ! Sorry, Emma." Liam rounds the corner like he lost the baby. Because he did.

"No problem," I say, passing the kid over to his dad.

"Alright, I've got one dirty Shirley for the birthday girl." Sandy, who is Liam's mom — I think — passes me what looks like a Shirley Temple. It's hard to keep track of who belongs to who around here.

"Thank you so much."

"Now, how is it that you've lived here almost a full year, and I haven't seen you around?" She stands with a hand on her hip and an eyebrow arched.

"I guess I'm just a hermit?" I shrug.

"Y'all are two peas in a pod, aren't you?" I assume she means Alex. And we are. Seriously.

"We get along well, yes." She laughs, this beautiful laugh. She has one of those great laughs that just endears you to her immediately. I like her. Innately. She seems like someone who is salt of the Earth, good people.

And then I'm reminded of someone else laughing and a soothing Southern accent wafting over to console her. *Jess.* Will I ever make it out of her shadow?

"Come get coffee at the shop sometime. I could always use a chat with a friendly face. Ever since the girls went back to school, and Jess and Eden moved away...It gets lonely in the winter around here." It slips out of her mouth without thought and no ill will.

But the sinking feeling is there all the same. *Eden.* That's a pretty name. I can picture a little girl toddling around the floral wallpapered room in our house. A room that we never talk about. The door is always kept closed. Like it doesn't exist.

But it existed for them.

"Yeah, I'll have to come by sometime. Usually, Alex makes my coffee to-go before I leave for class so I don't have to stop." *So I didn't have to stop...*

"Hey, sorry. Was talking to Brit, what'd I miss?" He puts a hand on the small of my back.

"Nothing." I give him a soft smile. It doesn't matter that he didn't want me going by The Grounds. I don't really want to go anyway. I just wonder if he did it for my benefit...or hers.

The stinging in my chest told me it was probably for hers.

————

"What would you do if Ray ever reached out to you?" I ask as we drive home from Brit's, way past our regular bedtime.

"I know exactly what I'd do. Because he did." I stare at him. He hasn't told me this.

"And what happened?"

"I visited him in prison."

"You did?" Picturing Alex visiting that man all alone breaks my heart.

"He was sober, and he apologized. I asked if he called Brit and apologized to her too..." I forget that Brit, with her happy, healthy, jovial family, came from that fucked up mess too. I feel slightly more sympathetic to her inability to be nice to me. Not that she hadn't been nice tonight. She had. She even gave me a birthday gift. Surprisingly.

"He told me she was probably better off not knowing him. So I got up and left and never looked back." Wow.

"He couldn't own up to his mistakes in the end, and I had no interest in a relationship. It's easy to forget he still exists."

"He said sorry, though?" I reach over, massaging his neck. "Yup."

"Did you believe him?" He inhales deeply, thinking.

He starts shaking his head, then says, "No." *Oh.*

"I think that's my fear. I'll go see her. She'll say sorry...but I won't believe her. OR she won't say sorry at all. She'll just brush it under the rug. Like one phone call for the first time in years would be enough to make it all okay. And then it'll just make me mad. Which would be a setback because I'm done being mad about it. I don't want to be mad *again*. I don't want her to even have that power over me."

"Some people, baby," he looks at me, "are irredeemable. And some are just people who have done bad things." I squeeze his neck tight.

"I hope you know you're a good man. You know that, right?" I tell him because I want it burned on his brain. I want to tattoo it on his soul. For all the disbelieving he does, or did, that he isn't worthy, he is. He is so good.

He pulls over to the side of the road, putting the truck in park, and Delta barks at the jolt.

"Come here." He takes my face in his hands and pours himself into me. A kiss made up of a lifetime of failures but good intentions. I would take it from him any day of the week. No questions asked.

Once we're home, we get ready for bed. Him at his sink, me at mine.

Afterward, I strip down, leaving my panties but opting

for a boxy cropped tee on top. He watches me. And then I watch him undress in turn, leaving only his boxer briefs on.

We come together in bed. His chest to my back.

And I whisper to him, "This was the best birthday I've ever had."

"I'm glad," he whispers back. Eventually I listen to his breathing deepen as his limbs get heavy, and his peaceful slumber pulls me into my own.

NINETEEN

ALEX

"Hey!" I call out before she makes it to the door. "Your coffee." Walking briskly, I pass it off to her with a final kiss goodbye.

"Thanks," she says quietly.

Since her birthday, things have been fine, but I noticed she's been even quieter than usual. Stressed maybe? Just tired from school? Still shaken up by her mom's call?

"What's wrong?" I stop her with a hand on her arm.

"Would you be mad if I wasn't here for Thanksgiving?" I sort of shake my head in surprise. That's not what I expected.

"Umm, no?" She inhales, trying to figure out how to say it.

"I think I'm going to visit her, and well, I don't have school next week..."

"Okay, do you want me to come with you?" I don't think

I'll ever be ready to be in the same room as the famed Darla Strait, but if Em needs me there, I will be.

"I actually think I want to go...alone..." She bites her lip nervously.

"Whatever you want, Em."

"You're not mad?"

"Not even a little." She makes a little nodding motion like she's relieved.

"You'll go to Brit's, right? You won't be alone?" I haven't told her about Jess coming. Seems pointless.

"I'll be fine. Don't worry."

"Okay, I'll probably book a flight and hotel between classes today. You promise it's okay?"

"I promise." I pull her in for one more kiss, my arms wrapping around her back. "I love you, Em."

She kisses me back and says, "I love you, too." Then she's gone.

Thanksgiving is next week, so I'm not expecting anyone to be free, but I give it a shot just in case.

A

Plans for Thanksgiving?

BLANKS

Nope, though Brit invited me.

Not going?

Didn't get the warm and fuzzies last time I was in town. Thought I'd let you two enjoy the holiday alone.

Emma won't be here.

> On the rocks?

> No. Asshole. In Vegas. To visit her mom.

> You're letting her go by herself?

> I'm her husband, not her keeper. She wants to go alone.

He doesn't text back. Delta and I would just spend the day together. And we'd be fine. Totally fine.

———

EM

> You didn't have to rebook my hotel.

A

> You can't stay at a motel, sweetheart.

> Well, thank you. What time are you heading to Brit's tomorrow?

> Not sure. If you want to call or text, anytime. Doesn't matter, okay?

> Okay.

> Have I told you you're the best husband lately? Because you are.

> I'll take it. Love you.

> Love you too

"You wanna walk?" I ask Delta, sliding my phone back into my pocket. He spins around in a circle, his tail wagging.

That's a yes. "Alright, let's go." I grab his lead but leave it off so he can roam free.

We opt for the path down to the cove and head towards the lake. Emma and I don't go every day like we used to. She's been tired the last couple of times I tried to wake her. I smile at the memory of her arms stretched overhead, baring her stomach in that cropped tee she wears to bed.

Damn, I miss her already.

I don't have enough cell signal on the trail, but the idea is there to check flights when I get back from the walk. Hell, maybe I'll even drive and surprise her.

Delta starts picking up speed as we get closer until I can't see him anymore, but I can hear him barking, loud, with alarm.

Picking up the pace, I jog to catch up but stop dead in my tracks when I round the last bend.

No.

Sitting on the boulder — mine and Emma's boulder — is Jess. Looking terrified of my rabid-looking dog. *Shit.*

"Delta, heel." He stops baring his teeth. "Sit." He takes a seat, and I slip the lead around his neck.

"Sorry." It's short, and I turn Delta and I around to leave.

"Wait!" The thought, *don't wait*, is there, but it's overridden by everything I try to keep repressed.

I turn around to face her, and *I hate it.*

Hate how fucking beautiful she is. Her hair has grown out since I saw her last year. It's longer and wavy, whipping around in the wind. Fucking teasing me.

She's wearing hardly any makeup, and with the wind coming in my direction, I can smell her perfume, unlocking memories I've pushed to the furthest edges of my mind.

"Hey, Jess," I say when she doesn't say anything. She starts climbing off the boulder to stand closer while keeping plenty of space between her and Delta. "He doesn't bite, just a bit protective, and sometimes an asshole, is all." She nods.

"Are you talking about you...or the dog?" She gives me a slight smile. I try to return it, but it's hard. Always hard with her.

"The dog."

She nods awkwardly again. "Y-you look really good, Alex." She's nervous. Strange to see her like this.

"Thanks, I am good." I hope it stings. I hope even just a fraction of the sting I felt when I opened that fucking invitation.

"Good." Her eyes widen with surprise before sliding down to check the ring on my finger. It's always there. I never take it off. Not in the shower, not working out. It's there as a reminder. A constant one.

I don't let my eyes stray, but I know she wears a ring now, too. A big gaudy one, like Damian needed the world to see it from space. Hope she likes it.

"I actually came down here, hoping I'd run into you." My heartbeat races. "Brit said you come down here a lot."

I nod, chewing on the inside of my cheek, an old nervous habit rising from the dead.

"I just wanted to, I guess...see if you're happy. And that... nothing's changed. For you." *The fuck is she getting at?* "Because sometimes I wonder...if you only did it to prove a point...and if you regret it?" She's looking down at her feet now. I don't regret a single second spent with Emma. I don't think I ever would.

Without her, I would have ceased to exist.

"I don't regret it, no." I don't tell Jess the whole story. She's also not asking. Out of nowhere, Delta starts growling at Jess, sensing that someone is encroaching on Emma's territory. "Delta, no," I command harshly, and he stops with a whimper. "Sorry," I apologize.

"Yeah..." She finally looks up, "If-" she starts, then stops. "If you ever-" she sighs. "This is your last chance...if you want to change things." I stare at her. *Is she fucking kidding?*

"I'm married, Jess." Her cheeks turn crimson, and I run my hand over my beard to hide any reaction.

"I know, but I can't help but think the marriage isn't actually real. And I guess...I don't want any regrets when I walk down the aisle in June." She moves her hands inside the sleeves of her sweatshirt, the anxiousness showing. "So I just want to be sure because...I got your note. On the prenup. And I haven't stopped thinking about it since." The post-it note I'd scribbled in my lawyer's office in haste. *I've always and only ever loved you, Jess.*

I remember it. I don't regret it. But that was a long time ago. It isn't even true anymore. I feel like I can barely recognize the man who wrote that. He's almost nothing like the man standing here today. With a dog, and a wedding ring, and a wife that I respect and care for. Deeply. A wife I love.

And yet, none of that seems to matter right now. My instincts are still as fucked as ever because the second I'm around Jess, I revert. I want the hurt. I want the pain. I want my heart racing and us fighting. I want to feel the burn. *But at what cost?*

"I'm glad you got the note. I meant it." I try to temper my tone; I try to bring the new Alex forward and push the old one back.

"*Meant* it?" she asks. I nod.

"I'm guessing if my wife had been with me today, this would have gone a lot differently, right?" I try to gently remind her that I am married. I am committed to Emma and not just in name.

"Yeah, it would have." She straightens her spine, trying to regain some pride. "Do you love her, though?" Her strength is back in her tone. She asks the hard question without a single quiver in her voice.

"Yes." I love Emma. Every part of her.

"Does she know that?"

"She does." I don't say it to harm Jess. I say it because it's the truth. It doesn't hurt to tell Em I love her. We don't have a history plagued with mistakes and betrayals that would make loving her hard work. We have trust and commonalities that Jess and I never did. We could have, but we could never move forward.

I look at Jess, and my soul wants to wither under the crushing pain of wanting but never having her. But I look at Emma, and I just feel free. To say what I need and what I want and have it reciprocated. I would give anything in the world to have that foundation with Jess.

Fucking everything.

She swallows, then says, "Okay, good. I hope both of you will come then. To the wedding."

I don't answer, unsure that we'll make it. "Is Damian back at Brit's?" I could give him a call. Maybe. Just courtesy. I'm not even sure we're friends anymore.

"Oh, no. He, uh, is in crisis. At work. The PE firm that bought the company a little while ago is pushing him out...so, you know, the sky is falling. But, it's probably for the best." She shrugs.

I'm glad to hear Blanks hasn't gone rogue. This is better than the alternative. I want to assure her of that, but that would be too revealing.

"Hopefully, it works out for him." I try to be polite even though every cell in my body is thrashing against one another, revolting like I'm making a mistake. The neurons are firing, slinging hot electrical bolts that all sing, *don't fucking let her go. This is your chance. Fucking take it!*

"Well, I should let you go. Get back to everyone at Brit's." I tighten my hold on Delta's lead so he won't pull after her when she leaves.

"Okay. Yeah. I will then." She starts to turn, like she's going to leave out the opposing path, but turns back. "I guess this is goodbye?"

She opens her arms, in question. I could say no, that it's not a good idea. In fact, that's what I should do. But instead, I move in, holding Delta firmly while lacing a hand around her back. She fits to me, molding her body against mine, and everywhere that she touches feels *ablaze*. We were a goddamn wildfire that, left to its own devices, would destroy everything in its path. She tightens her grip, and I tighten mine. Pulling her harder against me.

I love you, Jess.

Don't say it out loud, though.

"Last chance," she whispers, with a hand around my neck and her forehead resting on my chest. Why is she doing this? Why the *fuck*? Why now? It sows a seed of hate for her. The way she's tempting me, does she even know she's doing it? Is she desperate, too?

"Jess, you'll regret this," I whisper the words once whispered to me. And I get it, at this exact moment, exactly what Emma had meant. That Emma had been thinking about me back then. That she saw *me*. She still sees me. I couldn't do this to her.

"I don't regret loving you, Alex. But this is really it. I can't carry the torch forever." I understand. Deeply. However, I likely *would* carry the torch, for her and me, forever. But I won't be doing it at the expense of ruined lives. Not Jess's, not Damian's, and certainly not Emma's.

I can't do it.

I pull away just a little. "I want you to know I'm sorry. For hurting you. You didn't deserve it. And I hope that you're happy. With him."

"Okay," is all she says back. That one-word answer is bullshit.

I try my best to let it go, though. Because this is it, the last time it will ever be just her and me. Fucking hate it, though. I should have been used to the idea. If you had asked me before if I would ever be alone with Jess again, the answer would have been no. But here we are, and I know next time I see her, she'll likely be Jessica Scott.

I watch her swallow, her hazel eyes looking up at me, and I know she loves me, too. I can feel it. This thing between us reignites. Not that it ever really went out. It was a pilot light flaring.

Our paths had forked, veering away from each other, yet here we were. Together, again. Was it the last time? Would we ever meet like *this* again?

The sinking feeling in my stomach is an ache, a different kind of gut feeling. *Was this really the last time?* My heart-

222

beat pounds in my ears to the beat of: *can't-let-go. Can't-let-go. Can't let go.*

She comes up, leaning in, staring at my mouth. *God, I fucking love her.*

The hand around my neck tightens and squeezes, and my heart beats for her. Only her.

Again. *Won't-let-go.* I've come so far, but one look, one touch, is all it takes for me to fall back into the depths of hell with her.

And then, her lips are on mine.

The kiss is ravenous on both sides. Pushing and pulling. I groan when she bites my lip, and she moans when my tongue slides against hers. I pull her in tighter, dropping Delta's leash so I can pick her up. *Why am I picking her up?* Reason has fled. All that's left is her. Her chest pressing against mine, her lips on mine, her hands on me.

She wraps both legs around me, never relinquishing my mouth. Then I'm guiding her back and up against a tree, and she's pushing her pelvis against mine. How far is this going to go? How far do I *want* this to? *To the ends of the Earth.*

"Fuck," I pull away to mutter, shaking my head. *What are we doing?*

"Please don't stop," she begs me. But I do. I ease away, dropping her legs back to the forest floor.

"Fuck!" I turn towards the lake to shout. I'm not yelling at her; I'm shouting at the world. At myself. How could I do this? *To Emma?*

Delta barks at me. The dog is wondering the same fucking thing.

"Why did you do that, Jess?" I ask quietly, fighting back tears over what I just ruined. It wasn't just her, though. "No, don't answer that." I hold a hand up. "It's my fault, too." I start pacing in the small clearing. Running my hands through my hair, pulling on it tight.

"You love me," she whispers. *No shit.* I look at her, inhaling deeply, my nostrils flaring, tears pooling in my eyes. I want to yell at her. *Of course I do!*

"Alex..." she says in a tone that wrecks me. Ruins me. She reaches for me...and I don't have the will to walk away.

She palms my face and pulls me down to her. In theory, she might be the one guiding this, but I'm an active participant. I place my hands on her hips, remembering the feel of her. I revel in it.

She feels the same. But I'm different. And at the same time, I'm not. I would always be this version of me with her. There's no denying it.

Our mouths come together again, only marginally less violently than before. Both of us just desperate for more.

The need for *more* feeling. She nips on my lip.

More skin. She sheds her sweatshirt and runs her hands underneath my shirt, her palms warm against my abdomen.

More pressure. My cock is hard and wedged between us, the friction never enough with the layers of clothing.

More *time.* There isn't any, this would be it. All we would have.

Jess starts unbuckling my belt, and my breath speeds up, our mouths clashing. She unwraps her legs from around me, never letting my mouth go, and she's pushing her leggings down. I close my eyes, fighting against my baser instincts, but lose the battle. I wouldn't not do this. Not in any version of this story. Not in any other universe. Because I would always be this Alex with her.

She frees me from my boxer briefs, and I lift her again, her cunt lining up perfectly with me. I walk her back to the same tree, pushing her against it as I slide in. With the motion, it's like going back in time.

"God, Alex," she whispers softly, grinding her hips, willing me to move. So I do. I watch her with open eyes as I fuck her, words warring in my head the whole time.

I hate you.

I love you.

I'll never get enough of you.

She says my name quietly, but her eyes stay closed. I need her to open her eyes, to look at me. See me.

But this is our game.

I won't ask. Instead, I'll set her up for tasks she'll always fail. And when she hurts me, it'll be just another tick in a column against her.

Open your fucking eyes, Jess.

Her mouth grasps for mine, and I kiss her with open eyes, waiting. My heart pounds as she races towards her finish line. My dick moves in and out of her, my body is on fire, but if she doesn't open her fucking eyes...

"Oh god, Alex!" Jess exclaims, arching her back into the tree as her cunt convulses around me. I don't stop, letting her strangle me for every last bit of pleasure.

When she finally opens her eyes...I hate what I see.

"Alex?" she asks. I swallow against the strain in my throat. The burn in the back of my legs. Instinct is telling me to redouble my efforts. To fuck her ruthlessly, to take without care. It wasn't that I would always be *this* Alex with her. It was that she could only ever see me a certain way, so that's what I would be.

When I look down, watching her take me, it doesn't make me feel the way it should. It's not the way I fantasized it would be. There would be no rejoining of our lives. There isn't a future for us where I get down on one knee again. Because Jess and I only exist in the terrible. In the fraught. In the pain. I revert when I'm with her. I become someone I hate. I hate myself now. And I hate her, too, though a little of that hate is misplaced.

No, the glorious euphoria doesn't find me. Instead, I'm met with monumental regret.

I slide out of her, refusing to finish. Refusing to make eye contact as I set her feet on the ground.

While she puts her clothes back on, I zip up my pants with disgust. I just did that. I can hardly believe it. Like it was an out-of-body experience, and now that I was on the other side of it...I don't even know who the fuck that other person was. It couldn't have been me.

But it was. It is.

I'm a fucking monster. *Jekyll and Hyde.*

"We can do this, Alex. If you want to," she says as she pulls the sweatshirt over her head. Then, walking to me, she grabs a hold of my arm. "I know this isn't normal, whatever we have. I know you know it, too." Yeah, I know. I nod, acknowledging what she's saying but not agreeing that we should blow up our lives. *It's too late. You already have.*

"I love you," she says, but somehow I don't believe her. I can't. "It'll be hard, yes, but...if you just let Damian stay on... it'll be okay." The gut feeling roars within me. It screams at me as cold fear slides through my veins, and I freeze.

"Excuse me?" My tone doesn't broker even an ounce of warmth.

"I know it's you, Alex." She looks at me with strength and poise.

"And? What are you implying?" My heartbeat thrums, the cold turning to heat. It's in my back, in my gut, in my head, and it says something — *everything* — is wrong.

"Let Damian keep his company, and I'll break the engagement." The words are blunt, but her delivery is subtle. And I know she really believes this is a win-win situation for all involved.

Which would mean she hadn't come here for me. She came here for him. A sacrificial lamb for her chosen one. I hate her, more than I ever thought possible.

"I have to talk to Emma." I see her struggle to understand what I'm saying.

Love no longer matters in this scenario. Sure, she loves me. And sure, I love her, too. But there are too many games. Too many secrets. Too many lies. I can feel the love I have for her slip. It bleeds into the past, wiping away our future.

"You're going to tell her?" she asks.

"I'm going to tell her what happened," I say blandly, zoning out, looking at what was our place.

"So, what does that mean?"

"It means I have to talk to my wife." Then, more so to the universe, I let slip, "She didn't deserve this." The tears that are being held back slip free.

Jess pulls away from me, realizing the tears aren't for her. They're for Em.

"Oh god, you really love her," she says again, her realization sounding fucking aghast.

"Yeah, Jess. We've talked about starting a family together. She's important to me...in a way you could never understand." I can't look her in the eyes as I speak, but it doesn't matter. She takes a step back, and then she takes another.

"I didn't know." *I only told you ten minutes ago!* I close my eyes, the self-loathing coming to a boil.

The anger and the hurt lashes out. "Damnit, Jess! When you're around, I can't fucking think straight. I see you and- and it's all I can think about. Is you. *You.* But it's not just me anymore. And this — *this* is going to kill her!" My stomach rolls. Jess winces, either from the words or my raised voice.

"Okay." Her stupid one-word answers were the bane of my existence. I want to shake her. I want to shake myself.

"Okay, Alex." She finds some resolve. "I hope you're happy together." Is she fucking clueless? Fat chance of that now.

"Yeah, I bet you do," I say under my breath. "Are you going to tell Damian?" She shakes her head no. That would be her burden to carry. Fuck both of them. *But fuck her especially.*

"I have to go." I take a step back. And I see the heartbreak in her eyes. It wasn't going to be our time. It never would.

I don't wait for her to leave first; I just turn around, walking back to our side of the path, calling out for Delta who comes running.

I love Emma. I really do. She's the best person I know.

I just also love Jess...even against my own will.

———

I stare at the text messages. *Have I told you you're the best husband lately? Because you are.* I'm not. I'm the fucking worst. I lean back against the couch, letting my head fall back as I debate: What to say? How to say it? Do I wait till she's home?

> A
>
> How was it?

She should be back at the hotel by now. Three little dots appear before disappearing, only to return a minute later.

EM

Not what I was expecting.

My stomach turns.

> In a good way or a bad way?

It wasn't good. It's been a horrible day. Can you talk on the phone? Or are you at your sister's?

I panic. Nausea and disgust with myself are the only prevailing feelings I have. I can't do it; she'll be able to hear it in my voice.

> In the middle of something, but if you really need, I can pause.

No, that's okay. Tell everyone I said hi.

> I love you, Emma.

I love you, too.

I'm going to hell. Straight to hell.

———

I don't end up flying to Las Vegas to meet my wife. I don't drive there either. The Friday after Thanksgiving, I pick her up from the airport.

She walks out of the secure area and into baggage claim, a soft smile planted on her face as she looks around for me. She looks tired but happy to be here.

But her smile falls when her eyes land on me. I hadn't slept in two days. I hardly ate. I wanted to punish myself. And now, all I want is to fall at her feet and beg.

Instead, the second she's close enough, I wrap her up in my arms wordlessly. *Would this be the last time I get to hold her?* Tears leak out as we embrace, holding her tight against me, one palm on the back of her head, the other on her hip.

"What happened?" she asks hoarsely.

I nod, not able to form the words.

Her hands tremble as she adjusts her backpack, then she picks up the handle of her carry-on she'd dropped seconds earlier. I offer to carry her bags for her, but she declines.

The gut feeling howls.

We walk to the car, both of us looking like death. Probably feeling like it, too.

As soon as we're both buckled in, she turns to me.

"Tell me, whatever it is. Please?" Tears are already forming in her eyes like she knows it's going to hurt. She's bracing for it.

"I...saw Jess." She inhales sharply, and I think I can't do it. But I can't *not* do it. I'm staring at the steering wheel when I finally say, "I slept with Jess." I don't want to look at her, but I force myself to as punishment. She sits back in her seat, not looking at me, absorbing the information.

Fuck, I want to take it back. I would rather live in a house of cards based on lies if it would keep her safe. If it would keep her from ever having to feel this feeling,

"Okay," she eventually whispers out. I want to ask so many questions. I want to tell her everything, but I don't know that she wants to hear any of it. I know I wouldn't. I know I hadn't when I was the one sitting where Emma is now.

The back of my throat stings, and I clench my jaw together. My palms are sweating as they curl into balls.

"Can you drive me home, please?" she asks, silent tears rolling down her cheeks. I nod and decide to wait till she's ready to talk. I drive toward the airport exit, but she stops me.

"Go left here. I want you to take me to my condo. Please." *No.* My heart cracks.

"Please, *baby*..." I'll beg. I would beg her to come home. She shakes her head, refusing to make eye contact.

"I'm sorry, Em-" she stops me, cutting me off.

"Where? Did she come to the house? Was she there at Thanksgiving?" She stares out the windshield, unable to face me.

"At the cove," I say, knowing the impact, hating every fucking second as I watch her shatter at that admission. That's our place. *It was.* It had meaning to us, and I defiled it.

"Did it mean anything?" she asks, her voice so low, it's almost a whisper. I swallow against the truth. When my answer isn't immediate, she doesn't need me to answer at all. "Right then," she says. "I need to get home."

"*Please*," she says again when I still haven't started driving. "*Please*," this time, the word is choked by a sob.

I roll my head back against the headrest, loathing every

second of this. Hating what I've done. Hating myself. But I put the truck in drive and head toward her house.

She cries silently the whole time. I look over every couple of minutes, just to watch what we were circle the drain. *Jess*, my unavoidable vortex, sucked all that was good about me out of existence. All that's left in the wake is me trying to love Emma while still loving someone else.

The closer we get to her house, the faster our relationship dissipates. She starts toying with her ring the closer we get to her building. She twists it to the left, then back to the right. I'm expecting her to take it off any second.

"He said you'd burn me," her voice is a taut whisper, straining under the pain, like she's not saying it to me, just out loud. "I didn't know it would feel like I'd been scorched by the sun." She would never forgive me, but I couldn't stop myself from trying.

"Emma...I love you. I'm so sorry. I'm not done. I don't want to give this up." I don't. We were good, her and I. Maybe if I hadn't been stuck in a fog of Jess, I could have seen that clearly while it was happening. Guess it's true; you don't know what you've got till it's gone.

"Give up what?" She finally snaps, finally looking at me. I hate what I see reflecting back because she's the one person who's always seen me, and now, she really has. And she hates it. And it's warranted.

"Alex?" Her brash tone grabs my attention again, "Give up *what*? The cycle of pain? The holding back? The never being fully honest with anyone, including yourself?"

She lowers her voice before continuing, "I think it's clear that giving me up was easy because you already did. It's everything else you want to hold onto." My eyes close at the searing truth. The second I gave in to Jess, I'd given up Emma. I shouldn't have done it. I wouldn't have if I'd thought the consequences through. *Would I? Or would I always be this monster?*

As my eyes reopen, I watch Emma tense, her hand bracing the truck door as she shouts, "Alex!" Her terrified voice hits me at the same time a car sideswipes the passenger side of the truck, pushing us into oncoming traffic. When the second car hits us, all I can think is: *Emma*. But then there's another impact, and it all fades to black.

TWENTY

EMMA

Everything is sore and stiff. The fabric feels rough, grating against my skin. My throat is burning, and I don't understand why I feel so miserable. Like death warmed over. Twice.

I raise a hand to rub the sleep out of my eyes, but it doesn't come. It feels held down by the weight of sleep and I groan at the exhaustion.

"Hey, *shh*. It's okay." It's a woman's voice, vaguely familiar but still foreign. So, I start the arduous task of opening my heavy eyelids.

"I'm right here, Emma." Again, the voice. I focus on it, using my curiosity to raise my eyelids.

The room is dim, but I still squint at the light, then stare up at a tiled ceiling with confusion. If I could turn my head, I would, but I can't. It feels braced, held tight. I can't tell if the brace is real or just a figment of my imagination.

"You're okay, Emma. *God*, he's going to be so happy," the voice says, sounding relieved. The voice's warm hand embraces mine, giving me a firm squeeze that I realize I'm unable to return.

And then her face comes into view. She's pretty, much like her brother.

"Brit?" I rasp out, feeling a level of dehydration that I didn't know allowed for life to continue existing.

"Yeah, Em. We're so happy you're awake. He's on his way, I promise. He'll be so mad he missed this." Alex isn't here? *Where is here?*

"Where are we?" My voice sounds brittle, maybe even muffled, and a slight edge of panic creeps up at my seeming inability to move.

"The community hospital. You've been...asleep. I'm going to call the nurse, okay?" *No!* I muster everything I can and squeeze her hand, not wanting her to leave. Brit's eyes widen slightly, but eventually she understands.

"Don't leave me," I whisper softly.

She nods and begins stroking my hand.

I feel my breath quicken, and then the beeping grows louder and more frequent.

"I-I don't understand," I whisper to Brit, confusion and fear radiating off my words. Britain's eyes fill with tears.

"You don't have to worry, I promise. Everything will be okay. Let's just try to relax, okay?" She tightens her grip on my hand, then brings her fingers up to my forehead, stroking gently, nearly lulling me back to sleep.

"Em?" The tears come involuntarily at the sound of his voice. I open my eyes to find Brit gone, replaced by Alex. And a woman wearing scrubs.

"Hi," I manage to eke out.

His eyes seem sullen and tired. His gaze filled with... *guilt*? An immense sadness and weight seem to bore down on him. I don't like it.

I can't see, but I can hear other people in the room. Another man, maybe older, is talking about "TBI," and occasionally, another man replies or asks a quiet question. The voice is familiar, but I can't place it.

Alex doesn't move away. He hovers over me, a hand in mine, the other wrapped around my upper arm like he's holding on for dear life.

"I'm sorry," Alex eventually manages to say in a tight voice that cracks at the end. My eyelids fall closed at the confusing words.

"Sorry for what?" I ask in between what feels like long blinks. Maybe even cat naps.

"Everything," is eventually whispered back.

"That seems unnecessary." I almost try to laugh, but the pain in my ribs halts me, and I wince instead.

"She still needs to rest. We need to wait for her to regain full consciousness before proceeding." The man's voice sounds a mile away and grows further still with every slow inhale and exhale.

———

I awake, seated on the bed in an inclined position. My eyelids flutter, feeling less heavy than the last time I'd done this. I'm still tired. Bone tired. But somehow it's a little better than the time before.

A gentle tug on my hair pulls at my scalp, and I tense as the soreness in my neck makes itself known.

"Ouch," I whisper.

"Em?" The brush sliding through my hair stops.

"Yes?" I can't turn my head to look, but this time, when I command my hand up to rub the sleep out of my eyes, my limbs listen, and tingly fingers rub against my eyelids. It feels out of body in a way. Like I'm me, but this hand is not mine.

Looking at the backs of my hands, it's obvious they belong to me, but they seem lifeless. Slight. My skin has lost its color, but I don't understand if the fluorescent lights are playing tricks on me or if I've somehow changed.

"What's wrong with me?" My hands flop down beside me in defeat, the weight of gravity greater than the strength I possess.

"Nothing, nothing at all. You're going to be fine." He brings his face into view, and I smile, but he doesn't return it.

Going to be fine?

"Why am I not fine now?" I try to run back in time, to replay the last thing I remember, but it's like trying to hold water in my hands. The strands of time and grainy images slip through my fingers before I even have a chance to make sense of them. "It's like there's nothing there."

"Y-you don't remember?" Alex takes a seat on the bed in front of me, holding my hand, rubbing absently like he's trying to warm it. Or maybe even will some life into it.

"Remember what?" Again, the images slip through the gaping holes newly formed in my mind. I remember...walking in a parking lot.

"Walking in the parking lot?" I ask, thinking back.

"You remember then?" *Remember what?!* I start to feel frustrated. The beeps grow in frequency around me.

"I remember walking to my car on campus. What am I missing, Alex?" It takes extreme focus and energy just to push the words into existence.

"You don't remember..." he whispers as I start crying.

"I don't remember," I sob.

"It's okay," he rubs my leg affectionately. "You will, and until then, I won't go anywhere. I promise."

I don't understand. I can't. I can barely keep my eyes open a moment longer...

———

A damp nose nuzzles into the palm of my hand, and for the first time in a week, I'm able to turn my head to look at the intruder. *Delta.*

"I missed you," I whisper to the pup, who whines in return. I catch sight of Alex, sitting hunched over in a chair, staring down at the hospital floor. His head hung, his elbows perched on his knees.

"What happened?"

"We were in a car accident." He looks up at me, revealing deep, plum-colored crevices below his eyes.

When I nod, I no longer have to wince through the pain. The progress has been slow, and I still have a hard time staying awake. Sometimes Alex is here, but not the last two days. I hadn't seen him for two whole days.

It makes me worried, and I can't fully understand why. I don't need him here, but I still want him here. When I wake up at four in the morning, I want to feel his presence. When I sat up on my own for the first time, I wanted his hands holding me. But he hadn't been there.

"Okay," I say, feeling far away from wherever he is because it certainly isn't in this room with me. "You can leave, Alex." I fight the pain in my throat that no longer has anything to do with my injuries and everything to do with whatever's happening between us.

"I won't leave again. I'm sorry." *Again*, there's meaning I can't decipher in his words and it bothers me. The uneasiness invades; the fear is here, too. I want to yell at him: *What am I missing?! Tell me!* But the strength to lash out doesn't come.

"I just don't understand," I say, crying.

Alex stands, scooting his chair closer to the hospital bed, and Delta circles to make room for him. Taking my hand in his, he leans forward and rests his head on my lap.

"I wish this was me and not you, Em. I'm so sorry." I don't know what to make of the words or his demeanor, but it doesn't matter because the exhaustion is back.

———

JANUARY

"What are you doing here?" His voice is lowered but hard.

"Is she okay?" The second voice is barely audible.

"No," Alex says back.

The second voice sucks in a hard breath, then the door clicks closed. My eyes ease open, but the lights are off.

I'm beginning to hate this place. The smell. The food. The constant noise and lack of fresh air. I begged a nurse to take me outside yesterday, but I only lasted five minutes before my head hung forward and sleep defeated me. My days feel strangely never-ending, even though I spend large swaths of hours asleep.

It's unfair that I'm stuck here. That Alex *has* to come visit. I've moved past the point of wanting him here. I don't want anyone here. *I* don't want to be here.

Testing myself, I push up, rolling onto my side. Then, I move my legs out towards the floor. Chances of this ending in disaster feel high, but the more I keep to this bed and this room, the more I believe I'll never leave it.

I don't have my phone or laptop. No one has even turned on the TV in my room. It's a prison, and I'm done.

When my feet touch the ground, I question my ability to do this, but mustering all my strength, and with a bracing hand holding on to the bed, I inch towards the hospital door.

One foot in front of the other.

With more clarity than I've had in the last...*god, I don't even know how long I've been here*, I stare down at the pj's Brit brought me and wonder what day it is. The pattern seems almost festive, and a turning in my gut has me wondering: *Is it almost Christmas?* Have I lost nearly a month of my life in this-*this in-between?*

With more assuredness, and likely adrenaline, coursing through me, I grab hold of the hospital door and pull it open to Alex and Blanks staring at me, shock written all over their faces.

"What are you doing here?" I ask Blanks, confusion likely written all over mine. I don't want him here. To see me like this. Again, I don't want anyone here. My anger simmers, just barely restrained.

"You shouldn't be up," Alex scolds me, taking my hand to keep me steady.

"I don't want to be here anymore." I try to say it calmly, but I don't think it sounds like it. Blanks just keeps staring at me, in shock, I think.

I try to get Alex to drop my hand, but he won't.

"I just want to go home." I look away from them both when the tears begin welling in my eyes. When I do finally look up, I hate the expressions on their faces. I hate it more than anything I've ever seen before. There's no lust and wonder. There's only pity and obligation. There's disgust and anger, or maybe that's me projecting.

"If you won't take me home, then leave." My voice is hard and urgent. But neither of them so much as twitch. "I said LEAVE!" I cry out, mad and hurting. *Why am I hurting? Why am I so mad?* The rage seems to find me out of nowhere. Desperately, I want to throw something and watch it break. I don't want to be the broken thing anymore. I don't want to be *this* anymore.

In the hallway, I crumple to the ground.

A warm hand comes down around my arm, lifting me, and I want to push it away and scream, but all my energy has been expended. I don't even bother opening my eyes. The warm hand becomes an arm around my back, then another arm under my legs, and all I can do is lean into their hold as they carry me back to the bed while I sob against their chest.

When soft lips press against my forehead, I open my eyes, and all my crying stops when I realize it's Blanks and not Alex. He holds my attention, looking at me like he's broken, too.

I want to tell him I'm the only thing broken here, but he

doesn't get the memo. A single tear runs down his cheek and I push him away to no effect. He doesn't budge. He stays in my face, bent over, staring at me.

"What are you doing?" I lean back into the pillow, trying to put as much space between us. "Alex!" I call out, but there's no answer.

"He said you can't remember. Is that true?" A burning in my chest ignites at the question that feels more like an accusation.

"Remember what?!" I yell in exasperation. "Why won't anyone just tell me what I forgot?" The sobs overtake me, turning into desperate attempts to inhale, then a choking fit.

Blanks stays, though, still invading my personal space.

"Do you want me to leave?" he whispers, then takes one of my hands, sliding it against his. The problem is, I don't want him to leave, but he would stay out of pity, and I never wanted that.

"Yes! God, just leave, please!" I scream at him, and he stands up instantly, drawing away from me. I hiccup, then cough over the angry cries I can't keep down any longer.

Blanks finally backs away from me when Alex and a nurse, whose name I can't remember, enter. I should be able to remember her name, right? It's been at least two weeks, and she's been with me every day. But I can't recall it. Why can't I remember her name?

"A-Alex," I stutter on a cry, "what happened to me?" The nurse looks at him, then back at me.

"Just like last time," she reminds him. Like last time? *Oh god.* How long has this been going on?

"We were in a car accident, Emma." *I know! What the fuck?* They're treating me like I'm insane or an imbecile.

"I know!" I yell at him, but he comes closer, grabbing both my hands in his own.

"You do?" he asks.

"Yes! You told me that, but I can't remember when or how long ago it was. And every time I try to think backward, my mind feels like mush." I sniffle, "And every time I think about now, or the future, I-I get so angry, and I don't know why."

"We should take her home," Blanks says, standing back behind the nurse now. My crying quiets at his voice.

He stares at me intently, seeing something that Alex can't. I swallow past the lump in my throat. "Please," I whisper to Blanks.

He nods, leaving us.

"She can't just leave," the nurse looks at Alex.

Alex stands still, staring at me like he doesn't recognize me. I don't blame him. I don't recognize myself either. I don't even want to go back to his house. I want to go somewhere and be alone, though I doubt they would let me.

"If she doesn't want to be here, she doesn't have to be," he eventually says solemnly to the nurse, relief flooding me.

I mouth to him *"thank you,"* and he gives me a barely sympathetic smile in return. I don't like it.

TWENTY-ONE

ALEX

Six weeks in the hospital. *I'd* cost her six weeks of her life already.

Blanks brings a wheelchair into her room, and a smile spreads across her face. She stares at him, and he stares at her, and suddenly I feel like a third wheel, an odd burn hitting my chest.

"Mr. Palomino, I still don't think it's a good idea," Becks, our night nurse, pleads with me. But it doesn't matter what she thinks.

Emma is floundering here. Or maybe I don't want to admit what's actually happening, that she's fading, not healing. She should be home, in a comfortable environment where she might actually get rest. I should have taken her home a week ago.

The guilt that weighs me down intensifies. I would work

on finding a nurse to live in, get extra help around the house. It's not as if I can't afford to do this for her.

"I-I don't have any shoes, do I?" she asks, looking at me then Blanks, who lifts her frail frame out of the bed, setting her in the wheelchair.

There's probably a bag of clothes from the accident somewhere, but I would make sure it got thrown away before anything that touched her body that day would touch her again. In a lot of ways, I'm jealous of her. I would do anything to forget that day. To forget the last six weeks.

"No, sweetheart," I say. If I'd known we were leaving, I would have prepared or at least had Brit bring something. Aside from a few stale floral arrangements, the room lacks anything that actually belongs to Emma. Per the doctor's orders, I hadn't even brought her phone here.

"Is it cold out?" she asks, and Blanks nods, removing his own jacket and placing it over her shoulders.

"Yeah, Angel, it is. I'm gonna go warm the car for you," he says. Then, turning to me with an open palm held up, he asks, "Keys?"

I toss them into his waiting hand, not missing the hard line of his jaw or the way his knuckles turn white as they tighten into a fist. I almost ask what his fucking problem is, but he shoulder-checks me on his way out, and it doesn't take an emotionally inept asshole like me to realize he's pissed. Still.

You just couldn't leave her the fuck alone, could you? His words from earlier in the hallway come back to haunt me.

I should have, I know.

"I need you to sign paperwork before you go," Becks says as she helps put a pair of socks onto Emma's feet. "And you

E.L. STEVENS

should know, she needs care, maybe even round the clock. She'll need help showering, and going to the bathroom, and eating. Do you understand?"

"You do realize I'm right here? Right? I haven't kicked the bucket yet." Emma looks between the nurse and me.

"I'm sorry, honey," Becks grabs her hand. "I just want you to be taken care of, okay?" *Fuck.* The words are like a knife to the back. I hadn't taken care, but I would. As long as she needs or as long as she wants. Whichever comes first.

I know that if her memory does return, she'll be gone without a second thought, especially after all this.

"I know, thank you. I-I keep trying to remember your name, but I'm so sorry," Emma's tears start to return as she fumbles, trying to recall.

"That's okay. It's Becks. It's a funny little name to remember."

"Becks," Emma repeats. Then she repeats it again, "Becks." "Becks, Becks, Becks."

She's trying to commit it to memory, and my fucking heart shatters. I turn away to hide the tears, pretending to shuffle through paperwork that doesn't really exist. It's just pamphlets they brought me on cognitive and occupational therapy. I slip them into my back pocket like this is all on purpose.

But on second thought, I pull out a card.

"If you're interested, I'll double your salary." I hold the card out for Becks. "Think about it."

She stands from where she was crouched down and takes the card. "I will."

"Okay," I say, moving closer to Emma to wheel her out.

As soon as Becks vacates the room, Emma turns to me.

"Thank you, Alex." She places a hand over mine that's wrapped around the chair's handle. Fucking hate the feeling that engulfs me. It's guilt and shame, regret and self-loathing all rolled into one.

Kicking away the parking brake, I finally say, "Let's go home, Em."

———

In the rearview, I watch her sleep. Her head is in Blanks's lap, his hand stroking idly through her hair, and the uncomfortable feeling returns. My mouth feels hot, and there's this tingling skirting up my spine.

My fingers wrap tighter around the steering wheel as I try to pinpoint what I don't like. The way he calls her Angel? Was it that he seemed to know within fifteen seconds what Em needed when I'd been there for six weeks? Is it paranoia? Jealousy over their familiarity?

Jealous about what specifically, though?

I should've been the one to pick her up off the hospital floor. I should have been with her in the backseat. There are all these *should-haves*, but I can't wrap my mind around the *why-nots*.

Jess.

The text messages she sent sat unanswered. I left her on read for six weeks, too. She finally gave up and was moving on for good now.

While Emma was lying in the hospital bed, I grappled. I debated. And in the end, I made the choice to let Jess go. It isn't a mountain easily moved, but I need to do it.

"I'd appreciate if you were slightly less hands-*on* with my

E.L. STEVENS

wife." *My wife.* I feel like a fucking fraud saying it after everything I've done.

Blanks's hand stills in her hair, then he looks at my reflection.

"Just making sure she's comfortable. I didn't see you exactly jumping into action to do the same." It's accusatory. That I hurt her. Like he has a sixth-fucking-sense about it.

"Say what you're actually trying to say?" My eyes narrow at him through the mirror, and my jaw tenses.

"You should let her go," he says back firmly. "She shouldn't have almost died in your car. She shouldn't be here right now. She-" He stops to scoff, "She deserves a hell of a lot better than an existence with you."

A fucking dagger to the heart.

All Emma ever did was bring me light, joy, and a reason to keep living. And all I've given her is pain, a near-death experience, and a broken heart, regardless of whether she can remember it or not. She sacrificed her life for mine, it seemed.

And Blanks is right. My throat turns viciously tight. My body tenses with knowing.

I don't want to abandon her, and I won't, but she deserves a lot more than a life beside me.

I look back at where Emma's fragile body is laid out in the backseat. Any trace of a smile is vacant from her face as she sleeps. Her skin has leached all its color and turned alabaster. With her hair just as light, she looks like an actual angel. Perfect. And pure. And it hurts seeing her. It hurts knowing I did this. Knowing we would have to relive it all someday. That I would have to tell her.

I don't want to stop being with Emma or give her up. I meant what I said in the truck that day. And every day since,

248

I've thought it to some degree, but all the signs point to me needing to step away.

Well, being away is something I do best.

I push the instinct to care for her down. I try to disregard the happy memories, the places that mean something to us, the moments that changed me, all the times she held me. And I mentally prepare that from this moment on, Emma is no longer mine. She deserved more.

———

Opening the door for Blanks, who carries Emma, I direct him to the first-floor suite. Emma's old room.

I help move the covers, pushing the extra pillows away, and Blanks deposits her. I step back and watch as he covers her, adding an extra blanket. And I keep taking steps back, silently, knowing I'm already closing the door. I step out into the hall and pace while I wait. Once Blanks is there, I give him a quick head nod.

"Can you sleep on the couch? Or nearby?" It pains me to ask. "In case she needs anything or wakes up in the middle of the night?"

"You're not sleeping in there with her?" he asks, surprised.

I swallow the bad feelings and shake my head.

"If she remembered, I doubt she would want me there."

Blanks's expression falls. With a lowered voice, he asks, "What did you do?"

"It doesn't matter what. All that matters is you're right. And I'll let her go. I'll, uh," I nearly fucking choke on the words, "try to do it slow and easy, and I'll keep making sure she's taken care of, but...I'm done."

I don't — *might be that I can't* — wait for his reaction. I just head straight for the stairs and up to our room. I shut the door, then turn and slide to the floor. I fist my trembling hands into my hair and try to fight the urge to throw something. To yell or fight. I fight against the desire to run back downstairs and hold her one last time as she sleeps.

Rocking on the floor, back and forth, I fight for breath. My fingers twist inside my palms, hot and damp. Extending my left hand, I slide the gold band off for the first time in over a year.

I'm sorry, Em.

———

FEBRUARY

Emma

"Good morning," her voice is soothing, "let's try and get going, yeah?" She's always gentle with me. I can feel the bed dip as she sits on the mattress beside me.

"Go away, Becks," I groan, turning my head into the pillow to block her and the light out.

"Nope. We are not starting today like this. Try again, Em." She's always gentle but firm. I flop back against the bed, still shielding my eyes from the sun, and I cave in.

"Good morning, Becks. Today is Friday, January 31st.

My name is Emmaline Palomino, formerly Strait, and I'm 27 years old. I currently live in Spearhead Lake, California, with my husband." *That's a lie and a joke.* "And we have a dog named Delta, and a rescue named Blanks."

"She seems fine to me," Blanks snorts from the doorway.

I ignore him. "And my goal today is to make myself breakfast. Alone. ALL Alone." I drop my hands from my face and catch Caleb giving me a smirk from the corner of my eye.

He's been here every day and every morning since I came "home" from the hospital. He's the one who carried me to the toilet to pee that first day. He was the one to feed me. He even bathed me once in a genuinely humiliating debacle that I made him swear to never speak of again.

And he's held me as I cried on more than one occasion over the absence of said "husband." My chest burns at the memory.

"Okay," Becks moves two fingers to take my pulse in her routine morning check. "And can you tell me how you got here?"

"Well, I was working at this diner, and this really hot guy sat down at one of my tables..." Becks shoots me a look. This isn't the first time I've tried this. "Fine," I say in faux-aggravation because it always pisses me off that every day I have to recount this story. A story that had to be told to me because two months after the fact, I still have no memory of it.

"I was involved in a car accident, or so I've been told, and I spent three weeks in a coma, followed by an additional three weeks of mild consciousness. I suffered a traumatic brain injury, and most would say I'm lucky to be experiencing this level of recovery."

I know I sound ungrateful, but I feel anything but. Lucky

I survived so I could...so I could what? Become an obligation to the man I loved? To be tossed aside? To know that every day I will wake up in more pain than I ever did while lying in a hospital bed with a brain injury and bruised ribs?

I hate it here.

My manna from heaven has turned into hell on Earth.

Becks gives me a sad sort of smile that's equal parts empathy and pity.

"Do you want help?" She means going to the bathroom, but I shake my head, feeling my throat grow too tight to speak.

Becks releases my wrist, typing my pulse into the chart on her phone as I roll out of bed.

Blanks is still watching from the bedroom doorway. He stands with a coffee mug in hand, leaning against the frame. He gives me the same sad smile as Becks and I want to flip him off for it.

I can't believe I ever thought I had feelings for him. Some days, I feel ashamed of it. But then again, once he ingrained himself in my life to the point he probably knows what day I'll start my period before I do, all I feel now...is angry.

I don't want him to take me on as some charity project, or step in because his best friend stepped out. I know what I am to him now, and that quickly dried up any residual or lingering feelings.

I know I told Becks my goal is to make breakfast, but my goal is bigger than that. Leaving *here* is the real goal. To move back to my little condo. To go to school and back to work at the library. I was happy-ish then. I was healthy then. And all I want is to go back to *then*.

After washing my hands, I stand at the sink and stare at

the waif-like being looking back at me. When I lift my shirt to change, I see ribs and bones I never knew I had before. My skin looks thin and crepey white.

I'm revolting.

I try to focus on my breath, on maintaining my calm, but all I want is to throw something heavy into the mirror to shatter the image of who I am. Of what I've become.

"Em?" Becks knocks on the bathroom door.

"I'm coming, just a minute," I try to say back politely while silently sniffing the tears away.

Leaning towards the door, I check in the off chance Blanks and Becks are still in the room, and they are. The faint conversation sounds pleasant. Maybe even fun. He flirts with her endlessly, and I get it; she's pretty, and he's stuck in the middle of fucking nowhere against his will.

"*Is he going to come back?*" I hear Becks ask him. That is the million-dollar question, of course.

I've seen Alexander twice since coming "home." Twice in the last four weeks and none in the last two.

"*I don't know,*" I can tell he's saying it quietly, almost a whisper.

I run my fingers against my lips, feeling them tremble. *What is Alex waiting for?*

Sometimes, it's the not knowing that does the most damage. It's why I always wanted him to tell me if he wanted out. I just want to know where I stand with him.

It's *all* I wanted.

My fingers shake as I hold them out in front of me. *Naked.* I was told they had to cut the rings off sometime after the accident. I haven't seen them since. I assume they were given to Alex, but maybe they're lost.

It seems like I've lost a lot since the accident. *Memories, possessions, abilities, people...*

I'm still not allowed use of my phone in the mornings. It tends to just result in debilitating migraines, but once I'm able to, I'll call. Or maybe text him and let him know I'm fine. Maybe I would lie and tell him I'm better and that I'm leaving.

Yeah, I'll do that.

I wipe the stupid tears off my cheeks and slip on my robe before opening the door. Thankfully, the two have cleared out, but I still try to think of tasks to keep me in my bedroom. And I fail; it's useless. I would have to grin and bear another day.

The great room is empty, but hearing voices coming from the kitchen has me on high alert.

"There she is!" *Oh, good. Company.*

"Hi, Connie," I reply sheepishly. "Niko," I nod to the man half sticking out of the fridge.

"Coffee?" Caleb holds a mug out to me, already with cream in it. I'll never make my own breakfast if he keeps doing it for me. I give him a look of annoyance and accept the cup.

"You have to start letting me do things on my own," I mumble under my breath as I move past him. His shoulders drop in disappointment. I'm always grumpy now, which is new for me. But today isn't going to be the day that being grumpy stops. I know that much already, as everything about this morning seems to set me on edge.

I don't want to be rude, but I also don't understand why Connie is here.

"So..." I say awkwardly as I sit at the kitchen island.

"Right, you're wondering why I'm here." *Ding, ding, ding.* Connie takes another mug of coffee and sits beside me.

"I'm always happy to see you, but next time, you'll need to buy me dinner first." I give him a wink and a poor attempt at a joke.

Being the gentleman he is, he still laughs.

"Deal. No, I thought maybe we could have a field trip today? Go visit Brit? Go get a pastry at The Grounds? You know, break out of jail for the day?"

As much as I hate it here, the idea of doing any of that feels daunting. I'm already tired, and all I've done is walk from the bathroom to the kitchen. The last thing I need is more eyes examining all my deficiencies. Feeling pity for me.

He watches my face fall.

"Or, we could just keep each other company?" He redirects. I give him as much of a smile as I can manage.

"I'd love to hang out, thanks."

Connie nods at Blanks. *Right. Shift change.* My babysitters need a break.

There's always someone here. If it isn't Blanks, it's Brit, or it's Carly or Sandy. Or some other proxy for Alex. But never Alex.

I stare straight ahead as conversation picks up around me, zoning out on the far wall of the mudroom. Like a one-way ticket to hell, the gilded invitation catches my eye.

"Do you want some eggs?" Caleb's hand on my back startles me, a chill racking my whole body.

"That would be really nice, thanks." I shift on the stool, grappling with the feeling of impending doom, blanketing me, then weighing me down. "You know what? I actually think," I sway slightly as I stand, "I think I need to go back to bed. I'm so sorry," I apologize, feeling the tears start.

Then Becks is right beside me, helping me walk.

I just need to go back to bed. Maybe tomorrow will be better.

———

"Why did you do all this for me? He asked. I don't deserve it. I've never done anything for you." The sound of a page turning draws me towards consciousness. "You have been my friend, replied Charlotte. That in itself is a tremendous thing."

I open my eyes to find Connie sitting in the armchair in my room, reading. Aloud. To me.

"She rouses," he beams. There's nothing for me to say, and I feel incapable of pretending, so I lie here, doing nothing.

"This was one of Alex's favorite books," he holds up a battered copy of *Charlotte's Web*. "I actually bought him this one. Even signed it in the front." He sort of flips through the book.

"Connie," I stop him. "Alex doesn't want to be with me anymore." He starts to protest, but I won't let him. "Can you just tell him that it's okay? Tell him for me?"

"I don't think that's very true," Connie placates me.

"It doesn't matter that you or me, or whoever else, doesn't *want* it to be true. It is. And I'd like to leave here, but as long as I'm stuck in this purgatory, I'll never get better. So just tell him. Okay?"

Connie nods once. "When would you like me to do that?"

"Today, please." I continue lying there, staring at the ceiling.

I hear his gentle sigh, and then the light taps as he types a message on his phone.

A moment later, a ping rings out. *Definitive.*

"What does it say?" I whisper.

"It says," Connie pauses, "all it says is '*okay.*'"

Okay. "Thank you. I think I'd like to go back to sleep now." I close my eyes, feeling the sting of tears.

I hear Connie leave a few moments later, and my eyes reopen. I roll to face the window, watching as flurries fly past the pane. It doesn't take long before my eyes flutter and close. And in my dream, I dream of him and the life I always knew we'd never have.

TWENTY-TWO

ALEX

CONNIE

Enough is enough. You need to come
home, or the best thing that's ever
happened to you is going to leave.

A

But what if I'm the worst thing thats ever
happened to her?

Are you trying to make it true?

She told me to tell you she knows you don't
want to be with her, and it's okay. So
congratulations, son. You've done it.

Okay.

The hope was there that she would hit a limit and be done
with me so I wouldn't have to be the one to be done with her.

258

It sounds like she's there. And now that it's happening, I... can't stand the thought of it.

I miss her, desperately. In a way I've never felt before. For *anyone*. It emanates from a deep part of my being that I keep trying to bury. It comes from a place only Emma has ever touched.

Without thought, I grab the keys hanging on the wall beside the garage. I give Georgia's house a quick once over, making sure all the lights are off, and then I'm out the door. Driven by desperation.

It's like I have no control. Every good intention is gone. I have one need left. I only have one purpose. And it's to see her. It's to tell her what she can't remember. The truth of it. And then I want to hold and love her and beg her to take me back. If she'll have me.

When the gate opens to my house, the sun is just setting. The air bites as I step out of my car and into the cold January night. Staring at the house, lit up from within, a choice lingers in the back of my mind, but I push forward. I push against the instinct to turn away.

When I push down on the latch, I expect to hear something. Talking, cooking, life...*anything*. But the house is ominously quiet. No movement, just a few side lamps lit. No one in sight.

Shutting the front door as quietly as possible, I walk deeper into the house, turning towards her room. The door is cracked, but it's dark, and my heart races. Will she look the same as she did in the hospital? Worse?

I push on the door gently, and it swings in silently. Emma is curled up on top of the covers, sound asleep, while Blanks sits in a chair beside her, scrolling through his phone. He looks at me sharply and makes no attempt to move.

The odd feeling comes back, the same one I felt bringing her home.

Not mine flits through my mind like lightning.

We stare at each other in some odd faceoff, wondering who will be the first to break. It's a game of will. I withdrew before. But now, faced with the very real end, I couldn't. I won't. Eventually, Blanks stands, passing me brusquely but without a word.

At the sound of his exiting footsteps, Emma rolls to her back, flinging her arms against the bed in exasperation. Her eyes are wide open, as if she's just been waiting for him to leave this whole time. Like she wasn't asleep at all.

I take one more step into the room, and she shoots up at the now unfamiliar sound of my boots.

"Alex," she whispers, sitting up in bed.

The knot in my throat feels tight. Even in the dim light, her pale skin practically glows. She looks only moderately better than the last I saw her. I fucking hate what I've done to her.

"Em," is all I can manage back, each swallow more uncomfortable than the last.

"W-what are you doing here?" she continues to whisper.

"I-um..." I struggle to find the right thing to say here. Because there is no right thing, that's the problem. "I'm sorry." It comes out gravely, my voice hoarse.

She seems to visibly swallow.

"I'm sorry, too," she whispers back words that damn near break me. She has not one thing to be sorry for. Not one fucking thing.

I take a few steps closer.

"You will never need to be sorry to me. Ever."

"I feel like I do-"

I stop her, though, "You don't." I stand there, and she sits in silence for more than a minute.

"Did you just come to say goodbye, or...." she chokes on her own words.

"No," voice is gruff, even worse than before. I take another step, then one more, until I'm standing beside her bed. "I'm not expecting to be forgiven, but I couldn't let go without at least telling you *why* I can't be here." This is it. I would tell her the truth, ask forgiveness, then make peace with whatever her decision is.

"I forgive you," she says, no longer in a whisper.

"I haven't even-" but she stops me again.

"It doesn't matter, Alex. I love you more than whatever it is you've done. More than your absence the last few weeks. I will always want you. No matter what. And maybe that makes me a fool..."

I fall to my knees beside the bed. "I-I don't deserve you, Em. Really-"

"Maybe, but I know *I do* deserve a husband who's here with me. And if you need my forgiveness for that to happen, then I'm happy to give it. I'm so tired of waking up angry and hurt. Every. Single. Day. So, please. Can we just forgive and forget? Well, I suppose I've already forgotten..." She laughs, then sniffles.

"Emma," I whisper, incapable of finding additional words. Incapable of telling her when she was offering me this gift. "I love you."

"You'll tell me when you stop, right?" I would never stop loving her, ever.

"Sure, sweetheart, just don't expect it to happen soon." I pick up her hand and kiss the top of it. She eventually lays back down while I stay kneeling beside the bed, holding her hand. Once I think she's drifted off, I get up to go sleep in the chair.

"Are you coming to bed?" she asks, eyes still closed.

"Of course," I answer, kicking off my boots, tearing away my shirt, and unbuckling my belt. I get into bed on the opposite side, giving her plenty of space. But as soon as I'm settled, she moves under the covers and finds me. Her body feels frail against mine, and I hate myself a little bit more because of it.

But it doesn't matter. I'll hold her like this as long as she needs. Like she held me.

———

I brush the stray strands of hair out of her face before placing a kiss on her forehead. *I love you.*

Then I leave her.

My mind is too busy, my body too restless to continue lying there until she wakes up. So I sneak out of bed to take the dog out and make coffee.

I missed Delta, too.

I throw on the same clothes I wore last night and exit her room as quietly as possible. Again, the main floor is eerily quiet, but when I round the corner to the kitchen, Delta rushes, full of surprise, to see me.

"Hey, boy." He jumps, licking me, tail wagging, like this is the best surprise ever.

In contrast, Blanks stands on the opposite side of the kitchen island, far less enthused.

"Changed your mind?" he asks, slipping his hands into the front pockets of his jeans.

"Yeah," I reply.

"Man, must be nice." I stand up from where I was crouched down to pet Delta.

"*What* must be nice?"

"It's just like Amy all over again." His words nearly send me.

"What's just like Amy all over again?" I hold my breath.

"You know what," he says, narrowing his eyes at me. "Guess you changing your mind is my cue to get the fuck out, right? Regardless of the fact that I've been the one here, every second of every day." He shakes his head in disbelief. "You're the most selfish man to ever live, you know that?" His words are like a vice around my heart.

He walks around the kitchen island to pass me, but I stop him. My hand hits his chest, halting him in his retreat. He looks down at my hand, then back at me. My breathing thick, matching his.

"You should have told me," I say, gritting my teeth.

"It wouldn't have mattered even if I did," he grinds out. I fight back the urge to curl my fist in his t-shirt.

He's right, though. It wouldn't have mattered.

"Don't go," I tell him, meaning it.

"And why shouldn't I?" he seethes back. He moves in closer, his face nearly in mine now, my hand still splayed across his chest.

"Mr. Palomino," Becks says with surprise. "You're here."

The moment shatters, and Blanks pushes past my hand and leaves me in the kitchen.

"Yeah," I turn to the nurse, "I'm back." She nods at me while following Blanks with her eyes.

"I'm going to shower, but when I'm out, I'd love to sit down and talk about Emma's progress. Can we do that?" She nods, giving me a look somewhere between annoyance and discomfort. "Great." On our last few nightly phone calls to review Emma's status, I thought I heard disdain in Beck's voice. Being in person confirms it. *Great.*

———

"*Caleb!*" I can hear her shout over the sound of the faucet running. I turn it off and listen to what sounds like muffled crying. Terrified and still half naked, I take off, running down the stairs, rounding the hallway corner following the sounds.

"It just felt so real," I hear Emma say, heaving a deep breath. "I don't know what's wrong with me. Just please, promise me you won't leave me." I stand in the doorway to Emma's room, not fully prepared for the sight in front of me.

The sight of Emma curled into a ball in Blanks's lap, her hands fisting his shirt as she cries nearly hysterically. His hands are threaded through her hair as he whispers back, "Never. I'll never leave you."

"Em?" I ask softly, drawing her attention.

"Alex?" she questions back. She slowly releases Blanks's t-shirt but doesn't move out of his embrace. Meanwhile, Blanks glares at me.

"Are you okay?" I ask, stepping past Becks, who is also in the room.

She sniffles before answering, "What are you doing here?" She couldn't remember last night? Of course, that was more than I deserved.

"I came home last night..." I try to remind her gently, "Do you remember?" She stares at me long and hard.

"Maybe..." she eventually rasps out. "I-I thought it was a bad dream."

"Bad?"

"Well, I don't know," she cries a little bit. "I was so relieved, but then I woke up and was alone again...it didn't feel real. I wasn't expecting to see you, I guess." As innocently as possible, she's taken my heart and stomped on it.

Becks gives me the side eye, a disapproving glare plastered on her face. The same glare is still plastered on Blanks's face.

"I'm here now," I say solemnly. What else can I do?

"Okay," she says, still shrinking slightly away from me. "I-I'll be out in a minute, okay?" She looks at me, asking for a moment. I wanted to curl in a ball myself, but eventually, I concede and back out of her room.

As soon as my back is turned, they're whispering to each other, my blood reheating from the conversation with Blanks earlier.

He loves her.

————

Emma

. . .

They must think I'm the biggest fool. "I'm so stupid, Caleb. I'm sorry." I can't meet his eyes as he holds me. Not unlike he has many times before.

"Shut up, you are not." He shakes me a little bit, trying to get sense back into me. I fear I will never be sensible again.

"I thought I imagined the whole thing."

"Yeah, well, that's hardly your fault, Angel." I nod against his chest.

"I meant what I asked, you know." I feel his body go still beneath mine. "Don't leave me," I whisper.

His hold on me tightens, and as much as I shouldn't want it, I do. I can't remember the last time Alex held me like this. I don't know if it's my shoddy memory or an actual fact, but Blanks was safe to me. I don't want him to go away like he did last time. When I spent months wishing he would walk through that door.

Granted, back then, I hoped he was around for another reason...but now, I just need him. Like everything will be okay as long as he's around.

"Whatever you want, Angel," he eventually replies, loosening his hands from out of my hair. "I think Becks has waited patiently enough." Jesus, I forgot she was still in the room.

"Right." I crawl out of his lap and onto the other side of the bed, and Becks approaches, taking my wrist in her hand.

"Do you need a minute? Or are you ready?" Becks asks while my eyes glaze over. I'm aware of where I am, but my mind feels somewhere else. Or like it wants to be somewhere else. There's an empty longing burning inside me that I don't understand.

"No, I'm fine." I stare out the window at the snow-covered ground. "Today is Saturday, February first. My name is Emmaline Strait." Becks startles slightly, and I look at her, as she looks at me with confusion. It takes me more than a normal amount of time to realize the mistake. "Oh, I mean Emmaline Palomino. I-I'm 27 years old, and I currently live in Spearhead Lake, California." I pause, trying to get a grip on how to say this next part.

"I currently live with Caleb, Alex, and my dog, Delta. And my goal today is to go for a walk outside." I chew on my lip nervously. "Do I have to go over the whole TBI thing today?" It hurt my heart to have to say it.

"No, not today." I nod. Becks records my pulse, takes my blood pressure and temperature, then asks if I need help with the restroom. I decline.

When she leaves, I turn to Caleb, who's staring at me with something I can't discern.

"I should probably take a shower or something so I can stop looking disgusting." I look down at my baggy t-shirt. Blanks's baggy t-shirt that I had worn every other day for a week.

"I don't think you look disgusting. I don't think you've looked disgusting a day in your life." I can feel my cheeks warm. I feel warm. Warm...down *there*.

We stare at each other, something left unsaid by both of us.

"I'm gonna run you a bath, okay?" I nod as he leans into me, stealing a kiss on the cheek. "I'm not going anywhere, not without you."

It's like a punch to the gut. Feelings flood back that I wasn't aware had been there. But here they are, the nearly overwhelming flood of affection crashing into me. Shaking me.

Where is it coming from? And why do I suddenly want him? I should feel ashamed, *be* ashamed.

My brows are drawn together in confusion and wonder because once the feeling breaks free, it's all I can think. I *do* have feelings. For him. Even uncomfortable ones, dormant no longer.

I mentally gasp. *Does it hurt because...I love him?* Love is a strong word. I don't know that these feelings match the definition. But overwhelming and strong nonetheless.

I watch as he walks towards the bathroom, seeing him in a new light. Why does he have to be so hot, and why do I have to be so...me? I follow behind him, watching how he bends over to turn on the water to just the right temperature. He's barefoot, in jeans and a plain white t-shirt, and I want him to fuck me.

Just like that day, that feels like a lifetime ago, him watching me lose myself on the ledge of this tub. I divert my gaze at the thought. I was a different person then. The old me. Not this version that would blow over from a breeze.

Why is he here? Why is he here *still?* I want to ask something. It's on the tip of my tongue to do it when he turns around.

"Want me to help you get undressed?" *Yes.*

"Umm, no. That's okay." He doesn't move to leave, though.

"I'll help you get in then." I want to say yes. I mean, he's helped me get in and out of the tub no less than ten times already, but looking back, all I feel is shame. Mostly about the way my body looks.

I look worse than Darla Strait did on her worst day, and that's saying something. I mean, it *really* says something. She was 95 pounds and looked like she'd been rode hard and put away wet.

"It-I should probably get Becks to do it...from now on." *Now that Alex is back.* He looks only slightly concerned but leaves without issue, quickly replaced by Becks.

Now Becks is someone who could pull a man like Blanks. Her hair is dark brown, but she dyes the tips teal. She has a figure like an hourglass and big lips that may or may not be courtesy of filler, but it doesn't matter because she rocks them either way. I would put money on her and Blanks having already fucked.

Good for them.

I drop the t-shirt and my underwear, and Becks helps me step into the tub.

"Can you hand me a razor and shaving cream?" I ask Becks before she leaves, and she hesitates.

"You don't—you probably shouldn't—" I shake my head at her attempt to deter me.

"I don't care if it takes me all day. I need to regain some humanity, Becks. Look at me, okay? No one wants this..." I say it quietly, and she scoffs.

"You're out of your mind," but she brings me the razor and cream anyway, leaving me alone. *Thank god.*

TWENTY-THREE

ALEX

I stand outside her bedroom door, waiting for him to exit.

"Is she okay?" I ask once he's shut the door behind him.

"No," Blanks says curtly, walking past me towards the kitchen. I slide my hand through my still-wet hair and follow behind.

"When did it happen?" I ask, bracing my hands against the kitchen counter while he pretends to make coffee. He doesn't answer.

"Does she love you back?" He stops, standing still.

"No," he nearly chokes on his own word and I sigh out in relief. Like I have a leg to stand on. Fuck, it was only a few months ago I slept with Jess. I was still in love with her. At least partially. Well, I guess I didn't know what it was anymore. I'd sat with it for a month. I'd wrestled with the what if, and every time I came to the other side of it all...I didn't know that Jess was the one I wanted standing beside me in the end.

"I would prefer if we didn't talk about this. She asked me to stay, and I will. Otherwise, I would've left. That's the end of it, okay?" He starts the coffee pot and finally turns around, his face hard and the message clear. That's the end of it.

I put the same hard face back on. "Understood." This isn't the first time we've both been into the same chick. Maybe it was the first time we were both in *love* with the same woman, but I knew Blanks would take a back seat. At least he had once before.

"Let's chat," Becks says. "She'll be in the bath awhile." I don't know what that means, but I agree, and Becks sets a folder in front of me.

"Honestly, I think this place is only moderately better for her than a hospital or rehabilitation facility." I know. She's told me every day since we brought her home.

"She's responded well to the small amounts of physical therapy I've done with her, but again, that's not really my area of expertise." Again, she's told me this every day.

"She's ready for real cognitive therapy, which I know for certain I am not trained to administer."

"What would that entail?" Blanks asks.

"Well, it would focus mostly on her memory loss. So, working on what happened before the memory loss, what happened *during* the loss. Recalling events to try and get her to remember. It's a lot of talk therapy as well." Blanks and I both shift uncomfortably.

"Pick the therapist, and let's get it scheduled." It's like signing my own death sentence.

"Okay, then." Becks pushes away from the table. "I'm gonna go check on her." I just nod.

"Bet you're remembering why you ran away in the first place?" Blanks stares at me over the rim of his coffee cup.

Yup.

Blanks passes me a mug, and we sit at the kitchen table together. Somberly. I love Emma, but do I love her more than he does? Would she be happier with him?

The sound of the bedroom door opening pulls my attention, and I watch her walk slowly toward the kitchen. God, it's fucking painful. It's painful to remember this is the same girl who could have lapped me up to the ridge. And now, she's only managing a hobble.

Would she ever make it to her little Airstream again?

Blanks is already standing, giving her his seat.

"Coffee?" he asks her, and she nods.

We sit beside each other like strangers. Instinct says to reach out for her, but she seems feeble. Like I might break her. I want to say something, but it feels like if I open my mouth, my voice will only manifest as a slight croak.

"How—" "I—" We both start at the same time, interrupting the other. I can feel Blanks watching. Judging.

I give a tightlipped smile with a hand up for her to proceed.

"I was going to say that I just want things to go back to normal, okay?" she asks quietly, almost sheepish. God, this guilt would kill me. *Could we ever go back to normal?*

"Sure," is all I manage to get out.

"So you're walking outside today, huh?" Blanks asks, setting a coffee mug in front of her.

"Yeah," she replies, smiling back at him. How the fuck is

she supposed to go for a walk outside? She can barely walk inside.

"That sounds nice," I add. "Want some company?" But she shakes her head.

"No, actually." She watches my face fall. "Maybe another time in the future, though. You know, once I get my land legs back to full working order." She looks down, pink staining the apples of her cheeks. She's embarrassed. My heart sinks. Mentally, I'm already carving my fucking headstone. *Here lies Alexander Palomino, who died of guilt.*

"Well, the second you do, I'll be there." I lean forward, putting a light kiss on her forehead.

Normal. She wants normal. Give her normal.

———

MARCH

Things couldn't be further from fucking normal. I hate it here because I know *she* hates it here.

I thought she loved it here. And maybe she did, but I don't think she does anymore.

I thought she loved me. And maybe she did, but again, doesn't feel like it anymore.

She's almost nothing like the Emma from before. She's angry and bitter and quick to temper. She cries over small things and big things, too. She sleeps a lot during the day but tosses and turns all night. It's killing me watching her like this.

But that's my penance to pay, isn't it?

"Ow," she says, staring at me.

"Sorry." I release the hold on her leg, releasing the tension of the stretch I'd been helping her with.

"This is pointless," she huffs, rolling her eyes. The daily routines are rote and monotonous. Every day looks a lot like the last, with little forward progress.

"Do you want me to get Blanks?" That's her M.O. lately. When she gets tired of me, she'll ask for him instead. Each time she does, it guts me. She's become incapable of hiding her annoyance with me. Even if she can't remember, it's like her body still does.

She doesn't spare me the same sympathy as before, and I feel each day like a pull on our bond. I don't know what that said about us if we didn't work when she couldn't be the one picking up my pieces. *I think it says I'm a piece of shit.*

"I don't know, Alex. I'm just..." She puts her hands over her eyes, either fighting back tears or exhaustion. "I feel dead. *Inside.*" When she drops her hands, I see it. The lack of life reflects back at me. Been there, felt that.

"What can I do?" I don't have the same innate ability as her, or as Blanks, who knows what to do without being told. I'm exhausted, too, from always seeming to do the wrong thing. I need her to tell me the right thing.

She closes her eyes and sighs, fighting off a tremble. "There's nothing you can do. I'm going outside for a bit, okay?"

I'm about to ask if she wants company when she stops me. "Alone, I'm going alone." I nod, then take her hand and pull her up. She glances at both our hands.

"Why did you stop wearing your ring?" she asks. *When I stopped feeling worthy of wearing it.*

Instead, I tell a white lie. "Our rings are together, at the jewelers, being repaired." She swallows, gives me a vacant look, and walks to the mudroom to get bundled up for outside.

Her rings *are* at the jeweler's. They've also been ready for pickup for two months now.

Her walk is less hobbly these days, but she wouldn't be running anytime soon. It hurts somewhere between getting a fingernail removed and a root canal to watch her, only slightly less painful than the full-blown cardiac arrest I suffered the first time I watched her move post-accident.

I can't help but keep watching her as she gets ready. Maybe it's because she's still a fall risk. Maybe it's because I broke her. But as I watch, all I can think is: *I don't know how to make her better*.

I don't know how to make anything better. That's sort of my whole life in a nutshell. I've never met a deed, good or bad, that went unpunished.

I only know how to be with her in the before. Before I ruined it.

Grabbing my coat off the hook beside hers, she stares at me.

"I'm going alone, Alex," she says defiantly.

"No, you're not," I give it right back, not meeting her eyes. When she sits down to put on her sneakers, I pull them out of her hands and kneel to help her put on her hiking boots instead.

"I can't wear those. They're too heavy." Another annoyed protest.

"Then I'll carry you," *literally or figuratively*. "When's the last time you went down to the cove?"

"I-I can't remember." Her memory loss mostly centers around the time she was in the accident, but sometimes, other bits are fuzzy for her. The ability to concentrate fully was still lacking, and her ability to recall with it.

Unfortunately, I can still remember vividly the last time I was there.

It's time to replace the old with the new, though. *Forward movement, right?*

———

Emma

He's out of his goddamn mind. A walk down to the cove would likely kill me.

But I follow him because I'm out of my goddamn mind, too. I miss the cove. Or perhaps I miss who I was when I was there last, but either way, I feel excited. For the first time in two months, it seems like I have something to look forward to.

The cool March wind whips around us as we walk. Though, my walk feels more like a crawl. It's just a constant battle for balance, and I fight hard to hide it from him, insisting he goes ahead of me. The struggle steals my attention from the scenery, but I'm hopeful that a long rest at the boulder will make up for it.

Still, the trees and damp earthy smell envelops me, sweeping me off my feet and away into a world where things are different. Things are better. My mind turns to a blissful zen-like state between the focus on where to step and the sanctuary-like nature surrounding me.

There's a stirring in my chest. A memory that feels warm, and my speed increases the closer we get. I need to get there. Desperately. Like *there* will fix me.

I remember to squint as I come around the final bend, shielding my eyes from the sun that's sitting in the mid-morning sky. And I want to cry happy tears for the first time in a long time.

I stand, heaving for breath but grateful for each cold inhale and exhale.

I made it.

Smiling, I look to Alex, who isn't on my wavelength, but I don't care. This is for me. I could barely walk to the bathroom two months ago, and now I'd just walked nearly three-quarters of a mile to my favorite place in the world.

"Help me up, please?" I don't care if Alex doesn't want to sit on the boulder and look at the water. I do.

He helps me, though, then takes a seat beside me. We sit shoulder to shoulder without talking for a long time. My elation fades the longer we sit, both of us thinking things the other probably can't even imagine. We sit with our silence until it feels like one word would be all it takes to shatter this forever. Was our special spell in this place finally over? Would he share anything with me today? Would I?

"You know, I never even told her I loved her. Never spoke the words." *What?*

I turn to look at him. His face is hard, like this hurts him to admit.

"Why?" I ask curiously.

He runs a hand down his beard before saying, "Everything about Jess is *hard*. Being with her was *hard*. She…uh, reminds me of someone. Someone I resent a lot." I can read between the lines and know he means Georgia. "And maybe I'm projecting, but I just needed her to say sorry about what happened with Damian. And she hasn't. Not once. And I guess, I felt like, if she couldn't say sorry, I couldn't say I love you." *Wow.*

"Have you told her this?" He shakes his head. It feels like this is the crux of all their issues. And I'm pissed he's telling me this. Why now? I want to shake my head and tell him to go tell her instead. *Go be with her already! Why is he doing this today? Why would he ruin this moment with this?!*

"Why do I need to tell someone to apologize? If they did something wrong, I want them to acknowledge that on their own. Otherwise, it doesn't mean anything." He has a point, but still, what is the point?

"The only person I've said 'I love you' to, aside from my family and my daughter, is you, Emma." My throat feels swollen suddenly. We used to throw "I love you" around some days like they were beads at Mardi Gras. At times, I even wondered if he was too cavalier with it.

It hasn't been like that since the accident, though.

"When I tell you I love you, Emma," he turns to look at me, reigniting a flame that's dwindled since I came home, "I mean it. I love who you are. I love who *we* are. I love that there's no one else in this entire world who knows me like you. And even when you didn't know me, you showed me a capacity for love I didn't know existed yet." He sneaks a hand down to grasp mine in his. He punctuates the statement with the half smile I used to adore.

My chest burns.

"Even when I was the one in the wrong, you apologized, Em." His eyes cloud with tears, and mine start to as well.

This is his fucked-up version of a pep talk. I know it. This is him trying at 110%. I give him a wan smile back. I meant what I said when I said I'd forgiven him. Whatever it was, it didn't matter. Not then. Not now.

The magic of this place bleeds into me, and I can remember the phenomenon surrounding us. It's that nothing else exists outside of this moment. It's just him and just me. The past dissipates, the future doesn't matter. It's just this existence that we're sharing together right here, right now.

"I don't know what the fuck I'm doing, Em. But I do know you're the only person on Earth worth trying for."

"Alex," I whisper his name, remembering why I love him. "I love you." He nods, then leans in to kiss me. His warm lips press against mine. A gloved finger tilts my chin up, and his warmth seeps into me.

"I missed you," I whisper across his lips when we take a break for air.

"I'm not done loving you, I promise." I nod back, and he kisses me once more. It's not the kind of kiss we used to share where it was a fight for dominance. This time, it's tender and filled with a caring, so deep I know he isn't done. And I'm not either.

"We should probably head back soon, before the B's send out a search party." The B's are Becks and Blanks. He stays close, his nose brushing against mine.

"Okay," he finally caves, climbing off the boulder first, then reaching up to lower me down. The second my feet hit the damp, pine needle path, I know I've overextended myself.

"Any chance I could get a piggyback ride?" He smiles, crouching down in front of me.

I hold on tight as he walks us home, feeling safe, cozy, and alive inside. When he sets me down on the mudroom bench, I let him know.

"That was exactly what I needed." Because I know him hearing *that* is what he needs, too.

"Need help dismantling the layers?" I shake my head, declining his offer. "I'm gonna go start some tea then," he pauses to kiss my forehead. "I'll be right back."

As he walks into the kitchen, I fling my scarf back off my neck, then throw my beanie onto a hook, clapping when it hits the pinboard like a backboard and sticks the landing.

Papers shift and fall, and I curse my own laziness.

Picking up the fallen papers off the floor, I sift quickly, my fingers catching on the corner of gilded handmade paper.

The invite.

June 14th. That's still months away...I could make a lot of progress by then if I work hard enough...

"Becks!" I shout, bringing her running into the mudroom. Screens and I still aren't the best of friends. I'll need to outsource help for this task.

"Are you okay?" she asks frantically.

"Yeah, I just need you to send an email for me, please?"

TWENTY-FOUR

ALEX

JUNE

I double-check the packages before signing. Looking at the delivery driver then back at the packages, I pass over his electronic signature pad.

"Em!" I yell over my shoulder into the house.

Following the sound of my voice, she and Delta round the corner.

"Wow!" she says excitedly.

"Were you expecting all this?" I ask.

She nods, smiling, then leans in for a quick kiss. *She's in a good mood.* I'm practically hard from her kiss and smile alone. *Not that I'll let myself do anything about it...* But I still can't help admiring my wife's ass as she stacks two boxes, one on top of the other, to carry inside.

"Stop, I'll do that for you." She shoots me a glare and I back off. I haven't gotten used to her more recovered state.

She's worked her ass off for two and a half months. 5:00 A.M. wake-ups for PT, hours of cognitive therapy, enough vegetables to feed a small country later, and she's clawed her way back to her old self. Mostly. She's gained an edge, but it's one that I appreciate, honestly.

"Oh my god, they're here!" Becks lets out a squeal I can hear from the entry. Picking up the last three boxes, I find them both in the dining room.

"What's all this for?" Emma isn't a package-a-day girl. She orders clothes when she needs them. And even then, most of the time, it's Blanks telling her she needs something and then him getting it for her.

"It's for next weekend," she turns around, letting the box flaps fall shut. She bites her lip nervously.

"What's next weekend?" I step forward, lifting a box flap, catching sight of garment bags. *With designer labels?* That's not really Emma's speed.

She clears her throat, and Becks steps out of the room.

"You might have noticed that I've been working really hard lately..." I nod because I'm not fucking blind. "I set a goal for myself." She steels her spine, putting her shoulders back. "I'd like to go to the wedding next weekend."

Whatever I was expecting, hoping for, maybe even just *thought*, whatever it was, it wasn't that.

Her face falls with mine. I shake my head. "I told you I don't want to go." Her brows draw together.

"Then why did you keep the invitation hanging up for so long?" There's that edge. That strength. Her brow furrows more, and she doesn't wait for a response. "*No*, you said you *probably wouldn't go*, not that you didn't want to." *That* she remembers?

I don't have a good answer. Not one to tell her.

I kept it hanging because it was the last thing I had of *her*.

I kept it hanging as a reminder that she made her choice, and I made mine.

I kept it hanging because I've been preoccupied with my wife's traumatic-fucking-brain-injury and hadn't thought to take it down.

I've never really been mad at Emma. Until now.

I drop the box on the floor, and it falls with a loud crash, sending Blanks into the dining room to come to Emma's rescue.

Emma gasps at my outburst.

"We're not fucking going." My words cut her. I can see it. Blanks sees it, and I immediately regret the harshness because I'm not mad *at her*. I'm mad at me.

"Don't speak to her in that tone," Blanks puts out a hand like I need restraining.

"Caleb, I'm fine," Emma barks back at him. "I don't need you to fight all my battles for me." He looks at her, and she looks at him. I watch her eyes drop, confusion taking over. That still happens occasionally. When she gets worked up. It's been far and few between lately, but I've pushed her.

I don't care. My word is final on this.

"Caleb, please leave," she commands him firmly. She's become a worthy opponent. She isn't going to cave easily.

When Blanks finally leaves, she starts in. "Tell me why you don't want to go. Tell me, Alex." It's like she *knows*, even though she doesn't. I could be convinced a hundred times a day she's gotten her memory back and has just been fucking with me all along.

"I don't need to defend my position. It's inappropriate for us to go."

"Why?" She's pushing because she's fuming, too. She crosses her arms, breathing hard until she suddenly turns contemplative.

"Oh..." she says, sounding crestfallen, "I thought you'd moved on. Sorry." She pushes a stack of boxes out of the way and heads for the mudroom.

Fuck.

Jess isn't something I think I'll ever really *move on* from. There are days when I think about her less. Maybe even days when I don't think about her at all. But still, it'll always be there.

Or, more accurately, there would always be a part of me missing, like she took one of my appendages with her. Sure, life goes on, and I can still function without the appendage, but I wasn't exactly whole either.

I would have to find Emma and talk to her eventually, but it wouldn't be right now. I need to cool down, and I need to stop wanting to throw my fist into a fucking wall first.

I walk out the front door, avoiding wherever the hell she went on the opposite side of the house, and open the garage to my bike. A couple of hours on the road to clear my head is just what I need. Hopefully.

———

Emma

.   .   .

My hands tremble as I struggle to put on the sweatshirt I found in the mudroom. I don't know whose it is, and I don't care. When my hand gets stuck in the armhole, I curse, "Damnit."

Telling Alex hadn't gone exactly as I thought it might.

I imagined him smiling, telling me how proud of me he was for setting this goal and getting there. I imagined after trying on all the stupid dresses for him, he would start seeing me as a fully functioning woman again. Not just his charge. Because aside from a few kisses here and there, he hasn't so much as touched me in a sexual way since before the accident. *Maybe hasn't even looked at me in a sexual way, either...*

I imagined a long flight, curled up against him, and leaving this place behind for a little bit. I imagined a lot of things, but none of them had come to fruition. Not even the scenes in my worst-case-scenario mental file.

There had been him being awkward as hell about it. There was the instance where I pictured him crying. I mean, I guess that's a little far-fetched, and it would have been fucking terrible, but I think today was worse.

Whether he says so or not, it means a lot that he can't do this. Sure, I knew he probably wouldn't jump for joy, but I supposed — I'd hoped — he would think of *me* first. Not *her*.

But I know that's not the case. I've known for some time.

My memory isn't back, per se, but I can remember these *feelings*. I can remember feeling gutted. I don't know when, where, or why, but even just thinking about it, I can feel it all over again. It's the turning-in-your-stomach, ice-in-your-veins feeling. It's the "I feel like I'm dying" feeling. It's the "I'll never be whole again" feeling.

He told me he wronged me, and I guess it doesn't take a

rocket scientist with three working brain cells, like me, to figure it out.

I'm panting when I make it to the cove. Feels like a record time. Five minutes max. I might have even run. Couldn't tell you, though; my mind was too clouded with pain and rage.

I shake my hands out to my sides, trying to get the trembling to cease, but, "Ugh!" I shout, standing in the small landing area in front of the boulder.

I inhale and exhale. I think of all the calming exercises I've learned in therapy. I try to think about happy thoughts. *Puppies and flowers and sunshine.* But the thoughts are overwhelming. I feel trapped. In this life. In this body. In these clothes. The June sun feels like it's baking me, burning me from the inside out.

Fuck this. I strip down to my underwear and climb the boulder.

Letting the cool mountain breeze blow my hair off my shoulders, I stretch my arms out and close my eyes.

Will the magic of this place still work without him?

I inhale the scent of the evergreens and the dry pine needles. I smell the water that starts to take on an earthier quality in the warm months. I breathe out the bad feelings. I breathe out the self-doubt and the jealousy. And then all I'm left with is...acceptance. I'm left with *this* moment. One I'll never get back again. I would hate to waste it being angry.

I raise my hands up, bringing the tips of my fingers together, and I dive.

The crystalline water is frigid, shocking my system, but instead of fighting against it, I push deeper into the water. I kick and strain till I can almost reach the sandy bottom. I reach out a hand to grab a fistful of it when I'm pulled back.

I panic, fighting against the intrusion. I thrash. I push. I kick.

When my head finally crests the water, I have to gasp for air after expending the energy to fight.

"What the hell?" I shout at Caleb, who looks like he's seen a ghost.

"I thought you were..."

"I was what??? Going for a fucking swim?" I shout.

He shakes his head. He actually looks scared.

"Oh god," I sigh and swim closer to him. "No, it's not like that at all. I was just hot, and I was trying to touch the bottom."

He nods like he's trying to calm down.

"I didn't mean to scare you." With both of us still treading, I lift a hand to wipe a bead of water away before it hits his eyes. Before I can pull away, though, he grabs my hand, surprising me. He holds it underwater, then threads our fingers together.

"Caleb?" My voice is slight.

"I've been waiting so long now, Em." My throat burns. Confusion lines my features. There's that feeling...

"I don't know what you mean?" His fingers tighten against mine.

"Try."

"Try what?" I ask back.

He looks stricken, and my gut turns, but my thighs also clamp together.

He starts pushing us to where we can both just barely touch the bottom while still keeping our heads above water. The gentle wake laps at my chin and the tops of his shoulders.

"I have to leave soon." *No.*

"You said you wouldn't leave," I argue back.

"Come with me." My stomach bottoms out. The trembling in my hands returns. "He still loves her, and if you could remember, you would know that. If you could remember—"

"I don't need to remember, okay?" My voice shakes, undercutting my biting tone. "Trust me, I feel enough as it is. I don't need to remember the details, too." I try to pull my hand back, but he won't let me.

"You do need to remember because the world doesn't revolve around Alexander-*fucking*-Palomino, Em. You're better than someone's runner-up, alright."

His eyes darken, boring into me. I want to wrap my legs around his torso. I want to hold onto him. Tight. I want whatever he's selling.

The feelings I have for him rage beneath the surface, just barely containing themselves. I'm not sure it's reciprocated, but then there's the hand entwined with mine, the other hand at my hip pulling me closer, starting to make me feel otherwise.

I shake my head even as my body willingly moves nearer. He'd taken off his shirt before jumping in the water, but his jeans are still on. So reaching my other hand out, I use his belt loop to reel myself in and close the distance. If I take one more step forward, I'll be forced to tether myself to him or tread to stay afloat.

With his hand gripping me tightly, he pulls me in the last few inches, and like instinct, my legs come up, wrapping around him. His hand comes under my ass, and my chest goes flush against his.

Both of our breathing turns labored as his hand roams beneath the water. Learning the curves that have started returning to my body.

He releases our entwined fingers so he can run one hand up my back and the other around my thighs.

With one hand on his shoulder to keep me vertical, I run my fingers across his chiseled chest. I've never been like *this* with him.

He's held me. I've curled up against him on the couch, but we've never touched each other before. Not like this. I haven't been touched like this since...

"Emma!" *Alex.* My legs quickly retract from Caleb, and I push him away, putting space between us.

I panicked, and now he's the one looking gutted.

"*I'm sorry,*" I mouth to him.

He doesn't say anything back, just pushing a hand through his wet hair. It's grown out, and the thick, dark locks come right back, dripping in his face. I want to take a step towards him.

I want...I want his hands back on me. But do I want that so badly just because Alex won't? It's wrong on every level. And I'm positive I just want what I can't have. *Or, more accurately, what won't have me.* My whole life has been wanting what isn't mine.

I turn away from him and walk towards the shore, further from Caleb, further from the fantasy, and back to reality.

Back into Alex's waiting arms. Arms that hug, and gently touch, but never more.

"We don't have to go." "We can go," we both say at the same time. I would laugh if I wasn't feeling like absolute shit.

Alex runs his hands up and down my arms, trying to

warm me. The mountain air is still chilly in the shade in June, and a shiver racks my nearly naked body.

"I don't know what I was thinking, sorry," I apologize to him.

He runs a thumb over my lips, pulling my face upwards, "We're going, okay?" *Sure, whatever,* is what I want to say because I don't care anymore. I would go stand in front of his ex, play nice, and pretend to be happy and a devoted wife, all the while knowing Alex would be wishing this was his wedding instead.

I have nothing to say, so I walk around him, squeezing the water out of my hair and grabbing my clothes. I walk back to the house, alone and cold. And I mentally prepare for my trip to hell.

TWENTY-FIVE

ALEX

Finding her at the cove was a no-brainer. It's her sanctuary.

What I didn't know was that he'd be there, too.

What I didn't *expect* was to find my wife wrapped around my best friend. It stirs something inside me. Jealousy, desire. *Her legs wrapped around me. My hand wrapped around his throat.*

But it's something else, too, something I've been ignorant of. *Maybe she loves him back.*

Blanks is still standing in the water, staring at me.

So, I stare right back. Like a fucking old western standoff, my jaw tenses, and his does, too.

"So much for that being the end of it." I slide my hands into my pockets and crack my neck like I'm ready for a fight.

"Fuck you, Alex," he says, then starts making his way out of the water and onto the shore.

Standing toe to toe, I want to throttle him. Blanks knows it, too.

"Do it," he dares me, his nostrils flaring with the taunt.

I want to beat him to a bloody pulp. Push his body out into the lake—

"You're a hypocritical son of a bitch, you know that?" He shoves me away and immediately starts pacing. He stops, though, his hand coming up, balling into a fist in frustration.

"You know what?" His fist falls, "I'm done with you." Some of the tension leaves his voice.

"What the fuck does that mean?"

"I mean, I'm *done* being whoever the fuck I am to you because it's abundantly clear that to you, I'm no one."

I scoff, "Sorry, I'm not congratulating you with a pat on the back for trying to fuck my wife."

"Yeah, well, if all I wanted was to fuck her, it would have happened a long, *long* time ago." He paces some more, stops, then paces again. "Also, calling her your wife is a privilege earned, and *you* don't deserve it."

"And you do?" That's fucking rich.

He starts pacing again, then finally decides. "You know what, yeah. I do fucking deserve it. And so does she." He puts his fingers to his temple. "Imagine that. Two people who actually deserve each other and could make each other happy. Imagine her husband not having to pray every fucking day that her memory doesn't come back. Imagine what her life would look like if she had a partner who cared about her even half as much as she did about them. And you know what? Every time I *do* imagine it — which is *a lot*, by the way — I *never* fucking imagine that happening with you."

"You think you can give her everything she wants then? Is

that right?" I ask, feeling the anger and jealousy fueling what I'm about to say.

"Yeah! I do it a hell of a lot better than you already." He thinks he's so much better than me. *Well, fuck him.*

"She wants a family." The words slip out of my mouth full of venom, harsh and offensive. Then they just hang there between us, festering. He stops his furious pacing and stares at me. Then suddenly, the words are like an anvil falling from the sky, crushing him. Decimating our 20-year friendship.

He sniffles, wiping at his nose.

"God, I can't believe I was ever friends with you." Not stopping for the shoes or the shirt he'd thrown off, he turns and walks away from me.

I shouldn't have said it.

———

Emma

After drying off and changing quickly, I head for the basement.

His room is empty, so I sit on his bed and wait. I bite my fingernails nervously, trying to prepare. Trying to think of what to say. All I can come up with is "sorry."

Sorry for putting him in that situation. Sorry for acting inappropriately. Sorry for being a shit person. But most of all, I'm sorry for pushing him away.

My eyes pinch closed at the fiery burn in my chest when I recall the memory. The look on his face. It was fucking horrific, and I'd done that to him.

"Angel, open your eyes." I don't. I keep them closed.

"I'm so sorry, Blanks."

He laughs, and my eyes open only to realize the insincerity of the sound.

"I'm Blanks now? Not Caleb?" His tone cuts me right back. I hadn't meant it like that. I mean, I know I chose not to call him Caleb on purpose. Maybe I've been leaning on him too much. I've been leading him on. This is my fault.

"You'll always be Caleb to me. It's just...I think I've messed everything up." He nods, then grabs a shirt and throws it on. Then he grabs a bag out of the closet and starts filling it.

I walk over to him at the dresser, placing a hand on his arm, and ask, "Please don't go?"

He looks at my hand but not at me. *Look at me, Caleb.*

"Can't stay, Em."

"Please?" I plead again. He ignores me. "Please, I can't do —" I struggle for the right way to say it. "I can't be...um." My fists clench and unclench, trying to fight through the mental haze. Trying to pick the right words to go with the right thought. "There's this feeling. I-it," I stutter, and my hands grow clammy. "I don't know where it's coming from, but it's telling me that I want you here."

"Jesus." He shakes his head, still without looking me in the eyes. I've hurt him. Terribly.

"Please. Stop packing, *please.*" My voice grows more urgent, more insistent.

He pauses, then says, "Beg." No trace of warmth in his voice. It's like it's from a man I don't even know.

"Isn't that what I'm doing?" I ask in exasperation. "I'm begging you to stay! Literally."

When he finally looks at me, I don't know whether to cry or start unbuckling his belt.

"On your knees." The intensity of his command nearly blows me over. My heart thunders in my chest. I stare at him, and he looks at me. "If you want me to stay, you'll get on your *fucking* knees, *Emmaline*." My brows pinch together. I want to, but I'm so confused.

What would it mean if I do?

"Why?" My question comes out whispered.

"Because I'm tired of being the one who's always on their knees for someone else." He looks away from me, and I feel it like a loss. *Please don't go.* My whole body shakes, and I want him with every fiber of my being. I want him to stay. I want him today. And tomorrow. And I can't pinpoint when that started happening, but it's so clear to me how it's suddenly a fact of life.

If he wants me to beg, if he wants me on my knees, I just need one thing from him.

"I can't get on my knees for you, not without you ask—"

"Knockity knock-knock," Becks chimes from the doorway, eyeing up both of us. "We have to leave for CT, girlfriend." She looks down at her smartwatch. "Like right now."

I look at Blanks, who's gone back to ignoring my existence.

As I go to open my mouth and tell her I'm going to miss today, Caleb beats me to it.

"You should go." Then, more so to Becks, he says, "She was just leaving anyways."

"I wasn't," I protest.

"You were." When I don't move, he says, "You should."

It's the most malice I've ever heard in his tone. It's chilling. It slices me in half it's so cutting.

The next swallow I make reminds me of the time I spent lying in a hospital bed, throat bone dry. Unable to move, unable to open my eyes. All I can remember is being in crippling pain. And this is exactly the same.

I cry as silently as possible as Becks drives me down the mountain to my appointment, then back up afterward. She pretends not to notice my sniffles so I can have some privacy. She's good like that.

I didn't see Alex before I left, and he isn't around when I get home, and I honestly consider that a blessing. I don't want him to see me like this. I don't want to know if he saw me with Blanks earlier or if he was just coming up on us.

I don't want to think about what it means either way. He saw us, and he doesn't care? Or he didn't see us, and I need to tell him?

The house is quiet. Too quiet. No one comes to check in on me after hearing the front door open, and I know what that means. *He's gone.*

"Becks, I'm gonna go for a walk before dinner, k?" She gives me a little nod, and I slip out the mudroom door.

With the sun up till nearly eight, I wouldn't need anything more than the light sweatshirt I'm already wearing. With absolutely no rush, I meander down to the cove. I don't feel any pull to the house anymore. In fact, it's the opposite. I don't want to be there at all. But I do feel a pull to *here.*

The pine needles underfoot have turned chestnut brown in the recent heat, and the nearly always damp forest floor has dried with it. The sun rays filter in between branches and vines, bathing everything in its path with a golden glow, and I sniffle the last of the tears as my nervous system settles in the new environment.

I let myself let it out, and I've officially run dry.

My cove is empty, aside from Blanks's t-shirt and shoes. Picking up the shirt, I climb the boulder, then sit crisscross to watch the water.

I pull the shirt up, inhaling his spicy, masculine scent. With it comes flickers of dreams I've had of him. Lately, it's been this recurring dream of him and me getting married. It looks just like my wedding to Alex, but it's Blanks standing in his place.

I've told no one about the dreams because *fuck*, they're embarrassing. But I still get a warm feeling when I think of them. Especially for what they are. *Dreams*.

It's nice to dream, but reality is where I live.

I once had a dream of falling in love, too. I never dreamt of falling in love with two men. Least of all at the same time. The irony.

I close my eyes and listen to the sound of a faraway motorboat and the rustling boughs on the trees.

This place is still my magical place, and it never steers me wrong or fails to ease the pain. The longer I sit, the more I can feel my mood shift. I can feel the acceptance take over.

This is the first place I've ever known sanctuary. Where I finally understood the meaning.

I don't doubt that there are other places that rival Spearhead's beauty, if not surpass it. But no other place would hold the same appeal. No other place would be the one that comforted me for the first time in my life, blanketed me in contentment. Made my heart sing with joy. Made me feel like I had started breathing for the first time.

E.L. STEVENS

Being in love with Alexander feels the same. There are others. There is better. But no one is him.

Blanks was a fantasy. Alex is reality, imperfect and messy. And I know I won't love another the same way I love him.

I hope the same is true for him. I know he loves me even though he still loves her.

Somehow, I doubt he loves me *more*. He just loves me different.

And that's okay.

Blanks was a distraction. He was the one I latched on to because, simply put, he'd been there. And he was my friend; I should have never let there be anything more.

But Alex...I couldn't imagine a time I wouldn't be in love with him. He would be my constant. Even when he hurts me. Even when he can't give all of himself to me. Even still, he'll always be the one who matches me in every way.

Eventually, the sting of Blanks's departure will fade just like it had once before. Alex and I will both apologize for the way everything happened today, and then we'll move forward. Because that's something he and I are good at.

With a sort of peaceful resignation, I head back towards the house.

When I open the mudroom door, I hear talking, and for a brief moment, I think he might have come back.

"She picked this out?" *Alex?* "Really?"

"Okay, fine. No, I did," Becks replies.

I find them in the dining room, sorting through the options for the wedding.

"Hey." They both look up at the sound of my voice. Alex gives me his signature half-smile.

298

"I think we've got things sorted into Emma-would-like-this and Emma-will-not piles," he says while pointing to two stacks on opposite ends of our dining room table.

I smile back. "That's great. I'll try them on tomorrow." My stomach twists at the thought of actually going, but I started this...

"I'm gonna head to bed. I'm exhausted." It's the truth.

"Emma," Alex stops me as I turn to leave.

"Yeah?"

He meets me in the hallway, leaving Becks in the dining room.

"About today..." he looks like he's thinking hard. My heart rate spikes with anxiety. "I'm sorry. I was an ass." I sort of laugh.

"I'm sorry, too." He pulls me in for a hug. One that feels extra tight and warm, albeit lacking the sort of sexual tension I'm craving. "We really don't need to go, Alex. I don't care about it."

"Sure, but we're going to." He runs a hand into my curls, tugging my head back to look up at him. "I want everyone to see how fucking beautiful my wife is." Then he brings his lips down to mine. It's slow and tender, and when I go to deepen it by swiping my tongue against his, he pulls away.

I give him a little frown, and I think he blushes. "Are we okay?" I ask quietly. He doesn't reply audibly. Instead, he gives me the slightest of head nods. I've never felt less okay with him.

"Okay..." I slip out of his arms to leave, but he tugs my hand before I'm completely free.

"I'm going to sleep upstairs tonight if that's okay? Just haven't been sleeping great, and I think it's the mattress."

Bullshit. He sleeps like a baby beside me. I know because I'm the one who hasn't been sleeping great. I'm also positive it's the same mattress in both rooms.

"I can sleep upstairs with you if you want?" I offer.

He declines. "No, I don't want to mess up your routine. I'll just see you in the morning, baby." I feel my chest cave in. Maybe Alex and I won't be moving forward after all.

TWENTY-SIX

ALEX

I don't make it upstairs and into our bed like I said I would. Instead, I drink the night away in my office. Occasionally, I slip into sleep vertically, but altogether, my shut-eye comes in under an hour. Easily.

Less easy has been the fight to stay out of her bedroom. I've walked up to the door no less than ten times. I opened it once but stopped myself from looking in. I'm struggling between wanting to make these last days the best we'll ever have or starting the shift as soon as possible.

I love Emma. That isn't the question. I don't think it ever has been. The question is whether we're right together. Or more so, whether I'm right for her. Whether I'm *good* for her. A question I debated all fucking night long, still arriving at the same answer as I had yesterday afternoon: I wasn't good *enough* for her.

Rubbing the lack of sleep out of my eyes, I take a swig of the rocks glass in front of me, draining it.

At the sound, Delta prances into the office carrying his bone. He sits in front of me, drops his bone, and starts whining.

"I'm gonna miss her too, bud," I sniff, pulling the stray water droplets back into my eye sockets, refusing myself the release.

I pat him on the head and stand, venturing to the kitchen to find Becks. She's always up by six, starting the coffee or reading the news on her phone.

"Morning," she says, more friendly than she's ever been to me.

"Morning," I say back, reaching for a mug myself.

She sets down her phone before starting. "I think Emma probably doesn't need me anymore. I think it's probably time to terminate my contract." I tense at her suggestion. That would mean her losing Blanks, Becks (her only friend), and us in a matter of a week.

"Would you be interested in staying on in a different capacity?" I ask, still facing the coffee machine.

"I'm a nurse, Mr. Palomino." She never could call me Alex.

"Emma might not need you physically..." I sigh. Luckily, she picks up.

"But emotionally?" I nod, turning around to face her.

"She needs someone to drive her still. Take her to the grocery store, that sort of thing."

"And that couldn't be you because...?" Becks angles an eyebrow at me.

"I might have to start traveling for work again." *Lie.*

She nods, renouncing the friendliness because she knows. "Twenty-five percent pay increase and I'll stay."

"Done." I leave the kitchen and head straight upstairs to pull out my tux for the cleaners. When I get to the bottom of the stairwell, I can hear she's up. Probably doing her yoga stretches.

The next week is going to be fucking torture, and I contemplate walking in and ending it right now.

No. She'll end it with me. In due time, she will. I can wait.

———

Emma

The fucking worst week of my life...and I'd spent *weeks* in a coma.

Alex had been...different. He'd been cordial, at most. Just polite enough. Just barely affectionate *enough* so as not to raise any real concerns. But we hadn't been alone in a room together once this week. We'd hardly talked at all. And at the last minute, he invited Becks to join us on our trip to D.C.

She was the one who held my hand during take-off. And landing.

Standing beside him at the hotel reception, I'm actually surprised to find out he didn't book separate rooms for him and me. So, I guess we will be in a room alone today.

He takes my tote bag off my shoulder and carries both our bags once Becks heads in the opposite direction towards her room.

Once we do drop our bags, I'm nervous about what comes next. Will he leave? Will we just sit there in silence and stare at the walls? Watch meaningless TV?

When he opens the door to our room, a suite actually, I know why he didn't need to get us separate rooms. We likely wouldn't cross paths once in the expansive space. My heart cracks instead of soaring over the beautiful rooms.

There would be no cozy hotel hangout sessions. He'll go to his corner, and I'll go to mine. Just like at home.

Even in all my pity, I can't help but audibly gasp at the view of the Washington Monument and rush towards the window in awe. D.C. is a different kind of pretty. It's not my cup of tea, but palatable in small doses. I can see that.

"This view is amazing. Come look!" I turn and gesture for him to come closer.

"You enjoy it, I've seen it before." *Right.*

I turn away from the view, taking a seat on the edge of one of the sofas in the living space. This was going to *kill me.* I stare at my Converse against the plush luxury rug and wonder what the hell I'm doing here. The question mark is back, hanging over my head, smothering me. I wonder what he's doing here *with me?*

Even a fool like me can see he's obviously not where he wants to be.

"If you're done, just tell me," I say with as much resolve as possible.

He runs a hand over his beard and sighs. He doesn't immediately deny it.

Suddenly, there's a weight pressing against my chest, and my hands grow clammy. *This is the end.*

Even though he looks like crap from not sleeping for a

week, and even though he looked like the unhappiest man alive, he was still going to look handsome in his tux. And I'm already hating that I won't get to see it.

I would miss seeing all the other versions of him because he's *done*. I know it.

"I'm done, Em." *Wow*. My eyes blow wide open in shock. "I wasn't planning to do this right now..." *Planning?* He had been planning.

I stand. "Wow. Okay," I say shakily, panicking.

There's just one thing I need to hear, and then I would leave. *Just one thing.*

"Okay, tell me you don't love me anymore. O-or tell me what I did wrong." He doesn't say anything back. "I just need a little bit of closure so I don't lose my mind, okay? Just give me an answer, an-and I'll go." Where will I go? Becks's room, maybe?

"Alex!" I startle him when he gives me nothing. The last thing I need is to end up a pathetic 35-year-old, still obsessing over why her first love dumped her. He just needs to give it to me straight.

"I don't love you anymore." I nearly bow over from the forceful pain his statement incurs. *Eviscerated*. His words *destroy* me. His words lay waste to my being. His words...are entirely void of any emotion. There's nothing there, no callousness, but also no kindness. There's no guilt and no shame.

Maybe he doesn't love me, but the Alex I know would at least feel bad about that.

He's lying to me. *Unbelievable*.

I scoff, then walk towards the door to grab my tote.

"You're a fucking liar, Alexander." My legs are wobbly, and my voice feels the same.

I shuffle through the bag for my phone as he towers over me, and I've never felt so small or insignificant in my entire life.

"Where are you going?" he asks, sounding nervous. Or maybe that's me hoping he doesn't sound completely indifferent. *His indifference would kill me.*

"For a walk," I huff. "And then, probably to an airport." I finally find my phone and slip my tote over my shoulder.

I don't even have a wedding ring to give back to him. Our ending feels anticlimactic that way. We aren't at home where him or me leaving would mean something. There are no suitcases to pack. They hadn't even been delivered to our room yet.

It's just...goodbye.

I stare at him, giving myself this one moment to see him. He's almost nothing like the man who stood with me in a cold parking lot in Las Vegas. He's changed for the better. And maybe that was my only purpose here. To get him to the other side.

Fine, universe. That's just great. Not my time. Got it.

I turn away from him, then reach for the doorknob and leave.

Walking towards the elevator, I commend myself for not crying. At least not yet. At least not in front of him. Sure, my hands might be shaking, my ears are ringing and hot, and I might be weak in the knees, but I'm still standing and not hyperventilating.

I press the down button and wait.

I don't even have time to process what's happening when

my back is slammed against the corridor wall. His hands are hard, and his mouth is on mine. It's feverish and manic and rough. He pulls at my hair and slams his body flush against mine, where I can feel him hard, straining for me.

"I didn't mean it," he says while fighting back tears. "I didn't mean any of it." He kisses my forehead and my cheeks. He kisses away the few stray tears that had run away after all.

I don't know whether to thank him, or punch him, or ask him to fuck me right now.

He takes the decision out of my hands, lifting me up and wrapping my legs around his waist. He walks us back to the room where the door is still propped open by the lock. He kicks it inwards, throws my tote on the ground, and walks us backward towards the primary bedroom.

He's panting by the time we're standing in front of the bed, his forehead pressing against mine.

"Say something," he commands me.

But I can't. I shake my head against his.

With one hand under my ass supporting me, his other hand comes up, clamping around the back of my neck as he lowers me slowly to the bed. He places me there almost reverently, never breaking eye contact. I feel our connection so intensely; it's a nearly tangible attachment to him, even though he's severed us emotionally.

"Please, baby," his voice quakes as he begs against my lips, kneeing my legs apart. He's making room to cage me in on the bed.

I say the first thing that comes to mind, "I hate you." And I mean it. And then he's kissing me hard again. He lifts my pelvis up, and his hard length runs back and forth across my covered slit.

My words say, *"I hate you,"* but my body says, *"I can't get enough."* My tongue seeks out his, and my hands are gripping tightly onto his biceps. There's hardly enough room to fit a single piece of paper between us.

I've wanted this for so long, but he's kept me at arm's length for months. And now *this*. I want to knee him in the balls, then lick his cock from root to tip. I want to bite him and draw blood, then have him fuck me so hard he draws blood, too.

My feelings are duplicitous as my body betrays my mind.

All it takes is one finger sliding down the front of my shirt, and every button pops off. I gasp as small, pearly white buttons litter the bed.

He breaks the lock on my mouth with a bite, then leans back to slide off my leggings and sneakers. He proceeds to lose his t-shirt and rip the belt out of his jeans, making me inhale sharply at the tight *whipping* sound. It has my walls clenching and yearning. My inner thighs already burn with anticipation.

Without him asking, I lose my shirt but leave the bra. It's a white, lacy demi-cup that barely contains my nipples. They strain hard against the fabric, and I watch his cock spring forward as he watches me.

And then his naked body is back over mine. Cupping a breast in one hand, he sucks the nipple straight through the lace. My back arches, and I claw to get closer to him, bringing his bare cock down between my legs.

He's warm and hard, and the more he pulls on my nipples with his teeth, the harder I seek out friction. My cunt lubricates his dick with each grinding motion, back and forth, bringing us both pleasure, but never enough. *It's not enough.*

Finally, his hand releases my breast and clamps around my throat, holding me as he positions himself over me. And then, he's pushing in, inch by torturously slow inch. I moan and writhe, but I don't say a word.

Once he's filled me all the way to the hilt, he releases his hold on my neck, instead cradling my head. He presses down on me gently, and then, with all the care in the world, he thrusts into me. I dig my feet into the bed, hoping it will drive him harder, but it doesn't.

He plants soft kisses across my collarbone, he sucks gently at my lip, he caresses the tops of my nipples through the lace, but he doesn't do a single thing *hard*.

It's infuriating that all *that* led to this. It's not that it isn't good. It's fucking incredible. At least it would have been if it had happened a week ago. Now, it's heartbreaking. *Now*, I'm just angry, and here he is, still treating me like an invalid when he has his dick inside me.

"Harder," I finally bite out. My first words to him since, *"I hate you."* He shakes his head while running his tongue up my neck and behind my ear. "Stop fucking me like I'm fragile, Alexander. I'm not delicate." I take his face between both of my hands so that he has no choice but to look at me.

"No, baby," he leans forward to kiss me. "Not delicate, *rare*." *Well fuck*. I don't need him to make me love him more.

"I hate you," I say it again, meaning it more this time. Still trying to get him to be rough with me, but it doesn't motivate him. If anything, it backfires, and he slows down considerably.

He thrusts his hips forward in a slow, fluid motion, pushing against me but holding me close. His thumb massages my neck while his other hand moves down to my hip, settling in the spot between my hip bone and my abdomen. It's the perfect indentation for his thumb to fit while his fingers wrap around my backside.

As one thumb pushes back and forth against my neck, he looks down, watching as he enters me, looking at his other hand holding me.

"This is my favorite spot on your whole body, you know that?" I shake my head because I didn't think Alex had a favorite spot on my body. "It's a perfect fit." He watches his cock sliding into my body, "Just like this." Why is he being like this? *Why now?*

"Just fuck me, Alex. Please." He shakes his head, and a tear rolls out of the corner of my eye.

"Let me make love to you," he whispers against my cheek. I want to push him off of me even though I would just beg him to come back.

"But you don't love me anymore, so just fuck me. Use me. You don't have to make this last on my account." I'm lying through my goddamn teeth. I never want this to end. Any of it. But *fuck.*

Both hands are off me in an instant. Then they're flying up, pinning my wrists above my head. He stops thrusting and holds me there. But I'm not going to be submissive to him. I would get my pleasure with or without him.

As he holds still, I move my hips, planting my feet onto the bed for better leverage. I give him a sick sort of smile because I don't want to buy into this version of Alex. I can't.

"I didn't mean it, Emma. I-I," he stutters, and I stop moving, staring at him. His breathing shudders before he says, "I love *you* above all others. And *that* I fucking mean." My chest seizes. *Above* her? *More* than her?

I don't believe him, but I can pretend. Maybe he thinks he's giving me mercy by telling me that, but it's the opposite.

"You're just making it harder, you know that, right?" He nods.

"Just give me tonight, okay? Just one more night," he asks. I actually choke on a sob and catch it with a crude laugh because I would give him every night if he asked.

But he isn't asking. So, one more night it is.

I nod even though I roll my eyes, and he starts kissing my tears away.

"I'm sorry," he whispers. I'm sorry, too, but I'm done telling him that. Done being the fool who apologizes for someone hurting me, who apologizes for the sins of someone else.

When he finally releases my wrists, I wrap my arms around him, running my fingers up his neck and into the back of his hair. *One night.* That's all I'd get. So, I let my hands memorize the feel. I let my eyes memorize the color. *The color of caramel*, I decide. It's the color of the sugar and butter right before it hardens.

I let my hands come down to his short, trimmed beard, and I run my fingertips against it, vowing to remember the feel of the short bristles.

I understand now. I get it. He isn't making love to me; he's trying to commit me to memory.

He begins moving against me again. And my hands don't stop. They roam over the "v" between his brows, where they always come together when he's deep in thought.

Then there's the freckle high on his right cheek.

The scar on his chin, where his beard grows, slightly hindered.

The length of his throat and the rounded nature of his Adam's apple.

I take it all. I hoard it, praying these will be memories that keep. That I can freeze this moment of him and me so when I look back, the solid ice won't slip through my fingers like water.

I don't know if I still think he's a good man, but he's beautiful. And he's mine. At least he had been. At least he would be for one more night.

TWENTY-SEVEN

ALEX

Could you fit enough love to last a lifetime into one night?

No. But I'm going to try.

She gave me an out. Ahead of schedule, no less. But it wouldn't stick, not like that. And now, we were getting one last night. To pretend. To savor the end. To try and pack as much good into the last few hours as possible.

"I love you more than *anything*," I whisper to her as I grind down. I watch the sadness leak from her eyes at the words. The tears run, turning her blonde hair dark at her temples.

I want to hear her say it. One more time. One *last* time. *Please, baby.*

She ignores my silent plea, instead keeping her hands in constant motion. She's strategically surveying me.

I'm telling her the truth, knowing she won't believe it. Knowing she's taking this all with a grain of salt, but still needing to say it. Needing to speak it for all the times I won't be able to in the future.

I'll tell her how perfect she is. How perfect we fit. I'll praise and worship every last inch of her body. Her amazing and perfect body that's gone through so much at the hands of me.

I won't ask her to return the favor even if I'm already being selfish. Blanks was right that I'm a selfish son of a bitch. I know I'm a fucking monster, but I won't force her to do something she doesn't want to. Doesn't *really* want to.

"Perfect, baby." I'm already missing her. I missed her all week. I hadn't slept, I drank every night, and I lied straight to her face day in and day out. It had been the worst week of my entire fucking life.

All I want is to just be present in this moment, but my mind keeps drifting. And I want to ask questions. Where would she go? Does she want to go back to California? She could have the house. She could empty our bank accounts. Fuck, she could take our dog, though that would probably kill me.

I don't care what she does, but I wanted to know. Not knowing how she would be was already killing me, and she was still with me. Physically, she's here, but I feel the vacancy. I feel her holding back. For once, she isn't giving. She's done, and that's good. I don't want her giving so freely to anyone else in the future.

Fuck. Her with *someone else.*

I pinch my eyes closed when the burn of oncoming tears is too much to bear. She's too busy tracing the scar on my abdomen from an exit wound to notice. It's one of those scars that's always just a little sensitive. It never healed right, so I shudder when she passes across it one last time.

"No one will ever see the scars you left on me..." she says quietly, "but they'll be there." I close my eyes again.

Like I said, I'm a fucking monster.

I can't do this. I can't do this slow-motion car crash again. I slam my mouth down on top of hers. If she wants hard, I'll fucking give it to her. If she wants me to fuck her like all the rest, I will. And because she's fucking perfect, she'll probably love it.

When I ease off for air, I tell her, "Get up." Her eyes widen at the complete 180 shift in my tone. But she does as she's told, sliding out from underneath me to stand beside the bed. I follow behind, pulling her in tight, my front to her back. "Now bend over."

"What if I don't want to?" Her bratty tone has me wanting to take her over my knees instead of impaling her from behind.

I wrap a hand around her neck and ask, "Are you mine?" I want to pretend she is.

With far less certainty, she replies, "Y-yes." It almost sounds like a question at the end.

"Then bend the fuck over."

This time, she complies, placing her elbows down on the mattress. My fingers trace her back, down into the swell of her spine, then out to her hips, where my hands settle in their spot. *My* spot.

I'm the only one who's ever had her like this, and as far as I'm concerned, every spot is mine. That isn't bound to last, but I feel pretty fucking sure *this* is always going to be mine.

No one else's hands would mold around her this way. No one else would fit together this perfectly.

I slam into her from behind, feeling her tight cunt sheath me. It fucking pulls me in. It practically fucking vibrates with the word, *mine*.

I think it over and over in my head. *Mine. Mine. Mine.*

I watch with each thrust as her hands clutch onto the sheets. I look at her left hand, knowing it was wrong that I hadn't given her wedding ring back, and hating myself for it all over again.

Mine. Mine. Mine. It runs through my mind again, like if I think it enough times, it will somehow come true. And then another thought zips back and forth. *Ours. Ours. Ours.* Another hopeless manifestation.

Our family. Our life. Our child. I kiss the thoughts good-bye, banishing them.

I slide out of her slowly and leave her standing with her ass in the air. She watches me walk to my duffle and pull out a condom before coming back to finish her off. If I didn't know better, I would think she almost looks disappointed.

"Can't be too careful, can you?" she whispers bitterly into the empty bed. I don't want to wear a fucking condom. It's the opposite. I want to fuck her so full of my cum, she leaks me for days. I want to finger it back in place with a prayer while I lick her into another orgasm. I want to watch her grow and know that we did that together. We are *going* to do it together. I would look at her and know we both wanted this.

A fucking fantasy.

I'm putting on a fucking condom to protect her from that future. A future shackled to a monster who will hurt her over and over again. I've already been reckless and selfish by fucking her bare, but I had to know the feeling. I need to know what I'll be missing. What *isn't* mine.

When I slide back in, I wrap my body around hers, bending at the waist so I can massage her clit.

"Come apart, baby."

I plant one hand down on the mattress, and she wraps her hand around my wrist as she pushes back against me with a moan. The second my finger lands on her hood, the sound is practically ripped out of her throat.

"Alexander!" she screams as I rut against her from behind.

"Emma," I whisper back into her ear. "Don't stop," I plead, her walls fluttering around me, feeling her tense. I can almost sense her tears that are half ecstasy, half misery.

"Keep coming, baby." I massage and stroke her from one orgasm into the next as my own builds to the point of no return.

"I love you, baby," I say one *final* time.

As my fingers begin to ease, she places a hand over mine and pushes, helping coax a third orgasm for her as the lightning strikes from within me, my finish nearly bringing me to my knees.

That's what this was for me. Lightning. *It never strikes in the same place twice.*

This feeling with her is like nothing before and will likely best anything after.

This was my *once*. If I thought I had it before, I was wrong. It was this. No earthly words could ever describe how I feel towards her, how I feel at this moment.

They simply didn't exist.

A sound somewhere between a moan and grunt, a feral growl slips from me as my final punishing thrusts work her. In turn, her pussy pulls from me every ounce of cum I have. She's still pushing my fingers down when she comes again, her pulsing turning to a lulling constant.

"Alex..." she whispers, the sound a mixture of exhaustion, bliss, and pain.

At this moment, I feel with absolute clarity that this was where I was meant to be. That *this* is where I belong. Where I have always belonged.

It's not hard when it's right.

She was my home, but more than that, she was my shelter. She was my best friend and the only person I trusted wholly.

Emma,

Wherever you are, is where I'd want to be.

Wherever you go, I'd happily follow.

Whatever you do, I'd be right behind you.

I sigh.

Never done.

———

Emma

When he stopped to get a condom, that's when I knew. As stupid as it sounds, it's the truth. My heart sank with realization. *He couldn't risk being stuck with me.*

And yet, once he was done fucking me like I was the other half of his soul, he had no qualms about keeping me in his bed all night. It was a wordless command, just a hand holding my hip tightly all night.

I always thought when *my* person was fucking me, claiming me, it would be violent, rough. Desperate. It would be a clawing and clamoring to consume the other. Maybe, in the end, it was a little.

But what *had* happened was him fucking me like I was *truly* the other half. He had been tender, like I was the *better* half of his whole, and he wanted to take care. He wanted to treat me better than he would treat himself. He gave me everything he thought he'd never be.

Silly, really, because he was more. So much more, and I saw it the first time I laid eyes on him, from the very first moment.

Our story wasn't one of love at first sight. Though maybe it was a little for me.

No, it was recognition at first sight.

I saw him. And he saw me. Not as I was. Not as some diner waitress, but as *me*. He saw Emmaline with the gentle soul, and she saw Alexander, the warrior. The good man. It was yin and yang finding each other after years of loneliness and despair.

And so our lives merged in the same fashion. It wasn't violent and fast. It was a melding. A slow transition to be reacquainted with the other half of you. There was a push and pull to our story, highs and lows, ins and outs, but I always thought it was us in the end.

But it wasn't.

He held my body tight against his until sunrise, when I felt our spell break.

We were this tangible living thing one moment, and then it was all gone in the next. Nothing changed aside from time moving forward. But for Alex, we passed some invisible threshold, and he released me. Literally and figuratively.

I could feel his body still near mine. He was still lying on the bed beside me, even though he was no longer curled around me. Somehow, I knew he was staring at the ceiling.

It took everything in me not to roll over and face him. To not face this head-on.

But I was still holding on. To him. To the idea of us. To the hope that I'm his tomorrow, and he's mine. And if I rolled over, I knew definitively those dreams would die.

So I held tight to the delusion and continued lying on my side, not looking at him, until the mattress shifted under his weight as he got up.

He asked me if I would still go with him to the wedding... and apparently, I don't know how to say no. Because am I going to hang on to this for as long as possible? *Yes.* Am I pathetic? *Also yes.* My age-old curse of not knowing when to leave was back with a vengeance.

I want to believe this is just a small lapse in judgment. I want to be absolutely delusional and hope beyond hope this whole wedding has just put him under undue stress.

But he pulled away from me. Ever since the accident, he's been someone else. Maybe because I'm someone else, too, but whatever the reason, he stepped back. And then took another small step, and then another, until we were worlds apart. Again.

Which is how we landed in this massive hotel suite, on

opposite ends, getting ready for a wedding reception neither of us even want to go to.

Impossibly, I'm done getting ready first. After double-checking the living space and finding it vacant, I step back into my room to do one last once-over. I don't want to risk not being absolutely perfect. Not for him, but for *her*.

I'm not dressed for Alex tonight. No, I'm dressed for her. The dress I chose says youth and sex, yet timeless and demure. I wanted a dress that left everything and *nothing* to the imagination. I wanted a dress she would *know*.

I still remember my closet filled with her expensive clothes. Clothes I never had, but I knew. After all, I am the daughter of Darla Strait. She might be white trash, but she still had her Oscar De La Renta gown she'd worn to the Opry. She kept her first pair of Prada heels, remnants of the good ol' days. I know what all the labels are and what they mean, but before now, I've never cared.

Never had a reason to care.

My silk Saint Laurent gown clings to me everywhere it should, then hangs perfectly like a sensual guessing game. I slip on the Amina Muaddi "glass slippers" and grab my vintage beaded clutch, the same one I wore on my wedding day. It feels like an iconic thing to do.

Perhaps I wasn't a queen in real life. I wasn't the one turning heads, but I would today.

My hair falls voluminously down my partially bare back, and my makeup — which I practiced no less than ten times — came out perfect. If my dress was white or ivory, people might have mistaken me for the bride. And yes, that's on purpose.

I'm not petty by nature. Normally. But today, I feel like

someone different. Less naive, more cynical. The glass is definitely half empty even as I stand in this suite, even in my $3500 gown.

With a last glance in the mirror, I fluff my hair and leave my room to wait for him. The living space is empty, though. Still.

Swallowing past the discomfort, I set my clutch on the entry credenza and pour myself something from a decanter of brown, hoping for the best.

And then I stand there, waiting for my date because I can't sit. Can't risk the wrinkles.

Instead, I stare at the monument. I watch traffic, both pedestrians and cars. I imagine a world where I'm someone else. I imagine a world where I wear a ring on my hand, and a man on my arm who adores me.

A chill runs along my spine.

When I turn away from the window, he's there.

In his tuxedo. Looking like someone I don't know. He shaved his beard. He's cut his hair short. He looks like someone I saw walking on the street half an hour earlier. I don't recognize him. And it feels like that's the point.

I hate him.

I wait, hopeful. Then, when the lack of communication becomes suffocating, I set my glass down on a side table and check the time.

We still have five minutes or so.

And then, finally, he approaches me slowly, almost methodically. Even his gait seems different. Or maybe I've just never seen him move in tuxedo pants and dress shoes before. I feel like I'm meeting a stranger.

He embraces me, though a smile never broaches his face,

and I almost push him away so he doesn't crumple the gown. But I'm a little more desperate than I am vain, and I accept it.

"You've rendered me speechless, Em." The pain in my throat roars; it burns.

"Same," I reply quietly, matching his volume.

The hug — if you could call it that — feels foreign...and wrong. There's no pressure behind his touch. No warmth. His cheek is smooth, and nothing bristles as he pulls away. Nothing catches, nothing lingers. He smells like he's wearing different cologne, too.

I want to ask questions, but I don't think I can handle the answers.

Is this who Alex really is? I wondered who he was when he wasn't dying. I craved to know that man, but maybe that man doesn't exist. It's just varying levels of discontent, and this one, standing in front of me, seems the worst of them all.

When he stands back, he drags his gaze from my head to my toes but doesn't say anything. No compliment, no sentiments.

I shake my head, regretting not drinking more glasses of brown.

Quickly grabbing my clutch, I open the hotel door, then hold it for him, like a test. He doesn't hesitate to exit, leaving me standing in the doorway as he walks to the elevator.

I don't know if it's real or pretend, but I won't let him make me look stupid tonight. *No.* I will be so fucking perfect, I will act so fucking happy. I will be utterly aloof so that no matter what, no one can feel bad for me after tonight.

Even if tomorrow morning Alex tells them all he dumped me, that's fine. As long as it doesn't happen in front of *her*. As long as she sees us together and doing fine, that's all I want.

The ride in the town car from our hotel to the restaurant lasts all of four minutes. Neither one of us talks. When we arrive, our chauffeur holds the door for me, saving Alex from his faux neglect.

I plaster on a genuine-looking smile in case other guests happen to see. Then, I extend a hand to him instead of waiting for him to offer, and he actually looks at my hand before taking it.

He was debating.

As we walk the few short steps to the restaurant, I whisper to him, "Whatever this is, just please don't make a fool of me. I'll never forgive you." He doesn't so much as nod, but he holds the door and gestures for me to enter first.

We follow a long corridor to a private dining room, where we're greeted with welcome cocktails and a mostly full room. The crowd amassed is small but loud. The ages range from toddler to 80. Multiple generations present. I only know three people here aside from Alex and CT, whom I don't count because they don't talk. Either of them.

Liam, Brit, and Elodie are the only people I know, and I'm glad about that. I can be someone else to the rest of them. Not the pitiful girl who spent last Christmas in a coma.

Slipping a hand into the crook of Alex's arm, I gesture for him to lead. These are his people, after all.

We make a quick stop to say hi to his nieces first. Elodie wraps me up in a warm hug, and miraculously, I stave off the tears. She introduces me to her sister, Caroline, who looks like a carbon copy of her mom. For a few minutes, Alex's mask drops. He jokes with them. He tousles their hair. He teases them, but as soon as we turn away, he reverts back to stoicism.

We greet Liam and Brit, and while they all talk, I take CT for a lap around the room. We stop at the bar, where he gets an orange slice. We stop to look at the paintings on the walls, where I point out birds and tell him their names. Admittedly, I make up most of them.

It quickly becomes the highlight of my night. I don't even care when he drools down my dress. I just grab a napkin and laugh as I clean us both.

When I toss the napkin in the trash, I think I catch Alex watching us. I *think* I see him with a look that's shot through the heart. But it could have just been the light distorting my vision, maybe even just *delusion* distorting my vision. Because in all my dreams, this would have been the life for us.

A blonde baby on my hip as my husband watched us adoringly.

A delusion indeed.

When I deposit CT back with his parents, I plant my hand back on Alex, making it clear that abandoning me is not the business tonight.

Next, we stop to talk to an older gentleman who's come alone.

"Allan," he introduces himself. He seems nice. Maybe even reminds me of Constantine, and I almost turn weepy that I would be losing him, too.

"Emma," I reply, shaking his hand when it becomes obvious Alex can't be counted on to do the courteous thing. "Alex's wife." I dig the stake in my own heart just a little bit deeper.

"I didn't know you got married!" Allan says with astonishment, giving Alex a pat on the back. "How long?"

"18 months," we both say in unison, and I give him an adoring smile. He continues looking at Allan.

"And how do you two know each other?" I ask.

"Allan is Damian's dad." He gestures to the older man. "We've known each other a long time now, probably 20 years?" he asks. "Does that sound right?"

The older man laughs. "I don't know if it sounds *right*. I think it makes me sound old as hell," he chuckles, and I smile.

"Where are you seated tonight?" I motion towards the table that has place cards already set out. He points to the end of the table where we are. However, we are at the *very* end. He's closer to the middle.

The private dining room has been set up with one long dining table for everyone to sit together. As far as weddings go, I think it seems small, but when it's your second or third marriage, perhaps the number of guests doesn't matter. Quality over quantity, I suppose.

The number of seats set out might be small, but there's not a single detail missed or underwhelming. The flowers are gorgeous, the place settings are immaculate, and the welcome cocktails are delicious, though not nearly strong enough. The whole setting and ambiance ooze class.

Alex, with his short hair and smooth, hard jaw bones, fits here. In his tux, hair done, he could have been the groom. Easily.

I thought he looked good on our wedding day, but I hadn't a clue he could look like this at the time. Even with the dark purple creases under his eyes. Even with the deep V creasing his forehead. It doesn't matter. He's beautiful. Painfully so.

I'm too busy watching him to notice the bride and groom

have arrived, their entrance ushering in a change. The volume of the room grows as everyone turns to face the guests of honor straight from the chapel. The lights come down slightly, and I watch as Alex becomes transfixed.

I've never seen him around her before. I've never witnessed the way he's wholly enrapt by her. The entire room looks on and even cheers for the newlyweds. And yet I can't help but watch him, as he watches her. The sum of our relationship boiled down to that one simple sentence.

He's devout in his tracking of her. He clocks her with precision, taking in her flowing silk dress, one that's not unlike mine. However, her long dark hair and olive skin are absolutely *not* like mine.

Once again, he is a man possessed. And once again, not by me.

No, I would not be the queen tonight. It was not my time. Would likely never be my time.

We watch as she slips into the room, seeming to glide beside her husband. She practically floats on air. A damn goddess amongst mortals.

I'm embarrassed how our dresses practically mirror one another. Because while I thought my dress looked amazing on me, it only lasted until I saw what it looked like on *her*. The way it dips down low on her back *and* her front. The way her hips hold the fabric on either side. I can't help but imagine him and her. Together. A fucking American dream.

I'm just a cheap Barbie you get at a dollar store — off-brand, poorly built, and disposable. I'm the pig in lipstick. The trailer park trash in a couture gown.

She's like fine china and your grandma's best crystal that

made it through the war. She's the Cartier jewels, a champagne brunch, an enchantress who never ages.

I feel my spine turn to steel as I release my hold on Alex because it's clear now that he's released me.

I take a small step away from him. I won't be fooling anyone into thinking that we're happy. It's obvious he isn't.

Realizing he isn't going to stop, I head towards the bar, pretending to take my time choosing a drink.

To fill the time, I ask the bartender stupid questions.

"What's Lillet's taste profile?" "How many ounces are in a martini glass?" "Do you have ginger ale?"

When an older woman stands beside me, I gesture for her to order first. "Can't decide what I want," I say to her with a smile.

She gives me a polite smile back and orders. While her drink is being made, she turns to face me and then extends a hand.

"I'm May." I swallow, then shake her hand.

"Emma. Palomino," I tack on at the end.

"Ahh, yes," she says, knowing. "I'm the mother of the bride." I want to curl up into a ball and die.

"Then, congratulations. They make a beautiful couple." May nods demurely while silently assessing me. Likely holding me up beside her daughter and deciding I couldn't possibly hold a flame to her. "What did you order?" I try my best to divert the conversation.

"A French 75." I recheck the cocktail list, thinking I might follow suit. "You'll want something stronger, dear." *Yes.* She's right.

"I think you're right," I mumble under my breath, then

give her a tight smile. My fingers tremble as I let my hands fall down to my side.

The bartender hands May her coupe glass, but as she turns to leave, she says, quietly, "Jealousy is for those with no value of self. You don't strike me as someone who should be lacking."

It's a compliment and a warning. She walks away, and I order a double Johnny Walker Blue, neat.

TWENTY-EIGHT

ALEX

I stare at Jess as she walks into the Cabinet Room, and I despise her. I see her for what I always thought she was. *Not mine.*

For the first time, though, I don't want her to be.

I keep my eyes trained on her, like tracking a target, and fight against the urge to lace my fingers between Emma's. To look her in the eyes and let her know that another woman doesn't hold any appeal to me. I want to reassure her, however pointless it is now.

While I stare at Jess, I can feel Em stare at me.

I feel her hand slip out from inside the crook of my arm. Her perfume wafts towards me as she steps backward, putting space between us, then walks away.

The finality of her absence shatters me.

Goodbye, darling.

When the newlyweds begin making their way around the room, I move in the same direction, staying out of sight mostly, only talking to someone once Damian and Jess have finished and are already moving on.

Once a near complete loop has been made, I find Emma standing beside her seat at the very end of the table. A rocks glass in hand and a sedentary smile that says nothing.

When I feel the hand on my back, I have to close my eyes like I can block out what's about to happen.

I turn to face the bride and groom and hate it. I hate everything about it.

"Hey, man," Damian says. I don't reply. Staying mute feels safer because under no fucking circumstance do I want to say, *"Hey, man,"* back. I don't want to talk about the weather or pretend like someday we might be actual friends again. I don't want to pretend to still be in love with his wife either. But here we are.

Emma, being perfect as always, saves me, moving forward to my side.

Jess extends a hand to her first, "Jess. Nice to finally meet you." Jess plasters on a fake smile, and Emma does the same.

Emma's voice conveys only genuine sentiment, though, when she says, "Hi, Jess! I'm Emma. Thank you for inviting us. You're a beautiful bride." Emma is far more gracious and kind than Jess deserves. And I love her more for it.

"We've gotta catch up," Damian says, and I nod solemnly because no-fucking-thank you.

Jess picks up the vibes and offers all of us mercy. "I think if we sit down, they'll probably start serving the food." To Damian only, she asks, "Are you hungry?"

Damian frowns first, before giving in. "Yup, let's, uh, circle back in a little bit, yeah?" I don't know who the fuck he means to ask that question to, but sure. I nod.

I watch them walk away to the two seats at the center of the table, where they whisper in each other's ears and share a laugh. I want to believe Jess and him deserve this, but it's a struggle. And then...I find myself thinking, *I don't love her anymore.*

I don't love the way she holds herself. I don't love the way she looks, or sounds, or smells. I don't think I can think of one thing I love about her.

I try to recall why I loved her in the first place. I fell in love with her without reason. It was miraculous how it even happened. She had just been there. And she hadn't stopped until she found someone better. Her insistent presence, in the absence of Amy and Tally, was the only thing that tied her to me.

But Emma, I love with a purpose for who she is and what she does. I love her strength and poise. I love that she's ultimately the best person I know. The only person I've ever let really know me. The real me.

This wasn't the end I pictured for Emma and me. No, I pictured headstones beside one another after a long, full life of building our family. Adventures with our children and grandkids lining the halls of our home in the form of pictures. And I hadn't told her any of this.

For as much time as we had together, she probably spent most of our days thinking I didn't want her, love her, need her. But I do.

"Have you been here before?" she asks me while we sit, waiting for the food to be served.

"Yes," I say solemnly. This is where it all started. Or, more accurately, where it all ended. When I don't expand, she stares straight ahead at Jamie, who smiles sympathetically at her. But she doesn't strike up a conversation with him, or try again with me.

I go back to playing my role, focusing on Jess. Ignoring Em. Wishing time would move a lot fucking faster.

Food is eventually served. And cleared.

Champagne is poured.

A large cake is rolled out.

My sister clinks a glass with a fork, and everyone raises a champagne flute.

I'm not really listening until she says, *"BUT!* I'd be remiss to not also thank my brother, Alex. For introducing the two of you. So, to Alex, too!" *The fuck Brit?*

Most of the table turns to look at me when I crack my champagne flute between my fist, sending moisture onto my and Emma's laps, her silk dress, likely ruined. I stare down at where the wine and broken glass have pooled in her lap, and I want to clean it up, but Em stares at my hand with wide eyes.

"Baby," she whispers, "you're bleeding." She's never really called me that before. It's endearing. I want her to say it again. I want to lean over and kiss her, but then she would have broken glass, wine, and blood to clean up, too.

Realizing everyone is still watching me, I say, "Sorry." Then scoot my chair back and leave without looking back.

I can hear the room devolve into a celebratory cheer as I leave, and that feels very apt.

In the restroom, I clean the wound. It's shallow enough it doesn't even need a bandage if I just apply pressure and wait.

So I wait, thinking maybe I should just ride this whole thing out here, in the bathroom.

When I stare at the man in the mirror, I hate him. "Fuck," my raspy voice echoes.

I check the wound and find the bleeding has slowed, and then I stand there a little bit longer, buying some time. I can't let the night go to waste, though. I have to get back out there and wait for my opening, for the right time.

As I open the men's restroom door, the women's door is easing closed. I smell her perfume, I see a glimpse of a silky ivory train, and I know, this is it. A gift from the universe. Divine timing.

With any luck, Emma will come looking for me.

I lean against the wood-paneled wall and wait. The hall is dark but not pitch black, and it's damn near fucking perfect.

My heartbeat races with anticipation. With dread. The adrenaline runs rampant in my bloodstream as she opens the door to face me. She almost seems scared, and I get a sick thrill out of that.

She was the one who came to me, fucking up my whole world. She's the reason Emma lost six weeks of her life. More, actually, and I feel like justice is due.

"Excuse me," she says brusquely as if she could just walk past me.

"It was supposed to be us, Jess." *Lie.* It would never be our time.

I sense the presence of others, and I hope it's who I want to see this.

Jess laughs harshly, insecurely, and says, "No, thank you to whatever *this* is. You have a beautiful wife waiting for you.

Go home, Alex." I know *my wife* is here now; I can feel it for sure.

So instead of waiting, I say, "Okay," then move in, pushing my mouth to Jess's. Feeling sick to my stomach the second we touch. Hating this. Hating her. Wishing she would be punished for fucking me and ruining Emma's life.

The worst part is, she fucking returns the kiss. Her tongue slides into my mouth, and I want to push her away.

Then Damian is there pulling me back. *Perfect.*

He starts yelling, and I hope to god it's at her, but I'm not paying them any attention. Out of the corner of my eye, I catch sight of a golden silky gown as light bounces off of it.

I'm sorry, baby.

Damian goes for a swing, and I let him land it. I deserve it, and the pain of a single punch is nothing compared to the shredding my heart is undergoing, knowing what waits for me on the other side of this.

They argue for a minute, then finally leave. I run my hand down my bare chin, and turn to bite the bullet.

Emma's complexion is blanched. Her hands tremble as she brings one up to her stomach, holding herself.

"Scorched by the sun," she whispers. *Yeah, baby, scorched by the sun.*

She remembers.

———

Emma

. . .

Why would Britain do that to Alex?

I watch him walk out of the dining room, and I want to run after him. I want to hold him once again like a wounded animal.

Can't she see he's hurting?

I might be hurting, too, but Alex still needs love and support, and it pisses me off that his family would always fail him.

I don't run after him, though, not wanting to draw more attention to him. I decide to let him cool off, or settle down, and then I'll find him.

I'll take his hand in mine, and we'll leave. And I'll let him break down, and I'll help put him back together, and maybe after all that, he'll want to keep me. But again, after tonight, seeing how obsessed he truly is with her, maybe he won't.

I clean up as best I can, feeling guilty over the death of this $3500 dress. My dress and I were never really long for *this* world anyway.

As soon as the toast is over, the cake is served. I take a single bite, then push it aside and wait for Brit to finish hers, needing to talk to her. Well, needing to stand up for Alex because it seemed no one else ever would.

I miss my opening by seconds when Jess beats me to Brit first. So I hang back, then approach as soon as she's free.

"Can I talk to you?" I ask Brit, pulling her to the side, then whisper, "What the fuck? Can't you see he's dying already? And you just put him on blast in front of all these people who probably mean the most to him?" She seems surprised.

"You're really sticking up for him? Right now?" She double-checks, and I nod.

"He might be broken, and he might not always do the right thing, but he is so good. And he deserves to be loved and supported by his family. That means you, and me." She stands there, shocked. "If you'll excuse me, I'm going to go find him and take him home, so goodbye, Brit."

I give her a formal half hug that she doesn't return. So I grab my clutch and walk out of the dining room.

The hallway is empty, so I head towards the bathrooms, hearing shuffling feet coming from that direction.

My feet slow as I get closer, my stomach tenses, and a nervous chill sweeps over my body.

Something is wrong.

My hand hangs onto the paneled wall for support. And as I round the corner to where the restrooms are, I see him.

Kissing *her*.

He's kissing her.

I gasp, my mouth falls open, but no sound is emitted.

The feeling comes back. The feeling I remembered but didn't know when or how I knew it. The feeling is here, but now it's paired with the image, a memory, of him and me sitting in his truck. I remember asking him, *"Where?"* I remember feeling like I was dying when he told me.

Our cove.

It feels like the sky is falling. It feels like the walls are closing in. It feels like having your heart ripped out of your chest, then trampled over a thousand times.

I step back, hiding around the corner so that she can't see me.

Oh god.

I remember. I remember my trip to see my mom. I

remember asking if I could call him, and he told me he was busy. I slam a hand over my mouth to silence a sob.

There's yelling in the hall, and I want to vomit. I want to disappear. I want the wall I'm leaning against to absorb me. Ceasing to exist feels like an ideal solution.

He did mean it, that he doesn't love me. He doesn't love me above all else. *Not me. Never me.*

I watch Jess and her husband walk down the hall, and I stand, trembling, as he turns the corner to face me.

I have to put a hand on my stomach to keep from throwing up.

"Scorched by the sun," I whisper, partly to him. Partly to the universe because I remember that, too.

He'll burn you, Blanks warned me. And here I am, "Scorched by the sun," I say it out loud again.

He stands looking at me like he's fighting the urge to throw up, too.

I was wrong. So wrong. About all of it. About him being a good man. About him being deserving.

"I feel sorry for you," I tell him in a shaky whisper. "She owns you. Your life isn't even your own, and for that, I *pity* you." Each syllable is laced with disdain.

I hate him.

"What a sad existence to live," I tell him as my eyes roam over him, seeing him for who he truly is for the first time. I turn, preparing to leave, giving him my back, but fuck. *Fuck!* I'm so *so* angry, and he...he's said nothing.

I turn around to ask, "*Why?* Why couldn't you just let me leave yesterday?" My chin trembles, and I blink hard to clear the tears out of my vision.

"I would have walked away from you. A clean break. But

you wanted..." I struggle for air. "You wanted to hurt me." The realization is soul-crushing. "Why would you be so cruel?" I stand before him, dismayed by his lack of response, at his unchanging expression.

"Say something!" I shout at him.

"I told you I'm not a good man." Like him warning me absolves him.

"You're right. I apologize for not believing you." *Christ, Emma.* I'm still saying sorry to him. "I'm sorry to have fallen in love with a monster like you."

When I turn away from him a second time, it's for good. I walk up the stairs into the lobby, and the whole time, I'm hoping he'll follow me. I'm hoping he'll stop me.

But he doesn't.

The warm June air hits me when I push open the large door. The air isn't refreshing like it is at home. It's pungent and heavy, and I stumble before folding in on myself and emptying my stomach onto the curb. I would be embarrassed if I could be.

While opening my clutch, I gasp, trying to catch my breath. I'm hoping to find a receipt, a small piece of paper, or anything to wipe my mouth, but instead, my shaking fingers land on a business card. Thick in weight with a raised emblem.

Caleb.

I choke on another sob as memories come back to me. *Crazy. Me, playing a guitar. A chapel. A hotel room.*

My breath catches as my still-trembling fingers type the number into my phone.

It rings, then rings some more. He isn't going to answer.

But then he does. He doesn't say hello or hi. But I know he's there, and he knows it's me.

"Angel?" he finally asks.

"I remember," I say softly, then sniffle.

"You do?" he asks.

"Yeah." I'm nodding even though he can't see me.

"Everything?"

"Everything..."

NOW

TWENTY-NINE

ALEX

The hotel room is empty. She's already cleared out by the time I get back. She'd done a quick turnaround, considering I didn't drag my feet getting here. I hoped I would catch her one last time. Not to say anything or stop her, but to just see her. To know she's okay. Not that she's okay.

Fuck!

I throw a vase against the wall, not feeling nearly satisfied enough with the destruction it causes.

BRIT

Are you okay?

She wants to ask me *now*?

A

I've never been okay, Brit.

Get a fucking clue already. And then I power off my phone because I can't.

I feel like I'm drowning.

No.

This is worse. It's like being burned alive. Like my skin is being seared off my body, my being charred to nothing more than a husk of a man. Everything good about me seems to melt away, only existing with her. I'm only good around her. For her.

And Jess is the fire that strips me. Jess and I were that wildfire of destiny, roaring and strong, tearing down everything in its path. Loving Jess was like that. It was like looking into the sun. So goddamn beautiful and powerful, but how the fuck were you supposed to not get burned?

Emma had the magic to take the ashes and the dust and mold it into something new. She took the fire and used it to forge us together. Like pain meeting pain, two halves making a whole. It happened effortlessly, easily, and she sculpted us into something that was greater than its parts.

Emma was the salve that healed you. She was joy. She was the essence of *my* life.

And now she's gone.

———

Every day bleeds into the next. Just nothing but an endless onslaught of waking, taking Delta out, drinking, napping, taking Delta out, then going back to sleep. Sleep isn't the right word, though. I hardly sleep at all. Can't.

If losing Jess was like losing an appendage, losing Emma

is like missing a vital internal organ. It's an invisible pain that yields for nothing.

After the first week, I turn my phone back on.

> **BRIT**
> Where are you?
>
> What did you do?
>
> Damian is fuming.

> **LIAM**
> Hey man, need anything?

> **BRIT**
> I'm really worried.

> **MAX**
> Connie wants me to come kick your ass, so maybe just call him back?

> **BRIT**
> I don't even care about what happened with Jess and Damian, okay? I just need to know that you're fine.

> **CONNIE**
> Alexander, call me back. Please.

> **A**
> I'm fine. Don't look for me.

I send the same message to every person and turn my phone back off.

There's nothing from Emma.

I slam the bottle of Johnny Walker down, and Delta whines at the noise. He cries a lot lately. The house is unfamiliar to him. His person is missing. Life isn't the same.

Same, bud.

———

"Baby," I can feel her hand against my shoulder. "Wake up,"
she whispers.

"Wake up." This time, it's with a shove. "Wake up," he
pushes again.

My eyelids are sore, my ribs are bruised, and my knuckles
worn raw. Between the fight and the tequila, I'd finally gotten
some sleep. But now, some asshole is here, taking it away
from me.

I lash out with my fist, pissed that he's taking *her* from
me. Sure, it's only in my dreams, but that's all I have. And I
rarely actually sleep.

"What the fuck, man?" I hear him walk away, so I try to
reach back for sleep. I try to reach back for her with closed
eyes.

And then water is being dumped on me.

"Fuck!" I stand up with a shout.

Blanks stands back, looking at me with disgust.

"I got a call from our lawyer this morning, about you
spending the night in jail. For assault?"

"You got here fast," I say, pushing the water off my face,
feeling the nine shots of tequila slam into my skull.

"No, I didn't. It's 7:00 P.M. and," he coughs, "you smell
and look like shit, Alex."

Ignoring him, I ask the only thing I care about. "Have you
heard from her?"

His expression remains impassive. "I'm done with all that

shit, Alex." My stomach sinks, roiling with disappointment. "I just came to make sure you were alive, make sure the dog was okay." Delta sits beside him, looking at me with the same level of disgust.

I sit back down before I throw up all over his Ferragamo loafers.

"Yeah, thriving," I say as I run my hand across my forehead, finding it damp with sweat.

"Alright then, take care." That's it? He's just leaving?

I take a long blink, and when I open my eyes to Delta licking my face, the sun has gone down. And I'm alone.

JULY

"Up." The voice is loud and commanding. "Get up, Alex." The sound booms in the living room, bouncing off the adobe walls.

Am I dead?

"Any day now..."

"Yeah, I'm getting up," I finally say. I know better than to disobey this voice.

"Jesus Christ, Alex. Take a shower and put some clothes on. We're going home." When I open my eyes, all I see is Constantine's disappointment shining back, and I pinch my eyes closed again.

"Why are you here?" I ask.

"Well, when your children can't take care of themselves,

you do it for them." He knows just what to say and how to say it. The guilt is unbearable.

When I turn around to head for the shower, Niko is standing, leaning against a wall with Delta at his side. *Traitor*.

He gives me a head nod as I pass by.

I actually stare at the window in the small bathroom and consider crawling through it to run away. It wouldn't be the first time I've done that here. But I won't do that to him. Constantine is probably the only person left on this Earth who could coerce me into leaving this shit hole. He probably hates this place as much as I do. If not more.

Which is why I'm here. Punishment.

Self-induced exile in middle-of-fucking-nowhere, Arizona. Ray's house. My former childhood home and hell on Earth.

I can't remember the last time I put on a clean shirt. *Do I have clean shirts?* Doesn't matter. If I can't leave because I don't have clothes, I'll just stay.

The hot spray hits my back as I hang my head, ashamed of who I am at my core. Ashamed of all I've done. Who I've hurt.

I can't say exactly how many days it's been since I last saw her. Keeping track of time wasn't exactly my strong suit right now. If I have to ballpark it, I'd say 45 days. That's a long time. Almost as much time as she spent in the hospital.

It's reminders like that that keep me drunk most days.

All the time I cost her. All the pain I caused her. For every one good thing I can remember, there are at least five bad memories standing right behind, yelling at me.

I pick up the only mechanism for cleaning myself in here, a single bar of Irish Spring. Likely 20 years old. *Fuck me.* I use the singular bar to wash my hair, my body, my face, and my beard that's grown out uneven and thick.

I try to pick the pieces of myself up off the floor before I exit the shower, but it's damn hard.

Niko knocks on the door, "Alright, bro, let's pick up the pace. It's 85 degrees in the house, and it smells like rotting food and wet dog in here. And it ain't Delta." The towel I grab off the rack is threadbare and thin, but I do my best to dry, and what I don't evaporates quickly into the parched desert air.

I find my duffle strewn across my old room, picking out a plain t-shirt and rough pants. No underwear, though, fuck it.

I don't bother with re-packing. I don't want any of this shit anyways.

Constantine and Niko are waiting for me, with Delta already leashed. I nod, grab my wallet and the pair of $6 aviators I bought at the gas station, and motion for us to leave.

I can practically hear Niko's gasp of relief.

I can practically feel him holding in whatever he really wants to say, and probably only for Connie's benefit.

Once we're in the black SUV and heading towards the airport, Connie turns to me, a grave look on his face.

"This is enough, Alexander." He holds my eye contact, and I can feel the firmness of his words. How absolute they are. I don't miss the slight tremble in the back of his voice. The worry. But I also hear the strength.

Enough is enough.

I nod, unable to say anything back because I understand. Georgia would have been disappointed. Connie already is.

The flight home takes us just under two hours. I vomit twice, cry once, and don't speak a single word to anyone.

Aside from Delta, who sat beside me the whole time, his head in my lap. *The perks of flying private.*

"Are you driving me home?" I ask Niko when we get into his SUV, me and the dog taking the back seat. He doesn't answer me, looking at his dad instead.

"First, you're gonna get some food. Probably something greasy as hell. Then, you're coming home with me. When you're ready, you can go home," Connie says while looking straight ahead in the passenger seat. *Great. I'm grounded.*

I let my head fall back against the hot leather headrest and watch as we pull away from the airport.

Feels just as shitty this time as it did the last time. With Emma.

Niko takes us through Foster's Freeze, and everyone gets something, even Delta. And then we drive the short distance to the Scala Family Home.

It's practically a prison between the tall iron fence and the guarded shack at the gate. When we pull up, Connie passes the guard a bag from Foster's. Through the window, he says, "Carl, you remember my son, Alexander, right?"

He nods, "Yes, sir."

"Good, he lives here now." I wave from the backseat without looking. Someday I'll be polite and say hi, but it sure as fuck isn't going to be today.

"Understood, sir," Carl tips the top of his baseball cap that's embroidered with "*Security,*" and Niko pulls away, up the circular drive, to park in front of the fountain.

The house reeks of old money and a life I hadn't known till recently. It's a large stone mansion in the old part of town, on a street that once hosted the Roosevelts as house guests.

It's a 1920s California palace with a gothic flair. Probably Connie's ex-wife's doing.

I shudder just thinking about Julie.

We file into the, thankfully, well-air-conditioned house and Delta bolts the second his paws hit the saltillo tile floor in the entry. Off to find Milton. Just happy as fuck to be back somewhere familiar, I'm sure.

Constantine takes the bags of food to his kitchen and then sets them on the island. Instructing me to sit.

He makes me a massive glass of water, then hovers over me with his arms crossed.

"There are rules while you live here." I want to roll my eyes because I can hear Niko laugh under his breath.

"No girls. No drugs. And you go to therapy twice a week. I get to choose the therapist."

"You know I've been a fully functioning adult for a long time, Con-"

He scoffs, interrupting me, "Could have fooled me, Alex. Hell, you could have fooled anyone." Turning his head, he says, "Niko, take a walk."

Niko grabs his bag and leaves.

"Listen closely," Connie's voice is low and rough. "When I saw you today, I nearly had a coronary episode. You looked just like *him*." He whispers the last part, and chills run along my extremities. "That is not who you are, son." Tears fill his eyes as he fights to keep them out of his voice.

My greatest fear has been turning into Ray, and here I am, one bad decision away from stepping into his shoes. I nod, feeling my throat swell uncomfortably under the weight of his truth.

"Eat. Then go to sleep, and tomorrow, we'll start over."

He gives me a pat on the back, then takes the seat right beside me. We eat in tandem, and then sit there for a long while after, neither of us talking, but neither one of us leaving either.

———

"Wake up, Alex." It's her voice, again.

No, it's their voices mixed.

Huh? Everything is foggy, but there's a gentle hand on my shoulder, nudging me, rubbing.

"It's time to wake up, my love." Today's the day.

I don't want to wake up.

I crack my eye open, and just like it was the day before, my mom's face is swollen and blackened beyond recognition. I look down at my body, the body of a six-year-old, in a wooden bed with an American flag quilt.

It's a fucking dream. The same one I've had for three decades. It's the morning I leave for Arizona to go live with Ray.

"Mom," I'm crying. "I don't want to go," I tell her like I wanted to that day but couldn't muster the courage to actually say.

"Oh, baby." Georgia leans over me, hugging me. "Then you won't go."

I can't go live with Ray, I can't. "I don't want to live with him, I didn't mean it!" I sob against my mother's floral robe.

"That's all you had to say. You'll never have to live with him if you don't want to, I promise."

I sniffle, "Okay."

"I love you, Alexander."

"I love you, too." Even in my dream, my stomach turns, and my mind laughs at me. *This isn't a dream, you fool; this is a nightmare.*

"Wake up!" I inhale sharply at the knocking on the door and then a woman's voice. "Listen, I don't really need to be babysitting another fully grown adult, so get up and get dressed. You have an appointment in 30 minutes."

I don't recognize the voice. Hell, I barely recognize the room I'm in. The dream felt almost tangible. I wanted it to be. I thought I could reach out and touch her...

It started with Emma, and then somewhere...it changed to Georgia's voice, and I was back in the same variation of the dream I've had for years. They *seem* like a dream. They lure me in by recounting the past, but always with new words and different outcomes.

It's a taunt, the dream always morphing into a nightmare. Because the nightmare isn't reliving what actually happened, the nightmare is waking up and living with what might have been.

What might have been...

I shower, trim my beard, throw on some clothes Brit dropped off for me, and head for the kitchen.

Still feel like dying.

My head pounds and my palms are already sweaty, but I'm here. Existing and on time. I don't know what more they could possibly want from me.

"Morning, Alex," Connie says from his seat at the break-fast table. "You've met Gina before, right?" Yeah, and I've heard about her, too. My sister isn't a fan, which means I'm not either.

"Yeah," is all I say.

"Great seeing you again, too," Gina rolls her eyes, then pours me a cup of coffee.

"Is it safe to drink?" I look at Gina, then to Connie, who bursts into laughter.

"At your own risk, but whatever you decide, hurry up," Connie says, nudging my cup closer.

"Why, where are we going?"

"Nowhere, but your first appointment is in ten minutes," Gina says, then places a plate consisting of an egg white omelet and fruit in front of me. "You can eat it or starve. And no, I didn't make it," she says when she catches me eyeing it warily.

It has more to do with the nausea than to do with her poisoning my food, though.

"I-it's great, thanks." I don't care enough to spar with her. I can give her basic politeness. Nothing more.

We all eat together, including Gina. It's awkward at best.

Then the doorbell rings; well, actually, it chimes.

I help clear the dishes as a woman in her late 40s, maybe, walks into the kitchen carrying yoga mats.

"Connie!" *Fuck*, she has a lot of energy. "Oh my god, who is this handsome man?" The woman asks, eyeing me like a prize at the county fair.

"That's Alex, my son. He'll be joining us today." Her eyes light up like the Fourth of July.

I want to die. Doing yoga with my aging guardian and his horny instructor is not how I pictured my life at 44.

"I'll be setting up. Come out when you're ready," she winks.

"Don't let her fool you, Linda's a hardass," Connie elbows me in the ribs. *I doubt it.*

————

I can't move. Hell, I never want to move again.

Isn't the purpose of yoga to open up? Isn't it stretching?

The nurse inserts the needle for the IV, and I wait for the fluids and vitamin B12 to work their magic.

Our second appointment of the day is IV therapy.

Then we're scheduled to have lunch with Max.

Then, I have actual therapy. And then I'm hoping I'll get to go back to sleep.

I'm still in the haze of the worst hangover of my life when my favorite person walks through the front door.

"What the fuck is *he* doing here?" We both ask at the same time.

Matt throws a pile of mail into Gina's waiting hands, then stalks into the living room, where Constantine and I are set up with bags of fluids by our sides.

"Dad?" He asks Connie again.

"My life is too short for this, Matthias. Move on. For everyone's sake." Matt scoffs at the instruction.

"I have to move on, but he doesn't have to?" I roll my eyes, but I don't miss how his nose slightly crooks to the right now.

"Alexander has already moved on, hasn't he?" Connie asks, looking at me. "He has bigger issues to manage than this." Don't we all?

"Pretend I'm not here," I say to Matt, leaning back and closing my eyes.

"No fucking chance of that," Matt whispers out the side of his mouth.

"Enough," Constantine warns. Again, I don't care

enough to do this with Matt. No use wasting energy on him. "Alexander will be staying here for the foreseeable future."

"That's just fucking great because I just closed on the house and need a place to stay for a bit." Gina groans in the distance. *Same.*

"Well, of course, this is your home, too," Connie says.

Jesus Christ, it's like the fucking Brady Bunch.

THIRTY

ALEX

After lunch, Max drops me off for therapy. I wasn't even allowed to drive myself, like I was a fucking flight risk. To be fair, I am.

The office is close to the Scala house, and I wonder if Connie chose her based on distance alone.

Her office is in an older building that has a courtyard with fig trees growing in the center. The smell in late July is almost off-putting.

But the inside is nice enough. It looks like most generic waiting rooms. Magazines on the coffee table. A small fridge filled with water bottles and several sound machines, all whirring at the same time.

It sucks here.

Therapy fucking sucks. I'll have to tell my story all over again. And talk about how I have attachment issues. Maybe even a smidge of PTSD. And it'll be the same shit as every other therapist for the last twenty years.

Just give it time. It'll get better. Newsflash: shit never got better.

I've seen so many therapists in my life, chances are slim that this will be the one to stick. And yet, I'm here because Connie told me to be.

"Alexander?" An older woman with long gray hair and purple glasses asks.

"Yeah," I stand, and she extends a hand to me. When I take her hand, her shake is firm. It's strong.

"I'm Maureen. Why don't you come on back?" Like I have any choice not to.

She closes the door to her office. The space centered around a large window, offering a floor-to-ceiling view of the fig trees. She motions for me to sit on a couch that looks like it's from the seventies but still pristine condition.

She pulls out a notebook, sits cross-legged in an egg chair, and looks at me.

"So Alexander, is that what you go by?" I nod. She makes a note. "So, let's start at the beginning."

"Which beginning?" *The beginning of my problems? The beginning of my relationship with Emma?*

"Yours. I want to know everything about you."

"That doesn't seem relevant. Would hate to waste your time."

"Not to me," she says, staring at me with hands clasped together, resting on the notebook.

"*Fuck*, I don't want to do this," I say, pushing a hand through my hair.

"What would you rather be doing? In the realm of reality,

what would you rather be doing?" Yoga? Fuck no. Sleeping? Maybe.

"Probably sleeping," I give her an honest answer.

"Is that something you do a lot?"

"Lately."

"What's lately? Last month? Last six months? Last couple of days."

"Last couple of months." She nods at my answer, making a note.

"What's something else you do a lot of?" *Drink, self-loathing, fighting.* She gives me a closed-mouthed smile when I don't respond. "Listen, my job is to help. But I can only be as helpful as you allow me."

"So let's just say, you're bleeding out, but instead of telling me that, you tell me you have a scratch. So...I give you a bandaid when you need a tourniquet. I don't know what I don't know. And I can't know unless you tell me." She's no-nonsense about it. Why waste her time when it's wasting my time as well.

Fine. "Well, lately, I've been drinking a lot, getting into fights. I spend a lot of time just thinking about how much I hate myself."

"And is all of this recent as well? As in the last couple of months?"

"Yeah, mostly."

"Is there something that's changed for you...in the last couple of months?"

"I miss my wife." She nods, making a note.

"You're married?" *Technically?*

"I don't know anymore." She nods.

"Do you want to be married?" To Emma? *Yes. Maybe.* Ultimately, no.

"It's complicated."

"Then let's uncomplicate it." I laugh at her suggestion.

"I wouldn't even know where to start," I say at the sheer immensity of it all.

"Then let's start at the beginning." Damn, she is good.

I sigh, "Alright then. I was born on January 3rd to Georgia and Ray Palomino. Newlyweds, middle-to-lower-class family. Georgia was a secretary, and Ray worked construction. My first memory is sitting on a diving board with a cabbage patch doll while my dad screamed at me. I was maybe two and a half or three."

Maureen makes a note. She ends up making lots of notes over the next 45 minutes. I only get through kindergarten when our time runs out.

"I'll see you in two days," She says with a gentle smile. *Can't fucking wait.*

———

AUGUST

Connie has me on a strict program. I work out every morning, we have some sort of family company for lunch, therapy or meditation in the afternoons, and then I have to cook dinner in the evenings. Maybe I don't have to, but it's not like there's anything else to do.

Matt moves in my second week at the house, but the

routine stays the same. He only eats dinner with us a few times and he never speaks, at least not to me.

My phone stays off, dead in some corner of my room.

With the nights cooling off, we've been taking the dogs on long evening walks after dinner. We don't talk all that much, Connie and I, but sometimes he'll tell me about Georgia. Sometimes he'll tell me how Brit is doing. Sometimes he tells me about myself, and what I was like as a little boy.

I always viewed Constantine as a father figure, but it never occurred to me that he *is* my father. Always has been. He'd been the one to drive me to boot camp in Arizona. He'd been the one that bought me the Jeep. He's always been there, loving me from the sidelines when I wouldn't accept it, and now taking care of me, when he knew I needed it.

"Do you ever miss Julie?" I ask him one night because I've never heard him speak her name, not once.

He rears back in surprise. "Well, no. I don't miss Julie. I miss the idea of her, but never her. I do miss your mother, though. Everyday."

It'd been three years since her death. "Yeah," I didn't share the same sentiment, though. "*Why* did you love her?" I don't mean to ask how I do. It almost sounds cruel.

"Well, she was undeniably the best person I knew. The way she endured... Alexander, she was so strong. And being with her was the only time I felt...*free*. It was the only time I felt like I was really me. The best version. Isn't that what love is?" *It isn't pain?*

I guess I hadn't learned about love the same way other people do. I learned it looked like a broken and bloodied face. Bruised ribs. Shouting matches that went late into the night.

"I guess," is all I say because the pit in my stomach is weighing me down. The pain and the guilt gnaw at me because I'd had that. With her. With Em.

When we get back to the house, Carl nods, giving us his nightly greeting. "Evening, sirs, uh, I just want to let you know," *except this is new,* "Miss Britain is here, I let her in."

Fuck, the last person I want to see.

"Thanks, Carl," Connie says, patting him on the shoulder as we pass.

We enter through the front door, letting the dogs off their leashes, then head for the living room.

I'm stopped in my tracks by the sight in front of me.

"Brit?" I ask. She's on her tiptoes, hugging Matt.

She lets him go at the sound of my voice. "Yeah," she blushes, pushing a few stray tears away. It's none of my business though. Whatever the fuck just happened... Whatever the fuck it means, I'm just going to pretend I didn't see it.

She walks over to me, going back on tiptoes to hug me. She holds on tight.

"I'm glad you're home," she whispers in my ear. She moves on, giving Connie an extra long hug, too.

"I just came to check on you, both." *Yup, well, this is it.* "You look like you're doing okay." She eyes me warily. Then does the same with Connie.

"I'm fine, Brit," I say, and she nods.

"Okay, I, uh, can't stay long. Elodie and I fly home tomorrow. And it's Caroline's Big senior year, so we're staying back East for a while. I guess I just wanted to say bye. And make sure you're good?"

"All good," I say with false confidence.

"Okay, then." She gives me one last hug, and another to Connie, putting a kiss on his cheek.

"Love you, Dad," she says to him, and Connie's eyes turn watery. His hand shakes slightly as he gives her one more short hug.

"Love you too, Peanut."

They both share a shaky smile and then she's gone.

I've never heard her call him dad before. Or say I love you. The moment...feels mournful.

I watch my sister leave, Connie excuses himself, and then I'm left with Matt, who also has tears in his eyes.

What the fuck?

"What-" I go to ask, but Matt stops me.

"Just not right now," he says before walking away. *What the fuck?*

———

"How does that make you feel that Georgia sent you to live with Ray while Britain lived with her?" *Pissed.*

"I don't know." Maureen smiles at my agitated response, like she's holding back a laugh because this is how it goes. I'm always holding the real feelings in. "Fine, I hate her for it." It's the first time I'm saying the words aloud. It's damn near freeing to let it go.

"I think that's fair," Maureen says. She never judges me once I do say the truth; in fact, she never makes me feel bad about anything, ever. There's no guilt, no shame, just validation.

"Did you ever talk to her about this *betrayal?* Can I call it that? Do you feel like it was a betrayal or neglect?" *Yes, to both.*

"Yeah, you can call it that, and no, I never talked to her about it." I hardly talked to Georgia at all once I turned 18.

"Did she ever say sorry or express guilt?"

"Not to me," I anger. Talking about this always ended with me angry.

"Do you think she was, though?"

"I don't fucking know, Maureen. I'm not a fucking mind reader." She gives me the same tight-lipped smile she always does.

"This subject seems to be particularly hard to digest. So switching gears, I'm going to give you a scenario, okay? And we're going to walk through it together. So close your eyes."

This is fucking stupid.

"Eyes closed." Reluctantly, I close my eyes, tuning out the woman with long gray hair and purple glasses sitting in an egg chair.

"I want you to picture Georgia. A version of her you'd look back on fondly." *She was wearing a dress, it was maroon with white polka dots, and she had on white high heels, and she was happy. Dancing in the kitchen while she cooked dinner, singing to me.*

"Now, Georgia, she's going to tell you she's sorry. She says it. See it in your mind as she says, '*I'm sorry, Alexander, for failing you.*'" *I can see it. I can see Georgia take my hands in hers and say it.*

"We're going to choose to believe her. That she *is* sorry. Can you do that, Alexander?"

I open my eyes. I don't know.

"Can you forgive her?" Maureen asks again.

I think about Connie telling me all she endured. I think about the morning she woke me up to go to Arizona and how her face was black and blue. I think of the woman who had to make choices and probably did the best she could with what she had.

"I don't know if I can."

Maureen hums, "I think that's fair, too," and then checks the clock. "I'll leave you with this to think about today: Forgiveness doesn't change our past," *no shit.* "*But* it does render our future." *Goddamnit, Maureen.*

———

It's all I can think about for two days straight. I think about it while I'm lying in bed staring at a ceiling fan. I think about it the second I wake up.

Forgiveness doesn't change our past, but it does render our future.

Forgiveness is another one of those childhood lessons I think I missed. How would my life look if I hadn't, though?

The difference is easy. I'd be married to Jess right now. And I don't even want to be married to her.

But maybe I wouldn't end up married to her, because she would still need to say sorry in order for me to forgive her. And she hadn't. Still hasn't and likely never would because I don't think she is sorry.

She's twisted our reality as such that she has no fault in our story.

I pictured Georgia and Jess as two sides of the same coin. I was always conflating the two of them, resenting one for the other's mistakes. But the difference is, Georgia was sorry and couldn't say it. Jess wasn't sorry and, therefore, never did.

I make the decision, right then, to forgive them both. Or at least try to because at the end of the day, I can't waste any more time thinking about either of them.

———

"How are you feeling today?" Maureen's classic opening line.

"Let's just cut to the chase?" I'm not in the best of moods today. Some days are better than others. This isn't one.

"You've been coming twice a week, for nine weeks now, and aside from telling me some very basic information about how you met, you haven't brought up your wife at all..." *Fuck*. I want to go back, and answer the first question with something that will distract her. Something along the lines of, 'How can I reparent my inner child?' Something she could monologue on for an entire session.

I don't want to talk about this. Anything but *this*.

I clear my throat, adjusting the way I'm sitting. I look up to the ceiling, and clear my throat, again.

"What do you want to know?" I ask Maureen.

"Where is she?" I don't know. I've looked too. She isn't at our house in Spearhead. She isn't at her condo in town. Hadn't gone to her trailer in Vegas. She hadn't used our credit card, hadn't touched our bank accounts. She isn't on social media. Becks hadn't heard from her, and neither had Brit. Blanks wasn't talking to me.

365

So I really don't know. My last resort is to call her...and I won't be doing that.

"No clue."

"Did she leave you?" Maureen asks.

"No."

"You left her?" *Not exactly.*

"Yes. Sort of."

"Did you break up with her, or tell her you want a divorce?"

"Sort of. I...I told her I didn't love her anymore..." Maureen makes a note. "And then I kissed Jess at her wedding...in front of Emma."

Now, Jess, Maureen knew. She knew everything. The good, the bad, the ugly. She knew about Damian and about Jess and mine's demise. She knew why I loved her, and hated her both. But Emma, no, I'd kept her close.

"May I ask why you kissed Jess at her wedding?"

"I needed to do something unforgivable." Maureen stares at me, waiting, unsatisfied with my answer. "I wanted to make sure she wouldn't come back. Because Emma would have kept coming back to me. No matter how shitty I was, no matter how much I fucked up her life. She would have kept coming back, and I couldn't let her do that. Couldn't let her throw her life away."

"The last time you were intimate with Jess, you were married then, right?" I look up to the ceiling before replying, the shame reaching unbearable levels.

"Yeah."

"And did Emma know?"

"Sort of."

"Explain?"

"I told her, and then we were in a car accident, and she was in the hospital for six weeks..." I bring my head down to finally look at Maureen.

"I think you should start at the beginning. It's time to tell me about her."

"Do I have to?"

"Yeah."

THIRTY-ONE

ALEX

"Baby, you're bleeding..."

And then I wake up. My room is still dark, but morning feels close.

I flip over the phone that I've started keeping on again, and check the time. 5:17. Delta readjusts in the bed at the disturbance.

I'm up and thinking about her, half wishing I could go back to the dream just to see her again.

I open the messages app and reread some of the last text messages she sent me.

> **EM**
>
> Have I told you you're the best husband lately? Because you are.

My stomach rolls, but I can't stop myself from going to the photos app because, apparently, I'm choosing to hurt myself this morning. There aren't many of her, but I have a few. The first one is her standing at our cove. It's just the view of her from behind, with her arms spread out as the sun rises.

The second is her lying on the couch with Delta. There's one of us at the football game. And then the only other photo is from our wedding day.

I forgot how fucking gorgeous she is. That's not true, I didn't forget, I just try hard as fuck not to remember. I try not to think about her long legs. I try not to remember her first time. I try not to fantasize about her tight cunt that had only ever been mine. Try not to fantasize about that fucking mouth.

No.

I try to push it all away because letting her go was the right thing. I still think that even as my whole body yearns for her.

Still holding my phone, I hover over her contact for a long time. Wondering what would happen if I just…call. Would she send me to voicemail? Decline?

No, I won't call. As I set my phone down, my thumb accidentally bumps the call button. *Fuck!*

It's already ringing. *Should I hang up? Should I see if she'll answer? Why would she?*

"Hello?" Her voice is enough to bring me to tears. It's soft and doesn't hold any anger or venom like the last time she spoke to me. "Alex?" *Shit.* Fuck, I don't know what to say.

"I don't know. Probably just an accident that he called. It's still early on the West Coast," she says to someone else in the background before sighing then hanging up.

Who was she talking to?

Early on the West Coast? She wasn't on the West Coast?

Emma didn't have...friends. Not on the West Coast, and definitely not on the East Coast... *Oh fuck, Fuck. FUCK!!!*

She was with him.

She was with *him*. I don't know if jealousy is the prevailing emotion or betrayal, which is rich coming from me, I know. I want to call back. I want to ask if she's happy now. Or happier? *Had she been happy with me at all?*

I wait an hour before finally texting.

A

> Sorry about the pocket dial this morning. Didn't mean to wake you if I did.

EM

> I was up. I've been meaning to call anyway.

She had?

> My divorce lawyer needs a copy of the prenup.

Visceral. Pain.

A

> Sure, I'll email you a copy.

> I don't need anything for a settlement, just so you know. It should be entirely painless. Just sign the papers type of thing.

Entirely painless? For who?

> Whatever you want, it's yours. Even the house in Spearhead.

The bubble of three dots appears before disappearing

again. I wait, hoping. Is there anything I could offer her that would bring her back my way?

No. Thank you, though.

Take care.

Take care? She may as well have slapped me in the face.

I can feel the doom spiral starting up, but instead of giving in, I heave my ass out of bed. It feels like I'm actually bleeding out as I drag myself to the kitchen.

"Woah, who pissed in your Cheerios?" Matt asks, standing at the refrigerator door, looking at me. I flip him off.

"Why are you up so early?" I ask, and he stares back at me like I should get it.

"I don't sleep." He looks away, maybe in shame. Embarrassment too. Yeah, I for sure got that.

"Right."

I start the coffee, and he pulls out yogurt.

Both of us sit, staring out the breakfast windows into the backyard when Connie walks in.

"Look at this, bright and early, no less!" Today is not the day for Chipper Charlie. "Hey, kiddo, I need you to drive yourself to therapy for the next couple of days."

"Sure. What do you have going on?" Maybe he finally made a move on hot yoga teacher Linda, whisking her off for a romantic weekend. It tracked that the only person getting laid in this house is the 70-year-old.

"Just a little bit of surgery. Nothing major." I practically spit out my coffee. Matt actually does choke.

"What the fuck, Dad?" Matt asks.

"What kind of surgery?" I ask.

"Just uh," he pauses to stretch out his back, "just having part of my colon removed."

"I thought we said–" Matt starts to protest.

"I'm not doing chemo again, so this is what I'm doing. End of discussion." It's hardly the end of discussion. Matt feels the same.

"No, Dad. We talked about this, and everyone on the team agrees that another round of chemo would be the most beneficial." How many rounds had there been?

"Colon cancer?" I finally ask. Matt ignores me, Connie nods. How had I missed it? Connie hadn't catered a wellness regimen to kick my ass; this was his pre-existing wellness regimen.

I haven't seen him eat a cold cut, or have more than half a beer since I started staying here. His meals are consistently 70% greens. He's active, walking, swimming, and lifting. He's staving off father time as best he can.

"Does Brit know?" I ask. Matt nods reluctantly. That's what they'd been talking about that day. It made sense. "Does *everyone* know?"

"Hardly," Connie says. "It's not something I need the world to know about, okay? I'm still here, I'm still kicking. Just, you know, I also have cancer. A very slow cancer." I felt like I was just getting Connie back...

"What does Brit think about surgery? Silas? What's his say?" I ask, trying to crowdsource Connie's cancer treatment.

"My health isn't a democracy, boys," he reminds us. "This is what I'm doing. You can both drive me, and one of you can even hold my hair if you feel the need to do that, too." He's joking. He's fucking joking about having a part of his colon removed.

"What a shitty morning this turned out to be," Matt says as he scoots his stool back.

"That's a little on the nose, son." He's still joking. Unbelievable.

When Matt shoves the yogurt back in the fridge, Connie stops him with a hand on his cheek. They share a moment, both with watery eyes. Then he pats him, and Matt leaves us.

"What's got your panties in a bunch?" Constantine asks, taking his spot in the breakfast nook.

"Emma. And I just found out you have cancer?" *Where to start?*

"Have you heard from her?" He asks, hopefully bypassing any conversation revolving around him.

My nod is slow as I run a hand down my face. "She just needed a document for her *divorce attorney*." The words taste sour against my tongue.

"Ouch." Connie looks at his watch. "Before 7:00 A.M.?" He whistles.

"It's not 7:00 in New York," I say, staring into my coffee, wishing it was a black hole that would swallow me.

"Double ouch," Connie says, shaking his head.

"Yup."

Gina walks into the kitchen, huffing. She sets a tray of drinks and a bag of bagels down, and says, "I swear to god, if you two are in bad moods today, I can't. I won't, O thíos. Matthias just—"

I turn around fully, and she sees my face.

"Aww, fuck! What happened to you?" Gina asks, Connie laughs. He's running a fucking halfway house for his own amusement.

"Don't worry, won't take it out on you, Gina."

"Yeah, right. I swear, you men PMS harder than any woman. I'm taking a personal day, best of luck to you all." She kisses her uncle on the cheek before walking out of the kitchen with her head held high in her five-inch heels.

———

On the day of Connie's surgery, I wake up in a cold sweat. I can just feel it. It's that gut feeling that precedes a shit storm. It's only 5:00 A.M., but I get dressed and take Delta for a quick run.

The chilly October air pushes against my face as we lap the neighborhood for a second time. Every time I think the feeling has abated, we take a break, and the feeling comes flooding right back.

After four miles, we head home when Delta looks pissed I forgot his water bottle. Carl is already at his station for the day, and he gives me a sympathetic head nod.

"Big day for the big guy, huh?" He asks.

I don't like the look on his face. He's too worried.

"Yeah," I say, continuing to walk towards the house.

"Alexander!" Carl calls after me. "Miss Britain is here. She just arrived ten minutes ago." God love Carl.

"Thanks for the heads up," I tell him.

When we crest the top of the inclined drive to see the fountain, as promised, Brit's Range Rover is parked beside it. She's talking animatedly, probably on the phone with the girls.

I knock on her window, and she startles.

She starts to roll it down, and the second she does, it hits me. *The smell of her perfume.*

She's here.

I step back from the window as Jess leans forward from the passenger seat.

"Didn't know you'd be here," my tone is sharp, pissed that Brit would bring her *here*. For this.

"Matthias texted..." I raise an eyebrow. I had texted, too, but she left me on read. "And I felt like I needed to be here." Brit, I understand, but Jess? Why the fuck did she need to come? *Unless she wanted to?*

"He'll be happy to see you," I say, letting her decide who I mean by that. The fact is they would *both* be happy. Connie and Matt. "Gonna get showered, make sure he doesn't eat anything. You coming in?"

"Is Gina here?" Brit whispers.

"No."

"Okay, then, yeah." She steps out of the car, and Delta immediately goes to jump on her.

"Off," I command, and when Brit turns, she reveals a bump.

"When were you going to tell me about *that*? Congrats." She blushes, looking down at her stomach, then rubs it affectionately.

"Thanks. I guess I would have told you when you started talking to me again." With Brit out on the driver's side and Jess getting out on the passenger side, she whispers, "No drama with her today, okay?" *Is she fucking kidding?* I'm not the one...

"I'm gonna act like she's not even here," I whisper back.

"Well, I didn't mean–" I turn and walk away before Brit can finish her sentence.

"Found some stragglers in the driveway," I say as I walk into the kitchen. Delta, Brit, and...her on my heels.

"Brit!" Constantine beams. Matt stands back, leaving room for his Dad to walk by. I watch him and Brit make eye contact, but other than that, they say nothing to each other.

"Hi, Dad," she gives him a kiss on the cheek. "Jess came with me today," she puts a hand on her bump, "She's on snack duty, so whatever we need, she'll grab it." Connie looks at Britain's hand resting on her bump, ignoring Jess.

"Congratulations, sweetheart," the tears rim his eyes, and he loses the fight to hold them in.

I can't help but check on Matt, standing on the other side of the breakfast nook with flared nostrils, a tight jaw, and a look of devastation written all over him. Fucking terrible feeling, I bet.

I try to imagine what it would be like if Jess had been the one to walk in with a bump this morning, and...I don't think I would have cared. Alright, I would have, but not like Matt is caring about Brit.

An image of Emma, with a small bump, fills my mind. I try to scratch it out of existence but fail, filing the thought away as something to ruminate over later.

"How long are you here for?" I ask Brit.

"Just till Constantine goes home from the hospital," she says, smiling confidently. Good, we need someone with even just a smidge of optimism to lift the mood.

I ignore Jess' presence, but I do notice she's quiet as a fucking mouse. That's perfect; she doesn't exist in my reality, and she's playing her role perfectly.

"I'm going to shower, take Milton out, and then we'll leave?" I check the clock.

"Yeah," Matt and Connie say at the same time.

Leaving the kitchen, I head for the guest suite on the opposite end of the house.

I strip, start the shower, and step in without waiting for the water to warm up.

The freezing water pricks at my skin, each drop a small zing, making me feel alive. Making me wish someone was here. My someone.

I bet if she was here, Jess wouldn't have come. It would have been better that way because Constantine actually likes Emma, fuck maybe he even loves her. Not that he dislikes Jess. He's actually said almost nothing about her to me. Ever.

I wonder what Em is doing right now. It's cold in New York this morning. Is she back in school? Is she stopping for coffee? Is she walking past Central Park, watching the leaves start to fall? I would give a lot to just be standing beside her doing the same thing.

I can see her now. Curly blonde hair, with a beanie on, her nose pink from the cold. Mittens on, holding a travel cup in both hands as she smiles at me.

"You're so fucking beautiful, baby." I'd tell her because I hadn't told her nearly enough in the past.

She would blush. Then say something back that would rip my heart out, like, *"You're so good, Alexander."* The worst part is she would believe it.

And then we'd walk home, and I'd start in on her before we ever made it past the door.

Her beanie would litter the walkway, she wouldn't have any mittens on once we were inside. The scarf around her neck would become restraints around her wrists. And I'd push her to her knees. I'd watch as her ruby-colored lips opened for me. I'd feel my heart beating out of my chest as she huffed a breath against my pelvis once she'd taken all of me to the back of her throat.

I stroke my hard cock in the shower, imagining she's the heat.

She would lean back, and my dick would drag across her lips as she'd say, *"Anything my husband wants, he can have."* *Fuck.* I want her to call me that again. I want to pull out of her mouth and bend her over. Fill her up with my cum as she cries out for me.

I want to tell her, *"Let me fill you, baby. I need to see you full. I want my wife carrying my babies."* Where the fuck is this coming from? *Babies, plural?* The thought has heat racing up and down my spine. My thighs pull tight as I grunt, letting my cum spray against the tile wall, wishing it was inside my wife's tight cunt because we weren't divorced *yet*.

I pant as the pulsing slows, scared at what that means. Scared of how much I wanted it. Just desperate as fuck to tether her life to mine. And it's killing me that it never would be. Never *mine*.

I dry off quickly, toss my towel over the shower rail, and walk into my room to get dressed.

"Fuck, sorry," Jess says as she covers her eyes, blocking my nudity. Why *the fuck* is she in here?

"You shouldn't be in here," I say coldly, grabbing underwear from a drawer and throwing a shirt on as fast as possible.

"I just wanted to say sorry," she says, dropping her fingers from her face. Her words stop me, slowing me down as I put on my jeans.

"For what?" For being in my room when she shouldn't be? That's probably it.

"For...everything, Alex." Moisture forms in her eyes. "Just everything I've ever done that made us like this," she motions between the two of us.

"Why now?" Why the fuck is she saying this now? Of all the fucking days. If ever there was a time in my life when I didn't need this, it's now.

And yet, here she is.

"Because I don't know if I'll get another chance, so it has to be now. Just know that I *am* sorry, and you deserved to hear that from me a long, long time ago." She just had this revelation on her own?

It's the apology I've been dying for. She delivered it to me genuinely. At least, I think she did; I could be wrong. But here it is, this mythical day finally arriving, and now that it has, it...it doesn't live up to the fantasy. The *idea* of Jess somehow always better than the reality.

It doesn't feel good or blissful. I don't have any desire to whisk her around in my arms or embrace her. I hardly feel anything for her at all. I don't hate her, *and* I don't love her. It's a relief to feel free of it. Free from her.

"Okay, well...I forgive you." I try to retract some of the harshness from my tone. Softening my delivery. I don't know if she wants more than that, but it no longer matters to me. I gave her the truth, and she set me free. As far as I'm concerned, though, we were done.

"I need to take Milton out..." I stand beside the door and motion for her to exit.

She nods, walking slowly towards the open door.

"I guess in another time, we might have been perfect for each other, huh?"

I shake my head. *Perfect* doesn't exist. Not for her and

me, not for anyone. It's just a commitment you make and see it through. You commit the time and the energy, and you ride the highs and dig out of the lows. Jess and I couldn't do that. So no, we wouldn't have been.

"There's nothing perfect about us, Jess. But I want you to know, I'm sorry about the wedding. I shouldn't have used you like that."

"Used me?" Her brows come together.

"It was just a means to an end, and you were the right person in the wrong place. I apologize." I say it sincerely, hopefully giving her the closure she needs, too.

"Oh," she hesitates halfway through the door.

"Listen, I do need to go, though." Milton runs into my room, his internal clock blaring that I'm running late.

"Right," I can see the confusion written on her face, but I let her walk away. And I go right back to ignoring her existence. This time, for good.

THIRTY-TWO

ALEX

The seconds creep by, merging slowly into minutes, eventually bleeding into hours. The anticipated 90 minutes comes and goes until the duration has lapped itself.

Silas eventually comes out, bearing a grim look. He's not working today, but he's been back, waiting for word.

Matt stands up before the rest of us, so we let the two of them talk privately first. Brit worries her lip, trying to figure out the right time to ask what's happening.

"It's *a lot more* than they anticipated," Silas says softly, not sparing our feelings.

I didn't have high expectations after feeling like shit all morning, but I had hoped for better than this. I had hoped they just needed to remove a slightly larger section. Instead of a laparoscopy, they would have to open him up. I thought the level of "worse" would be marginal, not devistational.

"He's still in there, so let's just wait, okay?" Silas says when nobody has anything else to add or ask.

Niko is the first to walk out of the waiting room. Probably for a smoke, but Max follows shortly after to make a phone call.

"Do you guys want me to go get lunch?" Jess checks the time. Everyone thought he'd be out by now.

"No one's hungry, but thanks," Matt says, taking a seat again. I sit beside him this time, and Brit does the same, taking the chair on his left.

"I'll be back as soon as I know more," Silas pats Matt on the shoulder and leaves.

Jess is still standing, looking anxious, when an unexpected guest waltzes into the waiting room.

"Mom?" Matt asks, surprised. Julie looks like she's dressed for an occasion — tall, high-heeled boots, tight black top, her hair and makeup done — but not this occasion.

"I just came to see if you needed anything...I don't want to stay. I know I'm not welcome," she glances between Britain and me, still flanking him. "But Silas text that things aren't going as planned, and I–" she shrugs, "I can get coffee as good as anyone."

"Here," Brit stands. "Have my seat," but Matthias grabs Brit's hand, shaking his head at her.

"Coffees would be great," Matt tells Julie, and she looks grateful for it.

"How many?" She looks around the waiting room, trying to count.

"Seven," Matt says quickly.

"Full house, okay. I'll be back in a few."

Brit sits back down, but I notice Matt doesn't release her

hand. Brit doesn't try to free it, either. She threads her fingers with his and whispers to him, "That's actually really kind of her, Matthias." He nods.

Matt is Connie's only blood-related child. Everyone else loves him and calls him Dad, but everyone also feels like Matt has the most to lose here. We all know it.

Jess takes the seat directly across from mine, so I pull out my phone and do the only thing that feels right.

A

> Hey, Connie is in surgery today, and I don't think it's going as anticipated, so I just wanted to let you know. I know you both care about each other. A lot.

EM

> I'm so sorry to hear that it's taking a turn. I'm already at the airport. I've been on standby for two flights already. I'm trying to get there.

I swivel my head to look at Brit, knowing she would have been the one to say something.

> You're coming here?

> Trying to.

Why didn't she just ask Blanks to charter her a flight? I don't hesitate to call in a favor. I'm on my feet before I can even think about it.

> Which airport?

> I'm at Newark. It has the most flights westbound, so I thought my chances would be higher?

It takes five minutes to bump someone else's charter heading west, then order a car to pick her up from Newark.

A

> There's a car waiting at departures. It'll take you to Teterboro airport. Just check in at the front, they're expecting you.

EM

> You don't have to do this, Alex. I'll get a flight eventually.

> The only thing that would make today better is for you to get on that plane and come here. Please.

Her bubble of dots comes and goes. My heart races. I hope, then pray, and then I hope some more that she was walking to departures, and that was the reason for the hold-up. It's ten more minutes before I get a response.

> I'm in the car. See you in a few hours.

> Okay.

I sit back down, tipping my head up to the ceiling, feeling relief. Feeling overjoyed that she would be here. I close my eyes and run a hand through my hair before sitting up straight again.

I could tolerate the waiting room purgatory knowing she's

coming. I could make it through anything knowing she's on the other end of it all.

Eventually, Julie comes back, bringing coffee and bottled water for everyone. She sits with us for five minutes, bouncing her legs, wringing her hands together, and then she's up again.

"I'm ordering lunch," she says nervously, the physical embodiment of what everyone else is going through. "Britain, Alex, any allergies? You?" She looks at Jess.

We all shake our heads.

"I'll be back." *What the?* What was that?

I shoot Brit a side glance, and I can tell she's thinking the same.

Niko and Max eventually rejoin us. Both of them eye Brit and Matt, holding hands, but neither says anything. Everyone seems too scared to address the elephant in the room.

Another hour goes by before Silas walks through the hall door with a surgeon beside him. This time, everyone stands.

Silas looks uneasy, but he doesn't look like he just found out his dad died. Small wins.

The surgeon speaks first, "I just want to let you all know, he's in recovery and he's stable." Everyone lets out the smallest of exhales of relief.

"We had originally planned on laparoscopy, but after an initial incision, we made the decision to do an open hemicolectomy, removing the right section of the colon and all the surrounding lymph nodes. But unfortunately, the cancer has metastasized," the words get blurry, and the room feels hazy, but he continues on, "It's spread."

There are more senseless words, "...peritoneum, which is the membrane that lines the abdomen." The ringing in my ears makes everything hard to hear. "...a biopsy from his liver. He'll need to recover from the surgery, then we'll figure out the treatment plan. But more than likely chemotherapy."

Fuck. No one lets out a tiny exhale of relief this time.

————

A

I'll pick you up.

EM

I need to rent a car anyway. I can meet you at the hospital.

I'm already here.

When her flight lands twenty minutes later, I'm standing in the private terminal, waiting. I watch her walk across the tarmac in leggings, an NYU sweatshirt, and Chuck Taylors. Her curly hair gets swept up in the wind, and she does a light jog to escape the chill.

The door of the terminal opens, and she's here. Pink cheeks, shy smile. *My girl.*

Waiting for her to come to me, I debate what the appropriate greeting is. A hug? A handshake? A kiss that would show her I love her, desperately? Now more than ever.

But then she's standing in front of me and going up on tiptoes to place a kiss on my cheek. Before she can back away, I slip a hand around her back and hold her against me, pulling her in for a hug.

"How is he?" She asks like a reminder. She's here for Connie, not me.

"Stable." I let her go.

She lets loose a long exhale, jostling a large tote bag on her shoulder.

"Let me." I take it from her. "Is this all?" She always seems to travel light.

She blushes, then says, "Yeah. I left in a hurry..."

"Well, we can get whatever you need–"

She stops me, "I'm not staying long. I just want to see him. Want to make sure you're okay." She looks away like the thought pains her.

I take her chin and pull her back to look at me.

"If you're here, I'm better than okay." Her cheeks flame, and her pupils seem to blow wide open.

"We should get going, I didn't mean to take you from the hospital..." I release her chin but grab her hand, leading her to the car.

"New car?" she asks.

"It's Matt's." I hold her door open for her, watching her ass as she climbs up. She appears to be back to normal. Her curves look muscular, her hips look wider.

"The infamous Matthias? He let you take his car?" she asks while we get buckled.

"Yeah, we sort of live together at Connie's. It's-we just have an understanding that the past is the past, and we're both over it."

"That's great, I can't wait to meet him," she says, adding a smile. I fight the urge to reach for her hand and hold it. I fight against the need to wrap my hand around her thigh as I drive, like if I keep holding on to her, she'll never leave.

The car is silent, aside from Emma humming beside me, so I turn on the music. She looks at me, shocked.

"It's okay, this doesn't need to be on." She reaches over to press the power button, but I stop her, holding her hand.

"But you like it, right?" She doesn't respond, letting her hand fall. Mine goes with it. And this time, I do hold on.

Matt's radio is tuned to country music, so that's what we listen to while we drive. We actually pass her old condo building on the way to the hospital downtown. I watch her look at it almost longingly. *Missing who we were back then?* I know I am.

We park in the underground garage, and I tell her to sit tight while I come around to open her door. She almost looks embarrassed. I'm the one who should be embarrassed for not treating her like this at the wedding.

She almost forgets her phone but grabs it at the last minute, stuffing it into the side of her leggings.

"Is everyone still here?" She asks, pulling her sweatshirt down over her butt, and bringing her hands into the cuffs of the sleeves.

"I think." I want to reach for her hand, but she's hiding them now, maybe for that exact reason.

We take the elevator to level two and then walk down a long hallway to the surgery waiting room.

"Emma, I–" I start, but she shakes her head and then turns to me.

"I'm just here to focus on Connie and to make sure you're okay. Just let me do that, please?" She pinches her eyes closed, like if she blocks the visual of me, it will make this easier.

"Of course," I say. Because I would do anything she wants, act any way she tells me to. If she said I only want to talk about beet salad and overrated karate moves for the next 72 hours, I'd say, 'Yes, ma'am.'

The first person to make eye contact with her is Jess. I watch as Emma doesn't even so much as flinch. She goes to Brit first, giving her a warm hug. I watch from the corner of my eye as Jess watches, too.

And then she's giving Niko a hug. And Max. And Silas, too.

She stands in front of Jess' chair, and I hold my breath, but Jess stands, and they embrace?

It's not overly warm, but it's a friendly enough greeting.

I move over, slipping my hand in hers just as she finishes.

"We'll talk later," Jess says in a hushed tone. *They would?*

"Matt, this is my–" *wife* dies on my tongue as Emma interrupts me.

"*Emma*," she says, holding out a hand to him. "It's nice to meet you. Connie's told me so much."

"Same to you," Matt shakes her hand right back.

"What did I miss?" I ask for an update.

"They're moving him to a room, and then we can visit, taking turns. You missed lunch, though." I shrug. Don't care about that. But Emma's stomach growls.

"Sorry. God, embarrassing." She runs a hand across her stomach. The motion sends heat to my groin for some reason. "Um, flying makes me nervous, so I didn't eat..." I picture her clutching onto the armrest in lieu of anyone to hold her hand, and I feel like I could cry.

"You should have said something. I could have stopped..." She shakes her head, though.

"No, you needed to be back here. I'll go find the cafeteria or something," she rests a hand on my arm, her thumb rubbing gently. "Don't worry about me," she says softly. She's saying softly what feels like a dagger to the heart. *I'm not yours to worry about anymore. I take care of me, not you.*

But I want to. My soul practically cries back. God, how I want to.

When there's space between us, I can pretend that I'm not thinking about her 24/7. I can pretend like I'm not worried about her in New York City. I can pretend that I don't need to know if she's still keeping up with her physical therapy.

But her in front of me... I would give everything for her to let me in.

Anything.

"There's a vending machine, down the hall, if you make two rights...Actually, I can just show you?" Jess asks, eaves-dropping.

"Uh, sure," Emma replies, excavating herself from me. "Lead the way."

"Wait," I stop her as she turns to leave. "You left your bag in the car." I pull out cash and a card and hand them over to her. I can tell she doesn't like it, but she reluctantly accepts.

It's still all hers, anyway. Well, it's ours.

"I can see why Dad likes her so much," Matt says, watching her walk away.

"Yeah. Me too."

———

As promised, everyone is allowed to visit Connie in rotations.

Matt and Britain go first. Then Niko and Max. Silas

doesn't count as a visitor, so he's already been back several times. And then it's mine and Emma's turn.

I hold the door open for her, and she steps into the dim space.

His eyes are closed, but I don't think he's asleep.

"Hi, Connie," Emma stands beside the bed, taking his hand in hers.

"Sweetheart, you came."

"If you told me sooner, I would have been here earlier," she chides him. He opens his eyes slowly, to look at her.

"Didn't want you worrying about me. How's school?" *What the fuck?* "Take a seat," he pats the bed gently. She perches on the edge, giving him plenty of space.

"It's good. NYU is a *bit* different than FSU, no surprise there. But it's a good different. I miss our lunch dates, though." Should I be concerned that Connie has more game with my wife than me?

"I miss them too," he closes his eyes again. Probably exhausted. Emma realizes it, too.

"I'm going to give you two some privacy, okay?" she whispers, giving me a pat on the arm as she walks out. I wait two seconds before starting.

"You texted her you were having surgery? This morning?" I watch him smile.

"The second I saw Jess was here, I sent a message." Fucking meddler. Though I'm grateful for it. I need her here. To just make everything feel okay.

"Well, thank you," I say, taking his hand in mine. I pull a chair closer, then take a seat. "I didn't know what I had..."

Connie hums, "Isn't that the truth, son. But now that you know..."

E.L. STEVENS

"I know," I answer back. "I know." He squeezes my hand.

"I just need all my kids to be okay, then..." *Then what?*

"Shut up, Connie. This lot will never be okay," I tease him, ignoring whatever it is he would have said. "Go to sleep. We'll be back in the morning, okay?"

"Yeah, yeah," he waves his free hand at me. "Go, take your wife to dinner or something. Don't waste it sitting at a hospital with me." I chuckle.

"If you insist," I squeeze his hand once more and get up to leave.

"Hey," he says, stopping me. "She likes the Italian place on West. It's close to the house, too." I shake my head but take his word for it.

"Love you, Connie."

"Love you too, kiddo."

THIRTY-THREE

ALEX

Matt is nice enough to catch a ride home with Niko, so I can borrow his car and give Emma a ride.

She and I are the second to last group to leave, with only Max and Silas sticking around till the very end of visiting hours.

"Take care, kid," Max says to Emma when I pull her away.

She looks tired, mirroring how I feel, but there isn't a chance in hell I'm taking her home without a decent meal.

"Come on," I pull her into the hall, then hold her hand as we walk. I can't believe she's *letting* me hold her hand. A fucking miracle.

Halfway to the elevator, I realize she's crying. Pulling her to a stop, I ask, "What's wrong?"

"H-he looked so weak. And pale. And my heart hurts for

him. A-and then I wondered, is that what I looked like?" She looks up at me.

She looked worse. She looked a step away from death. Connie looked like a fucking warrior compared to her.

"You were...things were touch and go for a while, and yes, I know the feeling." I push a piece of curly hair behind her ear. "My heart hurt then, too."

Her nose scrunches, and she turns to keep walking.

I help her get in the car, hold her door, and follow right behind her.

"Can you drop me off at the condo? Is that alright?" *No.*

"I-I thought you would just stay with us?"

"Oh...um, I don't...I think it's probably wisest if–" I can't handle this.

"Em, I *want* you to stay with us. There's an empty guest suite beside mine." She's still quiet, looking out the windshield and not at me. "*Please*, I just need to go to sleep knowing you're safe tonight."

I lay my hand out flat, my elbow resting on the center console, like an offering. Would she take it?

Her fingers slowly slide against mine in acceptance.

I thread our hands together and head towards the Italian restaurant on West, just like Connie said.

"I love this place. How'd you know?" she asks. I hadn't known. There's apparently a lot I don't know about her. Like that, she goes to NYU. Is she still studying anthropology? Fuck, what's even her favorite color?

"Connie's suggestion. It's also close to the house." She knows that though; she'd been there before at least a dozen times with me. Maybe more just to see Constantine.

I get her door for her when we arrive, and she leads the

way. The place is small and quaint. The lights are dim, and there's an open booth calling our name. One of the servers seats us, and I debate ordering a drink to take the edge off my nerves.

"Can I get you something to drink, a bottle of wine?" Our server asks, and I look at Emma, but she shakes her head.

"Just a Sprite, please, if you have it. If not, club soda is great." Since when did she drink either of those things?

"Water is great," I say. They hand us menus, set down a basket of bread with a dish of olive oil beside it, and walk away.

I pick the first thing I see on the menu so I don't waste time figuring it out when I could be spending that time focusing on her.

The candlelight from the votive makes her literally glow, and I can't help but notice how healthy she looks. She's more beautiful than ever. Looking full of life, she looks... free.

She takes a little longer than me, but when she sets the menu aside, I give her a smile.

"NYU, huh?" She glances down at the sweatshirt.

"Yeah," she says, almost bashful about it.

"Why there?" As soon as it's out of my mouth, I wish I could retract it. I want to avoid her talking about him at all.

"It seemed like a once-in-a-lifetime thing to do. To live in New York and go to school, so I took the jump." Dodged that fucking bullet. Or she evaded nicely. Either way, we aren't talking about him.

"Still anthropology?" She nods.

"Still love it. Umm, actually, Jess' mom, May, is one of my professors." She laughs gently. "Small world."

"Huh, yeah. Small world." I most certainly didn't want to waste any time talking about Jess.

"What else have you been doing? Or what'd you do this summer?"

"I've been busy, Alex." She tears apart a piece of bread, dipping it into the oil. I could feel her holding back, trying to spare me.

"Yeah, same." I can't help the laugh that breaks free because, no, I hadn't been busy.

She laughs, too. "Oh really? Please indulge me."

"Okay, I will. Let's see...we've got a packed schedule Monday through Friday. I've got yoga with Linda three times a week. I've got therapy with Maureen twice a week. On days I don't have therapy, there's either meditation or tai chi. Both of those are with Sammy. And then, I have lunch with my family every day, and I cook dinner for whoever's around every night."

"Connie and I walk the dogs in the evenings, and sometimes I work out or run afterward, and you know...Life is *pretty* full." *Lie*, it's empty without her, but the routine has helped. It isn't anywhere near as awful as I make it sound.

"Wow, you were not lying. That is a *full* schedule, and it sounds amazing," she says genuinely. "And you live with Connie? And Matt?" I nod.

"Yeah," I do, and oddly, it works.

"You seem happy," she says. *Fuck*, no. I don't want her to think I'm happy. I'm not happy. I'm surviving.

"Are *you* happy?" I ask. It's something I'd asked once before, long ago, when we sat across from each other at her condo.

"Well, we're basically the same person, Alex..." She

lowers her voice, "So tell me, are we happy?" My smile falls. I shake my head.

"Not without you." I watch as her chest rises and falls in response.

"Did you know what you'd like to order?" our server asks, setting down our drinks. I motion for her to go first.

"Chicken piccata, please."

I take her menu from her, then order, "The exact same." Just desperate to get back to what we were saying, but once our server is gone, the air is cleared.

"So, how long have you been at Connie's?" She buries the former topic of conversation easily.

"Since August."

"And before that? You were?" She asks.

"Busy, Emma. I was busy." I could play games too. She swallows.

"Right," she says, dusting off her hands. "I think I'm going to use the restroom. I'll be right back." *Fuck.* I probably made it seem like I was out fucking someone. Everyone, for all she knew. Obviously, I wasn't. There hadn't been anyone since her.

I stand when she leaves. Then again, when she comes back, looking slightly paler. I stop her before she sits, my hand slipping around her waist.

"Are you feeling okay?" She arches away from my touch, though.

"I'm fine. Totally fine." *And I'm the king of England.*

It takes a few minutes before we start talking again, but once we do, the conversation flows. Effortlessly. Like it used to.

She tells me all her favorite things about New York. So

far, Central Park's turning colors are the leader. But she also loves people watching on the subway. She loves walking everywhere. But hates the lack of scenery and hiking.

She loves being able to order Thai food at 1:00 A.M. and have it delivered, "But no one makes pancakes as good as yours. At least not that I've found, and I have looked," she says, laughing.

I'll make her pancakes tomorrow.

"It's been a fun segue to live there..." she trails off.

I hope it's because it, "Doesn't feel like home?" She shakes her head.

"Not in the slightest," she says almost begrudgingly. I understand that.

The food arrives, and she eats entirely too fast.

"I really haven't had much to eat today." I believe her, then ask if she wants any of mine, too.

She laughs, "No, thank you, or I might toss my cookies." I finish my dish just so she doesn't feel weird about it. We both decline dessert, though. And after I pay our bill, we walk out into the cold fall night. It's not freezing cold like it is in Spearhead. But it's cold because we aren't dressed for it.

I rub her arms as we walk to the car, making sure she's buckled in before coming around. It's a short five-minute drive to the Scala's house, but I still catch her eyes falling every now and again.

It's only 8:30, but I guess 11:30 in New York.

Carl is gone for the night when we get back, so I enter the gate code and then park in the empty driveway.

I grab her tote from the backseat and then come around to get her door, but she's already passed out cold.

"C'mon, baby," I say as I unbuckle her, slinging her tote

over one shoulder. I lift her with an arm under her legs and one at her back and she instinctively wraps her arms around my neck.

The house is quiet when we step in. Both dogs still at Gina's. Lights are off, so I head straight to the guest wing of the house. I drop her tote on the ground, then lay her gently on the bed. Unfortunately, it's not my bed, but I would probably sleep like a fucking baby knowing she's right next door.

I help her kick her shoes off, then pull a blanket over her.

"I love you," I whisper. "I'm right next door," I say, dropping a kiss on her forehead before turning off the light.

Once the door clicks shut, I lean against the wall and sigh. Tonight was...great. Perfect even, but I want more. I want to know so much more. To be there. Holding her hand in Central Park. Dropping her off for class. Cooking her dinner at night.

And I wanted her to be honest with me about Blanks. As much as it would kill me.

But I don't deserve any of it. I should just be grateful for tonight and the couple of days she's here. And then I can recommit to letting her go.

Because she looked free...at the very least, happy. Healthy. Content. She looked like the best version of herself. And that's what love is, right? Isn't love wanting that for the other person even if it means it isn't with you?

She's my version of freedom. She's my happiness and joy too. She made me *want* to be better, but the problem is I would never be good enough for her. At least not by my standards. I want more for her than she knows she can have herself.

That's what love is. It isn't crippling pain. It isn't wanting to hurt.

It's doing whatever it takes to get her to be *this* person. And that means without me.

Resigning, I step away from her room and into my own.

I throw my clothes in a pile, slip into bed, and wait for sleep to take me.

At some point, I doze but wake to the sound of a gentle knock on my door.

"Yeah?" I sit up partially, worry thrumming through my bloodstream. The door cracks open, and Emma steps a bare foot inward.

"I can't sleep," she whispers into the dark.

I immediately move over, pushing the covers back to make room for her, letting her take the warm side of the bed.

She closes the door behind her and pads into the room, then into bed beside me.

"Thank you," she whispers.

"No problem," I say, then settle so I'm lying on my side facing her, even though she settles, lying on her side, facing away from me.

I consider rubbing her back or scooting closer, but ultimately, I decide to just let her sleep. Assuming she can. And I assume correctly because, after a few short minutes, I hear her breath deepen, then turn into a gentle snore.

I smile against the pillow and let the sound lure me to the same state as her.

When the color of the room starts to turn gray, my inner alarm clock rings, and I wake up to find myself curled around her. My bare cock is shoved in between her bare ass cheeks, and my hand covers her breast under her shirt. *For fucks sake,*

Alex. My dick twitches, digging deeper, and she pushes back against me.

Wait, does she want this? Is she even awake?

I go to move my hand away, but her hand comes over the top of mine, keeping it there.

"I hate how much I miss you," she whispers, then releases my hand. I'm positive she can feel the pounding in my chest or feel it in my cock that presses and twitches harder against her.

I'm fumbling with what to say and how to say it. Do I tell her the truth? Do I push her away? I want her back so goddamn bad...but I'm not good for her.

"I-I," I stutter and stumble.

"It's okay if you don't feel the same, Alex." She gently removes my hand from her breast and scoots her hips away from me.

But I grab her hip and drag her back, whispering into her hair, "I miss you with every fiber of my being, Emma. I miss you while you lie beside me because I know you're not mine. But I don't hate that I miss you; sometimes missing you is the only thing that reminds me I'm still alive."

It's a burn in my chest, a constant fire that just won't die.

She rolls over to face me, still in my arms.

"Then why do you insist on pushing me away?"

"Because you can do better than me. I'm not your happiness and joy, Em." That belongs to someone else.

"Are you serious, Alex?" I nod. Then, unable to stop myself from touching her, I push her hair off her face. "Sitting in the cove with you was the first time I ever felt truly free and safe. I feel that with you all the time. I feel happy when you let me take care of you. I feel joy every time you laugh.

Why?" She strokes my face in turn, "Why do you keep me out?"

"Because you'll be disappointed if I let you in."

She shakes her head, then leans in hesitating, but I close the distance. I let her lead, unsure what to expect, and she gently kisses me, wiping a tear off my cheek.

"No, I won't," she says with absolute assurance. "In fact, I think I'll be the one to disappoint you." I shake my head.

"You could never."

"You might be surprised—" I cut her off from talking, dropping my mouth onto hers. I try not to consume. I try to just kiss her, but it's hard. Especially when she's here, pushing back, trying to take everything I can give her.

I push her onto her back, rolling closer, putting a leg between hers. I thread one hand into her hair while the other roams down, groping a breast, then trailing over her abdomen. And she tenses.

She stops kissing me, and I lean back.

Her eyes are clenched closed like she's in pain. Like she doesn't want this. My heart races.

"Alex...I have to tell you something." In the blink of an eye, I'm ready for the heartbreak, the plummet. Only this time, there'd been no forewarning. No bad gut feelings, just straight to terror.

"I-I'm pregnant."

TO BE CONTINUED...

ACKNOWLEDGMENTS

I can not stress this enough: thank you. For reading Alexander. For reading Georgia, and Constantine, and June too. The readers make all this possible. You drive me to write and to continue on this wild path of indie author life. So, thank you.

Thank you to my editor, Sara Brown. She is a real-life Wonder Woman who never fails to support me in this endeavor. Her time, which is precious, is given to these books time and time again. I don't know how I'll ever repay you.

Thank you to my beta readers: Alix, Kristie, Merissa, Aubrey, Laura, Ellyn, and Morgan. Your advice and feedback is incredibly essential to making these books readable and not just a wild rambling of my mind. I appreciate the care and time you have poured over my manuscript. Your dedication and generosity humble me entirely.

Thank you to my two incredible PAs, Emily and Morgan. You guys blow me away time and time again. Thank you for pushing me, for supporting me, and for continually showing up for me.

Thank you to Erica Anderson for assisting me as I grow my readership and street team. She is an integral part of what makes the Hurt So Good Street Team run. Without her, there wouldn't be a team at all!

Thank you to the entire Hurt So Good Street Team, my

people, and my friends. Thank you for your continued support and for loving these books and characters. Without all of you, my readership would be no where near what it is today.

And thank you to my family. For accepting my need to put these words down on paper. For accepting all my mini breakdowns and for putting me back together again.

Thank you to my C & E for inspiring me to keep going.

And last, but not least, thank you Mr. S for supporting this adventure.

ABOUT THE AUTHOR

E.L. Stevens is a book loving low-key sneaker-head with a mild obsession for baked goods and Dr. Pepper.

Her love affair with reading and romance novels started in the seventh grade with Jane Austen's Pride and Prejudice and hasn't stopped since.

An overactive imagination and obsession with the genre led her to want to write her own books incorporating life experiences love of her hometown, and of course, baked goods.

When she's not writing, she's voraciously reading, walking her labradoodle, Maggie, chauffeuring tweens between sports and extracurriculars, shopping for sneakers, or baking in the DC exurbs.

 instagram.com/e.l.stevens

ALSO BY E.L. STEVENS

Spearhead Lake Series

Georgia

BOOK 1, BRITAIN'S STORY PART 1

Constantine

BOOK 2, BRITAIN'S STORY PART 2

June

BOOK 3, JESS' STORY

Alexander

BOOK 4, ALEX'S STORY

Emmaline

BOOK 5, EMMA'S STORY (COMING SOON)

———

Say Something

NEW STANDALONE ROMANCE NOVEL (COMING SOON)

The Scala Brothers Series

NEW SERIES FOLLOWING MATTHIAS, MAX, NIKO, AND SILAS
(COMING SOON)

Made in the USA
Columbia, SC
19 March 2025

55415719R00252